SEVEN

YEARS
A SEVEN SERIES NOVEL

DANNIKA DARK

Second Print Edition
ISBN 13: 978-1491065624
ISBN-10: 1491065621

Formatting: Streetlight Graphics

Cover design by Dannika Dark. All stock purchased.

http://dannikadark.blogspot.com/
Fan page located on Facebook

ACKNOWLEDGEMENTS:

Much love to all the readers who have been there every step of the way, eager to start a new paranormal love story with fresh new faces. Big thanks to Viviana Izzo and Nina Lillard for being my guinea pigs and giving me the thumbs-up. Thanks to my amazing betas for not just your hard work, but falling in love with the stories I write. And where would I be without the crazy support I've received from book bloggers, reviewers, Facebookers, and book junkies? You know who you are, and you rock.

Seven years ago, my world ended.

Seven years later, my new life began.

CHAPTER 1

—⊙◦⟨∕∕⟩◦⊙—

I DON'T CARE WHAT ANYONE SAYS, every girl needs to have a good long cry once in a while. The kind that weakens you, swells your eyes shut, and strips away every shred of emotion from your body until the pain subsides. The pain of… *whatever*. Death, heartbreak, solitude, desire, jealousy. All the crap that becomes a badge of honor among women—like those little merit badges Girl Scouts have sewn on their uniforms, only *these* badges are stitched across our hearts.

Of course, the last place I needed to have a meltdown was in a candy store by the gummy worms. Sweet Treats had closed half an hour ago, and I was restocking the shelves while April handled the cash drawer.

It used to be a fun place to work… when I was twenty-one. But now I was twenty-seven and this shit was getting old. Maybe it was the smell of chocolate in the air playing tricks on my hormones, or watching all those rug rats screaming up and down the aisles and wishing I had one. Or maybe it was the fact that Brooke Worthington (although in high school she went by Brooke Jenson) had walked into the shop wearing a business suit with three kids in tow and asked, "Is this what you've been doing since high school?"

"Alexia, what's the matter?" April peered at me from around a stack of canisters, her charcoal-lined eyes wide. "Did someone die?"

Which brought another gasp to my sob.

Yeah, that too.

Tomorrow will be the seven-year anniversary of my brother's death. My older brother by three years, who taught me how to ride a bike because our dad was a total dick and ignored me. My older brother, who piled our beanbag chairs in front of the television and made awful microwave popcorn while we watched a scary movie whenever our parents went out. My older brother, who was into muscle cars and hung out with all the bad boys my best friends for *life* (whom I haven't seen since high school) wanted to marry. My older brother, who gave me Indian burns, hid my pink razors, and intimidated the hell out of my boyfriends when I started dating in high school.

My older brother, who was killed in a motorcycle accident when he was twenty-three and found two days later by passing motorists when they spotted his bike in a ditch off Highway 71.

"Alexia?"

April didn't know about my brother, Wes. Sometimes there are chapters in our lives we don't want others to read. She'd started working here a year ago when she was twenty-one, but the girl had plans. She had been submitting her résumé to the top companies in the area in hopes of getting her corporate career started. Her long-term goal was to be a project manager, but handling the register and the books stretched her experience in the meantime. Our boss even added on a few additional duties to give her an incentive to stick around. Plus, she had a backup plan of becoming a store manager if the corporate gig didn't pan out.

I didn't know much about April's personal life because she wasn't one of those girls who put it all out on the table. I once asked about her mom and she clammed up, so I never brought up the topic again. All I knew was she was a workaholic who talked about books, complained about her younger sister, adored animals, and possessed a charismatic laugh that turned heads. I always found myself doing or saying silly things to bring a smile to her face.

"I'm fine," I lied, but it came out all garbled, so I cleared my throat.

"You don't sound fine. Does this have to do with Beckett?"

I glared.

She smiled innocently and lifted her shoulder. "You're still separated, right? Sorry, but he's *hot* and you can't blame me for assuming you worked things out."

"He's also an asshole with a temper, not to mention he has a disturbing obsession with professional wrestling."

"Thought you liked the bad boys?"

I bit my lip. *Yeah, I kind of did.* Not that I sought them out intentionally, but maybe I was subconsciously searching for a tough guy—one who would help me forget how out of control I felt at times.

"Learn from my mistakes, April. You're a sweet girl and guys like that will only drag you down. They'll make you forget you ever aspired to do anything meaningful with your life. Then one day you'll be crying over the kitchen sink, scraping at a piece of dried macaroni that's stuck to a plate because the dishes haven't been washed in two days."

"Holy smokes, Alexia. You really need a happy pill in the worst way."

Her fingers dragged through the chunky strands of her blond hair. She styled it short with fashionably long bangs angled over one side of her face. The duality with April was interesting because her appearance was trendy and rockerish, but her personality was anything but. She kept her hair a platinum blond that looked so natural I wasn't sure it came from a bottle—I'd seen girls born with that hair color before. It was a stunning look. She often wore smoky eyeliner that added an allure to her jaw-dropping hazel eyes, and I would have killed for her flawless complexion. April was as pretty as a pixie but lacked a social life from what I had gathered. Her personality shined at work, but in private conversations, she possessed a shy demeanor.

Maybe shy wasn't the right word.

Sensitive. I caught onto this because April was clumsy, always bumping into things or stumbling over her feet. When kids made fun of her, she'd laugh it off. It only bothered her when someone our age or older made a joke. Men in particular, but I could relate to that. A few years ago, I stepped in a hole on the street and almost broke my ankle. All I could think about was how embarrassed I was that everyone saw me fall on my face. Never mind the fact I almost ended up in an ambulance. Only later was I mad no one had bothered to help.

April was an introspective girl with a big heart, even if she didn't have the gift of gab. A bird had once slammed into our shop window and died on the sidewalk. She'd tried to help it, but it was pointless. I'd ended up sending her home when I saw how upset she was. I'd never had any pets, so maybe I just couldn't relate. But it spoke volumes about her character.

"I'm closing up; are you done restocking the supply?" she asked.

I glanced at a jar of circus peanuts and nodded.

Normally, the black cloud of depression didn't follow me. I'd learned to embrace life no matter what was thrown my way, but today was one of those off days when rolling with the punches just meant getting beat up.

It usually did at this time of year.

I wiped away my tears and stood up, straightening out the wrinkles in my skirt. I'd been mistaken for a waitress on more than one occasion while wearing our uniform—and *that* was a compliment. Nobody was impressed when I told them I sold candy for a living, especially not anyone with two kids and a mortgage. My white skirt stopped two inches above my knees, paired with a tight-fitting orange shirt. To top off the ensemble, we wore white aprons and looked like we'd been slaving away in some magical candy kitchen, creating fantastical sugary treats.

We opened a bag and poured candy in a jar. End of story.

Our boss emphasized presentation: perfectly aligned canisters, attractive displays, and a well-groomed staff. He even gave us plastic hairclips to use if we wore our hair up. Cherries, orange slices, or little multicolored candies were our options.

Needless to say, I always wore my hair down.

"Are you sure you're okay, Alexia?" April asked, touching my shoulder as I walked by.

"I'm outta here," I announced, grabbing my purse from the drawer behind the register and digging for my keys. "You coming?"

"I'm going to be five more minutes," she said from behind me. "Go ahead and take off."

"Okay. Just remember..."

"Yeah?"

A lump formed in my throat. "Just remember you're taking my shift tomorrow."

"Will do. Remember you're taking mine on Saturday," she sang melodically.

Damn. Saturdays sucked. The store was like a zoo because we were located near a pizza shop, not to mention the movie theater was just a short walk up the street. Parents often dropped their kids off in herds, and telling a bunch of rowdy eleven-year-olds to behave when their moms weren't around was an exercise in futility.

"I won't forget," I replied with a sarcastic smile. "Can't wait."

"Liar."

The silver bell at the entrance jingled as the door closed behind me.

Then the sight of my own damn car made me want to start crying all over again. "What the hell is wrong with you, Lexi? Can't you keep it together for one day? It's not even *the* day and you're already a hot mess," I muttered.

"Alexia!" April yelled out. Only my close friends and family called me Lexi, but at work and otherwise, I went by my full name.

April held her thumb and pinky finger up to her face in that universal "you've got a phone call" gesture.

"Now what?" I murmured. My stomach knotted because nobody called me this late. It was well known I was probably the only twenty-something living in Austin without a cell phone. But hey, I never liked being accessible.

"Who is it?" I asked, walking past her to the counter. We had one of those ancient rotary phones, except ours had push buttons. Charlie, our boss, liked the retro look. There were small touches throughout the store and customers often shared memories of things they remembered from their own childhoods.

April eased up to the counter, blatantly eavesdropping to her heart's content.

"Hello?"

"Lexi, it's me. Let's talk."

The asshole.

"We don't talk anymore, remember?" I bit out. Not since Beckett had cheated on me with another woman, in my car.

My car.

I'd put the car up for sale two days ago and hadn't received a single inquiry. The thought of driving it made my stomach boil, and the memory of catching them having sex in it was unbearable. The whole thing was still fresh in my mind. Beckett's Mustang had been in the shop, so I'd lent him my car. One night, a friend of mine swung by Sweet Treats and I asked her if she could give me a lift to the bar where Beckett worked. I wanted to surprise him and play a little air hockey until his shift ended.

We pulled into the parking lot of Ducky's Dive, and as we passed my car, I yelled out for her to hit the brakes. It looked like a shadow was moving around inside, so I stuck my face up to the window. I saw Beckett stretched against the back seat with a brunette straddling him and riding him like a pony.

Oh yeah, it was *over*.

But not *as* over as when he saw me and panic flooded his eyes. I relished that moment, because it was the one that had "busted" written all over it. But that cheap little whore saw me and rode him even harder. He didn't push her away because he wanted to finish off. He later claimed it was out of his control—that you simply cannot take a man to the edge of ecstasy and expect him to stop.

Whatever.

"Lexi, I'm two blocks away and we're going to talk. It's been two months and I think I've suffered enough."

"Suffered?" I exclaimed. "Are you kidding me? You had sex with *Rhoda,* for God's sake."

Rhoda had been given the nickname "Rhoda Commoda" because she'd take her conquests into the bathroom and have sex in a stall.

"That woman's had sex with every man this side of Texas. *And* you did it in the back seat of my car," I reminded him. "This breakup isn't a temporary thing until I get over being pissed off at you, Beckett. We're over. As in, over and out."

I slammed the phone down and lifted my purse over my shoulder. "I have to go, he's on his way," I said in a hurried voice, jogging out the door.

The engine of his electric-blue Mustang was gunning down the road so ferociously that I took off in a mad dash to my car. My coffee-colored hair tangled in the summer wind, and I stumbled in my new white sneakers, dropping my keys on the pavement. Just as I bent down, the front end of his car vaulted off the concrete as he jumped the curb. He had barely put it in park when the door swung open.

"Lexi, come on. Don't be pissed."

Any words in my mouth disintegrated and turned into kindling for the fire raging inside me. I wanted to open my mouth and spit out a fireball, singeing all the pretty blond hairs on his oversized head. His arms stretched wide—large arms, because he bench-pressed free weights—and I felt corralled like a horse.

"Get out of my way."

"Look," he said calmly, "I know why you're upset. Your brother—"

"You don't know a damn thing about my brother; you never met him!" I screamed, pointing my finger. "Don't you dare wave my past at me like some kind of party trick that's going to make me vulnerable so you can try to smooth things over. You lied to me, cheated on me, and had sex in my car!"

"Dammit, Lexi, I'll buy you a new fucking car if that's the deal."

A hard sigh flew out of my mouth and I walked around him. He grabbed my arm and I shoved him away. "Let go," I said, fuming. "I'm warning you, Beckett. You do not want to mess with me tonight."

His jaw clenched and he surrendered, holding up his hands. "Fine. But we're going to talk," he said slowly, meaningfully, in a way that said we both knew this wasn't over.

"Fine," I lied. It wasn't fine, and we were *definitely* over.

April lingered by the door, cupping her elbows with a wistful look in her eyes that expressed her desire for a man who would tear up his prized vehicle to stop her from running away. She didn't mind about the cheating part and had once declared that no man could be faithful to just one woman. I wasn't having much luck disproving her theory, but I wanted to believe integrity and honor existed. Her acceptance of that lie would only make her a doormat for love. Never expect anything less than devotion from someone who has claim on your heart.

That's why I cut Beckett off like a malignant mole.

The key slid in the lock and the cheap vinyl creaked when I sat on it. I glanced in the rearview mirror at the back seat and shuddered. Memories infiltrated my mind like a plague and I throttled the engine, threw her into gear, and eased up on the clutch.

The car lurched and died.

God, the embarrassment. I could see Beckett laughing in the mirror and I flicked a hot gaze at him. After two years, I still fought with that stupid clutch. Beckett had bought the car as a surprise and I'd had no say-so in selecting it. We'd argued for a week while he tried to teach me to drive a standard.

"I hate you," I grumbled, finally speeding away.

I didn't know if that was true or not, but I'd never get over what he did to me. Not when memories of him holding me at night and telling me there was no other girl were still fresh on my mind. Women flirted with him all the time at the bar because he was the bouncer with all the muscles. But when I was there, he only had eyes for me.

Apparently, his dick had eyes for someone else.

CHAPTER 2

WHEN I SHOWED UP AT my mom's house the next morning, it felt like the funeral all over again. The yellow sun glimmered off the black mailboxes, and a light breeze knocked some of the hot pink blooms off the crepe myrtle trees. It created the fantasy of a summer snowfall, and I stood on the cracked sidewalk staring at the front yard, remembering the tire swing that used to hang from the oak tree on the right side of the lawn. Wes had loved spinning me around on that thing until I got dizzy. Sometimes I could still hear his laugh.

The door swung open and little Maizy came dashing out of the house in a bright yellow dress that was three shades darker than her hair. "Lexi! Lexi!"

As soon as she made it to me, her exuberant face tightened with all kinds of excitement. Her blue eyes widened with anticipation when she saw my right arm curved behind my back.

I bent over and whispered in her ear, "Don't tell Mom." As soon as I brought my hand around, she grabbed the bag of assorted candy, giggled, gave me a kiss on the cheek, and stuffed it inside the top of her dress. I snorted, following close behind as she ran back inside.

Maizy was the result of my brother's passing. Sometimes good things come out of tragic events, and she reminded us of that every day. I'd never seen a child so full of life and happiness as my Maze. Our parents weren't very sprightly to be dealing with a new baby, but they'd had Weston when mom was sixteen, so they weren't *that* old. The pregnancy came not long after his death, and Mom called Maizy her little miracle baby because five months later, she had a medical scare and underwent a hysterectomy.

"Mom," I called out, "I'm here."

"Yes, I just saw my well-endowed six-year-old dash into her bedroom and thought as much," she said, coming out of the kitchen. "I'm going to assume that's a bag of candy tucked in her dress and not an early growth spurt."

She was wearing a dark blue dress with a black belt and a silver necklace I gave her two years ago on her birthday. Mom had been lightening her shoulder-length hair since it started going grey and put it in rollers at night so it would hold a curl. We were close to the same height but looked nothing alike. I hadn't inherited her generous cup size or her Montana-blue eyes.

"You really need to stop bringing that girl candy. I'm too old to be chasing after her when she's all sugared up."

I kissed her cheek and breezed into the kitchen. "Oh come on, Mom. She *just* turned six. Who else is going to spoil her if not her big sis?"

Her kitchen had pale blue tile on the floor and a matching backsplash behind the sink. The cabinets were red oak and lined the wall above the counter all the way to the window on the left. Mom loved blue and the kitchen looked like a bluebird's nest. Tiny vines branched out across the wallpaper like an enchanted forest, but everything else was accented in blue, including the knitted toaster cover she'd bought at a craft fair. I reached in the fridge and grabbed a bottle of cold water.

"Lexi, it's just going to be us today."

I stared at the counter. "Why?"

"Your grandparents put their foot down." Mom sighed deeply, painfully. "I had a long talk with your grandma and she said it's too difficult and they don't want to relive this every year."

I whirled around. "Relive the fact they had a grandson?" I said in a hurt voice.

She calmly placed her hands on my shoulders. The dinner had become a tradition, although I was usually upset by the end of the party.

"*We're* his family, Lexi. That's all that matters. If your father were here, he might have agreed with them. I called off the dinner, so no one will be coming. It's just going to be a quiet day with us three girls."

I should have been happy because dinner always consisted of a few aunts and uncles, not to mention dysfunctional cousins I saw only at funerals or weddings, and several neighbors my parents had known for years. My biggest complaint was that no one talked about Weston at the party. It was just a casual get-together and then a sorrowful "damn shame that happened" goodbye at the door. Now it felt like this was evidence that no one really cared about remembering him but us.

Which was a lie. At some point, people had to move on from grief and tragedy. I knew this, and yet I struggled more than anyone with accepting his death. Over the years, my mom had acquired a coping mechanism I just didn't have when it came to Wes. He'd been more than a brother—he'd been my protector, my friend, and someone who would be there for me long after our parents left this earth. Wes and I had been as close as siblings could be. I'd confided to him that he was going to walk me down the aisle because our dad would probably pick his butt and then give some embarrassingly long speech about how I'd never amount to anything but a barefoot and pregnant wife. Dad had never been the most encouraging man, and maybe that's why Wes took over that role in looking out for me.

Three years after Wes died, my dad left us. All of us, including Maizy—who would never grow up with a father. Maybe it was for the better, all things considered, but it stung. Mom was in constant denial, and it showed in the way she talked about him like he was deceased and not living in Florida. At least, that's where we last heard he was. I tried thirty-six times to contact him via phone and mail, but never got through.

Sometimes I wondered if Wes would have liked the idea that Dad split. I should have been upset, but we girls made a great team. Mom was much too young to retire, so she held a part-time job in order to take care of Maizy. I'd helped as often as I could in the beginning because daycare was too expensive. Now that Maizy was in school, life was a little easier.

Aside from our family tragedies, we led normal lives. I talked to Wes in my head a lot and didn't pine over his death, except on *this* day, because it had always been made into a big production. It was the only time I visited his grave, because seeing it made his absence too real.

Maizy's white shoes clicked on the blue tile and I lifted her up onto the cabinet, twirling my fingers in her blond hair. It wasn't bright like April's—more like the color of sunshine smeared across the floor at sunrise.

"You look *garjus* today. Like a little diva fashion model."

She squealed out a giggle. "Mommy bought me a pretty ring. See?"

Maizy held up her little fingers so I could admire the pink stone. I winked at my mom. "Mommy has good taste."

"Someday, I'm going to marry a prince and he's going to give me one just like this."

I softly kissed her cheek. "Yes, you will. Now why don't we… race to the car!" I splayed my fingers across her belly, tickling until she screamed, jumped down, and went flying across the house.

"I'm going to beat you!" she called out.

"Lexi!" my mom scolded. "The whole neighborhood can hear that child when she screams."

"Well, guess that means you don't need the tornado sirens. Just give her a bullhorn and we can put her on the roof—"

Mom popped me on the butt with her hand and I chuckled. I might have been in my late twenties, but that woman still saw me as the smart-mouthed little girl who once stood up on a counter at a department store, folded my arms, and announced to everyone that perfume made you smell like a stinky pig. It was a protest because my mom wanted to buy me a bottle of the little girl's stuff that smelled like overripe bananas.

Ever since then, I've despised bananas.

"Let's go before it gets hot," I decided. "Do you want to eat at Dairy Queen or come home and make sandwiches?"

Mom grabbed her purse and wiped a tear from the corner of her eye. I reached out and hugged her tight.

"Let's eat out." She sniffled against my hair. "Maizy can get a chocolate-dipped cone. She likes those. I don't ever want her to go through life not having the things she wants. Sometimes I still feel guilty for not buying Wes a skateboard when he was nine. I should have given him *everything*," she said in a broken voice.

Tears welled in my eyes and rolled down my cheeks. "It's okay, Mom. I know. You gave him love, and that was all he needed."

We sniffed, sighed, and laughed at each other.

"My makeup is ruined," she said, sliding a finger beneath her lashes to wipe away the mascara.

"That's okay, Halloween is only four months away."

"You're never too old to be grounded, young lady."

We made a brief stop at the cemetery to lay down a bouquet of beautiful white lilies. Maizy climbed on the statues for a while and then we watched her pluck tiny yellow flowers (which were really weeds) from an open patch of grass and place them on Wes's grave, arranged in the shape of a heart. She'd never met her big bro, but he would have loved her to pieces.

Afterward, we swung by Dairy Queen. It was a new location that had opened earlier that year, and we stopped in once in a while to pick up a sack of burgers and fries, and of course a hot dog for Maizy.

We were sitting at a table by the window, watching Maizy color with a green crayon, when my mom gasped and covered her mouth. "Oh my God, is that who I think it is?"

I swiveled my head around in the direction she was looking. Sunlight reflected off the glass as the door opened and made me squint. Stepping through the front door of Dairy Queen... was Austin Cole.

Also known as my brother's "best friend for life." They'd met in the first grade and had been inseparable ever since. He and Wes had run with the same crowd, sometimes dated the same girls, and could finish each other's sentences. Austin used to spend the night at our house and we'd treated him like a member of the family. In fact, when I was thirteen, I secretly decided we were going to get married. I had doodled Alexia Cole inside my notebook where no one would find it.

As kids, Austin used to pick on me without provocation. He once plucked off all the eyes on my stuffed animals and would dip his finger in my juice glass at the breakfast table and flick the drops at me. He didn't have a sister, so he probably didn't know how to deal with girls. Austin wasn't doing it to be cruel—he just enjoyed getting a rise out of me. I *was* a dramatic little girl.

"He's changed," Mom said in a quiet voice.

Her sullen expression at his unexpected appearance told the story. The last time we had seen him was seven years ago at the funeral. He'd left town that week without any explanation. No phone call, no letter, and that hurt. We'd been like his second family.

The visual of his body standing in front of the door burned into my retinas. His swagger in those loose jeans, the way his tight T-shirt had come untucked on the right side, the black leather Oxfords, and most notably, the ropes of muscle in his arms. Austin no longer resembled the boyish young man I had last seen seven years ago. He had filled out in all the right places. While I couldn't see his eyes behind those mirrored shades, I knew they were still crystal blue and the most remarkable feature he possessed, although the slight cleft in his chin came in a close second. Something about those pale eyes against his brown hair and thick brows could make a woman forget her own name.

He was dangerously handsome and held the attention of every woman of age in the room.

"Is she pretty?" Maizy asked, holding up her picture.

I blinked.

Princess in a green dress with an orange face. "She's beautiful, Maze."

My heart pounded against my chest and Mom stabbed the ice cubes in her cup with a clear straw. When her eyes lifted and locked, I knew right then and there he'd spotted her and they were engaged in a staring match. I waited expectantly for him to come up from behind and say an awkward hello.

Instead, I glanced out the window and saw Austin walking briskly to the adjacent parking lot where he had parked his classic

Dodge Challenger. It was a badass model with black paint and tinted windows.

"Mom?"

I didn't even know what I was going to ask. I just felt like something had to be said to deaden the moment.

He had been a second son to her, and maybe having him around after Wes's death might have helped her get through it. I knew that thought crossed her mind, so I shot up to my feet. "I'm going to get some ice cream."

"Yay!" Maizy cheered.

I marched over to the counter and right out the door, staring at his tinted windows with my hands on my hips. The tires spun, throwing gravel across the parking lot as he tore off.

But I knew Austin had seen me.

A boy named after the city he was born and raised in. A kid who ate dinner at our house three nights a week. A man who now sped off like a bona fide chickenshit when faced with the option of talking to his dead friend's sister.

A man who'd kissed me passionately the night my brother was killed.

CHAPTER 3

B Y TEN O'CLOCK THAT EVENING, we'd eaten pork chops, watched a movie, and I'd left the house with a bottle of Mom's whiskey. It wasn't a favorite drink of mine, but she never touched the stuff and I needed something to help me sleep through the night. My wine collection at home was reserved for good times, and I didn't want to taint my favorite beverage with sorrow.

This anniversary was never officially over until I was rip-roaring drunk.

On the way home, I made an unplanned visit to the cemetery. It was closed, but no one ever locks up a cemetery so tight that you can't get in; it's the getting out part that proves the most difficult.

Wes had a flat grave marker and I hated it. I tried to talk my mom into getting one of the raised ones to replace it, but she'd refused. Maybe that selfish part of me wanted something at eye-level to look and talk to, or maybe even hug.

"God, Wes. You should see how much Maze has grown," I said, sitting Indian style over his grave. It was dark as sin, and the only light illuminating the grounds shone from a tall lamp near a marble statue of an angel. "She's so sweet, not like me. I was a little terror and *you*," I said, waving my unsteady finger at the ground, "should have never let me go out with Josh Holden when I was fifteen. What were you thinking?"

I hiccupped and screwed the cap back on the bottle.

"Just because he was on the football team, you thought he was cool and he passed whatever test you had for the guys who called me up. Josh thought he was going to score a touchdown that night." I snorted. "That was the first time I'd ever been to second base and when he started to slide into third, I slapped his face and walked home. Josh works at the gas station now. But then, who am I to talk?" I yelled up at the trees. "I'm just a *candy* girl."

The grass met with my back and I gazed up at an infinite blanket of stars. Smog dimmed their usual brightness because I wasn't far enough out of the city. Plus, I was three sheets to the wind.

"Guess who I saw today, Wes? Your best friend."

I quietly lay there, thinking about how it made me feel.

"And?" a voice asked.

"And what? He pussied out and drove off in his tough-guy car." My fingers yanked on the grass angrily and then it dawned on me— the voice I'd just heard wasn't my imagination.

I rolled over and saw Austin leaning on his left shoulder against an aging tree. Austin always liked to do an ankle-cross while scoping out his surroundings. I used to think it was sexy as hell when he wore his leather jacket and fingerless gloves.

It took years before I realized that most girls probably had a crush on their brother's best friend at some point in time. No big deal—just a childhood thing.

But *damn*, that lean was hot.

My eyes blinked a few times, as if I could make him disappear.

"Only time I ever saw you drunk, Lexi Knight, was the time we drove to San Antonio to a concert. Not even old enough to order a drink. Do you remember?" Austin pushed off the tree and stepped forward a few paces, arms crossed. "Wes was pissed when he found out those guys were buying you beers and he pulled you out of their truck before they decided to take the party to a new location. Good thing we found you when we did."

"Oh? And where were you? I don't even remember you *being there*."

I emphasized the last bit and by the look on his face, he got my meaning.

"Kicking the shit out of every last man in that truck, that's where I was. Got my nose broke in the process."

The air stilled.

The only thing about that night I remembered was going to the concert, some guys giving me drinks from their cooler, and then hanging out in the parking lot cracking jokes. The next day, I woke up sick as a dog and Austin hadn't returned to the hotel room. Wes drove my hung-over ass home and told our parents I had caught the flu. Since Austin had taken a separate car, I just assumed he left without us or was banging some girl all night.

"That's right," he said, carefully watching my stunned expression with shadowy eyes I couldn't see in the darkness. "Bruised my knuckles knocking out the third guy, but he deserved it."

"Why?"

"Because it was *his* lap you were sitting on," he said in a low and dangerous voice.

A muscle flexed in his jaw and he lifted the bottle of whiskey, taking a slow swallow as a lightning bug flashed beside his shoulder. Austin screwed the cap on and I closed my eyes. I could have slept right there, sitting up in a graveyard with a ghost of my past in front of me.

"I'll take you home."

"No."

"I'm not letting you drive in this condition."

"What are you even doing here?" I finally snapped my eyes open. "Seven years, not a word, and you just show up and think everything is okay? Get away from me, and get off Wes's grave."

He flicked his eyes down and stepped to the side, shoving his fingers through his hair in a frustrated manner. "I think you've had too much to drink."

I fell back and curled to my side, mumbling myself to sleep. "I don't care what you think anymore. Leave me and Wes alone."

———◦◦◦◦———

When I opened my eyes, it was morning. I was asleep in the back seat of my Toyota with one leg stretched between the front seats and the other pressed against the glass.

"Shit," I murmured, rubbing the crud from my eyes. My long hair was all over the place. *Thank God* I was still at the cemetery because I was wearing a dress and lying in a position a gynecologist would endorse.

Then I sat up and found myself staring at a neighborhood, or more accurately, my mom's front yard. *Nope, I wasn't at the cemetery.*

A curse flew past my lips and I quickly glanced around and made sure the neighbors weren't out mowing their lawns or calling the police. The last thing I needed was my mom waking up and wondering why the hell I was giving the neighborhood a peep show in the back of my Toyota.

I leapt into the front seat and headed home.

During the drive, I gave myself a lecture, mostly going over the stupidity of driving drunk, even though I couldn't remember a thing. What was I thinking? Even worse, my stomach was churning like one of those hand-cranked ice cream mixers and if I didn't get to a bathroom soon, I was going to be sick in my car.

After arriving at my apartment, I dragged my feet up the second flight of stairs, stumbling twice.

"That good, was it?"

I glanced at my neighbor, Naya, and she caught the irritated look in my eyes. Naya threw world-famous parties in her apartment and invited everyone in the complex. She did it to give them fair warning there would be loud music, probably a few broken bottles, maybe a fight, and a drunk playing *Urinator* in the pool. Naya worked as a stripper and once came into the candy shop looking for an oversized pinwheel lollipop. She invited me to a party and that's when I found out what she did for a living. But off the clock she dressed like everyone else, and we hit it off as friends even though we had little in common.

We recently ended up living next door to each other when I needed a place to live after my breakup with Beckett. I wondered if she'd paid off her neighbor to break his lease, because the timing was impeccable.

Naya didn't have a man, at least not a permanent one. She was a huntress and hung out with some wealthy and dangerous men she'd met at work. Trouble usually came with money, but Naya said she'd paid her dues and wanted a better life.

My dues were about to wind up all over the landing if I didn't get my ass inside.

"Later, Naya."

I slammed the door and made a World Series slide to home plate in the bathroom, regretting every second of the previous night as I retched. After my humiliating porcelain moment of the day, I stripped out of my dress and debated whether or not I wanted to take an unsavory nap on the bathroom floor. Instead, I hopped in the shower and washed pieces of grass out of my hair. It felt delicious to stand beneath the spray of hot water, and after towel drying my hair, I snuggled up in my favorite pink robe.

I hadn't been that drunk in a long time and wondered why I never learned my lesson. The only thing on my mind after that was coffee, so I headed into the kitchen to brew a pot of Italian roast. That's when I saw Naya sitting at my bar playing solitaire. My wet hair squeaked when I pulled it around my shoulder and ran my hand down the long length of it.

"Don't you knock?" I said grumpily, staring at a pot of already-brewed coffee.

"Don't you lock?" she countered. "We don't live in Bel Air, missy. You don't think there are a few thugs in this complex that wouldn't love to find an unlocked door and rob you blind?"

"Oh God, you're right," I muttered, sliding my feet across the cold tile. "I don't think I could live without my nineteen-inch television or the transistor radio I bought at a garage sale."

I poured a steaming cup and sat on the wood cabinet inside the kitchen, facing Naya who was on the other side of the sink. I was being facetious because I did own a laptop and some small electronic toys, but I wasn't exactly living large and a thief wouldn't make off with much.

Her broad mouth twisted as she placed a card on the bar. "Someone's in a funk."

Naya had a curvy figure like a young Salma Hayek in one of those old movies where she's dancing seductively on tables. She had glossy black hair in beautiful curls and exotic eyes. Naya once tried to teach me how to dance at one of her parties. It got out of control when two idiots thought they were getting a free show with a personal lap dance to follow.

I went home five minutes later.

"Rough day at work?" she asked with a smile. That was an inside joke because my rough days consisted of screaming kids while hers ended up in fistfights between horny customers and the bouncers.

I never brought up Wes with anyone, so I shrugged. "Just felt like cutting loose for a change."

Naya had a way of staring me down to the very fraction of a lie I just told, and the moment my eyes darted away, a smug look of satisfaction crossed her face.

"Everyone is entitled to a night out," I continued, sprinkling a little sugar in my cup before taking a sip.

"Glad to hear you're alive and kicking. That means you'll be coming to my party on Tuesday."

"Don't people have to work?"

"Not the people I hang out with, darling. You know that. Tuesdays are my Saturday, and I know for a fact you don't work every other Wednesday. There's going to be a great crowd—lots of fat wallets and alcohol."

"It's not the size of a man's wallet that counts, Naya."

Her ruby lips turned up in a carnivorous smile. "Hon, that's the only bulge in the pants that *really* counts in the long run."

We both laughed, although deep down I had a feeling she wasn't joking. As sexual as Naya was, she didn't seem to care about a guy fulfilling her physical needs. She wanted stability—a man who could offer her a better way of life. She equated security with money. Some women just liked being taken care of; I was not one of those women.

"I'll come," I agreed. "But no dancing. And don't do your thing."

"What thing?" She laid down a queen and the tip of the card made a snapping sound against the bar.

"You know to which thing I refer." I took another slow sip of my beverage. "The match game. *Don't* do it. If my destiny is at the party and I can't find him myself, then clearly I should go home without a parting gift. It's embarrassing."

She lifted two fingers. "Promise." Naya glanced at her watch. "Ooo, I've got to run. Will you feed Misha? I'm working a double shift tonight."

I groaned and padded into the living room. "I don't know why dry food is such a big no-no. It's a cat, Naya."

She swung the door open and glanced over her shoulder. "You're the only person I've ever known who didn't like my pussy."

I snorted and didn't bother to respond. I had a love-hate relationship with her cat. I loved to hate it.

"The wet food is by the fridge—"

"I know. Go on, I'll take care of little Misha."

Naya blew a kiss and slammed the door.

"Lock it!" She yelled from the outside.

I turned the bolt, set my coffee on an end table, and collapsed on the sofa. All I could think about was Austin. Did I really see him at the cemetery? Maybe I dreamed it. I never could hold my liquor and it didn't take much to get me drunk, not to mention I was one of those people who blacked out if I drank too much. Not passed out, but conscious and sometimes belting out old rock songs. At least, that's what Naya told me, as did a girl I used to party with when I was younger. That's why I avoided binge drinking.

No one needed to hear my rendition of "Feel Like Makin' Love."

Still, the conversation had seemed so real.

I was angry and kept hitting the stupid rewind button in my brain, causing me to replay the scene at Dairy Queen. Except in episode two, I got up and cussed him out. By episode three, I told my mom to take Maizy outside and I tore him a new one for walking out of our lives. By four, I managed to get information on where he'd been all this time before slapping him. Somewhere around episode twelve, I started making out with him, and by eighteen, we were having sex all over the hood of his Dodge Challenger.

That's when I got up and took another shower.

CHAPTER 4

THE NEXT DAY AT WORK, we were slammed with orders. I don't know if there were a lot of cheating husbands or sick grandmas or what, but Sweet Treats was hopping. Aside from selling candy, we customized gift items. You could choose from a number of candy combinations and have them packaged for different occasions in the container or basket of your choice. It wasn't just a store for kids—we also sold expensive chocolates and gourmet popcorn. I'd sampled them to death over the years and officially murdered my love for sugar.

If a guy ever gave me a box of candy (not that one ever would, all Beckett ever gave me was a box of Victoria's Secret lingerie), that would be the equivalent of giving me a box of anchovies. It's not that I hated candy, but the magic was gone. A man should be more original than a bouquet of roses and a box of chocolates. Flowers die and sugar sticks to your hips like a permanent record to a criminal.

However, all superheroes have a kryptonite. I had one weakness.

Lollipops.

Our store only sold the cheap flat ones for the kids and those pinwheel multicolored novelty items. But my *favorites* were the large round suckers that came in various flavors, including gourmet. We tried carrying them but they never sold. Kids always wanted the chocolate bars or some of the newer candy based on their favorite cartoons or movies. Older generations wanted the hard-to-find items from their childhood or gourmet products. So things like lollipops, peppermints, and butterscotch just didn't sell.

The only person who knew how much I loved them was Wes. It's how he used to bribe me to stay quiet whenever he was going to sneak out of the house or if I caught him in a lie. I was a sucker for suckers, and bribery came at a very reasonable price for him. Our parents never bought junk food unless we went to the movies. Only in recent years had Mom let go of the reins when it came to sugar and offered Maizy an occasional treat.

April bounced into the room holding a beautifully wrapped basket with a yellow ribbon. "Here you are, Mrs. Lee."

"Oh, that's just gorgeous! Ellie's going to love it," the older lady gushed. "She hasn't tasted some of these candies since she was a little girl." Mrs. Lee took a moment to admire the packaging before heading out the door.

"Come by and see us again," April said with a wave. "Thanks for stopping in, and be sure to tell all your friends to visit Sweet Treats!"

The bell jingled and I glared at her from behind the display of gumballs. "That's a bit much."

So were the cherry earrings she was wearing and the matching pin clipped in her bright blond hair.

April tilted her head and the earrings swiveled. "You could learn something from me, Alexia. It's not just about sales, but returning customers. You *want* them to tell their friends about us and feel like they need to come back here again for more. Charlie doesn't offer coupons and we don't do any marketing, so word of mouth is all we have. Relationship building is important for an independently run business."

"We sell crack, April."

A kid went jumping by as if there were invisible hopscotch lines on the floor. I nodded at him to illustrate my point.

"You don't think this place could ever go out of business?"

I shrugged. "If the movie theater or pizza shop closes, then yeah. But this street is a freeway of hyperactive kids between the ages of Winnie-the-Pooh diapers and high school saggy pants. Not to mention the fact we offer pick-up through the Internet."

"Not everyone likes picking up when they can have it delivered to their house by another company," she pointed out, refilling a display of Ring Pops.

It was near closing time and I sanitized the counter, wiping away all the grimy little fingerprints and germs.

After hours when we closed the shop and turned on the dim accent lights, it became pure magic. Long canisters lined the walls and we had several short aisles with packaged candy and other items. We didn't have any fancy neon sign—just a pink board that ran over the doorway with the store name painted in black. We were open from ten to ten—at least those were the advertised hours. Everyone on this side of town knew we'd stay open as long as there were customers. Night owls loved it because the colorful displays in the window would catch their eye and draw them in for a late night snack before or even after their movie. I mentioned to Charlie once or twice that he should consider making us a hybrid business—perhaps buy the space next door to open a coffee shop and offer sweet treats for the adults, with a door connecting the shops. "Pipe dreams," he would say. Charlie might have gone for it, but he probably didn't have the money.

We admittedly got some peculiar customers wandering in; some of them looked like hardcore criminals while others just had strange eye colors. But sometimes there was a single guy and that's how I ran into Beckett. It was hard to pass by our shop at night because the beautiful displays in the window brought out the child in everyone.

The last customer left the store and I stretched out my stiff muscles. "You feel like going to a party, April? It's a little wild and crazy and there's no telling who will be there. My neighbor is throwing one on Tuesday. You can swing by after work if you want; it'll be going on all night."

She considered it and scrunched the ends of her short hair. "Maybe. Where?"

"You've been to my apartment once or twice; it's the one right next door. Stop by and keep me company. I told her I'd show up, but sometimes those parties can get a little nuts and I'd rather have someone there who's…"

Her eyes narrowed. "Who's what?"

Um—extracting foot from mouth. "Who's sensible and won't end up dancing naked on the balcony."

April shrugged. "I might. Depends on how tired I am."

I twirled my keys around my finger and stood at the

door. "Coming?"

"No. My sister is picking me up tonight and I have a book to finish reading."

I furrowed my brow and leaned on one of the display counters by the front window. "Something wrong with your car?"

April fidgeted with a stretchy bracelet on her arm. "I think it's the transmission, but I don't know anything about cars."

"Come on; I'll give you a lift."

She averted her eyes. "Nah. I already got a ride."

A grin crept up my face. "Actually, I happen to have a viable solution for you. See that *beautiful* Toyota out there in the parking lot? It can be yours for a reasonably low—"

"Save it," she said with an outstretched hand. "I don't want your cootiemobile."

Damn that hurt. "See ya, April."

Standing on the curb, I glared at the car. Not one single inquiry. At this point, I'd consider selling it for a dollar just to get rid of the memories. But I needed a way to get to work so that wasn't an option.

The lights shut off in the shop and April locked the door, waved, and went into the back room. I was crossing the street toward the parking lot with a slow, reluctant gait when a familiar voice called out from behind.

"Sexy Lexi?"

I cringed. I hadn't been called that name since high school when Michael Hudson deflowered me. After that, he called me Sexy Lexi and all his friends thought I was a slut. Isn't that always the way it goes?

"*Please, please, please*, don't let it be him," I murmured as I turned around.

"It's me, Mike Hudson. Remember? We dated in high school."

He smirked, lingering by the fire hydrant in a pair of jeans and a blue sports jersey. He still looked the same with curly brown hair and a light dusting of whiskers, but he'd put on a little weight around the gut. Without missing a beat, Michael walked in my direction and I began to get nervous.

"Still lookin' good, Sexy Lexi."

"Don't call me that, Michael. I never liked that nickname."

"All in fun," he said defensively, easing up to my right. "So, you work at Sweet Treats?"

When his eyes slid down my body and up again, I stepped back. "Yeah. Do you work around here?"

Michael stepped forward. "Nah. I'm in town visiting my parents and decided to take a tour down memory lane—hook up with some of the guys. Want to join us? We're having pizza and beers over there," he said, pointing three shops up the road.

"No, thanks. You guys have fun. I have to go, but it was good seeing you," I lied, turning on my heel and walking briskly toward the car.

"Wait a minute," he protested, jogging up behind me. "It's been how many years and you're giving me the cold shoulder? I thought you liked me?"

I whirled around and pressed my finger against his chest. "You gave me a bad reputation and then after my brother beat your ass, you had your friends jump him when he got off work. Then I was tagged with that sorry fucking nickname that stuck for three years. *Three years*, Michael." I glanced down at his wedding band. "Go home to your wife and kids, and just pray some idiot doesn't ever do that to one of your daughters."

I finally had my moment and it felt really damn good as I stormed to the car, ready to do my victory dance. I'd waited a long time to tell him off, and it didn't require a ten-minute speech. The less time I had to spend with him, the better.

But then he caught my wrist.

"You're still mad over that?"

I turned around and tugged my arm, but he kept a firm hold. Memories of our relationship flooded back. Something never felt right about our first time, but I assumed that's how it went with all the girls. The boy pressuring, the girl saying no, the boy insisting, the girl squirming because it hurt, the boy telling her it was always like that the first time and holding her wrists, the girl wincing in pain and crying. "*Next time it won't hurt as bad*," he'd said to me.

There *was* no next time with Michael. Maybe I was naïve in thinking the first time should have been special, but he was an insensitive jerk and I regretted giving myself to him. When I had refused to have sex with him again, he broke up with me.

That's when he made up the nickname and harassed me for the rest of the school year with obscene gestures in the hallway and spreading rumors.

I snapped my arm back again but he kept hold of it. The streets were empty and most of the shops had closed down except for the pizza place and theater.

"Look, I'm sorry," he finally said. "We were just a bunch of dumb kids. Let me walk you to your car and we'll go our separate ways. It's been a long time and I don't think it's fair you're holding me accountable for something I did when I was a teenager."

We were moving toward the car and I was too confused to react because of how reasonable he seemed.

"If it's any consolation, your brother had his friends kick the living shit out of mine as payback."

I blinked. "No, he didn't." Not that Wes would have told me, but it didn't sound like him.

"Yeah, he did. I don't know who did it, either, because none of the guys talked about it. Someone must have threatened them because I can't even get them to talk about it today. They stayed out of school for a week with their faces all messed up."

We approached the car and I sighed. "Thanks, Michael. Look, what's done is done. Have a good life."

Damn, that sounded cold, and I opened the door to my cootiemobile.

That's when Michael gripped the hem of my skirt and yanked it up, pushing me against the open door. My heart raced and I couldn't breathe from the sudden shock of being forcefully pinned. Either I'd have to stand there and let him grope me or get in the car. I sure as hell wasn't getting in the car with him right behind me. My hands rested on the roof and I started to push back when he grabbed my hips with a painful grip.

"Still feels good, Sexy Lexi. *Real* good," he growled in my ear, running familiar hands over a place where they had once been. "Just like old times."

The next thing I knew, Michael was yanked off me quicker than a heartbeat. I pulled down my skirt and turned around, confused by the abrupt cessation and silence.

Oh, my God.

Austin was straddling Michael, his brutal hands wrapped around his throat, squeezing tightly. Michael's face swelled up until it turned an ugly shade of bluish red, his mouth agape as he struggled to get air in. He tried to punch Austin and buck him off, but that was about as effective as moving the Great Pyramid of Giza.

I tackled Austin, knocking him onto the cement and falling on my side. Michael made a sound like a donkey as he pulled air into his lungs and Austin rolled over to finish what he started.

I climbed on his back and curved my arm around his neck in a viselike hold. "Austin, no! You'll kill him, you idiot."

Michael catapulted to his feet while holding his throat and jogged the hell out of there. When Austin stood up, I lost my grip and fell on my back. He turned to go after Michael but changed his mind when he saw me laid out on the concrete.

"Christ, Lexi. You okay?"

He knelt down and looked me over. I disappeared in his frosty blue eyes—so pale they resembled a Siberian Husky's. They were rimmed with inky black lashes and wolfish brows, which furrowed with concern.

"Lexi?"

"What are you doing here?" I asked, propping myself up on my elbows.

"Besides saving your ass from a dead man? Walking."

I lurched up and pushed myself off the ground. Austin slid his large hand beneath my arm to help and I knocked it away. "I can do it myself," I said.

"You always were stubborn," he mumbled.

"Capable," I countered, glaring up at him.

Up. Because I swear Austin had sprouted a few inches in the last seven years. I mentally measured him to be just over six foot, but when we last saw each other, he was probably around five-eleven. I knew this because I was five-feet seven inches. And a quarter.

He stared down his nose. "Stubborn."

I raised a brow. "You really want to fight with me in the middle of a parking lot? Why are you here, Austin? I know this isn't the side of town you hang out in."

He rubbed his jaw and scanned the parking lot once more. "I followed you to work."

I blanched. "My shift started nine hours ago."

Austin folded his thick, tattooed arms and belted me with a judgmental glare. "Can you drive?"

"Texas Department of Motor Vehicles seems to think so."

Austin's lips twitched. "Get in the car, then. I'll wait."

I brushed my dirty apron and lifted my purse from the ground, grabbing the lipstick that had rolled behind a tire. I peered over my shoulder; Austin stood with his hands deep in his pockets and I heard the sound of coins jingling as he looked around.

"Do you normally leave work this late?"

I didn't answer because after what had just happened, I was too flustered and didn't think it was an appropriate time to have a conversation.

Once inside my car, I started the engine and fought with the clutch. She sputtered and immediately died. I expected to see Austin laughing the way Beckett often did.

He wasn't. His brows knitted and he looked like he was about to step in until the engine turned over and I got her running. What bothered me was the distracted look on his face. Austin looked like a man who was three ticks away from beating the holy shit out of someone.

And that someone was going to be Michael Hudson. I should have said something, but I drove off and watched him in the rearview mirror as he stalked toward the pizza shop with a heavy swing in his step.

I always believed Karma would come back to Michael for how cruel he was to me in high school. Karma just happened to be a man named Austin Cole.

CHAPTER 5

ON FRIDAY AFTERNOON, I PICKED up Maizy for our playdate. It had become a tradition to go to a movie and then stop off at Pizza Zone. It gave my mom a break from reality so she could get a manicure or just take a nap. Maizy was such a good-hearted little girl, one who from an early age considered the feelings of others. She didn't like to see anyone cry and always cleaned up without being asked. Maizy had her moments like any six-year-old, but she was my Maze, and I loved her unconditionally.

"Lexi?"

"Yeah?"

"Can I go play now?"

I took another sip of my soda and admired her sparkly blue eyes. Wes and I got the brown hair and eyes in the family, but Maizy was a little ray of sunshine who had the same enviable features as our mom.

I glanced at her plate. "Are you finished?"

She had only taken a few bites of cheese pizza and I knew the excitement of the noisy games and hyperactive kids was too much to resist.

Maizy flashed a bright smile. She'd lost one of her bottom baby teeth and the Tooth Fairy had paid her a visit.

I hated to be one of those people who force-fed a child, so I nodded and watched her run over to the play zone. It was a walled-off area with plastic tunnels and ropes to swing on. She kicked off her shoes by the entrance and waved before disappearing inside the first series of yellow tunnels with the other kids. Maizy mostly played by herself because even though she had just turned six, she hadn't yet come out of her shell. It seemed like yesterday we were changing her diapers, and before too long, I'd probably be helping her pick out a dress for prom.

I thought about Austin. Had he gone after Michael, or was I reading too much into that? Austin had no right appearing out of nowhere and fighting my battles, although I was glad he'd shown up when he had. Still, he'd never once tried to contact me in all the time after Wes's death. It shouldn't have bothered me as much as it did, but he was such an integral part of our family that it was as if I'd lost two people that year instead of one. Austin had parents and siblings, but I'd never met them. I wasn't even sure if they lived in the area.

I twirled my pigtails around my fingers while watching Maizy swing on one of the ropes.

Before I could draw a breath, Beckett slid in the chair in front of me. "Knew I'd find you here," he said smugly.

Beckett had on that damn T-shirt I hated, the one that said "Meathead." It was just the sheer principle of a man proudly labeling himself as an idiot.

"Beckett," I warned. "Let's not do this here."

He narrowed his lashless eyes. "You got a right to be mad, Lexi. I fucked up. But I'm not perfect—no one is. You've got your fair share of baggage, and I've got mine."

I crossed my arms and leaned back in the plastic chair. "Are you calling your infidelity… *baggage*?"

He snorted, staring at my head. "You look ridiculous with your hair that way. Take it down so we can have a real conversation. I can't talk to you like this."

"How about you not talk to me at all? We're done, Beckett. That's nonnegotiable."

"Lex," he said, placing his hand firmly on my arm.

I bolted out of the chair and headed in the other direction. Leaving him was one of the most difficult things I had done in my life, and we had already gone through all this. Now he was picking at a scab and trying to make it bleed again.

"Lex, wait," he called out. I passed the pinball machines and he caught up with me by skeeball.

I turned around, tired of all the running. "Stop following me,

Beck. It's creeping me out. I don't want to keep reliving this over and over. Don't you get it? There's no going back and undoing what you did."

He gripped my shoulders. "Look, babe, I'm sorry. Please forgive me. It was a mistake and I won't—"

"Save it," I interrupted. "You'll never know what that did to me, and it's not something I can easily get over. Maybe some women can, but you've always known that was the deal breaker for me. Not only would I always be wondering where you were when you came home late, but I'd always know that I wasn't enough for you. I loved you, Beckett. I trusted you, and you broke that."

His grip tightened when I tried to shrug him away. "Lex, you know you're the only girl for me, right? You're the girl I want to marry."

I snapped.

My hands flew out in a karate-chop move I must have seen on one too many Kung Fu movies. A stunned look crossed his face when his arms were knocked away.

"Fine! Goddammit, I'm just trying to make it right again. Fucking *bitch*!" he yelled, storming out of the room.

There I stood amid ringing bells, screaming kids, and arcade machines.

Shaking.

I had to pull it together before my sister saw me have a nervous breakdown.

"Maizy, stay right where you are and don't go anywhere," I shouted, holding my finger out. "I'm going potty."

She nodded and I walked to the restroom, only a few feet away. But once I entered the empty hall, I couldn't go any farther. I allowed my body to slide down the wall and I covered my eyes as a tidal wave of pain surfaced.

I'd been with Beckett for *two* years, and through our ups and downs, I had started to imagine a life with him. One that might have involved kids, or maybe even going to college and figuring out what I wanted to do in life besides working a cash register. It took me two years to give him all of my heart, and he threw it away in one night. I'd thought he loved me. How many other times were there? Didn't matter.

Once was enough.

"Lexi?"

Two heavy hands covered my knees. "What's wrong?" The controlled anger belonged to Austin Cole.

My stupid tears. Damn them. I was already trying to get myself together and now my emotions switched gears to another part of my life that was an open wound.

"Why did you leave us?" I finally asked. The words felt like a sword because I'd said them a number of times over Wes's grave. It hurt to breathe for the first year after his death.

Austin sighed hard. The kind of sigh that had a long, regretful story behind it. "Lexi, I can't talk about this with you right now. Are you okay?"

Finally wiping my tears, I glanced up. Austin crouched in front of me wearing a white shirt and a leather-rope necklace with a round medallion made of silver. The tattoos on his upper arms briefly caught my attention, but when his sharp blue eyes cut through me, I looked away.

"I'm fine," I lied.

He lowered his head with a doubtful glare. "No, you're not."

"What are you doing here? Why do you keep showing up out of the blue at the worst times?"

"I'm back for good, Lexi. I want to set things straight and there's a lot I need to tell you, but this isn't the place. You tell me when's a good time and we'll get together."

I sniffed and gave a barely perceptible nod.

Austin let go of my knees and reached forward, sliding his hands down my hair with a short grin.

"It's Pretty Pigtail Day," I said in a small voice. "I do this with Maizy a couple of times a month." I didn't even bother explaining who Maizy was.

Austin didn't laugh. "It reminds me a little bit of you at that age. I remember you wearing your hair like this, or sometimes braided in the back. Come on, let's get up." He hooked his hands beneath my arms and lifted me to my feet. "You sure you're okay?"

Before I could answer, his thumb slid across my cheek, wiping away a tear. All those stupid rehearsals I'd played out in my head of telling him off were stuck in pause, and I felt ashamed I'd later be rewinding this moment, wishing I had tossed him into the bin of plastic balls.

He reached in his back pocket and pulled out a business card, placing it in my hand. "Call me when you're ready to talk, Ladybug."

I lifted my hand and admired a plain off-white card. Austin's name was on the front with a phone number beneath. A symbol of a bow and arrow filled in the right-hand corner, but nothing indicated what he did for a living. Did that mean he was Robin Hood?

When I looked up, Austin was gone.

The card went into my purse and I decided to take Maizy home. Austin had left the ball in my court, and while it felt good to know the mystery of his disappearance would be solved, it also irritated me. Now in order to get any answers, I'd have to go crawling back to him, and that didn't leave me in a position of power. I didn't know how to feel about it, but I knew one thing: panic flooded my veins like rocket fuel when I didn't see Maizy in the play zone.

"Maizy?"

My heart raced and I whirled around, dizzy with fear. I frantically searched the tunnels, peering through the clear plastic domes just to make sure she wasn't hiding.

"Maizy? Come out from hiding! It's time to go!"

When she didn't answer, I went into a complete state of panic, screaming her name and pacing around. Kids were turning to stare and a few moms lifted their chins and glanced around the room.

Oh God, I've lost her.

After I'd combed the room five times and scoured the bathrooms, I ran out of the restaurant to the brightly lit entrance in front of the parking lot.

"Lexi! Lexi!" a bright little voice yelled out.

My head swung to the right. Beckett stood motionless beside my little sister, holding her hand.

"Maizy," I gasped, my arms flying out. She let go of his hand and ran into my outstretched arms. "Don't you ever leave me like that, do you understand?"

"Uncle Beck gave me a ring," she said, holding up a plastic toy affixed to her finger.

I glared at him and he shrugged, walking away.

But something else made me uneasy—Maizy would have never left that room by herself. Beckett lured her out of there on purpose just to scare me.

It worked.

He'd resorted to a low tactic by taking advantage of my sister's trust in order to threaten me. At least, that's what it felt like. Beckett wasn't aggressive, nor did I take him for the kind of guy who would kidnap a child. He had a mouth on him when he drank, but I'd never seen him do anything like this before, and what gave me chills was how smooth he was when I caught him in the act, and how casually he walked away.

"Let's go, Maizy."

I tossed her ring in the trash and she started to cry, so I picked her up. "Sweetie, don't be mad at me."

Tears streamed down her ruddy cheeks and her mouth was agape. "But that was *my* ring," she whined.

"Maze, can I tell you something? It's a secret."

She nodded and wiped her nose.

"Never take a ring from a boy unless he's your prince."

Something sparked in her teary eyes.

"Remember how you said you wanted to marry a prince? Well, if you take a ring from another boy before you meet the prince, then he won't marry you."

Panic flooded her eyes. "But I took *that* one!"

"No, it doesn't count because I threw it away. That's the rule. Your big sis has to take it off and then the spell is undone."

She smiled and hugged my neck. Maizy loved stories about magic and spells. In her eyes, the world was nothing but a fairytale. Adults were blind to the magic that existed and only little kids could see it.

"Come on, little girl. Time for us to go home. You know, you're getting way too heavy for me to carry," I grunted out dramatically. "Are you sure you're not hiding a moose in your pocket?" She giggled and rested her head on my shoulder.

That did the trick, and Maizy hummed one of her favorite songs for the rest of the ride home.

———⊸•⟨∽∅∽⟩•⊷———

After a grueling day at work on Saturday, I threw my keys on the bar and collapsed on my sofa. The neighbor downstairs decided to have a party and the music thumped against the floor, rattling one of the pictures on my wall.

All these months, I'd managed to successfully avoid telling my mom about my breakup with Beckett. She liked him, and that made it more difficult. After the other night, I decided to let the cat out of the bag because I was afraid of him showing up at her house. When I finally confessed, I left out the part with Maizy because I still didn't know what to make of it myself. It wasn't a deliberate threat, but it just left me with a sick feeling. Mom didn't say anything and it was probably for the best. If she had defended him and gone on about forgiveness, I might have sped out of there at ninety miles per hour in "angry mode."

A woman screamed downstairs and laughter followed. I wondered what Wes would have thought about my life. I still saw him as the cool guy and he might have gone downstairs to join them. But he would be thirty and who knows… maybe married. It was hard to imagine him as anything but the young man I once knew.

I could still remember the last time I saw him, two nights before the accident. I was living at home and he stopped by to have a talk with Dad. He walked me into my bedroom and told me I needed to get a full-time job and move out. I'd been slacking off at my job because I hated flipping burgers. Wes shared his concern with me and wanted to know if Dad had been giving me a hard time. He told me about a job at Sweet Treats and suggested I could move in with him until I found a place. *"Call me tomorrow and we'll go to a movie,"* he said.

God, why didn't I call him? I ended up blowing him off and it had become one of the biggest regrets of my life. A last chance to see him, or maybe that could have changed his fate and he would never have gone out on the night he died.

Suddenly, a knock sounded at my front door. I catapulted off the sofa and grabbed the fireplace poker—my weapon of choice.

Through the peephole, I watched Naya impatiently pacing in circles with her arms folded.

I opened the door.

"This is the last straw. I called the police this time," she announced, rushing past me and going straight for the can of Spanish peanuts in the kitchen.

"The party girl called the cops?" I smirked.

Naya strutted into the living room and plopped down on the floor, leaning against one of my chairs with her long legs crossed.

"Lexi, on more than one occasion I've invited them to my parties, but they've never *once* returned the courtesy."

I flopped onto the couch and grabbed a magazine from the coffee table. "Do you really want to party with a bunch of college kids?" My gaze flicked up. "Wait, don't answer that."

She popped a peanut into her mouth and brushed the salt from her fingers onto her tight shorts.

"Crash it," I suggested.

Naya rolled her eyes. The root of her irritation wasn't the noise but that she wasn't a part of it. Naya hated exclusion. "I have more class than that, chickypoo. So are you going to tell me what's been bothering you?"

I slowly turned the page, glancing at an article about the top twenty ways to turn on your man. "Nope."

She set the peanuts down and hopped on the sofa beside me, lifting my legs onto her lap. "Ooo, it's a man, isn't it?"

"Naya, it's—"

"A *man.*"

I snorted. "Drop it."

"Dish, Lexi. I can tell it's not about Beckett because you have a totally different look on your face when you're stewing over him. So who has your feathers all ruffled up?"

I hurled the fashion magazine to the floor. "A ghost from my past. Just someone who took off years ago and never once contacted me." Now I was irritated all over again and sat up with my knees against my chest. "He just showed up out of the blue and now he wants to talk."

"Someone you dated?"

"No. Just an old family friend."

"Hmm," she pondered, setting her feet on the coffee table. A silver anklet slithered down to her foot and a tiny heart dangled from her toe ring. "Maybe he was in trouble."

Something I'd considered. "Maybe he was in prison."

"That's kind of sexy."

"That's kind of not," I said. "I have no desire to graduate from a cheating bastard to an ex-convict."

"So talk to him. Either that or sit here night after night, wondering what happened while wearing your bitchy face."

"I don't have a bitchy face," I argued, trying to conceal my smile.

An unexpected knock at the door startled the both of us. I glanced around but forgot where I'd set down the fireplace poker.

"Shhh." Naya tiptoed over to the door and peered through the peephole with her index finger pointing up.

"Who is it?" I whispered over her shoulder.

"I can't tell. Oh, shit."

"What?"

Naya looked at me and winked. "It's a cop. He flipped a badge."

After using her pinky finger to pick a peanut skin from her teeth, she casually opened the door. "It's about time!"

The man raked his gaze up and down Naya before looking in my direction. He wasn't wearing a uniform, but his stature was tall and he had a short buzz cut many of the cops sported. When he held up his badge and folded it back into his pocket, Naya leaned comfortably against the doorframe.

"That's been going on for two hours," she pointed out.

Cops turned Naya on. Period. If there was a reason she could call them, she would. Even at her own parties. I tried not to laugh when her right leg rubbed against the other, as if she were scratching her left thigh with her right knee and beckoning her panties to drop.

"I'm Officer McNeal, responding to a report of a noise disturbance. Are you the one who made the call?" he asked.

"Guilty," she purred.

"I'll need your names for my report." He took out a tiny notebook and I backed up, folding my arms. I didn't want to get involved in this shit.

"Naya." She spelled it out. "Naya James."

"And?" he said, locking eyes with mine. It made me nervous. More nervous than it should have since he was the good guy.

"Um, is this necessary? I didn't call."

The tip of his pen remained firmly pressed against his little notepad. "Name?"

My stomach knotted. "Alexia."

He didn't move his pen. "Alexia what?"

Why was he making me so nervous? "Alexia Knight."

"Do you live alone?" he asked.

I glanced at Naya.

"Ma'am, if there's anyone else on the premises, I need it for my report. If we come back for more information, we'll need to know the names of all residents within the building."

"I'm alone, she's alone," Naya quickly said, smiling with her ruby lips. She stepped a little closer to him. "Were you on your way home? Sorry if we pulled you back on duty, officer. Can I make it up to you?"

She batted her lashes and I gave her *the look*. Not that she noticed since her eyes were eating up Mr. Undercover Cop.

Without writing down my name or any additional information, he tucked his little notepad in his back pocket. "I'll go down and have a talk with them. If they bother you again, give us a call and you can come down to the station and file a formal complaint. Have a good evening." He tipped his head and walked off.

"Damn," Naya said, slamming the door. "He was kind of hot, and so not into me." She put her arm around me. "But he sure had his eyes all over you."

"Yeah. In a creepy way."

"I'm going to have to put in a personal request for Officer McNeal next time," she said with a giggle. "I'd love to rub my hands all over his head."

"Which one?"

She slapped my arm and feigned a shocked expression. "A little seasoned by the look of salt and pepper in his hair, but I bet I could crack a smile on that stern face of his. Try to get some sleep, and don't forget about my party on Tuesday."

Naya shut the front door behind her. "Lock it!"

I turned the bolt and wondered how I could possibly forget about the party she reminded me of at every opportunity. That night, I slept with a pillow over my head.

The music downstairs went on until four in the morning.

CHAPTER 6

T HE NEXT DAY, I FOUND Naya's cell phone on the floor by the sofa. I decided to swing by the strip club and drop it off since she had tiny conniptions whenever she misplaced it. I never understood how a man could walk into a strip club on a Sunday and not turn into a puff of smoke as soon as he crossed the threshold of the establishment.

Club Sin was on the far end of town and I had a few other errands to run, one of which included laundry. I stuffed two large bags of clothes into the trunk of my car. We had a laundry room in the apartment building, but it was dark and had only one door. The Laundromat I frequented had televisions, ample seating, and a few classic arcade games in the back. I felt safe in there and it gave me time to read my magazines or paint my toenails.

Her phone was tucked in the back pocket of my shorts along with Austin's card, because I planned to call him on a phone that wasn't mine so he wouldn't have my number.

And wasn't *that* childish?

Before going to a strip club on a Sunday, I made a detour over to the cemetery because something had been bothering me, and that was the possibility of having left a whiskey bottle on top of my brother's grave. I parked the car on the little pathway and walked across the stretch of high grass until I reached his marker. There were a few blades of grass on the plaque, so I dusted them away, but no signs of a whiskey bottle or vomit.

Thank God.

That's when every muscle in my body froze.

A merciless snarl stirred the balmy air behind me. A prickling sensation touched the back of my neck and I slowly stood up and turned around.

A menacing dog with matted brown fur bared its sharp canines at me. Dog? Who was I kidding? It was too big to be a dog. With cautious steps, I backed away.

My throat dried up as it paced in my direction with stiff shoulders, malicious eyes, and a drip of slobber dangling from one side of its mouth. *Could I take down a dog? Maybe kick it or punch it? Shit. What if I got rabies? Wasn't that a bunch of shots to your stomach?*

Then I remembered all the stories about people attacked by dogs who ended up with their faces torn off.

Without batting an eyelash, I spun on my heel and leapt for a branch on the tree beside me. I swung my legs up just in time as he snapped his massive jaws, then climbed as high as I could, as if Mr. Big Bad Wolf could grow arms and come up after me.

It felt like thirty minutes had crawled by, and the dog continued to circle restlessly around the tree like a soldier. The unrelenting heat planted frightening thoughts in my head that I might die of thirst in a cemetery. Could *I live off leaves and bark?* My fingers clawed at the trunk and I shifted my hip uncomfortably on the angled branch where I squatted.

Then I remembered the phone.

Very carefully, I reached around and pulled Naya's phone out of my back pocket. I dialed her work but no one answered. The thought crossed my mind to call the police, but I had reservations about calling 911 over a dog. The city was full of crime and car accidents, and after Wes's crash, the last thing I wanted to do was take a cop away from helping out someone in serious need.

Although, being stared at like a T-bone steak felt pretty serious.

I put the phone in my mouth and pulled Austin's card out of my pocket. Maybe now was a good time to talk and by then, the dog would be gone.

He immediately answered, which took me off guard.

"This is Cole."

I mentally wrestled with the thirteen-year-old inside me who wanted to hang up on him.

"Austin?"

After a brief pause, I heard the sound of rustling sheets. "I wondered if you'd call."

"So, talk. Now's your chance."

His voice was kind of soft and growly, like he'd just woken up. I could hear his skin rubbing around, as if he were stroking his face with a tired hand. "I don't want to do this on the phone. You pick a place and I'll meet you there."

I snorted. "I'm a little tied up at the moment."

My foot suddenly slipped and I lost my balance. A piece of bark tore off the tree and the dog barked ferociously. I pulled my leg up and resumed my squatting position.

"What's going on?" he asked in an alert voice. "Where are you?"

"I called so we can talk, Austin. I don't know if we should continue accidentally running into each other before I finally want to kill you. Was it that easy to cut ties with us? We've moved on with our lives, but I think I'm entitled to an answer. Losing my brother was the hardest thing I've ever had to go through, but you were like family to us. You didn't think we'd care that you just took off without a word?" I licked my salty lip and waited for an answer.

When he spoke again, the tenor in his voice gave me chills. "*Where* the fuck are you?"

"Up a tree. I'm at the cemetery with a dog eyeballing me like I'm a meaty bone. Guess I'm in the right place if something goes wrong, huh?"

The line went dead.

Did he just hang up on me?

I was so upset that I threw the phone, which was a completely stupid idea because now I'd lost my chance of calling animal control or 911, thanks to my temper. I cursed and thumped my head against the trunk, which roused another bloodthirsty snarl from the dog below.

"Oh, shut up!" I yelled.

That pissed him off. He stretched out on his hind legs and showed me how tall he was. His predatory eyes were enough to make me hug that tree even tighter, and I was never a tree hugger.

He didn't just look mean, he looked *mad*.

Time drifted by with no signs of life in the cemetery. A couple of ants bit me on the ankle and I continued scratching it as the heavy afternoon sun became a scorcher. Sweat trickled down my brow and my upper thighs began to get stiff. The cicadas in the neighboring trees were chanting up a song that lulled me into a state of relaxation.

I jerked back to alertness when thunder rolled in the distance. No, not thunder, but an engine. It sounded like King Kong roaring as the car increased in speed and a cloud of dust appeared on the other side of the cemetery, moving around the winding road.

Down below, the dog perked his head up and grew skittish, pacing frantically in a circle. The car ate up the road in my direction and I waved to get their attention. The dog suddenly hauled ass and relief swam through me.

The engine cut off and heavy footsteps crunched across the gravel road, treading over the soft grass until Austin came into view.

For a fleeting moment, I wanted to stay up in the tree. There he was, looking sexy as hell with his shaggy brown hair, all disheveled with bedhead. His black T-shirt was thrown over a pair of jeans.

Thrown. Wrinkled and untidy, like a man who had been pulled out of bed and barely had time to zip up his pants. I even glanced down at his zipper before giving myself a mental slap.

Austin's style had always been casual and cool. Back in the day, it was all about muscle shirts and jeans that were shredded at the knees. Now he filled out his clothes like a man, and they wore him more than he wore them. There I was, sitting in a tree wearing flip-flops, black jogging shorts, and a pink tank top. Not to mention I was wearing a ponytail and sans makeup.

Perfect.

Austin scanned his eyes around the cemetery. "Where did he go?"

"Who?"

He slowly looked up. "The wolf."

"The dog," I corrected. "I don't know. To take a piss, I guess."

After a quick glance over his shoulder, Austin rubbed his jaw and then looked up at me again. "Climb down. I got you."

Well, getting *up* a tree is a piece of cake. But I can testify to the fact that going down is no easy feat. Now I knew why cats got stuck in them and needed a fireman to come to their rescue. Of course, having seen some of the sexy local firemen in their gear, I'd pretend to be stuck in a tree too. *Damn, that story would have totally made Naya's day.*

As I swiveled, my shoe fell off and I froze. "I can't."

"You will. Sit on the branch and put your feet on the one below it."

My legs were locked up and stiff, and what scared me was the branch below was farther down than I thought. I'd have to let go of the trunk and sit down, but as I did this, I wobbled. "I'm going to fall," I warned.

"Then I'll catch you," he said, not attempting to conceal his soft laugh.

Screw it, I thought. I spun around, lowered my legs, gripped the branch, dangled in midair, and slipped.

I squeezed my eyes shut and Austin caught me from behind.

His right arm tightened around my stomach and it punched the air out of my lungs. My legs were shaky and he held me for a minute before I noticed my tank top had slid out of place. As he let go, I quickly pulled it down and wiped pieces of bark off my shorts.

"How long were you up there?"

I picked a leaf out of my hair and turned around. "Long enough that I have to pee."

He spun on his heel to give me privacy. I walked over to Naya's phone and stuffed it in my pocket, then limped toward the car and grabbed my shoe.

"I'm not sure what kind of girl you think I am, Austin, but I'm not going to pee in a graveyard."

"I seem to remember you having no problem reliving yourself behind a church." Austin looked away, no doubt to hide his smile.

"Hey, you said you'd never bring that up again. That was supposed to go to the grave."

Then I looked around at where we were and snorted.

The back of my arm burned and my joints were stiff. Austin

jogged up beside me and pulled a piece of bark from my hair.

"What were you doing out here?" he asked.

"Making sure I didn't leave a mess behind."

"I cleaned that up," Austin replied matter-of-factly.

I broke my stride and studied his thick brows that framed the clearest eyes I'd ever seen. "Why did you let me drive home drunk? I could have been killed."

He folded his arms and I stole a glimpse of his tats. They disappeared beneath the sleeves of his shirt.

"I didn't. You think I'd let you drive off in that condition?" He huffed with irritation and shook his head. "I didn't want to rifle through your purse to find out where you lived, so I left you in front of your mom's house."

"How did you get back home?"

"Meet foot one and foot two," he said, pointing down at his shoes. "Let's go somewhere with air conditioning."

"I have to do laundry. You get one rinse and spin to tell your story and then I have errands to run."

Without another word, we got in our separate cars and he followed me to the Laundromat. Austin said he'd join me in a minute and took off toward a convenience store across the street where I sometimes grabbed a hot dog and soda. The laundry bags weighed a ton, but the handles at the top allowed me to drag them across the polished floor. I put in the first load and pumped a few coins into the washer.

Minutes passed and I hopped up on one of the machines to read a magazine.

"Let me see your arm," Austin said, coming up on my left. He held a bottle of peroxide in one hand and a box of bandages in the other.

"Huh?" I spun my left arm around but couldn't see anything.

"Your arm is bleeding, Sherlock. Lift it up and let me have a look." He set the supplies down and raised my left arm over my head. That's when I could see the scrape on my upper arm. It was deep and pretty gnarly-looking.

"So, are you going to tell me your life story, or are you stalling again?" I prodded.

"*Christ*," he said under his breath.

"What?"

He shook his head. "I forgot to buy cotton balls." He set the brown bottle of peroxide on the washer.

Before I could make a suggestion, Austin peeled off his shirt, wadded it into a ball, and doused it with peroxide.

I was pretty sure I would never buy another cotton ball again if this was the alternative solution.

Austin brushed my long hair away from my shoulder and eased between my legs. While he dabbed at my cut with his T-shirt, I got a bird's-eye view of his torso. He smelled musky and everything about his body was different from the man I remembered. Not bulgy steroid-looking arms like Beckett, but solid. Then there was that sexy six-pack down below, and I tried not to look because I felt Austin watching me out of the corner of his eye. I lifted my gaze and focused on his tattoos instead.

Nope, that wasn't helping either.

They weren't so much on his bicep as they were on his shoulders, with tribal patterns sharpening down his upper arms and branching onto part of his chest. The last time I'd seen him, he was twenty-three and leaner. Austin was always tough by nature, just not in stature. He had always been the guy you didn't want to mess with, and his nose was slightly crooked from one of his many fights.

Time had changed him, and in all the right ways.

"So?" I pressed.

"Is this where we're having the talk?" he asked, dropping his arms and tearing the wrapper from a bandage. His blue eyes flashed to mine as a warning. If I said yes, there was no going back. We were going to have some kind of important talk in a Laundromat.

I'd never seen Austin wear jewelry or watches, so I leaned in and admired his necklace again.

He grinned and looked down. "You like it? It's a family heirloom—a talisman that brings good fortune. My dad gave it to me about a month ago."

"Does your family still live here?"

"My parents moved away years ago, but my brothers—we're back for good."

I quieted and Austin tapped beneath my chin with the crook of his finger—something he used to do whenever I was moping.

"Mom was really hurt when you took off," I said. "She thought of you like a second son, and it destroyed her when Wes died and you left too. It was like she'd lost two kids."

He put his hands on the washer and leaned forward. "Wes didn't die in an accident; he was murdered."

I gasped. My heart rate took off and the room closed in. "What did you just say?"

"Wes was tangled up with some bad people. I tried to keep him away because he was getting too deep into my world. He tried to cut a deal with the wrong man—someone you don't make deals with—and when he didn't follow through, they put a hit on him. They staged it like an accident, but I tracked down the piece of shit who did it."

"Wes was *murdered*?"

I shoved against his chest and he stepped back, rubbing his jaw. "That's why I left town—to track down his killer. It took me six months to find him and…"

"And what?"

He folded his arms and lifted his chin. "And I took care of him." His brows popped up when he said "took care of," and I knew what he meant. "Not long after that, I was offered a job as a bounty hunter. I made a career out of tracking down the worst kind of men. It was too dangerous for me to stay here."

"If you took care of him, then where was the danger?"

"I took care of the killer, not the man responsible for putting the hit on Wes." Austin rocked on his heels and briefly grasped his talisman before dropping it again. His cheeks were red from the heat and he rubbed his jaw, looking around. "Sorry, I can't explain everything to you here."

"Cat and mouse. I see how this is going to be."

I tried to hop down, but he stepped so close I had nowhere to go. Austin flattened his hands on either side of my legs. An electric charge hummed between us—or at least it felt that way. Maybe it was just me, or the vibration of the nearby appliances, but something felt so very different about Austin and I couldn't put my finger on it.

He leaned in close. Hard. His chest pushed out and we were nose to nose.

"I didn't say I *won't* tell you everything, I just can't do it *here*." His eyes motioned to the people sitting nearby.

And then it happened. A shift in the way he looked at me. His clear eyes softened and his nose twitched as if he smelled a perfume I wasn't wearing. His eyes hooded and I leaned away, uncertain of how I felt about him looking at me like that. Austin was my brother's best friend.

But then again, Wes wasn't here. And we weren't teenagers anymore.

A couple of young women by the door giggled and broke the silence between us. Austin backed up, tossing his bloody shirt into a nearby trash can.

"You just going to walk around like that?" I asked, as he was the only half-naked man in the Laundromat. Not that the two women by the door raised any complaint.

He answered my question by sitting down in one of the plastic bucket chairs in front of me, casually spreading his arms across the back of the seats and widening his legs. Whenever he was in one of his thinking moods, Austin's brows pushed together and formed a crease in the center of his forehead.

When we were younger, it made him look pensive and angry. Now it just made him intimidating.

"So, are you married?" I tapped the back of my flip-flops against the washer and watched his Adam's apple undulate as he swallowed. The hum of the machines gave us a little privacy.

"No. I never settled down," he admitted.

Then he flicked a hot gaze up to me and I shivered.

"Casey got married," I blurted out.

Now he looked interested. Slightly. Casey was the girl he'd dated off and on in high school. I had a feeling they still hooked up after high school, although I had no proof, just friends who'd seen them together in random places.

"Good for her. She got kids?"

I shrugged. "I don't know. I just heard she married a year after... Well, not long after you left."

Austin was never one for small talk; he had always preferred deeper conversations. So his uncharacteristic silence put me on edge. Something was on his mind, and by the way he kept looking at me, it wasn't about Wes's death.

"Why were you crying?" He didn't move an inch. Just kept his eyes locked on mine.

I cocked my head to the side.

"At the pizza place," he said.

Oh. *That.*

"My ex showed up. I flipped out a little."

The ropes of muscle in his arms tightened, as did his jaw. "You're divorced?"

"No, I never married."

Now Austin looked pissed. He leaned forward and scraped his fingers through his hair, staring at the tacky pattern on the floor tiles.

"How're your parents doing?" he asked, switching topics.

"Mom's great. She doesn't work as much as she used to. I'm sure dad's great too. Wherever he is."

His head snapped up. "What do you mean by that?"

"My dad left us."

He stood up and erased the distance between us. "When?"

I laced my fingers together. "About four years ago. I don't know."

"He *left?*"

"Yep. One day he packed up all his shit and told my mom he'd had enough. It came out of the blue because I don't remember hearing them argue that much, but I wasn't living at home at the time. Who knows what was going on; she never talks about it."

"He left his wife and daughter unprotected?" Austin repeated through clenched teeth.

I narrowed my eyes. "Yeah. Sound familiar?"

A low growl vibrated in his throat. "I had no choice. It was the only way to keep your family safe."

"Look, I'm tired of playing this game," I said, pushing him away.

I hopped down from the washer and felt trapped because of that damn laundry. I was tempted to pull out every last sopping-wet towel and just go home. But instead, I paced. "You're the same, but you're not the same. I know it's been years, but have you been in prison?"

Austin stirred with laughter and tiny crinkles pinched the corners of his eyes. There he was—the guy I once knew. The one whose laugh was contagious because you rarely heard it, and it gave him such a sweet expression. With his right arm, he leaned on the washer and I turned my back to him.

Damn, that lean.

"No, I'm not a convict. I'm the same guy, just older and a little fatter."

I snorted. *Hardly*. I didn't see an ounce of fat on his well-proportioned, nicely tanned—

"Lexi?"

I spun on my heel and folded my arms. Austin tilted his head and spoke softly. "I want my hug. I've got a lot of baggage, and you look spooked, but we need to mend the rift between us. I can't undo the past, but I want to make it right with your mom. Fuck your dad, because he can rot in hell for leaving you the way he did. Had I known, I would have come back sooner."

My knees weakened a little. There was fierceness in his declaration—an honesty in his voice I couldn't ignore. As pissed off as I was, I owed him the benefit of the doubt as much as he owed me an explanation.

With my arms still folded, I shuffled forward and leaned into him.

Austin wrapped his arms around me tight and kissed the top of my head.

"I missed you, Ladybug," he murmured in my hair.

CHAPTER 7

I N THE SPAN OF A rinse and spin cycle, I'd managed to get Austin caught up on seven years' worth of gossip. Who was married, who was divorced, who was gay, who had five children, who lost all their money on a gambling trip, and who was arrested for public indecency in a museum. Austin's eyes were brimming with amusement; I always had an animated way of telling a good story.

We slid into our groove just a little bit more, although in many ways, Austin still felt like a stranger to me.

I offered him one of my warm T-shirts to put on, fresh from the dryer, but he smirked and held it up to his broad chest. Unless I wanted the stretched-out version, Austin was going shirtless.

Not that I had any complaints.

"I'll follow you," he said, slamming my trunk closed and walking back to his car. We agreed to head over to my place and he'd tell it all. My stomach twisted into a knot because I wasn't sure I was ready for the truth—not after what he'd already told me.

I wrote down my address in case we were separated in traffic, and to be honest, I was *trying* to lose him. I needed at least five minutes to run a comb through my hair and look halfway decent.

As soon as we arrived, I ran up the stairs and left my trunk open for him to haul up the laundry. Halfway through the living room, flip-flops were flying left and right as I kicked them off and hauled ass into my bedroom, yanking a pair of denims from a dresser drawer and changing into them. I stripped away my tank top and pulled a form-fitting brown shirt with retro lettering over my head. Austin's heavy footsteps tromped up the stairs.

"Shit," I muttered, dashing into the bathroom. The door slammed and I sprayed myself with cucumber body freshener. The heat had done a number on my face, so I brightened it up with a dab of tinted lotion and mineral powder, then rummaged through my drawer twice until I found my favorite tube of lipstick. Nothing dramatic, just enough color that I didn't look like a hot mess.

"Lexi? Where do you want me to put these?" he yelled out.

"Hi, there. I'm afraid we haven't had the pleasure. I'm Naya James."

I tossed my lipstick on the counter. "Well, so much for that," I murmured.

Now that Naya was in the mix, there was no point in—wait, what was I even doing? Once again, reverting to my sixteen-year-old self and trying to hit on my brother's best friend. That's what.

If Naya wants him, she can have him.

I swung the door open and they were standing in the middle of my living room. Austin held a heavy bag under each arm as if they weighed nothing. Naya had on her favorite black heels with ribbons tied around her ankles several times. All you saw were legs that went up to a pair of tight black shorts. Her red blouse was a favorite—the shredded material looked like a yeti had tried to make out with her.

"Naya, this is Austin Cole. He's an old friend who just got back in town and we're doing some catching up. Austin, this is Naya, my good friend and neighbor. She also makes some really kickass baklava."

"Yes," Naya confessed, "I *love* to cook. Do you love to eat?" she asked, sliding a glance my way. "I think we should have him for dinner tonight. You two can talk and that'll give me plenty of time to whip up something delicious. I know just the thing a man like you needs."

Naya had her kitten motor on purr. Men responded to it without a doubt. She was testing the waters to see if I'd react, which I didn't, thus giving her full permission to pursue. We had an unspoken agreement about that kind of thing.

Austin's eyes were fixated on my shirt. "Are they still around?"

For a second, I thought he was talking about my breasts and I looked down to see if I still had them. Then I noticed the logo on my shirt.

"Yeah, believe it or not, they're still in business."

A nostalgic grin slid up his face.

The Pit was the best barbecue joint in town. At one time, it was a popular hangout for the teens. I'd go with my friends, or sometimes tag along with Wes. Their food was great, and it had become a place where we congregated to talk about school, guys, concerts, and stuff that didn't matter. So many memories were tied to that place and I hadn't gone back in all these years. We used to tear the ends of the straws and blow the long wrappers across the room. The owner must have hated us.

"Let me take those," I said, reaching for one of the bundles of laundry.

He swung away. "I got it. Where do you want them?"

I wrapped my arm around a large bag and he swiveled away. "You act like I don't know how to handle something that big, Austin. Just *give it to me!*"

"Now *that's* what I like to hear," Naya said with a wink, and the door closed behind her.

"Your bedroom or right here?"

His question startled me and I let go. Austin paced into my messy bedroom with the laundry. "I'm not folding your clothes," he said with a chuckle. He dropped the bags on the floor beside the closet and glanced around with inquisitive eyes.

He was curious about my life. I saw it in the subtle way he scoped everything out, from the pictures on my walls to the comedy movies on my shelves.

"Why don't I get us a drink," I offered, disappearing into the kitchen. I could see him over the bar and he was looking at the back door that led to my balcony. "You want a beer? I don't have your favorite, or at least, what you used to like."

"Sounds good."

This conversion was going to require more than a beer. It was too early in the day to get lit, so I pulled out two bottles and set them on the rectangular table in my quaint little dining room.

Austin had his back to me, still shirtless.

I quickly dove into the bedroom and fished out one of Beckett's shirts from a bottom drawer. There was no way I was going to be able to carry on a conversation while staring at his six-pack.

"Here," I said, tossing him the shirt.

He caught it and sharpened his eyes. "Whose shirt is this?"

"My ex's."

His fists tightened around the red material but his voice stayed smooth and relaxed. "How much of an ex is he?"

"What is that supposed to mean?"

He lifted the shirt. "You're still keeping around a spare set of his clothes. You tell me."

I sat down and took a swig of beer. "He had sex in my car with another woman. I'm not a forgive-and-forget kind of girl. I just forgot I still had it in there."

"You just said you didn't forget."

I turned my mouth to the side and drummed my fingers on the bottle. "I can forget a T-shirt pretty easily. I can't forget my ex getting ridden like a mechanical bull in the back of my Toyota."

Austin suddenly ripped the shirt in half and the sound of the material tearing made me jump.

He calmly walked into the kitchen, dropped the shirt into the trash can, and returned to his seat across the table. Then he casually drank his beer as if nothing weird had just transpired with him going Hulk and shredding my former lover's favorite "I'm an idiot" shirt.

The bubbles in my empty stomach were already working their alcoholic magic. "So tell me what happened to Wes. Don't dance around the truth, Austin. I've invited you here and I want you to be straight with me."

Austin sipped his beer and grimaced, setting the bottle in the middle of the table.

"I'm a Shifter," he said.

"Shifter," I repeated blandly. "You move around? What does that mean?"

"*Shapeshifter.*"

My shoulders sagged. "I don't have time for jokes."

He didn't break eye contact and those pale blue eyes polished me off like a dog licking his bowl clean. "There's another world that exists that would surprise the hell out of you. Wes knew what I was."

I sighed angrily. "Don't drag Wes into your pathological—"

"Lexi," he said in a hard voice, "I'm a Shifter."

My eyes narrowed. "Then turn yourself into a zebra."

He slowly shook his head and rubbed his jaw. "My animal hasn't met you; I don't trust him alone in your presence just yet."

I threw my head back and slapped the palms of my hands on the table. "Oh my God. You're *kidding* me! All these years I've wondered what happened to you and if you were even alive. I'm such a fucking *idiot*. Now you show up out of nowhere and the only thing you have to tell me is you're a *werewolf*?"

"Shifter," he corrected with a suppressed grin.

※

Austin didn't back down. He was convinced he was some kind of a paranormal but assured me he wasn't a werewolf because they didn't exist and the moon had no effect on him. His revelation also came with a warning label: those who knew about their secret were entrusted not to reveal it to the human world. There were consequences, and I really didn't want to ask what those were. He made me promise I wouldn't tell a soul. I didn't have a problem with that.

I was never a fan of padded walls.

There were breaks in our conversation when I'd walk off to do the dishes, leaving him alone so I could allow the facts to settle in my brain. It was a lot to digest in one day, particularly after spending an hour in a tree. He went out on the balcony a few times to make phone calls, and I finally collapsed on the sofa and flipped through the TV channels. A tapestry of light blanketed the room, fading to nothingness as darkness dominated the sky.

Then my idiot neighbors cranked on their stereo. Austin flew in through the back door and sat in the chair beside me, rubbing his hand across his bare chest. "You should move into a house and get away from this lifestyle—too many drifters coming in and out of this place. It's not safe."

There he went again, talking about *safe*. Although I couldn't deny it was nice to hear someone showing concern about my safety. As much as I wanted to roll my eyes, feeling protected by a man was an undeniable soft spot with me.

A knock—or more precisely, a shoe—tapped on the door. "Lexi, darling, open up. Dinner is served!"

"I'll get it," Austin said with a hint of curiosity in his tone.

From my lying-down position, I couldn't see over the back of the couch when Naya came in and started her kitten purr. It was a cute little growl she put at the end of her laugh that was just as provocative as her figure.

"It's nice and hot, so if you two want to eat now, it's ready. Lexi, would you mind opening a bottle of wine?"

I peered over the edge of the sofa. Naya was dressed in a black skirt with a slit all the way up to her thigh, although it looked more like it went to her appendix. Her blouse was fashioned the same way, with a slit that stretched all the way down to her navel, probably held together by a single thread made from the cheapest material in Taiwan. One snap and boobage would kick this dinner from low to medium-high. She offered him a full-lipped smile, staring at his bare chest and looking as if she had plans to feast on something other than what she brought over for dinner.

Go, Naya.

I sat up, patting down my tangled hair. Austin was open game and I had no interest in exploring those old feelings all over again. People say time machines don't exist, but they do. They're your friends, and being around them takes you right back to that place in time you had long since put away.

"I'll set the table. Mmm, smells good. What is it?"

Naya proudly held up the foil-covered dish. "Chicken spaghetti."

I almost snorted. For some reason, I had expected her to pull a fiesta out of her hat, but chicken spaghetti required very little preparation and involved a couple of cans of soup. My guess was that Naya had spent the better part of her afternoon giving herself a wax and shine.

"I'm starving," I declared.

"Let me get the candles," she said, digging in one of my drawers.

I grabbed a few wine glasses and hesitated. Did she want me to leave them alone? Naya dimmed the lights and a flick of a lighter sounded. As I poured the wine in my narrow kitchen, Austin brushed up against my back.

Tiny little hairs stood up on my neck when he leaned against me, reaching in the cabinet overhead and pulling out the plates.

"I'll get these," he said in a rough, sexy voice.

And there it was. Something I was totally not expecting when he lightly pressed his body against mine.

Tingles.

"Where are your forks and knives?" he murmured.

"Drawer on the right," I said in an embarrassingly breathy way. "But I can get them. Go sit down."

He ignored me, taking everything into the dining room. I snatched the glasses and followed behind.

Naya was setting the table and using her spoon to dish out the food. "So tell me about yourself, Austin. Where are you from? What do you do for a living?"

I bit my lip and set the glasses on the table. Austin stood behind his chair and Naya sat down across from me, placing one of the candles in the middle. She did the infamous stretch that usually gave men a good whiff of her heavenly perfume and sometimes a peek through the opening of her blouse.

"I'm an investigator. I'm originally from around here, but I've been traveling for the past few years as part of my job. Decided I missed home and it was time for a change." His eyes dragged over to mine and I continued arranging the silverware beside the plates.

"Have a seat, Austin," I said. "Shit—I mean shoot. I forgot the napkins. Be right back."

"I work as a dancer, but it's just a temporary thing until I find something better," Naya went on. "I know exactly where you're coming from. We all want something better for ourselves. Is your family here with you?"

"My brothers are here."

"Not married?"

I almost cringed as I grabbed a stack of paper napkins from the kitchen and returned. Austin was still standing beside the table. When I sat down and took a sip of wine, he pulled back his chair and relaxed in his seat. The legs creaked as he settled.

Austin stared at my finger as it tapped repeatedly against the wood table. If he remembered anything about me, he knew I was a finger-tapper whenever something was irritating me. On a table, on a wall, on my leg, on a keyboard—didn't matter.

It was just my thing.

Naya and I had grown used to the music blaring from the neighbor's apartment, but with company over, it was embarrassing. Apparently, the cop hadn't put enough of a scare into them, so we sat there listening to the Who singing about a teenage wasteland.

"Naya, you left your phone over here last night," I said conversationally.

Relief washed over her lovely face. "Oh, thank *God*. I was looking everywhere for it this morning. I get so many important calls and half of them don't leave messages. That's my biggest peeve."

"Naya doesn't have a home phone," I pointed out.

She shook her head and savored a small sip of Merlot. "Who needs a home phone? You don't even have a cell phone. Get with the times, girl. Where did you put it?"

"On the bar next to the deck of cards," I said, pointing over my shoulder. "Hope you don't mind that I used it."

Lucky for me it didn't break when I threw it earlier, thanks to the lawnmower man who hadn't cut the grass in over a month.

"Damn, Naya, this is really good." I took a second bite of creamy noodles and made an approving moan. Only Naya could whip up something decadent from a can of soup. "Naya's a great cook," I said to Austin, giving her a few brownie points with him. "If you ever taste her lobster, you'll probably want to make babies with her."

"Lexi," Naya said with a giggle.

Austin twirled his pasta but didn't take a single bite of it. That was his pissed-off look. I'd seen it plenty of times. He'd given it to a guy who called me a hot piece of ass when I was seventeen and walking out of a convenience store. Austin had left me in the car with my Popsicle while he and Wes got out, locked the doors, and yanked that redneck out of his green Ford pickup truck. They dragged him around the side of the building and when they returned, Wes had a bloody lip and Austin's knuckles were bruised.

"Don't you like it?" Naya asked.

The fork clicked against the plate and Austin stood up. "I'll be right back."

"Where are you going?"

He lowered his chin. "Stay here."

When he left the apartment, Naya finished her wine. "He's a beast of a man, Lexi. *This* is your old friend? Hot tamale, girly. You've been holding out on me. Any feelings still there?"

"I don't even know him anymore," I said with a pitiful sigh.

"Can I get to know him?" She lifted her hands defensively and laughed. "If you want him, Lexi, just say the word and I'll take my dinner and go."

"Nah. He's practically family."

"I thought you liked big, strong men?"

"Beckett was the exception. I don't usually go for all the roughnecks," I lied. Well, at least not all the time. "Remember Lance, the guy who worked at the coffee shop?"

"The painter?" she said with disdain. "Come on, Lexi. Aspire to something greater."

"Muscles don't make the man."

"True, darling, but they give you something nice to hold on to," she said.

"I just can't be with a guy who worships his body more than mine."

Naya raised her hand for a high five and we laughed.

Which abruptly stopped when the silence became deafening.

"The music cut off," she said, stating the obvious.

I swiveled around to look at the clock. "That's a first. It's not even close to midnight."

Naya chewed on a bite of spaghetti and froze when the heavy sound of footsteps came up the stairs. Naya got nervy about unlocked doors. We knew it was probably Austin, but when the knob turned, her eyes went wide.

But it was him.

Austin gave us a demonstration of swagger as he crossed the room to claim his chair. Naya did a little finger swirl around the rim of her glass. She must have been used to crystal, because mine was made of glass and barely made a squeak.

"You forgot to lock the door," Naya pointed out.

Austin scooped a giant forkful of pasta into his mouth. "When I'm here, you don't need a lock."

His chiseled jaw worked hard, making Naya crumble like a cookie at the sight of a handsome man devouring her food. Austin was better looking than he'd ever been in his youth, even if it *was* mixed with a tough exterior like a street fighter looking for action.

"Did you confront my neighbors?"

After chewing his last bite, he put his tanned forearms on the table and leaned in, nodding with an arched brow. "I wouldn't worry about them. Just a couple of college kids with a bong, some kind of black light, and all these posters and shit of Led Zeppelin and—"

I burst out laughing and when a snort escaped, I covered my face. The laughter couldn't be contained any longer. On top of this crazy day of getting chased by a dog, sitting in a tree in a cemetery, having my best friend hit on my old flame—who by the way was in town to tell me he was a bounty hunter and shapeshifter—there sat Austin, pointing out how weird my downstairs neighbors were.

"God, I love her laugh," he said to Naya, licking the prongs of his fork. "When she really gets going, she sounds like Beaker from *The Muppet Show*."

Which made an embarrassing sound escape my throat. I waved my arm to get up and knocked over his glass of wine. Naya flew out of her seat and covered her mouth.

That sucked all the humor out of the moment. So much for sophistication at twenty-seven. I stood up and sighed.

"I'm sorry, Naya. It's been a long day and I've had more to drink than eat. Let me get something to clean up the mess."

"How about the shirt in your trash can?" Austin suggested.

CHAPTER 8

T HE NEXT DAY, I FELT sick as a dog. It was probably a combination of the alcohol from the night before and everything else going on that made my head spin and stomach churn.

Thankfully the shop wasn't busy, and April kept the customers happy while I worked in the back, wrapping up gift orders. During the downtime, I'd sit outside in the sunshine on the wooden bench, listening to music until a customer wandered into the shop. It was slow on weekdays, which is why we desperately needed new ways to attract customers.

Truthfully, it only took one of us to run the shop during certain hours, but our boss wanted two workers on site during peak hours. We had two other girls who worked part time and rotated shifts as needed.

Charlie, our boss, frequently stopped in to see how things were going, but not so much lately. He spent a lot of his spare time reading if not telling stories about Greek mythology or the truth behind ancient Egyptian culture. It was riveting to hear his spin on things and it was too bad he never pursued a career in teaching.

Charlie wasn't just the owner, but also the manager on call. He'd never hired anyone to fill that role because it would have meant paying out a higher salary, so I had become the designated lead. Whenever someone had a complaint and asked to speak to the manager, it was me they saw.

Luckily, we didn't get many complaints. We sold sugar. That made most people pretty damn happy.

"You feeling okay, Alexia?" April came into the back room and sat on the bench beside me, patting my shoulder.

"Not really."

"Want me to call Beth to come fill in for you today?"

Guilt crawled up and took a seat in my lap. I hated doing that to someone on their day off. In fact, I was notorious for taking other people's shifts and Charlie made it a point to reprimand me for it. Not in a way that jeopardized my career in the candy field, but he didn't want me to get burned out on work at a young age.

When my relationship with Beckett got serious, my private life had become more of a priority than work. Now that I was single again, work was starting to fill that void, and not in a good way.

"Oh, I almost forgot." April dashed to the register, reached in one of the drawers, and returned with a slip of paper. "I got a call this morning from someone; he was trying to get a hold of you about your car. Did you advertise our work number in your ad?"

"Guilty. And don't tell Charlie. I didn't want my home number splashed in the paper for all to see, and I'm up here most of the time anyhow."

April twisted her hair between her fingers. "I won't say anything, but you could get us in trouble if someone calls when he's up here."

I took the paper from her hand and stared at a name and number. "What did he say?"

"To call him?" She laughed quietly. "Go see if he's interested. I'll cover for you if he wants to take a look at it today."

"You're a godsend," I said in a miserable voice.

I sat in a very unladylike position in my white skirt, hugging my stomach, my legs spread wide. We were in a private back room with our very own vending machine and luxurious water fountain. April didn't mind the enclosed space, but I preferred sitting on the benches outside during my breaks. She handed me her phone and I called the number.

◦◦◦◦◦◦◦

Lorenzo (the potential buyer or hapless victim, depending on how you looked at it) didn't converse much over the phone, but he did want to hear the specs. Manual transmission, new tires, ninety thousand miles, and semen in the back seat.

I left out the last part.

We agreed to meet at a mall I'd been to once before when I was twelve to have my ears pierced. Lorenzo stood next to a big black truck like he'd described to me. He wasn't what I expected. He wore a pair of pale green khakis and a black tank top with writing on it. Something just didn't feel right as I pulled into the parking space and looked at his expensive truck. But those moments are when you convince yourself that you're overreacting and maybe he was purchasing the car for his girlfriend.

Lorenzo towered beside his sharp, heavy-duty truck with chrome wheels and tinted windows. His straight hair was as black as the truck and fell past his shoulders. He looked Native American with his tanned skin and high cheekbones.

I wiped my brow with my clammy hands, still feeling sick. When I turned off the engine, he slowly paced around the car and began appraising it. I stepped out and felt the scorch of heat from the asphalt.

"Hi, I'm Alexia Knight. You must be Lorenzo."

"How does she run?" he asked.

"Like a dream."

His eyes briefly darted to mine. I stepped back with my keys in hand so he could sit in the driver's seat and check out the interior.

Lorenzo looked at every detail and then glanced at the back seat. I wondered if there was a sex aura back there that psychics could see.

"Has anyone ever worked on the transmission?"

"Nope. But the alternator was repaired, or replaced. Don't ask me which; I didn't handle that."

"Let me see the keys," he said eagerly.

I hesitated, looking around.

Lorenzo's hands slid down his pants and stopped at his knees. "If I drive off in your car, feel free to take my truck," he offered, tossing me his own keys. "Is this in your name or do you have a boyfriend on the papers?"

Was he asking me about my situation?

"It's my car."

"How are you going to get around without it?" He laced his fingers together and watched me carefully. "Is someone going to drive you, or do you have another car lined up?"

Had I been sitting, I would have squirmed in my seat. "Do you have an offer?"

Lorenzo pinched his chin, tassels swinging from the leather bracelet on his wrist. "Your asking price and dinner. You didn't mention a boyfriend, so I'm going to take a chance and guess that you're just as available as this car."

I threw his keys and they hit the concrete with a jingle. "I'm not for sale. Get out of my car if you're not going to buy it."

"I'll double the price for a date."

"What the hell do I look like, a prostitute?"

Jesus, maybe I did. His eyes scraped down my stupid miniskirt and tight-fitting orange shirt that said Sweet Treats on it. For anyone who wasn't familiar with the area, he might have just assumed *I* was the sweet treat. I did a mental facepalm and tightened the grip on my keys.

"It looks like this was a waste of your time and mine. I drove all the way out here hoping I would get a serious offer. I don't come with the car and this isn't a sex transaction. Get out of my car or I'm calling the police."

Lorenzo stood up and approached me. I nearly fled, but that stupid impulse was quashed by the logical voice in my head, once again, trying to convince me that I was overreacting.

Except the skull and crossbones tattooed on his arm caught my eye. As did the matching design on the back of his truck window. Men who had skulls on their bodies were usually trouble.

I backed up and he caught my arm. But gently. Not in the way that would make a girl throw her knee against a man's balls. It was a soft touch with just the very tips of his fingers, and his features no longer appeared hard and unpredictable. Lorenzo's brown eyes were as warm as his hands and melted me like caramel in the summer sun. To look at him, Lorenzo was a very handsome man, but I hadn't made up my mind on his personality.

"My offer is serious. I won't hurt you, Alexia. I just think you're exceptionally pretty and I want to show you I'm interested."

Well, *hell*. What's a girl to say to that? I almost wanted to ask if he was still going to pay me double for the cootiemobile.

"Do you really want to buy my car?"

He glanced over his shoulder and chuckled warmly. "Not really. Sorry, it's not what I'm looking for." And then his eyes melted over me and my breath quickened. He really wasn't so bad if you didn't notice the skull inked on his left arm.

"I need to go," I sputtered.

"Alexia, please don't go without giving me your number. Let's have one conversation and you can decide if I'm a bad guy or not. Unless you have a boyfriend."

Maybe it's the mouth-twist thing girls do when someone brings up a boyfriend who doesn't exist, but he read my expression and a satisfied look glittered in his eyes. Lorenzo pulled a pen from his back pocket and held the tip to his palm. "Number?"

And like a freaking zombie, I found myself reciting my home number. Why not? I'd met the worst mistake of my life in a shop full of sugar. Maybe I'd meet the man of my dreams in a rundown parking lot by a shoe store and an overflowing dumpster.

"I'll ask around to see if anyone I know is interested in the car," he promised me. "I know what it's like to have something you want to get rid of, but for some reason, it keeps hanging around like a curse."

"Thanks," I said. "The car needs to go, so if anyone you know wants to take a look at it, give them my *work* number. Tell them about the car before they show up and change their mind—you've seen it, so you'll be able to sell it better than I can."

He smiled. Not the kind with teeth, just a broad smile with his lips pressed together. "I'll do that, Alexia. It was a pleasure to meet you," he said, raising his hand in a wave. "And my name is Lorenzo Church. Friends call me Enzo, business associates call me Church, but you can call me anytime."

He bowed his head, and I listened to his black boots tread heavily on the pavement as he walked back to his truck.

The next day, I called in sick. I'd caught a bug of some kind and it was slowly taking my body hostage. My fever hovered around one hundred degrees Fahrenheit for most of the day. Stuff like this happened a lot when I first started working at the shop. Kids collected germs, which is why I became vigilant about wiping down the counters with sanitizer. But lately, I'd been lucky with my health. I'd managed to accrue about twenty sick days, so I made the executive decision to use some of them.

I also handled food and giving our customers Ebola wasn't high on my list for the top ways to earn a promotion.

It was the night of Naya's party, but I'd already told her I wasn't feeling well and wouldn't be able to make it. I called April at work to let her know she was still invited, but she shied out and made up an excuse about painting her bathroom the color of lemons. I really wanted to see her cut loose and have a good time. She was too young to be sitting around the house and not going to parties and dating. The strange thing was how little I knew about her, but sometimes people don't like to show all their cards until they're ready to go all out.

All my blankets were piled on the floor so I could stretch out across my bed. I had turned down the air conditioning, but nothing soothed my fever and restless legs. The blinds and drapes remained closed, submersing me in darkness.

My skin crawled, sensitive to everything. I didn't have any violent fits of vomiting—thank God—but there was a gnawing sensation in the pit of my stomach. Not hunger, but almost like when you're at the top of the hill on a roller coaster, three seconds from going down a steep track. Odds are I had the latest bug going around, as the symptoms mimicked what I had heard about—minus the vomiting.

The music cranked up at Naya's apartment as her festivities were in full swing.

Of all times to get sick.

A knock sounded at my front door and I sat up, listening. Sometimes partygoers got lost and wound up on the wrong doorstep.

My stringy brown hair covered my face and I flipped it back. Getting dressed wasn't high on my agenda that day, so the only thing I bothered putting on was a long black tank top that fell just below my panties. I would have never worn a silly shirt like that in public because of the giant pair of red lips on the front in the shape of a kiss. Due to my fever, I would have preferred to sleep in the nude, had I not been afraid of an apartment fire and having to run naked into the arms of a fireman. Not that it would be a bad outcome.

But then the knocking sounded again.

"Dammit," I murmured, dragging my bare feet across the carpet. Too tired to look out the peephole, I pressed my cheek against the painted wood. "Who is it?"

"It's Beckett."

I made some kind of a growl and thumped my head against the door.

"Come on, Lex. Just give me *five* minutes and you'll never have to see me again. I saw your ad in the paper for the car and you won't be able to sell it without the title. I brought it over; you left it at the house."

Double ugh. I'd never sold a car before. Did I need a title? Damn.

"Five minutes," I warned, turning the locks and opening the door.

"Jesus, Lexi, you look like shit."

"Thanks," I said as he shouldered past me and casually walked inside.

Beckett flipped on a small lamp beside the balcony door and I squinted. "By the way, you shouldn't put your full name in the paper; that's just fucking stupid."

My living room was modest with a cozy sofa facing a small window, two tan chairs, and a couple of end tables. The dining room, bedroom, and kitchen were all connected. You could essentially stand in the living room and see my entire apartment.

A chill rolled through my body and I leaned against the cool door. "Where's the title?"

Beckett involuntarily dropped his eyes to my legs. *Involuntarily*, because Beckett had no self-control when it came to tits and ass.

A sign I should have paid attention to from the beginning, but I'd naively thought I could change him.

"You look *damn* sexy in that shirt, Lex. I always liked it when you wore it to bed."

Beckett brushed his hand through his bristly hair. It was dirty blond and styled close to his head. He just got off work because he was still wearing his black work shirt with a logo of a red duck on his left breast. The name of the bar where he worked was Ducky's Dive.

He walked right up to me and intimately rubbed his hands over my bare shoulders. "Let's try it again," he suggested in a smooth voice. "I fucked up and I want a second chance, Lex."

Beckett was encroaching on my space and had that look in his eyes—the one that was dripping with lust. Before I could protest, he peeled off his shirt and slid his arm around my waist, grinding his hips against mine. His mouth trailed along my neck and I felt feverish, as if it were a dream. I wanted to object, but the fight was hardly in me.

My body trembled.

Beckett's hands slid over my bare hips and his fingers bit into my ass. "Ah, shit, Lex. You feel so fucking good. You have no idea how hot it feels to be near you."

It was a familiar feeling that suddenly made me uncomfortable. I no longer liked the way he touched me, his smell, or even his whiskey voice. My stomach knotted; I was trapped. I didn't want this. I didn't want his hands on me.

A knock on the door made me jump.

"Fuck off," Beckett yelled out.

I flattened my hands against his sticky bare chest and pushed. "Beckett, no."

Sex-filled eyes devoured me as the music from Naya's apartment pounded like something you'd hear at a strip club.

The light knock at the door turned into a hammering fist. "Lexi, open up the damn door," a dangerous voice demanded.

Austin?

Beckett's eyes narrowed. "Who's that?"

"No one."

"Good. Get rid of him. I want to talk, and you don't look like you're up for watching an ass-kicking tonight." His muscles flexed as he laid down the threat. Being a bouncer, Beckett knew how to handle himself, not to mention he loved starting shit with other guys for no reason. All that wrestling he watched had gone to his head.

He backed up and stood beside the balcony door with his arms folded in order to draw attention to his thick biceps. I turned around and cracked open the door. "Austin, what are you doing here?"

Austin's eyes hooded as he studied my face. "Are you okay?" His voice maintained a frightening level of control—a little bit like a gun about to go off.

"I've got a virus. You should go; it might be contagious."

Being that Austin was taller than me, he had the vertical advantage of seeing over my head and into the apartment. When I heard his knuckles crack, I knew he'd caught sight of Beckett, shirtless in my living room with the smug expression he always wore.

"Who's in there with you?"

"It's just my ex. He brought the title to my car and…"

"And he decided to mend fences by groping you in your condition?" Austin slid his jaw from left to right, something he did whenever he was pissed. Perhaps it was the slight lift of my brow, but his answer flashed across my face. Austin had a gift at reading people.

"I want him out," he demanded.

I tried to shut the door, but Austin wedged his foot in.

"Just go," I whispered. "He's a big guy with a temper and I'm too sick to deal with a fight."

Austin Cole lowered his head as well as his voice. A muscle tightened in his jaw and I knew he meant business. "You may not realize this yet, Lexi, but you're in my pack. And *nobody* fucks with my pack."

The door pushed open and Austin stood beside me. Beckett had never looked so small.

"Time for you to get the fuck out of here," Austin said in a calm voice, the kind that made all my hairs stand on end.

Beckett looked intimidated just for a split second before going into stupidity mode. "Says who?"

Those two words had started more fights than I could even remember.

Austin reduced the space between them to nothing and I became nervous about what was going to go down. All my furniture in ruins, lampshades torn, curtains ripped, tables smashed to pieces...

Austin threw a hard fist into Beckett's face and knocked him out cold. It sounded like bones cracked. I gasped when it happened and covered my mouth. There was no warning. No words were exchanged. Beckett fell to the ground like a tranquilized deer and Austin grabbed him by the ankles.

"What are you doing?" I exclaimed.

He dragged Beckett all the way outside. I cringed with every thump of his body down the steps but remained inside my apartment, peering through my door. Naya's partygoers were scattered about, enjoying the balmy night air and barely paying attention.

Austin Cole walked coolly into my apartment, closing the door behind him. "Did he hurt you?" He placed his large hand across my forehead and then touched my feverish cheek. "He put his hands on you, didn't he? I could smash his face in for trying to take advantage of you."

"I think you did smash his face open," I murmured.

Before I knew it, my feet were off the ground. Austin lifted me in his arms and carried me to the bedroom. I mumbled incoherently and everything became hazy and dreamlike. He placed me gently on the bed and kicked off his shoes, climbing in.

"What are you—no, Austin. No," I said firmly, trying to roll off the bed.

He tucked himself against my back, holding my body in a tight grip. Something strange began to happen. The sensation was similar to having hunger pangs and taking that first bite of a cracker. My body filled with relief, and I suddenly craved more of Austin, as if he weren't just a cracker, but a Ritz.

"That's it," he said, brushing his hand through my hair. "Relax. It's my power you feel. Perfectly natural."

My left leg slid over his and he hissed, pushing it back. Austin was essentially spooning me and trying to hold me still at the same time.

"I need to see a doctor," I groaned. "I'm sick."

His chest filled with air and a deep sigh warmed my shoulder in the most delicious way.

Oh, God. Austin was turning me on.

That's when I knew I must have been running a high fever, because the control button in my brain was out of order.

When his hand curved around my hip, I brought it between my legs. A deep growl rumbled in his throat and he immediately pulled it back to my waist.

So I arched my back until I pushed against his groin. He didn't move, but I could feel how much he enjoyed it. A deep ache filled my body, one that made me desire the man behind me like never before. Now he was in my bed—all these years, something I'd dreamed about for so long. I reached around, clawing at his jeans with my fingernails.

"Lexi, *no*," he said firmly. Something compelled me to obey. He gently pulled loose strands of hair away from my face with his right hand. "I need to tell you something." Austin swallowed thickly. He played it cool and stayed absolutely still. I could smell his skin and taste his power. "When we had the talk in the Laundromat, I got close to you and picked up on something I hadn't before. You're a Shifter."

I stopped moving while Austin spoke against my ear.

"I didn't know it when we were younger, but now that you're going through the change, it's like turbulence on my body. It explains why you were so drawn to me, Lexi. I'm an alpha wolf, and females respond to alphas. It's instinct. I've always felt protective of you and now it all makes sense. Humans are naturally attracted to female Shifters, but it's sexual, and some are weak and unable to control those urges. Most of our women don't date humans because they have trouble letting go and become obsessive. It's why we're protective of our women when it comes to humans or any other Breed."

"I'm not a Shifter," I protested, struggling to get free.

He kept a tight hold and threw his left leg over mine to tether my legs down.

"A Shifter can only come from Shifter parents—no exceptions.

You must have been adopted or something."

Finally, my mouth began to work. "What are you saying? Why are you doing this to me? I'm sick, Austin. Don't fill my head with—"

"With the truth. We don't shift until we're adults, and it's different for everyone. Usually the first time occurs in our late teens to early twenties. You're a late bloomer; maybe your animal was suppressed for so long because you've lived with humans all your life. If you've felt sick the past day or two it's because your animal is getting restless and trying to come out. It's nothing to be afraid of, and it won't hurt. You're going through the change, Lexi. Don't fight it; just relax and let your animal free."

I wriggled away from him and he finally let go. I wasn't thinking straight and everything felt like a dream. "Are you the cause of this? Are you the trigger that's making me change because you're some kind of an alpha wolf?"

Had I a non-feverish cell in my brain, I wouldn't have even entertained the idea.

Austin sat up and leaned forward on his knuckles, lowering his dark brows. I flinched a little from his intense stare and he spoke in a rich and textured voice. "If that's true, then this is the proudest fucking day of my life."

And then I blacked out.

CHAPTER 9

M Y TIRED LEGS STRETCHED BENEATH silken sheets, and my limp body relaxed on the soft mattress. The wooden ceiling fan rotated above my head, swirling a cool breeze around my bedroom. It was a quaint little room with a shelf full of movies and photo albums sitting below a painting. Two black lamps were on either side of my bed, and the dresser had a few photographs of my family.

I touched my cheek and blinked a few times. My fever must have broken.

"How you feeling?"

Oh shit. It wasn't just that Austin was in my bedroom, it was the feeling of complete nakedness beneath the covers.

I scrambled beneath the sheets and sat up, my hair a tangled mess.

"Eat this," he said, carrying in a large plate of food.

As he sat on the edge of the mattress, my stomach did a flip. Austin had several bandages patched to his left arm and a gnarly cut on his chin.

"Where are my clothes? What happened to you?"

He wasn't listening. He held a sausage between his fingers and tapped it against my mouth. "You need your strength."

"Tell me what happened," I ground through my teeth. "You're scratched up, I'm naked, and I have no memory of last night."

That's when I noticed the condition of the room. The curtain rod was hanging down at an angle and the drapes were shredded. There were long scratches on the bedroom door and tiny feathers covered the bed from a torn pillow.

"What happened to my room?" My tone wasn't hostile, but accusatory.

"Before you get riled up, Lexi, it's not what you're thinking. You know me better than that. I didn't dress you because it would have meant handling you naked. Better that you just slept it off. We have all day to talk about this, but right now you're going to eat."

Thanks to my voracious appetite, I bit into the most delicious piece of meat I'd ever put in my mouth, as if I'd been on a deserted island for years and it was my first taste of home. It was gone in five seconds.

He chuckled and cocked an eyebrow. "You're ravenous this morning. Any unusual cravings?"

What an odd question. Although now that he mentioned it, I *was* having a severe, unexplainable craving.

"So? Tell me what you're hungry for, Ladybug."

"Why are you still here?" I said with a mouthful of food. I started to eat a pineapple ring, but couldn't remember buying any in the past year, so I tossed it to the side.

"Do you have any memory of what happened? Most don't."

I frowned and pulled the sheet tighter. "What's that supposed to mean—most don't?"

He set the plate on the bed and wiped his hands along his jeans. "Do you remember our conversation last night?"

I thought about it through the hazy fog and shook my head. "A little bit, but... was Beckett here?"

His jaw tightened enough that it sharpened the angled line of his jaw. Austin always had strong features and maybe that's why I was attracted to him. There was nothing soft or feminine about his face... except when he smiled. Then his pale eyes sparkled so brightly that it became difficult to remember what the hell he was even laughing about.

"We're going to talk about that later. You're a Shifter, Lexi. Do you remember our conversation?"

"Oh, hell," I grumbled, falling onto my back and throwing my right arm over my face. "I was really hoping that was part of the dream. Why did you come back here, Austin? To show me how crazy you've become? I don't have room for crazy in my life right now."

The sound of him chewing filled the quiet room. When he

spoke, he was calm, as if we weren't about to begin an argument. "You're a wolf. *That* came as a surprise. Most of us know what our animal is before our first change because of what our parents are, unless they're mixed, and then it's a fifty-fifty thing. It usually shows in how we socialize with family. If both parents are leopards, the kids will be too. Not many Shifters mate outside their animal; it creates a shitload of friction in the house, from what I've heard."

"Then why don't I remember anything?"

"Few do," he said. "The majority of Shifters either remember nothing at all, or just the first few minutes after the shift. A few outliers can remember more, if not all. Our animal prefers to be in control and there would be too much internal conflict, so they block us out. Let her out every so often or she'll get restless and try to take over. You're going to have to learn to be in tune with her needs, because you're two halves that make a whole."

He took another bite of something and sucked on his fingers.

"Are you going to eat all my breakfast?" I managed.

He set the plate on my stomach. "There's more in the kitchen. Trust me, you're going to want at least three helpings before it's all said and done," he added with a smile in his voice. "The first time is always like that. Tell me what you're craving and I'll have it ready for you the next time you shift."

My chin touched my chest as I looked down and picked up a few scrambled eggs with my fingers. My appetite was waning; this was too much to accept.

"Did Beckett bruise up your face?" I cringed at the thought. Beckett was the kind of guy who held grudges against any man that showed him up, which wasn't often.

"No. *You* did it."

I blinked in surprise and Austin stood up and stretched out his toned arms. His dirty blue T-shirt was thin, faded, threadbare, and way too sexy for me to be ogling while naked in bed. It looked like one of his favorites—washed a million times. We all have a favorite shirt that the love's been worn into.

"You can't trust your animal until you bond with her. Introductions to someone new are usually supervised because there's a potential for them to attack. I swear, Lexi," he said laughing. "I seriously thought you were going to be a panther or some shit. The way we fought like cats and dogs sometimes, and hell… the way you *move*."

Just then, scarlet bled into his face and he spun around, staring at a picture of sailboats in a harbor.

When I looked down at my plate, I noticed something else. Hairs on the bed. I pinched one between my fingers and it was silver.

"You can't be serious," I said, beginning to feel my own doubt.

"What I don't understand is why you attacked me," he said to himself. "I'm an alpha and you should have submitted. Most will, except for other alphas or wolves who are no good for pack life. I've heard about women who have alpha personalities, just never thought it was true. I've never met a female with as much bite as you." He peered over his shoulder and his dark brow slanted in a way that made my toes involuntarily curl. "No pun intended."

I stared at the hair again, rolling it between my fingers. "You're serious? Then why don't I remember? Seems like I'd remember turning into a dog."

"Wolf," he corrected with intolerant eyes. "We're not *dogs*, Lexi. It's something to be proud of."

He scolded me with his tone and turned around, stuffing his hands in his deep pockets. "Don't ever talk down about your animal, especially not around me. I won't tolerate it. I've always considered your family my pack."

"What do you mean by that?"

"It's common for an alpha to find his own pack outside the family, although usually it's just a bunch of friends. That's why I hung out at your house a lot. My brothers sure as hell weren't going to let a nine-year-old kid try to boss them around. My parents were careful not to… damn, what's the word? Reprimand me too much, I guess. It would be a detriment to the leader I'd one day become. I needed another family unit. I was born to lead, and having older brothers trying to put me in my place went against every shred of instinct I had. Now that I'm grown, it's cool. Everyone knows their rank."

"And your brothers are wolves?" I couldn't believe I was getting sucked into his delusions.

"Yeah. In fact, that's why I'm back in town. I'm ready to settle and they're ready to be led."

A mockingbird sang outside my window and a smile wound up my face.

"You don't believe me, Lexi. But you will. I'm going to take you to meet my brothers and I'll introduce you to one of them in their wolf form."

"Why not you?" I scraped my fingers through my matted hair and frowned when I snagged a tangle. Damn, I must have looked like a nightmare.

He pulled his hands from his pockets and folded his arms, pacing to the door. "My wolf is dangerous." He paused, dropping his eyes to the floor. "He's aggressive, and I don't completely trust him around someone new. I can't risk hurting you."

"How is it my mom didn't notice I was changing into a wolf?"

"Because it's kind of like puberty. Your body goes through the change when it's mature, and we're all different. It's not triggered by anything except your own hormones or genetics. You wouldn't want a bunch of little kids who were mad at their parents to shift into a wolf and attack them or run away. Their animal would be volatile and hard to control."

"Austin, you do realize you're dropping a bomb on me, don't you? You're not just telling me I'm a Shifter, but that I'm not even related to my family. I don't believe this."

He turned on his heel and leaned against the door. "Family isn't blood—it's who has your back."

I chewed on my lip. The only way to know the truth was to talk to my mom. I'd know it if she was lying to me—she was a horrible liar and had a habit of doing dishes or cleaning if I asked her a question and she was untruthful. It's how I knew that the separation between her and my dad wasn't amicable. He'd left her, and that infuriated me almost as much as the fact he'd left his daughters behind.

"I'm going to take a shower and go to my mom's house. Then we'll see what's what."

"You need help?"

"Austin, I've been taking showers for twenty-seven years now. I think I got it."

A full-bodied laugh filled the room as he struggled to contain it. "I meant to talk to your mom."

When I clenched my teeth, he took that as a no. My mom was going to be giving me a straightjacket for Christmas after this convo. A sinking feeling settled at the possibility they might not be my real family. I loved Maizy and my mom with all the fire in me. I'd die to protect them. When my dad left, I was around as much as possible to make sure my mom didn't succumb to depression. We joined art classes, went shopping, and I spent a lot of time watching Maizy so she didn't overwhelm my mom, who wasn't exactly in her prime for motherhood.

I was the glue in my family.

<hr />

I'd been stalling the conversation ever since arriving at my mom's house. She sensed a serious talk coming and plopped Maizy in front of the TV with one of her favorite fairy princess movies. That was one little girl who had her heart set on marrying a prince.

The coffee burned against my upper lip and I blew off the steam, pensively watching my mother across the table.

She smiled and touched her hoop earring. "I remember when you made that cup. You were so proud of it and I thought it was the most hideous thing ever created."

I snorted and admired my mug. It was a regular coffee cup, but we'd painted them ourselves. In kindergarten, my obsession with dragons began. While Maizy adores fairy tales and happy endings, I used to want to slay dragons. So, my half-assed attempt at painting a dragon on the mug ended up being the family joke for years. It curved around the mug and looked like a green anaconda with spider legs, throwing up mustard. I'd never seen a dragon, so in my defense, I wasn't sure how many legs they had.

Apparently, seventeen was too many.

"Mom, I have something serious to ask you and I want the

truth. I'm not even sure where to begin."

"You know you can ask me anything," she said in the way all moms do when they have no idea you're about to drop the mother lode of bombs on them.

Maizy giggled in the other room and I scratched my neck nervously. "Am I adopted?"

"Now why would you ask a silly thing like that?" she said, rising from the table and turning on the faucet. She rinsed out her mug, then wiped it dry with a paper towel. "Would you like some pie with your coffee? I think I'm more in the mood for iced tea—it's too hot today for coffee."

"Mom, turn off the water and sit down. I don't want pie or anything else."

That's when I knew Austin had told me the truth. Maybe not about being a Shifter, but now it was clear my life had been manufactured from a lie.

"I'm not going to get mad about it. I just want to know who I am and where I came from. You'll always be my family, Mom. Please, don't lie to me. Not now, not after everything we've been through."

When she turned around, tears stained her cheeks. "I never wanted you to know. You were our baby and *my* little girl."

I covered my eyes before she made me cry. I needed to keep my head straight. "Mom, please sit down."

She quietly sniffed and took a seat, avoiding eye contact. I reached across the table and held her hand. "You're my mom. You'll always be my mom and nothing will change that. I promise. I just… I can't believe this is true. How did I not know? I always thought I kind of looked like Dad, but…"

"Lexi, we never wanted you to grow up feeling separate from us—different. I was afraid that's how kids felt in your situation, so we decided not to tell you."

"What exactly was my situation? It's not like you couldn't have your own children. Why was I adopted?"

She pulled her hand away and laced her fingers together. "You weren't."

Just then, Maizy came bounding into the room. "Mommy! Can

I please have some cookies?" She lifted her shoulder and tilted her head to the side in that innocent way kids do to turn on the charm. Few could say no to her adorable dimples.

"Just one, sweetheart. It's almost dinner."

Maizy skipped over to the bright yellow jar by the sink and pulled out a small chocolate-chip cookie. Seconds later, she went flying into the living room wearing her pink skirt and white shirt with all the sparkles. She was in princess mode.

I warmed my hands around my mug. "What do you mean, not adopted?"

Her voice lowered. "I don't know where you came from. Your dad brought you home one night. He used to stay out late sometimes, and I convinced myself he was having an affair. But occasionally, he came home with—with blood on his clothes." She pulled her hands in her lap and shook her head. "Not a lot, but spatters around the sleeves. I was afraid to ask what he was up to because he was a serious man—you know that. I don't know what he was involved in, but we argued for weeks. All I could think about was your poor mother, worried to death about where you were. He assured me you had no mother, and that frightened me."

"Why?"

She pulled the salt and pepper shakers to the middle of the table, lining them up neatly and never once lifting her eyes.

"I'm an adult now, and there's no need to lie anymore. Whatever you've been carrying around for years, we can talk it out. Maybe it'll help. But I can't go on not knowing the truth. Everything."

My heart galloped and I placed my hands on my lap to hide the fact they were shaking. Had Austin never come back into town, I would have gone on thinking my life was normal.

"The night he brought you home, there was blood on his clothes. Only this time, I found them in the trash instead of the wash, and they were just *soaked* in it."

"You didn't know what he was involved in?"

To my knowledge, my dad had worked for a shipping warehouse. He was a bossy guy, but otherwise, family life seemed as normal as it could be. He took Wes fishing in the summer and we had a barbecue every Sunday. I didn't have a close relationship with my dad, and he was strict when it came to punishment, but this revelation came as an unexpected shock. I felt disenchanted with my life, knowing that nothing was as it seemed.

She shrugged and pulled my cup away. "Do you want something else, hon? Chocolate milk?"

God, my weakness. "Sure, Mom. That'd be great."

The table sat in a room connected to the kitchen, but a partition wall with an opening in the center separated the two rooms. My mom put her favorite fern on it to add a sense of privacy. Light blue paint colored the top of the walls and wood panels covered the bottom. Outside the window on my left, the hummingbird feeder swung like a pendulum in the breeze. I'd never seen any hummingbirds, but Mom always kept it filled with bright red liquid.

I watched her through the divider as she stirred the chocolate into a tall glass. As calm as we were, I had a feeling I'd be in tears later on once everything sank in.

She set the glass down on the table and I took a sip, hoping the coffee wouldn't complain. Mom eased into her chair and peered around the corner, listening for Maizy.

"When I first met your father, he was involved with some dangerous people. He used to work as a middleman, and I don't know what exactly he did, only that it was illegal. He quit that life when he proposed, and I thought we were going to have a new start. I wouldn't have to worry about something happening to him, or the police showing up. That's not the kind of home I came from. He changed, or at least I thought he did. It started up again a year after Wes was born, when we were struggling financially. Suddenly, your dad paid off the bills and things were okay. How could I complain? Everything went back to normal until the night he brought you home. He was panicked that night and then for weeks, he barely slept."

Tears threatened to slide down her lashes and she averted her blue eyes. "Only he knows the truth about where you came from, but I fell in love with you, Lexi. I had to buy you little gowns and booties since you were only wearing a onesie with Talulah stitched on the front. I always wanted a little girl. You were such a sweet little thing, didn't cry much at all even though you must have known we were strangers."

"Did you keep my clothes?"

Her voice fell to a whisper. "There was blood. I had to throw it out. Your dad somehow got a fake birth certificate; I just didn't ask questions."

I buried my face in my hands. "Did Wes know?"

"At first," she said. "But he was a toddler and after a while, he forgot where you came from. We told him the stork brought you and in time, I guess he just didn't remember. Your grandparents never knew because they were living in Seattle. We told them we had been keeping it a secret because the doctor warned us the pregnancy might not go to full term and then we said you were born premature. They didn't come down to visit until you were five anyhow, and two years later, they moved down to San Antonio."

I circled my finger on the smooth table. My mom had lost her parents when she was ten, and my dad's parents never came around much—especially after he split. "Are Wes and Maizy yours, or—"

"Yes, they're ours. Maizy is the spitting image of your great-grandma from the childhood pictures I've seen, and Wes looked just like Grandpa Knight. Oh, God," she whispered, covering her eyes. "I'm so sorry."

"Mommy?"

Maizy wandered into the room and worry filled her blue eyes. Mom discreetly wiped a tear away from her smooth cheek and smiled. "Mommy has allergies. Do you need something, sweetie pie?"

My sister might be a child, but she knew something was wrong. Mom held out her arm and Maizy walked forward until Mom hugged her tightly and kissed her on the cheek. In fact, she started kissing Maizy all over her face and it switched on her gigglebox.

"Go in the other room, Maze," I told her. "I'll be in there in a minute and we can watch the best part together." I knew which part was coming up because I could hear the song playing and practically had that movie memorized. Maizy skipped out of the room and I rubbed my eyes.

"I need to get a hold of Dad. Do you know where he is?"

She shook her head adamantly. "I have no idea, honey. A friend of mine even tried searching for him on the Internet. He just... disappeared."

"Then I'm going to find a way to make him reappear, because he has the missing piece to my puzzle."

CHAPTER 10

THE NEXT DAY AT WORK, I kept popping jellybeans into my mouth. Normally I stayed away from the candy, but I deserved a few extra pounds after my unforgettable week. Instead of eating my sack lunch, I walked down the street to the deli and ordered a chef salad. While staring at the glazed sugar cookies in the display, a familiar voice called out from behind.

"Alexia Knight, is that you?"

These are the curses of living in the same town you grew up in. Either your old classmates still lived there, or they eventually returned to visit family. I was always running into someone from my past and it felt weird, like you weren't supposed to know what happened to everyone when they grew up.

I recalled some of the most turbulent times of childhood. I got in a fight at school with a girl who called me Flatass, my brother and Austin took me to prom because no guy had asked me, and a couple of my besties either slept with my boyfriends or ended up going to college and never called me again. While I'd been avoiding class reunions, they didn't seem to be avoiding me.

I turned around and laid eyes on Josh Holden. He now worked as a manager at a gas station. I'd run into him a few times when I lived with Beckett because the station was on my way home. Usually I just paid at the pump, but a couple of times Beckett wanted me to go in and pick up some lottery tickets.

When I was fifteen, Josh had tried to get me a little more experienced with older boys than I was ready for, but chalk it up to teenage hormones. Up to that point, my version of dating was handholding and a few French kisses. I'd never had a real boyfriend or done anything sexual. Then Josh took me out on a date and couldn't keep his hands off me.

"Haven't seen you in a few months," he said. "Your hair looks different."

"So does your face. What happened?" It was bruised up and his left cheek was green.

"Uh, got jumped by some psycho," he said, scratching the side of his nose. Josh was once a buff guy on the football team, but time had worn away all that brawn. Now he stood around five feet ten inches and had a potbelly. His reddish-blond hair was shaved close to his head, and his once golden skin was now mottled and freckled in places.

"Sorry to hear that," I said. "Robbery at the gas station?"

"Nah. I was driving around and, I don't know. So how you been? You still seeing that big dude with the pythons?"

By pythons, he meant Beckett's arms.

"No, we split up."

"That's too bad. I just broke up with some chick I met online. Stay away from those dating services."

"Why's that?"

He nodded at the man behind the counter. "Ham and cheese to go. And a pickle." Josh put his hand on the counter and scoped out a blonde who walked inside carrying a small dog under her right arm. "Most of them use pictures they took ten years and two babies ago."

What a pig. "You don't have kids?"

"Hell no. At least, none that I know about."

I impatiently glared at the manager. He was putting the last toppings on the salad and I suddenly wished I had ordered my lunch to go. *Please do not let Josh get the bright idea to join me.*

"I love kids," I declared in a bright voice. "Can't wait to have a bunch of them."

His brows popped up.

"Miss, here's your salad."

The man behind the counter slid my tray forward and I grabbed the ends, looking back at Josh. "Well, take care, and good luck with everything." What else could I say? It's not as if he was an old friend, and the conversation was just weird and a little sad.

I walked to the back of the quaint little deli and set my tray on a small wooden table beside the soda fountain machine. When the heavy legs of the chair scraped back, Josh sidled up beside me. "Can I join you? I've got the afternoon off and we can catch up on old times."

Old times of him pawing me in the front seat of his dad's Pontiac? No, thanks.

"Sorry, Josh. I have a lot on my mind and I'd rather be alone," I said, sitting in the wooden chair.

"Maybe we can talk about it," he suggested, leaning forward with his hand on the table, obscuring my view.

I poked my plastic fork in a boiled egg and sat back. "No offense. I really need to be by myself right now."

"Problem?" a deep, scary voice rumbled from behind him.

Josh stiffened and looked over his shoulder. Austin stood with his arms folded and the most volcanic gaze I'd ever seen. He looked wolfish, like a predator stalking his prey. His dark brows sank over his bright eyes, and the way he looked at Josh gave me the chills.

Apparently, it gave Josh the chills too.

"See ya, Lexi," Josh mumbled, walking swiftly to the door without waiting for his sandwich.

"You seem to always show up at the most convenient times," I noted. "If I didn't know better, I'd think you were following me." My statement was a question in disguise.

Austin pulled out the chair across from me and slowly sat down, resting his forearms on the table. He was wearing a sleeveless black shirt and my eyes stole a glimpse of his remarkable tattoos.

"How did it go with your mom?"

"Are you following me?" I repeated.

Austin rubbed his jaw and gave himself away. "What did that asshole say to you?"

I tapped my finger on the table and something clicked. "Are you the one who put those bruises on Josh's face?"

"I heard everything you said at the cemetery and that's all I needed to know. I didn't like hearing about the way he treated you."

"I was fifteen, Austin. He was just doing what boys do."

That pissed Austin off something fierce as his expression tightened and he scorched me with his eyes. "Time doesn't erase stupidity. You should have told us back then and we would have taken care of it. Do you think I treated girls like that? Do you think Wes did?"

I snorted. "Yeah, I'm sure you rolled out the red carpet and showered them with rose petals and poetry before popping their cherries. Don't play knight, because boys are boys and all boys think about is s-e-x." I stabbed a tomato with my fork.

His voice became smooth like molasses as he leaned forward. "I'm not a boy anymore, Lexi. Are you going to sit there and tell me you never think about sex?"

Damn if that didn't make my toes curl.

"If I had known all this was going on when we were younger, you might have wound up seeing a darker side of me, Lexi. I didn't have sex until I was nineteen, and fuck it if that makes me a big pussy because I waited so long, but having sex with a girl who wasn't even a woman never seemed right, even then. That's the difference between Shifters and humans," he said in a quiet voice. "I got a lot of shit for it back then from Wes and some of my human buddies in school, but none of my brothers said a damn thing. That's just the way it is in our world."

"My mom confirmed what you said. I'm adopted." I bit into the tomato and sighed. Suddenly, it didn't taste as good as I'd hoped. It had all the bitterness that was already in my mouth from learning the truth.

"You okay?"

I flicked my eyes up and my heart skipped a beat. Austin had that look.

The look.

The swoon-worthy look that made my palms sweat. All the rough edges in his voice were gone, and it was the smooth timbre of concern I'd heard on rare occasions when he was being soft and not treating me like his best friend's kid sister. Except now, with his broad shoulders and bold tattoos, he was shrouded in mystery.

"I guess." My shoulders sagged and I set the fork down. "She doesn't know where I came from because I wasn't adopted. My father brought me home and my mom doesn't have a clue who my real parents are."

"Palmer, your order is ready," the cashier called out.

Austin rubbed his hand across his mouth. "Shifters, of course. But we don't give up our own." Austin ran his index finger along his eyebrow and glanced at my salad. "Eat your lunch."

"I've lost my appetite."

Austin leaned in closer and slowly pushed my bowl toward me. "It's not good to starve your wolf," he warned. "They get angry and pace until they're ready to take over. Don't try to deny what you are, Lexi. It won't go away just because you choose to ignore it. I need to talk to you later about this—tonight. I'm here because I've been keeping an eye on you today. I don't want anything upsetting you or else you might shift."

I licked my dry lips and held my breath. Something in me was starting to believe him and I didn't know if it was brainwashing or insanity.

"Could that happen?"

Austin slid my salad to the side and leaned across the short table, curling his finger for me to do the same. I leaned in and his mouth grazed against my ear.

"I'm a bounty hunter, Lexi, and I protect what's mine. You don't have anything to worry about, because if you shifted in this room, I'd lay to waste any man who tried to capture or kill your wolf. Are we clear?"

My cheeks flushed and the bristles of his jaw immediately rubbed against my skin. Something had changed in Austin, all right. There was raw power in not only his words, but in his presence. I felt it, just as sure as I felt his whiskers prickling against my cheek. A thick tension built between us and something inside me began to pace.

Austin was offering me more than his friendship—he was offering protection.

"Just so we're clear," I pointed out, "I'm not yours."

I felt his smile stretch across my cheek and his breath melted against my ear like hot wax. "What time do you get off work? I want you to meet my pack."

———————⋙⋘———————

"This is where you live?"

I scanned our surroundings in the dark woods, leaning against Austin's black Dodge Challenger. The gravel road led to a rather large house nestled in the middle of nowhere. The front yard was dirt and pebbles, and to the right, a couple of cars were parked beside horseshoes and a rusty metal pin staked into the ground. A crooked light pole lit up the side of the house and the woods were thick with native trees. I cupped my elbows and a twig snapped beneath my foot.

Austin chuckled. "Come on, Lexi. You don't have anything to worry about."

He took a few steps and looked over his shoulder at me. It was out of character for me to be so timid, so he walked up and held my face with his strong hands. "You're always safe with me, Lexi. I want you to know I won't let anything bad happen to you. My brothers are good guys, even if they are rough around the edges. You can trust them."

"Pack or brothers?"

"What's the difference?"

Austin took my hand and led me to the front door. A motion sensor light clicked on and he slid the key in the lock. I could already hear rowdy chatter inside and found myself gripping his hand tighter.

The door swung open and I stared into an entryway with a view of an atrium that was in the middle of the house. It was a small, grassy enclosure with a barbecue grill in one of the corners. I might not have seen it had the light outside not been flipped on, and there was no roof, so it was open. The wall on the right stopped at an entrance to another room, but I hadn't moved from the front door because I was a bundle of nerves.

"That must be Austin," someone said from the room on the right. "Hey, Aus, I hope you brought some beer because dickhead drank the last of it."

I stepped back a little and Austin shut the door, kicking off his shoes and adding them to the pile in the corner. As a courtesy, I took off my white tennies.

A barefoot guy who looked about my age walked up on us. "What's up?"

Austin smirked. "Lexi, this is my brother, Denver. He can serve a mean drink, but don't ask him how to heat up a can of soup because he doesn't have a clue. Denver, this is Alexia Knight, Wes's little sister."

Denver jerked his head back in surprise. He was an inch shorter than Austin, and his stylish, dark blond hair was arranged in disheveled chunks all over his head. He had the sort of face that was handsome and soft with smiling eyes—like a man who didn't take life seriously. I tried not to look, but there was a scar on his temple about three inches long, right above his left eye, angling from the hairline toward his left ear. But his indigo eyes melted away any curiosity about a scar that barely marred his handsome face.

"How's it going?"

I shrugged.

"I take it you didn't bring beer?" His smile morphed into a contagious grin—definitely the pretty boy in the family. Denver had acquired the genes that propelled him to runway-model status.

"Gather the boys up, Denver. There's something we need to talk about."

"The boys are all out. Only the men are here," he said with a cocksure grin. Then he touched his scar when he realized Austin was serious. "It's just me and Jericho. They're having another ladies' night down at the bar and you know how that riles up all the uh…" He looked at me and switched up the last word. "Men."

"That's fine. It's Jericho I need to see; Lexi can meet everyone else later."

Denver shrugged and disappeared around the wall to the right.

"It's better this way," Austin said with a sideways glance. "A large group of men watching might spook your wolf, and I don't want you shifting in front of them." He hung his keys on one of the nails lined up in a row. Each had a letter directly below, and his was an *A*.

"Nice place," I said. "Do you guys live together or is this just the hangout?"

"Packs live together, but this place is getting too damn crowded. I can barely get my car in the driveway without hitting one of the other cars. I've clipped Denver's truck twice and he's getting pissed about the scratches. Not to mention we only have one bathroom, and that's an issue I'd rather not go into. I'll be scouting for a larger place pretty soon."

"Where do you get the money to pay for this?"

His thumb stroked my cheek and my breath caught. "We'll talk about that later. You ready? There's no going back once you learn the truth, Lexi. But you need to see it for yourself and know what you are."

"Sexy? Beautiful? Smart? I know *that* already," I said facetiously.

He sniffed out a laugh and lightly gripped my elbow. "Let's go, smartass."

CHAPTER 11

⊸◦〇⌇〇◦⊱

AUSTIN LED ME TO THE center of his modest living room. A long brown couch on the right side faced a massive television on the left. Just to the right of the couch was a hideous maroon recliner that matched nothing in the room. Sprawled across an oversized round carpet the color of cocoa powder was a guy who looked like he needed a guitar and a bottle of whiskey.

And maybe a shower.

He glanced up and Austin kicked him lightly. "Get up, Jericho. Company."

Denver collapsed onto the sofa and pulled a pizza box across his lap. A couple of messy tomato stains colored his white T-shirt. "Jericho, don't be a dick. That's Wes's sister," he said with a mouthful of pizza.

Jericho slowly dragged his jade eyes over to mine. They were milky green with black rims—the kind of eyes that could stare into your soul. He sized me up and rolled over onto his feet. "*That's* Alexia?" His eyes glided down my body and the corner of his mouth hooked up. "I thought you said she was a pipsqueak."

Austin slid his jaw to the side and tilted his head, causing Jericho to look away. I was a little irritated because these men knew who I was, and yet Austin had never talked about his family with us. At least, not to me.

Jericho was leaner and taller than Austin, and his grungy hair fell around his shoulders like he was channeling Kurt Cobain, only his was different shades of brown. He looked innocent and damaged all at once. Especially with the charcoal liner smudged beneath his large, expressive eyes. But they looked haunted, like a man who lived through or had seen things he shouldn't have. He carried an easygoing smile. A smile like that should come with a warning label and a list of side effects.

When he stepped forward, Austin touched his shoulder. "Disrespect her and we take a long walk. That goes for you too, Denver."

"Austin, Denver, and Jericho," I said softly as something finally clicked. "I'm sensing a theme."

Denver spoke with a mouthful of pizza. "Family tradition."

"To be named where you were born?" I asked.

"Our parents traveled a lot in search of a pack," Austin explained, his hand sliding down my back. It felt overly intimate with his brothers closely watching his every move. "They bounced around but never settled for long if one of the local packs didn't take them in. We're all named after the city we were conceived in, not where we were born."

"Tell her what they almost called you," Denver urged his brother.

Jericho cocked one eyebrow in an irritated fashion. "They were in Utah at the time. I was almost named Beaver; thank the fuck they kept on driving."

"That's fucking epic," Denver said with a chaotic laugh. "It never gets old."

"You guys don't look older than Austin," I said observantly.

They smiled and looked at one another. "Shifters age slowly," Austin explained, his thumb stroking my lower back. "I may look a little older than some of these guys, but we all age at different rates."

"How old do I look?" I wondered aloud.

"Twenty-delicious," Jericho replied with a sex-laced grin.

"You'll meet everyone else later." Austin turned his attention to his brothers. "Lexi is family to me, so watch your P's and Q's. As it turns out, she's also one of us."

"No fucking way," Denver breathed. Both of them seemed to freeze up and really study me, as if they'd never laid eyes on a woman before. I folded my arms and looked to Austin for a little reassurance.

"What's your animal?" Denver blurted out.

Jericho tilted his head. "I bet she's a deer. She's got them doe eyes."

Austin's voice changed, becoming like a sergeant giving orders. "Jericho, cut the bullshit. I want you to shift."

"Now? What for?" he asked apprehensively.

"She needs to see what we are because she's still skeptical. Lexi's never been around our kind and just went through the change."

Something wild stirred in their eyes and they looked at me like a succulent steak they wanted to pour sauce all over and devour.

"Fine. But put me outside before I shift back. This better not be some fucking joke to get me naked in front of a girl."

"Yeah, like *that's* never happened," Denver said with a snort.

Jericho took off his socks, slowly slid his belt out of the loops of his jeans, then pulled his shirt over his head—scorching me with his gaze the entire time.

And *all* while retaining a panty-dropping smile on his face.

Jericho possessed an ample supply of charisma and confidence—a vibe that drew women to a man regardless of what he looked like. Before tossing the shirt down, he glanced up at his brother. Something transpired between them, as if Austin wasn't happy with the striptease act.

"Sorry, Austin, but it's one of my favorites and I'd be pissed if it got torn. It was a badass tour."

He neatly folded the Pink Floyd concert shirt and set it on the armrest of the couch.

"My neighbor would worship you," I said, watching him stretch out his arms.

Jericho might have been lean, but one had to admire his physique. There was something compelling about the way he carried himself, or maybe it was the awesome tattoo of a guitar on his left arm. It was black and wavy—the neck looked like a lick of fire—and one side was not filled in. It resembled one of those yin-yang designs.

Without removing his eyes from mine, he asked Austin, "Sure you want me to shift? I've got a pretty wolf, and she just might take a shine to me."

Austin cleared his throat when Jericho unbuttoned his jeans. "Drop your pants and I'll shave your wolf."

Jericho's expression darkened. With a wink of his eye, he shifted so fast I could barely comprehend what had just happened.

I gasped and leapt back. Standing before me was a brown wolf with rust and cream-colored markings. He was bigger than I imagined a wolf should be—as big as the one that chased me in the cemetery. Holding my attention were milky-green eyes with black rims.

"That's impossible. *That's just not possible*," I babbled, stepping back even more. Austin caught my arm.

"Don't run from a wolf, Lexi. This is who you are," he said in a patient voice.

I stood there shaking, palms sweating, heart racing, knees close to buckling. This was too much. All this time he'd been telling me the truth.

"Damn, Austin, she doesn't even know what she is?" Denver tossed a green pepper into his mouth. "Maybe you need to explain why a Shifter was living with a human family."

"Later," Austin snapped, his eyes still on me. He reached his left hand out—palm down—and the wolf stepped forward and sat down submissively.

"I'm the Packmaster, so you don't have to worry. They won't attack as long as I'm in the room."

"And when you're not in the room?" I asked, wide-eyed and looking at Austin as if I'd just stepped into the Twilight Zone.

A shadowy crease appeared between his brows. "Then *you're* not in the room. Trust has to be established with the animal, and that's one reason I don't want you shifting around them. You lunged at *me*, so there's no telling what you'd do to these sorry asses."

"She did that to your arm, bro?" Denver grinned. "'Bout time someone put you in your place."

Austin swung his eyes up at Denver, who quickly shoved a pepperoni in his mouth and suddenly became engrossed with a *Golden Girls* rerun on TV.

"You believe me now?" Austin asked in a soft voice.

I nodded. The evidence was panting in front of me. Jericho had the same haunting eyes in human form.

"Doesn't he have control?"

"Did you?" Austin asked. "Only alphas have the gift to remain in control when they shift and remember everything. Not all, but some do. Once the animal's in charge, then that's what we're dealing with. An animal. Jericho's in there, but he's not in the driver's seat."

I reached out to pet him and Austin snatched my wrist. "No, Lexi."

He tapped Jericho on the snout and called out to Denver. "Take him outside; I need to be alone with her."

Denver obediently got up, dropped the box of pizza on the floor, and walked Jericho outside. When the door slammed, a few glasses tinkled on the bar.

"You okay?"

I stared like a zombie at the spot the wolf had been.

"Lexi?" He dipped down and tried getting my attention. Then he lifted my chin and grinned. "It's pretty exciting stuff, admit it."

Then my head began to shake. "No, no, no. I *can't* be one of you. I can't do this, Austin. If it's true and I shift in front of Maizy…" I began to panic. "How could I have not known?"

"Calm down," he said, taking hold of my arm and leading me to the sofa. "I know it's a lot to take in. Here, sit down." Austin knelt before me and placed his hand on my knee.

I didn't know whether to laugh, cry, or throw up. My hands were shaking uncontrollably and I was suddenly thirsty. Austin smoothed his hands over mine and patiently waited until I simmered down. Or until my heart rate stopped breaking the sound barrier.

"If you don't develop a relationship with your animal, then you can't be trusted with your own family. I can supervise your visits, or…"

"Or what?"

He stood up and walked to the other side of the room, where he leaned against the doorframe.

Damn, that lean.

"Or we can tell them. We can sit down and show them what you are. It's something you should be proud of, and while we keep our world secret from humans, this would be one of the exceptions. She's your mom, and eventually she'll notice you're not aging.

But it's important they don't tell anyone, and I don't know about your daughter."

I blinked.

"My daughter?"

"She's young, and you know how kids are. Not that anyone would believe her, but they won't tolerate any disloyal—"

"Wait a second, Austin. My *daughter*?"

He furrowed his brow and his blue eyes flashed. "Yeah. And if that piece of shit I dragged down the stairs was her father, then I don't want him hanging around or there's going to be trouble."

"Maizy isn't my daughter, Austin. She's my sister."

Something shifted out of place in his expression, a new look I'd never seen before.

He closed the distance between us and instead of kneeling down to eye level, he leaned forward and put his hands on either side of the sofa cushion behind my head.

"Your sister? *Wes's* sister?" he asked in disbelief.

I nodded.

I'd never really been scared of Austin until that moment. His eyes bored into me and I looked away. For a minute there, I thought he was going to yell, or maybe I fantasized a little bit that he was going to lean down and kiss me fervently.

But he came to some kind of conclusion after a hard stare and straightened up with his arms folded.

"I don't want your ex coming around again. If I find out he has, I'm going to track him down and personally deliver the message."

A knuckle cracked.

"Don't worry," I assured him. "I have no intention of seeing Beckett anymore. We're over."

I stared at Jericho's belt on the floor, then at Austin's. I remembered the slow precision with which Jericho unlatched the leather and slid it out, imagining Austin doing a move like that. Maybe it was for the best he didn't shift after all.

I really wanted to kick myself.

"Does he have anything of yours? You mentioned the car title. I don't want anything holding you to him."

"Yeah," I said. "But I read up on it and I can get a new one."

"One of my brothers may be looking for a car," he suggested.

"No."

He titled his head. "And why not?"

"Beckett had sex in that car and I'd rather see it burn. I want to sell it to a stranger so I never have to see it again."

"Tell you what. I'll see what I can do about taking the car off your hands, and I promise—it'll be gone for good."

That was a relief. Buying or selling a car was stressful, and I didn't really know how to handle those things. "Thanks, Austin. I'd appreciate it."

Denver appeared and his voice boomed. "We got company!"

"Who?" Austin's eyes were bright and alert.

"Jericho's hunting them down." Denver hopped on one foot while shoving the other into a sneaker. "We were twenty yards from the house and—"

"Shifters?" Austin peeled off his shirt and his abs tensed.

Denver flicked his eyes to me. "Yeah. One of them said we have an unclaimed bitch and he wanted to meet her."

My eyes narrowed. "Who's he calling a bitch?"

"Word's out then," Austin muttered. "Doesn't take long. How the hell do they know about her?"

Denver shrugged as he tied his laces. "Only an alpha would have smelled her if she was close to the change. You been near any alphas?" Denver asked.

"How would I know? I get a ton of customers coming in and out of my store and I couldn't tell you an alpha from a beta. Are you saying you can smell me?"

Denver quirked a smile and quickly switched over to a serious face. "They didn't state what pack they belonged to. If Jericho tracks them down, you should have a talk with their Packmaster. I wouldn't recommend going after them yourself," he said, eyeing Austin who was squeezing his hands into fists. "You know the consequences if an alpha attacks another pack on the offense without provocation, especially if they're not on our turf. Rules, bro. Play by 'em."

In that moment, I saw wisdom in Denver as an older brother,

even though he didn't look it. Austin was in charge, but their experience would serve to provide him with invaluable advice.

Austin pointed at him and replied in a chillingly cool voice. "He'd *better* find them. Stay outside and keep guard. I don't want anyone sniffing around my territory. Have Jericho mark the perimeter and leave a warning."

"Let me just go get him some Gatorade," Denver said with a suppressed smile and a song in his voice, hitching up his jeans in the back as he sauntered out of the room.

Austin looked me over and released a breath he must have been holding in. "You're staying here tonight."

I sprang up. "I have to go to work tomorrow, Austin. I feel better and my work clothes are at home."

"Call in sick and I'll go pick up your things. They're not going to fire you for having the flu."

"Wait a second," I protested, inching my way toward the hallway. "I'll agree to stay here the night, but I go home tomorrow. Period. This isn't a request. You can't waltz into my life and start making decisions for me. I have a job, a family, and a life to live. Okay, so maybe I'm dealing with a little bit more… like the fact I'm a wolf."

I paused. This was too much.

"Do you guys really call us bitches?"

Austin made a little grunt that sounded like he found my question inane. "It doesn't have any negative connotations with Shifters. It just is what it is."

"I still have a problem with it." The bottom of my feet were sticky against the wood floor as I paced in a small circle. "Better warn your brothers, Austin. I'm dead serious. I've been called a lot of things, but bitch is one name I don't tolerate very well."

He leaned forward. Just a little. "Who's calling you names?" he asked, and I didn't care for the darkness in his voice.

"No one. Since when did you become so concerned with my life?"

There was an uncomfortable silence between us as he swallowed thickly, like he wanted to say something. "I'm going to check the locks on the doors and windows. If you're hungry, there's plenty in the kitchen. The boys will be out all night; that's usually the deal when it's Shifter's night at the bar. Denver will let us know if something's up. I don't have any concerns. This is *my* turf. Sounds like they were just checking you out. Someone got them riled up about an unclaimed woman in town—someone knows about you."

I shrugged. "I don't know who that could be. I wouldn't know how to spot a Shifter."

"I'll be back." When Austin stalked out of the room, the stupid teenager in me actually turned my head to stare at his ass.

As alarming as it was to know a bunch of strange men were snooping around to get a look at me, I felt safe with Austin. I was never the kind of woman who sat around dreaming of a man protecting me, but since Wes died and my dad left, I'd missed out on all the luxuries most other girls got. Having someone help change the oil, sell the car, or shop for a new apartment. A man to stop by and figure out what was going on with the leaky faucet or have my back whenever someone gave me shit.

Not that people gave me shit. I wasn't a troublemaker and didn't hang out with the rowdy crowd. Those were Beckett's friends, and usually I dodged their parties and went out with Naya. Maybe the whole "tough guy" thing was why Beckett was so appealing in the beginning. Then I realized that sometimes being a tough guy simply meant you were a jerk.

He never changed my oil, either.

I had a small panic attack in the bathroom and spent a long time digesting the facts. Nothing would ever bring Wes back and over the years, I'd accepted his death. But now that sorrow was replaced by anger that his life was cut short unnecessarily. Maybe I wasn't related to my family by blood, but I loved them fiercely. Being a Shifter? A whole other ball of wax. I didn't even begin to know how to process it.

I found a chicken potpie in the freezer and heated it up. After devouring the entire meal in less than five minutes, I curled up on the sofa with a bag of Doritos and fell asleep watching *Die Hard*. I'd found the movie stacked in a large box labeled "Reno."

The bag crinkled and someone jostled me around.

"Stop," I mumbled.

"Time for bed," Austin said, and then I was in his arms.

He set me down on top of a comforter and I nuzzled into the pillow, listening to the sound of a window unit circulating air.

The bed moved in the darkness and my eyes popped open. "Austin?"

"Yeah."

"You're *not* sleeping with me."

He threw the comforter from his side over my legs.

"It's my bed, so I'm pretty sure I am. Plus, it's the only room in the house with a window unit," he murmured sleepily. "I run hot."

Then I heard a zipper and the bed moved some more. I stayed very quiet, because honestly, I had no idea how to react. I felt a connection with him that time never erases with someone you know, like when you hear a song on the radio and all those old feelings of a special time in your life come flooding back.

That was Austin—he was my song.

I still remembered the sleepovers and how I'd pretend to doze off beside him while we watched a movie on the couch. It was strategic, of course, so I could slide against his shoulder. Wes always had to play bad guy and drag me off to bed, but Austin never seemed to mind. I loved those moments, because when he laughed, I could feel it.

Austin released one of those long sighs with a satisfactory moan once he settled beneath the sheets. Then I started wondering things like what kind of underwear he wore, or if he slept Tarzan style.

I immediately threw the blanket over to his side.

His warm laugh filled the chilly room. "I'm not cold, Ladybug."

"Why do you call me that? You've been calling me that name since I can remember."

He exhaled through his nose as if he were going to tell me something he didn't want to.

"Your freckles."

"Oh. Those."

"Yeah, those." He was quiet for a minute and then his voice changed up, softened a little, but had an edge like maybe he was embarrassed to talk so intimately with me. "One summer when you were about five, your mom bought you one of those moving sprinklers. You practically lived outside and ended up with a sunburn."

I smiled. "I don't remember."

"That's when you first got 'em. It was just a little spray across your nose and high on your cheeks. I was being mean when I gave you the name, but then it kind of stuck. Not in a mean way."

I still had them, but they were small and faded, and invisible whenever I wore makeup.

"You shouldn't cover them up," he said, as if he could read my mind. His voice was soft like melted chocolate, and I turned on my right side, giving him my back.

"Why did you kiss me that night?" I finally asked. That question had plagued me for years, ever since the night Wes was killed.

The cover snapped off the bed and Austin rolled over behind me. "I planned on leaving town that night; I was trying to talk Wes into going. Hell, I thought he *was* going. We had a deal, but Wes wanted to be Breed, wanted immortality so much it blinded him from making the right decision."

"What decision?"

"He got mixed up with the wrong people, and they asked him to be a hitman. I told him the last thing he ever wanted was to be in debt with one of us. Breed don't mess around when it comes to paying debts. I guess he didn't have it in him to do what they wanted, and he paid with his life."

Tears sprang up and I pressed my face against the pillow. Austin's hand touched my hip.

"Don't," I warned him. He immediately retracted. "Is that all, or are you hiding something else?"

"There's nothing else." Then his voice switched over to dark and threatening. "One of these days, I'm going to find out who he was bargaining with, and they're going to pay with their life."

"So why did you kiss me?" I asked again.

Austin didn't answer but rolled over and pounded on his pillow a few times before settling in. I had a feeling I might never know the answer to that question, and maybe there was no answer. Maybe all these years I had built up in my head something that had meant nothing to him.

I sat up, unhooked my bra, and tossed it to the floor.

"Take off your pants," he said.

God, if those words didn't heat me up. "I'm fine."

"Lexi, I can't see in the dark. Get comfortable," he insisted, shifting in the other direction. *Indifferently.*

I mentally sighed and tugged off my jeans, sliding between the crisp sheets. The window unit chilled the air with every passing second.

"Promise to take me home tomorrow?" I asked.

Silence, at first.

"Austin?"

"I promise."

CHAPTER 12

"**S**HHH."

I nuzzled my head against something warm.

"Damn, she's got a *nice* ass," a man's voice whispered. "Not really my type, but I'd tap that."

"What, Jericho has a type now?"

"Tits and tats, that's where it's at, Denver," he said with a chuckle.

"Well, I like a nice ass. And *that's* top of the line. Look how it cups just below the panty line." Then the sound of air hissing through teeth. "*Damn.*"

"First time you been close to one of those?" Jericho asked with a chuckle.

"Shut it."

Then I blinked my eyes open and realized what I was nuzzling against that was so warm and solid.

Austin.

He was on his back, arms spread out, and I was covering him like a tablecloth at Thanksgiving. My right leg was hooked around his hip, and my body fit snugly against his right side.

I lifted my head and saw that my red hipsters were a little too close to his black jockeys. Not only that, but we had an audience. Denver and Jericho were standing at the door admiring the view and watching us like a double feature.

"Get out!" I shouted so loud Austin flew up and nearly flung me off the bed. His arm snaked around my waist just in time and pulled me onto his lap.

So there I was, bent over Austin's legs like a bad girl about to get spanked.

Chuckles from across the room were cut short when Austin

spoke. He didn't yell like I had, but it was contained, controlled, and quiet. "Get the fuck out."

The door closed.

I scrambled to get away and yanked the comforter over my legs.

Austin got out of bed and slowly hitched up his jeans, yawning hard and ending it with a growl. I could still smell him all over me.

"Why didn't you wake me up?" I complained.

He cleared his throat and combed his fingers through his hair a few times. It was messy and nice all at once. I admired the medallion he wore around his neck that dangled when he bent over to pick up his shirt. "Because I was busy sleeping?"

His indifference only made me look desperate, and it felt like we were right back where we started. My old feelings toward him needed to end. I was tired of chasing a shadow of my past. Time had changed both of us, and I didn't have much of a heart left to give to a man who didn't want it.

I leapt off the bed and stepped into my jeans, yanking them over my hips angrily. Didn't even care if he was watching me. I tucked my bra into my back pocket—straps hanging out and all.

Austin circled around the bed and blocked my exit. "Where you going?"

"Home. Remember?"

"Lexi…"

"Don't do that. You promised you would take me home."

"Why are you mad?" He still sounded sleepy and the fact he wasn't wearing a shirt wasn't helping any. Not when I could see his defined abs, and then one of his pecs twitched.

Damn. It wasn't fair that after all these years, Austin still looked as hot as he ever did, while I just looked like the same old Lexi. I'd filled out a little more as I used to be a beanpole with long legs in high school, but some men just got better with age.

I pulled on the doorknob. "I'm not mad. I just don't like being controlled."

His body language altered and I could almost feel the heat licking off him. "Is that what Beckett did?"

"No, no. You're taking it all out of context. Don't go beating up any more of my old boyfriends, okay? You're not my brother. That's what Wes should have been doing."

Oh, God, I was going to cry again. When my bottom lip quivered, I quickly looked away.

Without warning, Austin yanked me into his arms. I fought against him but he held on tight. "I'm sorry I couldn't save him," he whispered in a broken voice.

My breath hitched as the apology summoned painful memories of the night they found Wes's body. Austin was over that night and lost it, slamming his fist into the wall. All I could hear were my mom's screams as I stood catatonic in the middle of the living room while the trooper delivered the news to my dad. Then Austin had tried to hold me and I broke free and fled.

I couldn't do this here, so I opened the door and pushed him away.

Denver was lying on the sofa in a pair of sweats with a bowl of cereal on his chest while Jericho sat at the bar on the right, smoking a cigarette.

"Do either of you have a car?" I asked hopefully. "I need a lift."

Jericho slid off the barstool, patted out the butt of his smoke, and flicked his eyes at Austin. "Come with me, honey. I'll take you where you need to go."

"She's not leaving." Austin's voice made the hairs on my neck stand up.

"Do you want to go with me?" Jericho asked, his voice sincere. He walked up and I suddenly felt sandwiched between the Cole brothers.

"Yes."

He looked up at Austin. "Free will, brother. You know it and I know it. She ain't your bitch, so you—"

That was it.

Austin swung a hard fist right over my head and it cracked against Jericho's face. Jericho spun around and hit the floor. Shocked, I stumbled forward and turned around. Austin glared at Jericho so hard he could have torched him with the fire in his eyes.

"Do *not* call Lexi a bitch, are we clear? Let that be the golden rule of this motherfucking pack. Spread the word."

And just like that, Austin Cole stood up for me. Not because of pride, male territorial instinct, family obligation, or even jealousy. But because it was something that mattered… to *me*.

Austin kept his word and drove me home to my apartment. We had a brief argument in the car because he'd left Jericho bleeding on the floor without so much as an apology. He reassured me a Shifter heals when they shift back and forth from their animal to human form soon after injury, but Jericho was too proud and he would probably wear that shiner. I didn't get the guy thing, and I especially didn't understand the dynamic between brothers. My brother had never punched me for calling someone a name.

Naya must have heard me tromping up the stairs and swung open her door. Cotton balls were stuffed between her cherry-red toenails.

"Why is your bra hanging out of your pants?" She snatched it and dangled it in front of my face.

I yanked it away and she widened her gossip-loving grin.

"Your hair isn't brushed, either!" she said excitedly. "Who were you with? I want all the juicy details."

"Not now, Naya." I fumbled with my keys.

"Someone was looking for you."

My back straightened and I curved around, watching her blow on her fingernails.

"Who?"

"That cop from the other night. Are you in some kind of trouble? This time it wasn't about the neighbor downstairs."

"Uh…" My mind went blank. Maybe Beckett was trying to get me in trouble. I bent over the railing to see if my car had been stolen, but it was still there. "I don't know. That's weird. Are you sure it wasn't about the neighbor? I'm not going to the station to file a complaint, if that's what he wants."

She hobbled toward her door, walking on her heels so her pedicure wouldn't be ruined. "He's either gay, has a thing for you, or you're in trouble. But the man wanted nothing to do with me."

"Did you tell him anything?"

Personal stuff is what I meant. I didn't know who this guy was and the last thing I wanted to worry about was him tracking me down at work. Of course, he *was* a cop, and I'm sure he could have figured it out.

"Nope. You know me better than that. He asked where you might be staying and that was a stop sign for me. Cops don't chase you all over town unless they have a warrant for your arrest, or want in your panties."

"Don't tell him where my mom lives," I said. "If he comes around again, just tell him I moved to South America or something."

"Will do, chickypoo."

I tossed the keys on the bar and slammed the door. The red light on my answering machine blinked with sixteen messages.

The first was from April. "*Alexia, where are you? It's ten and you're still not here. Hello?*"

The next two were also from April, with the last one saying to give her a call because she was worried. We didn't hang out together outside of work, but April was a likable girl and I knew she was genuinely concerned and not just bitter about having to run the store by herself.

The next eight were from Beckett. Two of the messages were apologies and on the rest he hung up, although one of them creeped me out because I could hear him breathing on the other end.

Two other messages were hang-up calls, and the number was blocked on my machine.

"*Hi, I'm trying to reach Alexia Knight. This is Officer McNeal; I dropped in the other night for a disturbance. I need to speak with you on an unrelated case. It's about your father. I'll be stopping by this evening.*"

He hung up and I hit pause and grabbed a pen, jotting down the number on the machine. When I resumed playback, I heard another familiar voice.

"*Alexia, it's Lorenzo Church. You tried selling me your car, but I was more intrigued by the driver. Sorry I missed you. I'll give you my number and leave the ball in your court. I'm interested, and I'd like to take you out. Maybe lunch and conversation, so give me a call.*"

He left his number and I scribbled it on a napkin. I wrote his name above it and doodled, making his *O*'s into smiley faces.

Then it was Maizy, and she sounded scared. "*Lexi? Someone took Mommy.*"

My heart stopped.

I don't remember anything after that. With my keys in hand, I fled down the stairs, running across the grassy lawn so fast I stumbled and skinned my elbow on the dry grass. Adrenaline filled me up like rocket fuel and I scrambled to get up before racing to my car.

Out of nowhere, I was tackled by a strong pair of arms.

"What's wrong?" Austin shouted, lifting me off the grass.

"Let me go! Let me go!" It was a feral scream, the kind no one wants to hear.

His grip tightened and I kicked him in the shin with my heel so hard that he shouted and my keys fell in the grass. When my teeth sank into his arm, he let go. I snatched my keys and took off again.

My heart was racing and I couldn't get the key in the lock. "Dammit!" I screamed, my hand trembling.

Austin came up from behind and pressed his entire body against mine, pinning me against the car. His mouth moved against my ear as his right hand reached around, stroking my neck soothingly. "Tell me what's wrong." It was that commanding voice again. The one that meant business. I'm sure he could feel my pulse beneath his fingertips because it was out of control.

"My mom; something's happened. I have to get home. Maizy—she called—I have to go!" I screamed. Austin lifted me off the ground by the waist and hauled me off.

"I'll drive," he insisted, walking swiftly to his car.

I didn't fight.

He set me in the passenger seat and reached around to buckle me up. I rocked in my seat, covering my mouth with my hands. My God, if anything happened to either of them, I wouldn't be able to hold myself together. I'd been the strong one when my parents fell apart after Wes's death. When my dad left, I kept Mom from going into a state of depression and living in her bedroom. No one had ever been there to keep me going; I just had to fight through my own pain and focus on keeping my family together.

The engine roared to life like a mad dog and he turned the corners so sharply that I slammed against the door and threw my hands forward to keep from hitting the dash.

When I told him about the message from Maizy, he pulled out his phone.

"Denver, I want you to get a hold of Reno. Tell him it's— … No, this can't wait. Level fucking red, now deliver the message. I better have him on this phone in three minutes."

Austin hung up and cursed. "He never carries his damn phone when I ask him to."

"Hurry, hurry, hurry," I started chanting as we approached a yellow light. It flipped to red, but Austin gunned it and we sailed through the intersection. Thank God a cop car wasn't around, but Austin knew how to weave around cars like a stuntman. The way he handled that Challenger was heroic.

We came to a hard stop and I was out the door and running toward the house.

"Lexi, wait!" he yelled out, but I was already on the porch. Worst of all, I didn't have the spare key with me. I tossed the mat and tipped over the flowerpot. I pounded on the door and desperately rang the doorbell.

"Maizy! Maizy! Open up, it's Lexi," I shouted. Locked from the inside was a good sign; it meant someone was home.

Austin's boots crunched on the patio and I glanced up at him, shaking.

He backed up a step, eyed the door, and kicked it in. It took two solid kicks, but the flimsy door cracked and flew open. It was an old house, and thank God for that.

Austin held out his arm to keep me back. "Stay close," he said. "Someone could still be inside the house. If something happens, take off and I'll handle it."

The sliding back door was left wide open, and the wind had lifted the curtains and pulled them onto the patio.

"Maizy hides," I whispered. "Please find her, Austin."

He did a quick scan of the rooms to make sure no one else was in the house. Then it was my turn. I looked in the closets, beneath the beds, and in her favorite hiding spot behind the pantry door. Austin walked around the perimeter of the yard.

Mom's purse was still on her dresser, and nothing looked disturbed.

I went into the kitchen and stopped at the table. Maizy's little juice glass with the frog on the side was half-filled with milk, and an uneaten cookie sat on a paper napkin beside it.

I doubled over and threw up on the kitchen floor. Austin came running in and God, how embarrassing was that?

Everything blurred through my teary eyes, and Austin helped me up and walked me to the guest bedroom that used to be mine. It was cheery and bright with yellow paint and white furniture. I sat on the edge of the bed and watched him peel off his shirt, using it to wipe my tears and mouth.

"Don't worry. I'll find her, Lexi. My brother's on his way and we're going to track them down."

Just then, a loud motor shut off outside and there was a ruckus at the front door.

"Stay here and rest for a minute while I talk to him," he said.

After Austin left, I wept so hard that my chest began to ache with fear. I needed to become emotionally spent before I lost control and went on a rampage through the neighborhood.

I walked into the living room and Austin folded his arms, staring at a man who favored him a little in the face, except his handsome features were stern. He matched Austin's height, but not his style. It was at least eighty degrees outside and he wore a long-sleeved black shirt with matching pants and shades, like he was ready to join a SWAT team.

Austin closed the distance between us and lifted my eyelid, treating me as if I were a patient. I jerked my head away.

"Just need to make sure you're not going to shift on me," he said in a low voice.

"Who's that?"

Austin approached the formidable man. "Lexi, this is my brother, Reno. This is Wes's little sister."

I was starting to notice that was how Austin was introducing me to everyone.

Reno removed his shades, tucked them in the collar of his shirt, and studied me with narrowed eyes. His brown hair was neatly styled with short sideburns and a little length on top, but not much. Chocolate-brown eyes, tough features, and he looked like a guy you just didn't want to mess around with. Deep lines were carved in his cheeks and around the corners of his eyes—the kind that are etched into your face from smiling hard. But Reno didn't look like the smiling type. He wore a gun holster strapped to his left arm as if he didn't have a care in the world if a cop pulled him over. We had a concealed handgun law in our state, but I didn't have a clue if that meant you actually had to conceal it. Truthfully, I never imagined I'd even be asking myself these questions. Reno might as well have put glitter on the handle and drawn a red arrow across his shirt to the holster.

"Are you going to find my mom and sister?"

His serious eyes flicked back to Austin. "You wanna search, or me?"

Austin looked between us. "I'll shift. Call up Denver and give him her address. I want him to pick up the tape on her machine, trace her calls, and set up a hidden camera outside her door. Keep an eye on Lexi, and don't let her out of your sight. She's one of us," Austin said in a deep, smooth voice.

Reno's eyes cut to mine and he sized me up. "No shit. I thought Denver was pulling my leg," he remarked, pinching his stubbly chin.

Austin handed Reno his wallet and keys. "Scan the house; do your thing. If I'm not back in an hour, take her to our place."

"Wait—" I started to say, but Austin interrupted in his take-charge voice.

"You do as I say."

How could I argue? I hardly had a plan of my own, and these guys didn't want to call the cops. Not that the cops would do anything except speculate my mom took off with Maizy.

Austin kept talking to Reno. "Tell Denver to sit tight and I'll be joining him. It's been a while since this happened; the milk on the table is warm and so is the house. The thermostat is set to seventy-two," he added. "If I pick up a trail then I'll stay on it, but

I got a feeling they're long gone. Maybe the kid wandered off to a friend's house or something. I'll mark the yard in case one of ours was involved; then they'll know who the fuck they're dealing with."

I watched him storm out the back door and out of sight.

"Mark?" I asked.

Reno straightened a picture on the wall and glanced around. "Leave our scent. He's marking territory. We might get some help this way."

"Someone is going to smell Austin's pee and help?" I threw my hands up. "This is ridiculous!"

"You don't know pack rules, do you?"

And I didn't care. I just wanted my family found safe. I called April and explained I'd had a personal emergency. Then I called Naya, because I'm sure she was going to immediately notice a hot guy outside my apartment rigging up a camera. She was at work on her cell, so I just told her I planned to stay away for a day or so and not to worry.

Naturally, she worried. Naya knew I wasn't a "stay away from home" kind of girl.

CHAPTER 13

R ENO WAS A HARD MAN to warm up to, but I had to give it to him, he was effective at distracting me. He gave me a brief lesson about Shifter rules and how things worked, and I wasn't sure if he was doing it for my benefit (being that I was completely ignorant of their culture), or his own so he wouldn't have to deal with watching me cry.

Men avoid women when the waterworks turn on the way a mouse avoids a rattlesnake. I could tell he wasn't much of a social talker since he kept the conversation strictly about *pack* this and *pack* that.

He made a few calls and reassured me they had everything under control. Denver would drive my car to their house for safekeeping, and they'd have surveillance on my apartment at all times, including when I finally went home.

Which was a strange feeling. I didn't even know these men and they were stepping in and taking over like I meant something to them.

But then again, maybe I did. We didn't know about Austin's family, but they knew everything about ours. They supported Austin's need to form his own "practice pack," as Reno put it.

We arrived at Austin's house in the afternoon, and despite the fact there were people inside I'd never met, I went straight to the bedroom and shut the door.

First I paced. Then I got mad and threw things around— including a silver clock, which I smashed to pieces against the wall. It quieted in the other room during my meltdown, but no one came in to disturb me. Once I released the anger, I gave in to the sorrow and cried.

Cried myself right to sleep.

I awoke, unable to move. A crescent moon shone through the window on the left, casting a buttery glow in the dark bedroom. A heavy arm wrapped securely around my waist, and the solid press of a man's body warmed my back.

I tried to get up and the arm tightened, restricting me from moving away.

"Don't move," Austin mumbled against my left shoulder. "Just go back to sleep."

I struggled. "What did you find out?"

He finally let go and I sat up to face him. Austin wearily rubbed his face, still in his jeans and one of those wife-beater shirts. It made his tattoos soften in the moonlight, like ancient shadows carved on his arms.

"I lost the scent by the street. I'm not so sure your sister ran away. Her scent is in the yard—front and back—but it didn't go any farther. I tracked an unfamiliar scent outside the house and if I smell that sonofabitch again in wolf form, I'll know it."

"You can't smell him like you are now?"

"No," he said. "No more than you can."

"So you found nothing?" My voice broke. I must have looked like a mess with puffy eyes and tangled hair. Not that I cared, but the thought crossed my mind. A woman could be stranded on a deserted island with no sign of life for thousands of miles, and as soon as a rescue ship comes her way, she'll be combing her hair with sticks and squashing berries to rub on her cheeks.

"I've got two of my brothers searching the house and making sure nothing was missed. We've put out an alert to all the packs and offered up a reward. That'll motivate the ones we don't usually deal with."

"Oh."

"I have a question, Lexi."

"Yeah?"

He sat up and drew his brows together. I got nervous and felt my cheeks flush from the intensity of his luminous eyes.

"Why is Lorenzo Church calling on you?"

Ah, he must have listened to the messages on my machine. "Lorenzo was one of the people interested in my car and then he asked me out. Or, he's trying to ask me out. I don't know; he seems nice. I might," I said with a weary voice. "Do you know him or something?"

Austin's voice dropped an octave. "You *do* know he's a Shifter, right?"

I hesitated. "So?"

"I got bad blood with him, and I don't want Church sniffing around my pack."

"Austin, I don't think I'm mentally capable of arguing right now, but let me put this to bed for you. Whatever I do in my life is my choice, and I'm not making those decisions based on whatever personal issues you have with someone. He seemed like a nice guy, and…"

The thought fell away, because I remembered my mom and little sister were missing.

"We'll talk about it later," Austin said, getting up off the bed. I watched him walk to the door and run his fingers through his messy hair. "You hungry?"

I shook my head.

"Feed your wolf, Lexi, or—"

We both widened our eyes at the sound of the doorbell.

"Austin!" a voice boomed.

He flew out of the room and I followed closely behind him. We hurried toward the front door where Denver stood beside a guy who was wearing a red tank top and long shorts.

We walked past them and when I looked at the man in the doorway, I frantically reached out.

"Maizy!"

Wrapped in the arms of a tall man with a defined jawline was my little sister. He glanced down at me with one sapphire eye and one brown, his dark hair pulled back tightly into a ponytail. Maizy slept soundly in his arms, dressed in her favorite pink skirt, white leggings, and princess shirt.

I scooped her up and smelled her hair, overwhelmed and sobbing like a baby. She stirred a bit and looked up. "Hi, Lexi," she said sleepily.

"Hi, Maze. How's my girl?"

She peered up at the man and back at me, whispering. Little did she know how loud her whispers were. "He's my prince." Then, after a few heavy blinks, she fell asleep.

"Thank you," I said in a broken voice.

Austin stepped forward and introduced himself, quickly explaining he was the leader of a newly formed pack in the territory. The man watched him cautiously and I realized it was because he was a Shifter. Probably a well-known one in the area by the way Austin was speaking respectfully to him. Even I could sense his power.

"I'll take her," Denver said over my shoulder. My hands tightened. "Let me put her to bed so you three can talk," he insisted. "I'll guard her window and make sure she isn't disturbed."

Maizy needed sleep and I had to find out what was happening, so I capitulated, kissing her cheek.

"Wait," the man at the door said. He reached around and pulled something from his back pocket, handing it to me with an uncomfortable expression. It was her princess wand. Just a small thing Maizy liked to carry around the house because she thought she could tap it on things and make magic happen.

"She kept hitting me over the head with it," he said with a lazy grin. Sure enough, there were red marks across his forehead.

Denver took Maizy and the wand to bed.

"Come in," Austin said. "My home is open to you."

Maizy's savior glanced down at the mountain of shoes by the door.

"No need," Austin said. "Let me get you a beer."

"Sounds good," he rumbled in a loud voice. He wasn't yelling; he just spoke at a volume that demanded your attention.

They walked a few paces to the right until they reached the bar just inside the living room. It was simple and seated three, with a black granite countertop and a canister of cashews. I glanced over at Austin's brothers who were watching with interest. Two I didn't recognize, but I could see they were identical twins.

Almost.

Austin strolled around the bar and pulled a few cold ones from a short fridge.

"Can we have privacy?" the man requested.

"Boys, out!" Austin bellowed. "You too, Lexi."

"Uh-uh," I protested. "Sorry, Austin, but this is my sister and mom we're talking about. You'll have to wrestle me off this stool if you want me out of here. No offense, mister," I said, taking the seat to the man's right.

He chuckled warmly. "She can stay."

"I'm Alexia Knight," I said, offering my hand for him to shake. He looked at it and Austin shrugged, setting the beer in front of him.

"My name is Prince," he replied, lightly shaking my hand.

"Prince? As in the artist formerly known as?"

"That's my name."

"Oh," I said with a growing smile, "I bet Maizy just *loved* that."

I wanted to ask if his last name was Charming but decided my humor might not be well received.

Austin popped the caps off the bottles and they clicked across the polished surface of the bar. He sat on a stool across from us, offering our guest a look of gratitude. "I appreciate you bringing us the girl. Where did you find her?"

Prince leaned on his forearms and tilted the green bottle. "She was wandering around on the side of the highway, dangerously close to the shoulder. A truck ahead of me nearly clipped her, so I pulled over. She refused to go with me because I wasn't in a uniform. My apologies," he said, looking at me. "I had to pick her up and put her in the car by force. It was the only way to get her off the road. She finally told me her name, so I made a few calls. That's when I got wind she was on the bulletin. Didn't find the woman. Didn't look." He took a long sip of the frosty beer, appreciating the import with a glance at the label.

"Did Maizy say how she got there or who took her?" I asked.

He shook his head. "All the little one said was that her mother left the house with a man and then they came back for her. They argued in the car and then the man pulled over, walked her to a sign, and forced her mother back in the car before they drove off."

I covered my face. "Oh my God."

"What kind of sick animal would do a thing like that?" Austin growled, pushing away from the bar.

Prince shrugged. "Sounds domestic to me. No signs of a struggle in the house and she didn't mention seeing a weapon."

"Did she say what he looked like?" I pressed.

He traced his finger over his left eyebrow. "Charlie Brown."

All the blood rushed from my head and I became dizzy, blinking a few times.

"Lexi?" Austin rose from his stool and touched my arm.

I looked up and drew in a deep breath. "What if it was my dad? He's bald. Maizy doesn't remember him, and Mom stuffed all his photos in an old shoebox. She wouldn't have recognized him."

"Why would your father leave his little girl on the side of the road?"

"I don't know!" I said louder than I should have. "He left *all* of us, and I still can't explain that. Apparently, there are a lot of things about that man I'll never understand. Who else would be kidnapping my mother, Austin? She works a part-time job and stays home with Maizy almost all the time. She doesn't have a computer, so it's not like she's hooking up with strangers online. This just isn't happening."

Austin leaned forward on his elbows, staring at his hands pensively. "I picked up your father's scent in the house but I didn't make the connection. I was so focused on the unfamiliar scent that I tuned out all the ones I recognized. *Damn.*"

"People are asking why you're protecting humans," Prince inquired in a private voice.

"They're part of my pack," Austin countered. "I grew up with them and anyone who fucks with them… fucks with me," he said in stone-cold words.

Prince looked at me and dragged his eyes back to Austin, nodding slowly. "I respect that, but *she's* not human."

"How do you know?" I asked. This whole Shifter thing didn't

make sense. First they couldn't tell, now they could. What was I to believe?

"Because I'm an alpha, and I can smell a bitch about to go into heat."

His words weren't meant to be rude, and when I noticed Austin walking around the bar to confront him, I hopped off the stool and wedged between them.

"Don't, Austin. Let it go. He saved Maizy and we owe him."

Fire blazed in his eyes as he stared at Prince, who rose from his chair.

"Didn't mean to step on your territory, friend. If she's yours, I'm not staking claim."

"It's not that," I said, turning around. "I have a thing about being called a bitch and he's just sticking up for me."

His lips twitched. "In that case, my apologies."

I was a little too embarrassed to ask what he meant about going into heat. That scared the crap out of me and I panicked my way right into Austin's bedroom where Maizy was fast asleep.

Denver sat in a corner chair with his legs stretched out, playing a handheld videogame in the dark.

I flipped on a small light, took off her buckled shoes, and set them on the floor. Then I removed her tights and folded them up.

"You should let her sleep," Denver suggested without lifting his eyes.

"This girl can sleep through an apocalypse," I said with a laugh in my voice.

What I really wanted to do was look her over and make sure she wasn't hurt. After a few turns of her legs and arms, she made a complaining moan and I covered her up with the blanket.

"Thank God," I whispered. My mom was still missing, and while that wasn't okay, I could deal with it better than the thought of this little girl getting hurt.

The door opened behind me. "He's gone," Austin said in a hushed voice. "I offered him the reward and he turned it down."

"*The fuck?*" Denver said. "Ten large and he turned up his nose?"

Austin shrugged.

"Ah, shit. You didn't," Denver grumbled, tossing his videogame on the other side of the bed. He didn't look so handsome when he was pissed off. The scar on his temple turned a little pink and his lip did a funny curl. "Are you a bag of nuts?"

"What's going on?" I asked, turning around.

Denver replied in a low voice. "He paid him with a favor, to be collected at a later date. Am I right? Dammit, Austin, you know how that shit can backfire on your ass."

"Watch the baby, Denver. We're going to bed."

We? I thought.

"I'm staying here," I insisted. *Who did he think he was, ordering me around?*

"No, Lexi. She needs to sleep and you… you're worked up."

"So?"

He stepped closer. "Do you really want your baby sister to be in the same room with a new wolf who doesn't know any of us and is amped up on adrenaline? Are you ready to take on that responsibility if she gets injured?"

Point taken.

"Maizy doesn't know Denver."

"But I do. That's my brother and I trust him with my life. Until we know what's going on, I want someone watching the window at all times while she sleeps. You don't have to worry," he said in a smooth voice. "No one's taking her again, not on my watch."

I kissed her cheek and followed Austin into the hall.

"Are those your brothers?" I asked, staring into the living room on the left.

He took my hand and gently laced his fingers around my wrist. "Later. We're going to bed."

We? There was a whole lot of "we" going on in his sentences these days.

"Aren't *you* afraid of my wolf?" I wondered aloud.

Austin led me to a room across the hall and closed the door behind us. "I'm not afraid of anything, Ladybug. Not a damn thing."

Tucked in the left corner was a small bed with black covers and pillowcases. Concert posters were tacked all over the snow-white walls and I knew by Pink Floyd hanging behind the bed that we were in Jericho's room. An oversized black beanbag chair sat on the floor with a leather jacket casually draped across it. To the right, a plain wooden dresser against the wall had been covered with loose change, guitar picks, cigarettes, and a box of ribbed condoms.

"We shouldn't sleep in here," I said apprehensively, staring at a bubbling red lava lamp beside the twin bed.

Austin pulled off his socks and unbuckled his belt. "Jericho's got a gig tonight and won't be back until tomorrow afternoon. He likes to get trashed and party after the show."

"What does he play?"

Austin pulled off his belt and tossed it to the floor. "He sings lead and plays guitar."

"Does he also sell his music online?"

Austin sniffed out a laugh. "No telling. The Breed bars pay them well and they're a hit with the ladies. Too much risk doing anything that would make him famous, because eventually people would notice he isn't aging very much. We try to keep a low profile around humans."

"I need a shower," I said, stalling and staring down at my day-old clothes.

"Denver set up a camera at your apartment and I packed you a small bag. It's in the bathroom. You can take a shower and brush your teeth if you want. I'm tired, my wolf's tired, and I'll be knocked out by the time you're done," he grumbled, crawling over the bed and spreading out.

The taut muscles in his arms flexed as he stretched his right arm and sighed. I turned on my heel and went for the shower.

⚯

Austin was right; when I got back to the room, he was sound asleep. Thankfully, he wasn't a snorer. He just breathed deep and growled once in a while.

I was a little embarrassed he'd paid a visit to my underwear drawer, but relieved when I saw he didn't pack my black garter belt or see-through red nightie. He'd chosen for my nightwear a knee-length T-shirt with *Ka-Pow!* written on the front. He'd had a wide selection to choose from, because that drawer had everything from *I'm ready for smokin' hot sex* to *It's my time of the month, so don't even think about touching me.*

Austin dressed me like his kid sister, and I mentally sighed.

He didn't stir when I crawled on top of the sheets. He was flat on his back with both arms spread out—just as I'd left him. I combed my fingers through my damp hair, feeling the energy drain from my body.

I pulled the covers up and found myself staring at Austin's chest. He had well-defined muscles in his abdomen that looked like I could have washed my clothes on them. Despite the fact he'd been out running all day, he smelled wonderful. Sometimes I wondered if men had any idea of what women found attractive. Like the small cleft in his chin, or the way his hands felt rough when they touched my soft skin, and even the way he had popped open the button on his jeans. When I heard a low growl—it was a sexy little sound that made me wonder what he was dreaming about.

I eased a little bit closer with my arms tucked against my chest. Then just a little closer, watching his breathing to make sure I didn't wake him up.

The closer I snuggled up to Austin, the more I craved that cozy familiarity—more than I would have cared to admit. I'd missed him. How do you not miss someone who was a huge chunk of your childhood and young-adult life who disappeared off the face of the earth? Almost every memory I had from kindergarten to age twenty involved Austin Cole.

The next thing I knew, my cheek rested on his bicep and I tucked my body against his like a puzzle piece. Just when I closed my heavy eyelids, he groaned.

Oh God, please don't let him wake up now.

It was deep and guttural, and he shifted on his right side, facing me.

"You okay?" he murmured.

I didn't reply. I played dead and pretended I was asleep. It seemed like a good plan to avoid the embarrassment of explaining why I was latched on to him like a man-sucking leech.

A rough, warm hand cupped my cheek and I felt him scoot down a little. Maybe he thought I had fallen asleep, because his thumb brushed over my right eyelid softly.

Five times. I counted.

When his lips lightly touched mine, my brain just shut down. It was a soft, almost nonexistent kiss, but I felt it all the way down to my toes. Then it zinged back up to my hips and damn if I didn't moan.

Now we were both aware I wasn't asleep and he was kissing me. But it didn't stop. His kiss pressed a little bit harder and tingles roared through my body, and my breath was shaky and erratic.

When his tongue touched my lip, I quickly opened my mouth and kissed him back.

Hard.

Deep.

Kissed him like I'd fantasized about doing for the last seven years. I gripped the back of his neck with my right hand and my fingernails bit into his skin. Austin was a phenomenal kisser with all the right tongue moves. Slowly stroking me like he meant to kiss me elsewhere. The next thing I knew, his hand slid up my nightshirt and down my panties in the back. He gripped my ass and rubbed it so hard that I made a strangled moan in the back of my throat.

"Take them off," I breathed against his mouth, pushing up to my elbow so I was leaning more on top of him.

"Christ," he whispered back. "I can't." He pulled his hand away and there I was, the desperate girl who was left wanting Austin Cole, who didn't want me back.

And boy did that piss me off. I nipped his lip hard enough that he "*ow*ed" in response, and I flew out of bed.

"*Fine*. I'll go sleep with one of your brothers."

I really didn't mean it that way. What I *meant* to say was I would sleep in one of their beds. Just not *with* them. Sharing a bed with a man who turned me on and shut me out wasn't in my best interest.

He caught me by the wrist and yanked me back to the bed. "Over my dead body," he said roughly.

I twisted my arm and he lost his grip. "I get that you don't like me like that, Austin. You woke up with a hard-on; big fucking deal," I said angrily. "But don't work me over and then make me out to be some desperate, clingy woman. That's right—*woman*. I'm grown up now, and I make my own decisions, including whose bed I sleep in. And whose bed I *don't* sleep in."

When I turned away, he grabbed my hips and pulled me back. Suddenly, my backside was pressed against his front, and his front was thick and hard.

His hot breath touched my ear and I shivered.

"You're too close to going into heat, Lexi, and it's driving me fucking wild."

The little hairs on my neck stood up.

"This will push you right into it, and it's too soon. I *sure as hell* don't want it happening in one of my brother's beds," he bit out. "You don't want me to go all the way. You have no idea what sliver of a thread I'm hanging on to right now to maintain control, because I could slide your panties down and slip inside you in less than three seconds. You hear me?"

"Yeah," I breathed, feeling his fingers clawing into my hips.

"And trust me, I *want* to. My body can't help but react to a woman in heat. But you're the good girl and I'm the bad boy, and we've both known that for years."

He released his grip and slid his right hand down to my belly while my idiot head fell back on his shoulder.

"Come back to bed. Sleep beside me. We have a long day ahead to find your mother, and us having sex in my brother's shitty-ass Pink Floyd bedroom is not going to be a magical moment for you. It's going to make things weird between us, and I look after my pack and make sure that they get what they need. A one-night stand is *not* what you need."

"There you go again, Austin Cole, making decisions for me."

He stilled, as if he were making up his mind. Then he came to his conclusion and spun me around to face him.

"Alexia Talulah Knight, get into this bed."

"I hate my middle name," I complained.

"I know," he said with a warm smile in his voice. "Now get in."

He scooted toward the wall and I crawled beside him. Every ounce of lust that was in my body had magically evaporated. I was too mad to be turned on anymore, and Austin decided to roll over and show me his back to prevent anything further from happening.

When I was almost asleep, I heard him mumble, "I like your name; it's Native American. I looked it up once."

I was too exhausted to ask him about the references to me going into heat, so we slept the rest of the night beside each other.

Just like old times.

CHAPTER 14

THE NEXT MORNING, I WOKE up in Jericho's bed, alone. I shuffled my feet down the hall, past the bar, the atrium on the right, and then into the kitchen.

"Lexi, look! I got marshmallows!"

I glanced at Maizy's cereal. Mom always bought her the healthy whole-grain stuff, which I'd argued defeated the purpose of childhood. Denver sat at the table with a glass of milk and the funny papers. He had dark circles under his eyes and nodded when I sat down.

I watched Maizy pick out the colored marshmallows from her cereal and eat them, saving the pink ones for last.

"You feeling okay this morning, honey?"

"Uh huh," she sang, as if nothing out of the ordinary had occurred the day before. I wanted to ask all kinds of questions, but I decided not to upset her while she was eating.

"Where is everyone?" I asked.

Denver put one hand behind his neck and stretched his left arm. "Hunting. I'm on chick patrol."

"You got chickens?" Maizy asked.

I snorted. "Did Austin go too?"

"Yep. I got a funny feeling he'll be going out of town."

"Why do you say that?"

Denver pushed back his chair and yawned a big, ugly yawn. "He knows a Packmaster who might be able to help. He's getting some gear together."

Austin still cared for my mom, even though he had no clue how mad she was at him. My heart warmed a little at the thought, knowing he was going above and beyond what the cops would ever do to get her back.

"Damn," he said, rubbing his eyes. "I have to tend bar tonight and I'm no good unless I can get in a nap. Maybe I'll call in and tell them I got an itch I need to scratch."

"So you guys always knew you were... you know," I said, glancing at Maizy. I didn't want her to hear every little bit of this whole Shifter conversation.

"Yeah. But as kids, we're just like humans. We don't howl at the moon or anything." For effect, he howled and Maizy giggled. Then he turned to me seriously and folded his fingers together, resting his elbows on the table to speak in a private voice. "A good pack is better than a human family. Alphas naturally form them and we spread out over the territories. Some cities have more of us, some less. Some are corrupted a-holes and the rest are committed to family. We look after our own. No matter how I feel about some of these dickwads in the house, I'd lay down my life for them. That's how it goes in this family. We protect our own. It's instinct—one I'm sure you've felt your whole life. That's one little characteristic where we differ from most humans."

"Yeah," I said softly, reflecting on the unbreakable bond I've always felt with my family. Maybe he was right. "How old is everyone?"

He snorted. "Shake their pockets and a few Mayan coins might roll out."

"I'm serious."

Denver snagged one of Maizy's blue marshmallows and nibbled on the tip. "I'm not much older than Austin, but the others are closer in age. Reno is over a hundred and—"

"A hundred?" I said in disbelief.

"He's got some wild stories, but we only get to hear them when he's tanked. The twins came next and then there was a stretch before Jericho. Your mind doesn't age much, Lexi. That's why you see all those eighty-year-old women acting silly. In their head, they're still young. Time doesn't change people, experience does. And sickness. You can't tell someone's age by just looking at 'em."

We sat for a quiet spell, watching Maizy pile a mountain of pink marshmallows onto her spoon.

"I need to go home for a little bit," I said.

"Chick patrol," Denver reminded me, wagging his finger.

"This chick has rent due today. I also need to pay my electric bill, take out the garbage, and check on my neighbor. There might be messages on my machine. Not to mention my boss is probably wondering where I am. Will you look after Maizy? Can I trust you?"

His blue eyes blazed, making his soft features even more striking. "I don't have a leash on you. Go do whatever you need to do and if Austin calls, I'll tell him you're in the bathroom with a book and a bunch of bubbles and candles. You got nothin' to worry about while I'm in charge." Then his voice grew uncharacteristically dark. "No one lays a finger on her. Maybe the man who dumped her on the side of the road like trash is your father, but you better pray I never meet him."

"Lexi's my sister," Maizy told Denver, as if he had no idea. Denver arched his brows and nodded at her.

"Is my car here?"

He pointed behind him in the direction of the front of the house.

I got dressed and went to pick up a few pieces of my life and put them back together.

⌦⌧⌦

"No, no, no," Naya chanted. "You cannot just take off like that, have roughnecks show up at your apartment, and then waltz in without telling me what's going on." She cocked her hip angrily and her pea-green dress swished at the knee. She had her hair pinned up in a messy knot and looked beautiful in natural makeup.

Definitely her day off.

"Naya, I don't think *I* even know what's going on," I said in all honesty.

After dropping off my rent, I had stopped by my apartment to pack my bag and listen to my phone messages when Naya came barging in.

"I was worried sick," she reminded me.

Before she went on a Naya mouthing spree and gave me a ten-minute lecture, I dialed my work number. "Give me a sec; I need to call work. April? It's Alexia."

"What's going on?" she exclaimed over the phone. "Don't tell me you're sick because you don't *sound* sick."

"Can you let Charlie know I'll be out for a couple of days? I'm so sorry to spring this on you at the last minute, April. Do you think you can handle the store by yourself? Call one of the girls in as backup if you need to."

"Of course I can handle it," she retorted. "I've just been worried is all. By the way, someone came in here looking for you."

"Who? Was it a cop?"

Which made me a little nauseous because all these people were suddenly looking for me and my mom was missing.

"I don't know. A big scary guy with long hair."

"Was his name Lorenzo?" I asked.

"Yeah, that's the one. He seemed worried about you too. He wanted to know where you lived—said you weren't answering your phone. Is he your boyfriend?"

I glanced at my messages and saw the number twenty-four blinking. *How did he know where I worked?*

"No, no," I said. "He's the guy who asked about my car."

"Don't worry," April reassured me. "I didn't tell him anything. He said he knew how to find you here because of your work shirt."

Ah, yes. Now it was clear.

"April, it's just some family drama and I need more time off. I've got a ton of vacation and I'm sure Charlie won't mind. He's always trying to get me to use it; I'm just sorry I wasn't able to give you advance notice."

Which almost made me laugh. Advance notice on a kidnapping?

"Alexia, it's under control. There's no need to call Charlie, I don't want him to get upset over nothing. He's been sick."

"With what?"

"I don't know," she said in quiet words. "Something doesn't seem right. He hasn't been coming in as much over the past few months, not like he used to. When I talked to him, it didn't sound like he wanted to be bothered with work stuff, and you know that's not like him. But no need to worry, I got it covered. I created a rotation schedule with the girls; Kelly even stepped up to work more hours in the week if needed."

"Good." I glanced up at the impatient Naya, leaning against the front door and picking her polished nail. "Gotta go. I'll call you later. And if you need anything…" I hesitated, because I wouldn't be home and didn't carry a phone. Austin hadn't given me permission to share his number with anyone.

"Don't worry about a thing, Alexia. Just do what you need to do," she said, and I felt the stress melt away with her reassurance.

"Thanks. And if Lorenzo comes in again, tell him everything's okay and I'm dealing with family business. I'll try to get in touch with him. Not sure why he even cares, we just met. Talk to you later."

I hung up and gave Naya the skinny. I left out the part about being half dog and decided she just needed to know about my mom's kidnapping and to keep an eye out for anyone suspicious visiting my apartment.

"What about the cop?" she asked.

"Was he here?"

"Last night."

I walked to the bar and got the information I'd scribbled on a napkin with his number. He had wanted to talk to me about my father, and that made me anxious.

She wrapped me up in a generous hug. "Find your mama. I'll keep an eye on your place and if you need anything, call me."

"Thanks," I muttered against her perfumed neck.

"And if any of those strapping young men you're hanging out with are single, slip them my number."

I laughed so hard it morphed into my silly laugh. Sometimes you just need to let go when things fall apart in order to keep yourself together.

Naya went back home and I called Officer McNeal. He didn't answer, so I began listening to my messages. Twelve were hang-up calls from Beckett, according to my caller ID. Lorenzo had left three brief messages, but I saw his number come up five more times. I was surprised he hadn't assumed I was just brushing him off. But before he turned stalker on my ass, I figured maybe I should give him a call and let him know this wasn't a good time for me.

What made me curious was wondering if Lorenzo was a Shifter, did he know I was one too?

"Church," he answered.

"Hi, is this Lorenzo?"

There was a brief pause. "Is this who I think it is?"

"That depends on who you think it is."

"Yeah," he said with a dark laugh. "It's who I think it is. I'm glad you decided to give me a call, Alexia."

"Call me Lexi."

"Why?"

"Look, I'm sorry you've been going through the trouble of calling. I've had some family stuff come up that I need to take care of, but I didn't want you to think I was being rude and ignoring your calls. I'm not like that. If I don't like you, I'll tell you flat-out."

Lorenzo laughed. "That I believe. Why don't you invite me over and we'll talk? Maybe I can help with your problem. I'm a good problem solver."

I suddenly remembered the cameras that had been installed. As in *plural*. I sure didn't see the one outside, so if there were any inside the apartment, I was going to have to get Austin to take them out. That was a little invasive, especially since I liked walking around in my underwear on Saturday nights while watching movies and making quesadillas.

"Alexia? Speak to me."

"I'm… what did you ask?"

"You were about to tell me your address so I can help you with your problem." Before I could reject his offer he said, "I think it's time the both of us come clean. I'm a Shifter, Alexia, and I know you're one too. I don't know what pack you belong to, but whatever trouble you may be in, my people can help. I'm a Packmaster. I got strong connections, money… whatever you need."

And that was an attractive offer. More help.

"Did you hear about a mother and daughter gone missing?"

"Yes."

"That's my mother. We found my sister, but my mom's still missing."

He covered the receiver and I heard muffled conversation. "Tell me where you are. I got thirty men I can put on this right away."

Thirty?

Lorenzo swung by in his monster black truck with the skull and crossbones on the back window and took charge of the situation. He was already on the phone with his pack, relaying information and barking out orders.

No pun intended.

He helped me into his truck and I felt like I was on a carnival ride due to being so high up. After a trip to my mom's house, he shut me up in the back bedroom while he shifted into his wolf to sniff things out. That was around the time I started to notice a restless feeling stirring within me. Something so primal it felt innate.

Thirty minutes later, I locked up the house and we sat inside his truck.

"Nothing?" I asked.

"I picked up a scent," he said, leaning his head back and sliding the key into the ignition. "Not the alpha who pissed all over the yard, but the one who took your mother."

"Can you tell the difference between a Shifter and human? There were other men in and around the house."

"Give me a little credit, will you? I picked up two Shifters and one human, aside from the feminine fragrance of your family. There's also another Breed scent outside, but it's faded. I think they were there before it happened."

He slipped on a pair of shades and hooked his right hand over the steering wheel. The air from the open window blew some of his long black hair around. Lorenzo didn't just look Native American, I was almost certain he was. His name didn't match up, but then I didn't know much about Shifters. I also knew a girl in school named Julie who was Cherokee.

Lorenzo pulled into the Dairy Queen parking lot and told me to wait in the truck. A light breeze blew in through the open windows and I watched a young teenage girl standing outside, chatting on her cell phone. How strange it felt to now be on the outside looking in, knowing that in this seemingly ordinary world, people like myself existed who weren't human. When Lorenzo emerged, he came out with two vanilla cones. This had been the hottest June on record, and sitting quietly in his truck while eating ice cream really hit the spot.

"You got a pack?" he asked, licking off a drop of vanilla from his hand. He had devoured his cone in less than five bites.

"Kind of," I said, dipping my tongue in the soft ice cream.

He wadded up the paper that had been wrapped around the bottom of his cone. "Kind of doesn't sound like *yes*."

"I don't know if there's some official ceremony, but someone has taken me under his protection."

"Hmm," Lorenzo murmured thoughtfully, sending a text message. He finally tossed the phone down and crowded my space, leaning over with his face close to mine. "Nashoba?"

"Umm, I don't understand."

Lorenzo never removed his dark eyes from mine as his tongue came out and licked a dollop of ice cream from my cone. His hands never touched me, but watching the animalistic look on his face felt intimate and magnetic.

He flicked his hot eyes to my mouth and asked, "Wolf?"

I nodded.

"I knew it. Only wolves refer to their family as packs."

Something Austin had never gone into detail about. "What other kinds of animals are there?"

A smile spread across his face. "Panthers, birds, deer, bears—you name it. Tell me why you don't know this?"

"Long story."

He took my chin with his fingertips and stared at my mouth for an uncomfortably long time. "Good. I like long stories. Makes for a long date." His finger grazed my cheekbone and Lorenzo analyzed my face. He pulled my straight hair around and smoothed his fingers down it before sitting back on his side of the truck. "Your mother is human?"

I kept staring at the little swirl on my ice cream that he'd made with his tongue. "Even longer story."

"Tell me where you're staying," he said. "I'll take you there."

"What about my mom?"

"That's what I want to work on," he said, starting up the engine. "You mated?"

I bit the inside of my cheek. "No."

He threw the truck into reverse and kicked up a cloud of dust. I tossed the rest of my cone out of the window and just as we hit the main road, a motorcycle pulled up beside us. It was a classic beauty with a long black seat, and the silver chrome gleamed in the sunlight as if it had never known a speck of dust. It didn't look like those big bikes I'd seen, and "Triumph" was written on the side. We slowed at the light and while Lorenzo was fooling with the radio, the rider lifted the face on his helmet.

"Shit," I whispered.

It was Reno, and by the look on his face, he wasn't surprised to see me. Nor was he happy.

When we finally reached Austin's secluded house, Lorenzo skidded to a halt. "Your friend isn't very subtle," he said, tilting the rearview mirror.

Reno sped around us on his Bonneville and parked beside a large truck. *Thank God the Challenger wasn't out front.*

"Is Cole here?"

"No," I said, scratching my cheek. "Thanks for helping out."

Maizy came bounding through the front door and Reno quickly corralled her back inside.

Lorenzo lit up a smoke and stared at the house, taking a few drags before he spoke. "You could be living a lot better than this."

"It's temporary until I find my mom."

He nodded. "Temporary's good. Real good. You should go back home in less than three days." Lorenzo took another draw of his smoke and I unbuckled my belt.

"Why three?"

Then his hot eyes flicked over to mine and made a long journey all the way down to my lap. I knew it had to do with that *heat*

word. Whether all the men could sense it or just the alphas was a
mystery, but it made me uncomfortable when it kept coming up
in conversation.

I used the side step to get out of the truck and almost tumbled
on my ass. Lorenzo stayed in the truck until I made it inside and
then he sped off with a few intentionally loud engine revs.

Reno cornered me in the front entrance, gripping his keys tightly.
His brows were low, but they weren't dark, and he looked like the
kind of guy who could star in his own action movie. A tiny scar on
his lip caught my attention, but not for long when his eyes narrowed.
"We got a camera hooked up outside your apartment, remember?"

I shrugged. "I don't really care if you have an issue with this.
Lorenzo's going to help."

"That's not how it works," he said gruffly, hanging his keys on a
nail above the letter *R*.

I kicked off my shoes and, in Naya fashion, put my hands on
my hips. "Then *how* does it work? My mom was kidnapped and my
little sister was abandoned on the side of a fucking highway. She's
lucky someone didn't snatch her or run her down. Tell me, Reno,
how does it work that I can't get more people helping out since you
guys won't call the cops?"

"Human cops aren't going to solve your problem," he replied in
a *you should already know that* voice. "And we don't bring other packs
in our business unless the Packmasters come to a mutual agreement.
That's problematic. You want to be beholden to someone you don't
know? He'll want the favor returned, and it's going to be a big
lump-sum payment."

"Well, he'll have to get on the payment plan because I'm
flat broke."

Reno blocked me from going into the living room and poked
my shoulder with his finger. "The plan is you."

Then he walked off.

Denver shot me a judgmental glare when I strolled into the
living room. Maizy rolled around on the floor while cartoon animals
on the big TV paddled across a river.

"Did she take her nap?" I asked.

"She's not tired. Are you, Peanut?"

I looked down at her restless legs and back at him. "Of course she's not tired. How much sugar did you give her? Maizy isn't used to eating sweets all the time; she gets hyper and then throws fits because she can't sleep."

He leaned back in his chair, crossed his ankles, and laced his fingers together across his stomach. "I'm not apologizing for giving her candy," he replied in a smartass tone.

"Ooo, Lexi!" Maizy squealed, whirling around. "Denny has a biiiiig yellow candy jar with lots of different kinds of candy. There were worms and bears and chocolate and—"

While Maizy listed off what she had for lunch, I smiled. "Uncle Denny is going to watch you all day, would you like that?"

She squealed a yes.

Punishment served. Once Maizy got wired and tired, Denver was never going to give her sugar again. Especially when her magic wand made an appearance and she started whacking him on the head to transform him into a prince.

He acted nonchalant, so I hauled my bag I'd brought with me into Jericho's bedroom. Austin had a point. Staying in the same room with Maizy was too risky. Even though I had no recollection of turning into a wolf, I knew I must have been dangerous by the scrapes I'd put on Austin.

"Well, well," a familiar voice said from behind me as I was bending over and making up the bed. The door clicked shut and I peered over my shoulder. "That's the position I like the *most*," Jericho said, holding the door up with his shoulder blades and staring at my ass.

"Long night?" I asked, noticing the hickeys on his neck. I tried to avoid looking at the shiner on his eye because I felt responsible. On the other hand, it didn't appear to have been of any hindrance to him getting laid.

He stripped away his graffiti T-shirt and tossed it onto a pile of clothes on the floor. There were more hickeys, and mostly around his navel area. I guessed groupies liked staking their claim on a rocker with their mouths.

"You sleepin' in my bed, Goldilocks?"

"I can't stay with Maizy for obvious reasons. Austin told me you guys have more control over your wolf and I'm new to all of this."

He moved his mouth around as if he were sucking on a piece of candy. "You're taking it pretty well."

I shrugged. "I've always had to be the rock in my family; I guess it's not in my nature to go apeshit over finding out I have paws and a tail. I'm handling it the best way I know how."

"Denial?" Jericho snorted and tossed a set of keys on his dresser. "I can say this because I'm his brother, but maybe you should stay away from Austin."

"Why?"

His eyes hooded behind the long strands of loose hair that had fallen free from the band he'd used to tie it back. "A girl like you wants a man who can control his temper. Austin's not quite there yet. He's good, real good. We've watched him grow up and become alpha material, but he has a switch in there and if you flip it the wrong way, then look out."

"Everyone has that switch," I argued.

"When Wes died, that switch stayed flipped for a long time."

Then I got it. Jericho thought I was going to push Austin over the edge again and tear apart the pack—that I'd hurt him the way Wes did by dying.

"We're not tight like that, so you don't have to worry."

He glanced down at the floor. "My brother's socks are lying on top of your lacey bra. That's pretty fucking tight."

A sudden knock rapped on the door and it cracked open. Jericho anchored his feet to the ground and pushed it closed with his back.

"Let me the fuck in," Austin growled.

When the door opened, Austin looked between us. He gripped Jericho by the back of the neck and guided him out into the hall before shutting the door behind him.

"What's this about you seeing Lorenzo?"

I stayed quiet. It seemed like the best way to avoid a fight and Austin had an agitated look on his face.

"Well?" he pressed, looming above me and closing the tiny gap of air between us.

I placed my hands behind me on the bed and gave him the "so what?" silent look.

"Always so difficult," he finally said in a softened voice. "Even when you were a kid."

"You were mean to me."

He tilted his head, rubbing that thick jaw of his. "When I was eight or twelve I might have been a jerk, but after puberty…"

Austin actually blushed and when I smiled, he turned around and stared at a Led Zeppelin poster.

"Lorenzo is searching for my mom. He doesn't seem like a bad guy, Austin. I don't have any reason not to go out with him, and no one else is calling on me."

He rocked on his heels and I stood up, unzipping my bag and grabbing my purple hairbrush. I stood in front of a dirty mirror and combed my hair, which hung just past my breasts. Guys liked my straight hair and invariably commented on it, so I usually wore it down. Otherwise, I didn't think there was anything remarkable about me. My eyes were the color of bourbon, my cheekbones high, and I had a few faded freckles on the bridge of my nose. My slim figure received a number of compliments, but I wasn't ample in either department. I worked what I had (my legs being my best asset), but always wished I had larger breasts or curvier hips.

"You don't trust that I can handle this and find your mom?"

"The more help I can get, the better, is all I'm saying, Austin."

He spun around, arms folded. "I have to take a trip tonight and I want you to come with me."

"I can't leave Maze."

"Denver and the boys got it taken care of. Shifters are protective of kids, even if they aren't our own. It's why Prince stopped his car for Maizy and didn't keep driving. You can trust my pack. They're older and have their wolves under control. They'll fight to the death to protect her, if that gives you any comfort."

And it kind of did. "Why do you want me to go with you?"

He flexed his jaw, staring at me in the mirror. Then his eyes slid down and I knew it was that *heat* word again. Austin didn't want me in the house with his brothers.

"Okay, so where are we going?"

The "we" in my question satisfied him immensely. "Oklahoma. It's about a six-hour drive and we're staying overnight," he said, looking at his watch. "We should be back tomorrow before dark."

"What do you have to do?"

"Talk to someone" was all he'd tell me.

CHAPTER 15

THE CHALLENGER'S MOTOR PURRED ALONG I-35 until Austin turned off at the exit and changed direction. Maizy hadn't revealed much about her adventure outside of what we already knew. What detailed information could I expect from a girl her age?

I had purchased all kinds of beef jerky from a gas station just outside Gainesville. Austin had merely watched as I piled the individually wrapped sticks on the counter. I'd never really liked jerky very much, but the long car trip was grueling and I was famished.

"Craving?" he asked with a twitch of his lip.

I ignored him, paid the cashier, and stuffed the bag in the back seat.

Austin played a few old songs that brought some forgotten memories to the surface. We laughed and shared stories, finding out little snippets about each other we had never revealed back in the day. When Aerosmith came on, it brought back memories of a camping trip we took to the lake one summer with a group of friends. I was stuffed in a tent with three girlfriends while Wes and his buddies camped closer to the wooded area. In the middle of the night, my friends decided to sneak over and raid their tent. What can I say? We were seventeen. I didn't go because my favorite Fleetwood Mac slow song had come on my portable radio. I walked to the shore and sat down, watching the moonlight slide over the waves like icing.

I still remember that night so clearly in my head. Feeling the warm summer breeze in my hair and listening to the water lap up on the shore as footsteps approached from behind, competing against the squeals of the girls and complaints of the boys in the distance. Austin had sat beside me that night, wearing his leather coat and denims with a hole in the knee. He didn't say a word. We just sat together and watched the waves until the song played out.

Of course, he was smoking a cigarette and looking all Joe Cool Badass while I was wearing a ponytail and pink pajama bottoms with strawberry designs. Nothing happened between us. It was just one of those beautiful moments in life that means something for reasons we can't explain.

Austin had quit smoking since then. You can always tell when you get up close to someone or check out the car ashtray and find loose change instead of cigarette butts. Strangely, he was even cooler now than he had been before. Maybe it's because back then he was trying hard to *be* somebody, and now he finally *was* that somebody.

"Does this mean I'm not going to age?" I asked, staring out the window as a billboard went by.

I felt his eyes on me in the dark interior of the car. "It slows. I'm guessing you'll look this way for a while."

I shifted uncomfortably in the seat and pulled my legs up. After a few scrapes of my fingers through my long hair, I put my feet back on the floor and tried to recline the seat.

"What's wrong?" he asked. "You need to go to the little girl's room?"

I laughed because he was serious. Then in the quietness of the cab, it just struck me funny and I laughed some more. When I felt him giving me the "what the hell is wrong with you" look, I completely lost it.

I went into Beaker mode.

Austin smiled wide with warm eyes that crinkled around the corners. He chuckled as I let out an exhausted sigh and rested my head against the seat.

"I've missed your laugh," he said.

"Only you, Austin. Only *you*."

"Wes said it was the very best thing about you."

I teared up and smiled, curling up on my side to look at him. "Why did he say that?"

Austin shrugged and rolled up his window. "He said it was uniquely you, and he was right. Wes didn't have plans after school and that's why he took the job with your dad. But he always knew you were going to be somebody. He also said you made the best chocolate-chip cookies and could bake your ass off."

"I still can," I bragged, lightly touching his arm and smiling. Baking sweets had always been a passion—I just never had any opportunities to show off my skills outside of Naya's parties. I had perfected my cookies down to an art.

"Maybe you should do something with that," he suggested.

The thought lingered. "Maybe."

"I called Church and requested that he back off."

"Why would you do that?"

Austin turned the radio down. "You don't understand the pack dynamic. Bringing him in only complicates things. He's going to feel a sense of entitlement if he finds her."

"It's not a race," I reminded him. "It's not like the winner gets a prize."

He regarded me with serious eyes. "For some, it is. Anyhow, he's not backing down. I can't go above him since he's the Packmaster. If he finds your mom before we do, it could get very sticky."

"I can handle sticky. I work in a candy store."

"You have a lot to learn, Lexi," he said, patting my leg. His hand remained there for a moment before he put it back on the steering wheel. "I need to teach you some of the rules before you get yourself in deep trouble."

I glanced outside. "Are we here? That was fast."

"Detour," he said, making a right turn. We drove up an old dirt road with only the headlights illuminating our way. "My parents bought some land out here years ago as an investment."

"Not to be the little black cloud on your picnic, but most horror movies usually begin this way. Couple goes down a dark road into the woods and the next thing you know, a guy with a chainsaw is chasing them down."

"Only when they start making out," he said. His eyes searched the dark woods, looking more alert. "You need to let your wolf run. We're camping here for the night. We'll head out in the morning to the Packmaster's house, but this is a safe place where you can shift."

I got nervous at the suggestion. "And why do I need to do that? You're not telling me everything, Austin. What's the worst that could happen if I choose not to?"

"There are some things in life you have to do, and letting your wolf out is one of them. Their spirit grows restless. They pace and get angry. If you don't let them run once in a while, they'll force you to shift and you won't be able to switch back until they're ready. This is a way of life, Lexi. It's not a choice."

"What if I can't?"

He bellowed a laugh. "Girl, if you can't figure it out, then class is in session. Every Shifter has to learn how to control their animal and that includes summoning it."

"Maybe I don't want to summon it," I said in a low voice.

"Chicken?"

I wrinkled my mouth. "I hope not. I'd look awful with feathers."

Austin laughed so loud that he turned his head away and coughed into his shoulder to muffle the sound.

After we turned off the road, we got out and he walked up to a storage shed and unlocked the door. I waved off a mosquito and cupped my elbows as Austin hauled some equipment to a clearing on the left and began assembling a tent.

One tent.

The jury was still out on whether or not it was a tent or a sombrero, because it was too small to fit the both of us. Once it was set up, he placed an electric lantern inside the flap and held my hand, leading me through the woods to a grassy area.

"Austin, I don't know about this."

His grin was nothing less than devastating. "Lexi, I promise you it's not as bad as all that. I know you feel your wolf pacing in there—I can tell by your restless behavior. We all feel it with our animal. Establish a relationship with her. She wants out, and that means you'll have to let her take over once in a while so her spirit is happy. You are two halves that make a whole. When she's hungry, feed her. I once knew a guy who didn't shift; he was one of those who lived in denial of what he was. He caged a wild animal, Lexi. He became aggressive, and eventually the wolf broke free and he didn't shift back for a year. What we are isn't like what you've read in books or seen in movies. Most Shifters can't remember what happens in their animal form, but the animals within us are always aware of what's happening. They're the source of our instincts." He tucked his hands beneath his biceps and lowered his chin, looking down at me. "It's easier than you think. Just relax and call to her."

"I don't know her name," I countered, kicking the toe of my shoe on the ground.

His smile faded and he stepped forward. "I can *make* you shift, but I'd rather you learn to do it on your own. I thought you were always the girl who wanted to do everything herself, without any help?"

Boy, did he put me in my place. That's exactly the kind of girl I was. I'd gotten better about it in recent years, but not much. Life kept throwing me in situations where I had to step up to the plate and swing.

And right now, I was up to bat without a clue of how to play the game.

"What if I run off?" I asked.

"Then I'll track you down," he replied matter-of-factly.

"Austin, I'm scared."

He cupped my face with his hands and moonlight glittered in his eyes. "No, you're not. You're Alexia Knight; you're not afraid of anything."

I studied the dark woods nervously, and a restless shadow paced beneath my skin, making me hop from one foot to the other. I finally shook it off and blew out a hard breath, staring down at my shoes and allowing every muscle to relax. I wasn't sure how to call my wolf, so I did something quite silly.

In my head, I whistled and said, "Here, girl."

And then I blacked out.

⌐◦⟶◦⌐

Austin's breath caught when Lexi shifted, just as it had the first time in her bedroom. Her wolf was *magnificent*.

Silver fur with a snowy-white face, black nose, and the tips of her ears looked like they had been dipped in ink. She was just a little bit bigger than most of the females he'd been around, which was surprising considering how slender Lexi was. But no one could explain the magic behind shifting. He admired her as she pawed the wet grass and lifted her nose, taking in the wild scent of the wilderness for the first time.

She was also showing him every white tooth in her mouth.

"Easy, girl," he said in a soothing tone. Austin summoned his alpha voice, the one laced with enough power to make the betas submit upon command, regardless if they were in animal or human form. He had to teach her to obey or else she could wind up in serious trouble someday by tangling with the wrong alpha.

Lexi's wolf lunged and snapped ferociously.

Austin stepped forward, never looking away from her fearless eyes. She hesitated for a moment, appearing uncertain of what he was going to do. Austin knelt down on all fours and looked her dead in the eye, throwing out all the power he could.

"*Submit*," he commanded in a heavy voice.

Something flashed in her pale brown eyes and her lips uncurled just a fraction. Austin didn't want to frighten her by shifting, so he waited her out—something he'd done with his own brothers when they formed the pack so everyone knew who was in charge. Surprisingly, Reno was the most obedient and Denver proved to be the most challenging. They'd fought until Austin caught hold of his throat and held down Denver's wolf. In human form, Denver couldn't be more opposite than his animal.

That wolf had issues.

"Come here, beautiful." Words he never thought he'd say out loud to Lexi, but she wouldn't remember this. He'd always thought she was a captivating creature, but nothing like now. She was once a young girl who wanted the world to see her, who craved love in ways that only young girls could understand. Lexi really looked at the world and noticed it. She was far more stunning now than ever before because of the womanly fire in her gaze, the subtle curve in her hip, and the compassion for others in her heart. She was fiercely protective of her family, and Austin admired her courage through adversity.

It's what did him in.

The truth of the matter was—Austin had loved Lexi for more years than he could count.

That bright-eyed little girl used to have stars in her eyes when she looked at him. Austin grew up thinking she was human, and most Breeds didn't associate with humans. His feelings for her began to change when they were teenagers, and by then, it was hard for him *not* to notice her. She was lovely with her long hair and sun-kissed skin. Lexi had an endearing wide smile, but even that didn't hold a candle to her glowing expression when she went into one of her fits of laughter.

Wes had been his best friend since they were tying sheets to their shirt collars and pretending to be superheroes. He considered him a brother, because Shifters bonded that way and blood made no difference in who you considered family. As attracted as he was to Lexi, friends didn't do that to each other. So Austin had kept a respectful distance from his best friend's little sister. Wes did a great job keeping the boys away from her, but he also kept a close eye on Austin. He looked out for Lexi because her father didn't.

What a bastard he was too. Austin had never seen a man less compassionate toward his daughter, but he had all the affection in the world for Wes. It should have made sense back then, but Austin just figured Nelson—their dad—didn't relate to girls.

One night after a party, Wes lost his keys and they had to sneak in through Lexi's bedroom window. She had tagged along with them, but they hadn't let her have anything to drink; she just had the giggles. Nelson was waiting for them, and he was drunk. He threw Austin and Wes into the hallway and locked himself in the bedroom with Lexi. Austin never knew what happened in that room, but he'd heard a smack.

That was the night Wes discovered what Austin really was. Rage funneled through his body and caused him to shift uncontrollably in the hallway. He was ready to tear her father apart.

Austin had some explaining to do. After that, Wes became obsessed with their world and wanted to be a part of it.

Lexi had become a handful when she started dating. That didn't sit well with either of them. Especially in high school when some of the boys started calling her Sexy Lexi and then Austin found out why. One of her best friends revealed to him that Michael Hudson had deflowered her. He went after Michael's group and did some damage to their faces.

Rage didn't quite encapsulate the feeling that coursed through Austin's veins. Michael was evasive and hard to find, but Austin knew he had all the time in the world.

That's how deep his respect for Lexi went; that's how much he revered this girl who didn't have a clue how he felt about her. She never had. Each time she entered a room, he tensed and felt a thrill move through his body as well as a fighting instinct to protect her.

A mockingbird sang in the distance and the night air called out to his wolf. Austin's eyes never left hers as she bravely stared him down in wolf form. It was a proud moment watching her shift for the first time, even though she destroyed her bedroom and tried to take a chunk out of his arm. Man, what a fierce heart, and that's something you never break.

"Come on, Lexi," he coaxed. "You got these woods to run in and no one will hurt you. I need you to trust me."

No longer baring her teeth, she snorted and stepped forward—tail high and proud.

Not a good sign.

He stiffened his shoulders and leaned forward on his knuckles, staring at her intensely. She whined a little and her tail went lower.

"I've known you for years, and this is how it's gonna be?" he asked, a little playfulness in his voice.

Lexi's wolf cautiously took another step, her silver-and-white coat even more exquisite in the moonlight. Recognition flashed in her brown eyes the closer she got to him. Maybe she knew his smell, but Lexi began to submit. She stretched out her neck and nuzzled below his chin. Just a few taps before backing off.

He smiled and sat back, hands on his legs, watching her nose lift in the air.

"Wanna go for a run?"

Her eyes glittered with excitement, fear, and all the wonder one would expect to see in a new wolf.

Austin stood up and stripped away his shirt. If you were careful shifting, it wouldn't become tangled around your head, but he didn't feel like worrying about things like clothes right now. He smirked when Lexi's wolf turned away and howled a haunting note that stilled every living creature within earshot.

The alpha power pumped through his veins, and a heat ignited his senses and made him hunger for life. Lexi was going to see his wolf for the first time, and now that he'd gained the upper hand, he was confident the two of them would mix well.

In the short time they'd spent together, it had been a struggle to suppress a primal urge to claim her in the Shifter way. It was a territorial feeling an alpha possessed in the presence of a worthy female. Feeling her body curled up beside his in Jericho's bed had awakened those instincts because he was protecting one of his own as a Packmaster should. But it also ignited other unexpected feelings, sending his blood in new directions.

Coupling with Lexi wouldn't be right, and maybe some of those old feelings were getting all mixed up. It would take something pivotal to force him to make that kind of decision. Only then would he know if she was someone he wanted to pursue as his mate. They'd both changed over the years, and he felt an obligation to watch over Lexi and her family. Messing it up with alpha lust wasn't the plan.

One of the most important lessons a Packmaster learned was control. He'd seen far too many packs led by the wrong wolf, one who used the old ways of mating by taking the female while they were both in wolf form in front of the pack to not only make her submissive, but to demonstrate to the men who she belonged to. He knew at some point women would come into his pack through his brothers, but he'd never considered how he'd feel about it if one joined their pack unmated.

Her wolf ensnared him. Austin shifted and they ran through the night.

Together.

CHAPTER 16

I RELEASED A LONG, EMBARRASSING MOAN as I stretched out my aching legs. I blinked my eyes open and felt my body tucked inside a warm sleeping bag. The sun hadn't risen yet and darkness swelled inside the tent. Albeit summer, sleeping outside in the deep woods was not always a warm experience. I think I shivered more with my voice than my body.

A zipper cut through the silence and someone stepped inside the tent, a chilly breeze floating in behind him. "I hear someone's awake. You feeling okay?" Austin asked in a tired voice.

"I don't remember what happened," I grumbled. "And I'm naked again."

"It's normal."

"Did you sleep outside?" I asked.

"I didn't sleep."

"Is *that* normal?"

He chuckled and I sat up, rubbing my eyes. "I feel good though. Rested. My feet kind of hurt."

"You ran hard. Why don't you get dressed and we'll head out."

I fell on my back and disappeared inside the sleeping bag, shivering. "It's too cold. Wait until the sun comes up."

Austin crawled down to my feet and then I felt his hands on either side of me. I wrapped my arms around my naked body and froze when the zipper was slowly pulled down.

"What are you doing?"

"I can't see a thing, Lexi. I want you to trust me."

I believed him whenever he said "trust me." I'd never had a reason not to trust Austin. So I lay there, fully exposed, and Austin Cole lifted my legs and placed my cold feet against his warm stomach.

He hissed and then quickly covered my toes with his large hands.

"Oh my God, that's heaven," I moaned with a sigh of relief.

"I run on hot," he said in a thick voice.

My nipples immediately hardened, and while I knew it was from the draft, I began to have serious doubts about how true that was. I could only imagine what we looked like—me lying nude in front of him with my feet on his...

"Austin? Are you naked?"

His stomach rocked and his whole body began to shake. A low laugh built up until he opened his mouth and puffed out my fire with his laughter. I smiled and wiggled my toes against his firm abs.

"I put on pants an hour ago," he said. "Today we're going to see Ivan of the Kizer pack."

"What's your pack's name? Cole Pack?" I snorted. "Sounds like a compress."

He squeezed my ankles and I moved my feet around to a warmer spot, mostly so I could hear him hiss again from the chill of my icy toes.

"It would usually go that way, but if the name is already in use, we have to choose another. Cole is an active pack in Houston, so I could either come up with a new name, or have one assigned. The Council was going to give us Skinner," he grumbled. "I didn't like that."

"Is it a big deal or something?"

His voice was low and raspy—that bedroom voice that made me shiver. "It should mean something. We're the Weston pack."

I scarcely breathed. The silence became so deafening that sunrise would have sounded like a volcanic eruption. After a few smooth strokes of his hand that warmed my skin, Austin crawled outside to allow me to get dressed. I rolled to my side and felt around for the lantern as he zipped up the tent. When the light switched on, it threw my shadow against the smooth lining, piercing my eyes. I fumbled around in my small bag for some clothes.

If we were meeting a Packmaster today, he was just going to have to accept me in a pair of jeans and my strapless shirt. It was undeniably a cute top with elastic around the edges and turquoise patterns mixed with black flowers. Summertime in the South was nothing to mess around with; I'd just thought we'd be sleeping in a hotel with room service and movie channels.

I didn't pack for *BFE at four in the morning* weather.

The hollow note of a wolf's howl sounded in the distance and goose bumps rippled up my arms. "Austin?"

The tent zipped open quickly. "Get out. Come on, let's go," he said hurriedly, grabbing my bag and hauling ass.

"What's wrong?" I asked, hopping in place and slipping on my sneaker.

"I marked the property and some sonofabitch is on it. There are too many rogue Shifters around these parts, so I'm not about to go after him and leave you sitting in my car by yourself. Lexi, *dammit*," he chastised, yanking my arm so hard I stumbled. My left shoe wasn't all the way on, but I managed to make it to the car in record time.

Once the doors shut, he rubbed his face and I looked around, noticing how quickly the yellow and lavender colors filtered through the branches overhead. The sublime beauty of early morning could rarely be matched in my eyes. I preferred mornings over sunsets because beginnings are always better than endings, even if you don't know what the day will bring.

His bright eyes were sharp and alert, but more relaxed. "You hungry?"

"Now that you mention it, I'm starving." My stomach gave an angry growl as if to agree.

He reached in the back seat and handed me a stick of jerky. I tore off the plastic wrapper and nibbled on the end. It wasn't half bad, although it was a little greasy.

Austin frowned.

"What's wrong? There's plenty if you want some," I offered.

"That's not what you're craving, is it?"

I held his glance and his crystal-blue eyes captivated me in the morning light. "No, but it'll tide me over until breakfast."

"Why did you buy so much of it?"

I shrugged. *Who knew why I bought anything edible from a gas station?* "At the time, it sounded really good. What's the big deal?"

"You'll know when you figure it out," he said with a frustrated sigh. "Try to think of what it is you're craving and I'll have it for you next time. You've got a picky wolf."

"Tradition? Or does the wolf like a little snack after walkies?"

He cut me a hard glare. "This isn't a joke. Being a Shifter is an honor. We get enough shit from some of the other Breeds, I don't want to hear it coming from you. There are a lot of prejudices, and many of 'em treat us like we're the lower end of the totem pole. Someday I'll tell you what they used us for."

"Sled dogs?"

He leaned over and restrained every spark of anger until it only glimmered in his eyes. Austin was nose to cheek with me and I lowered my eyes, feeling immediate guilt for my predawn sense of humor, not to mention his alpha power flowing over me like a punishment.

"Slaves. We were chained, whipped, beaten, slaughtered, raped, and the wolf packs were used as guards or bloodhounds. We were forced to kill and do other people's dirty work. It was before our time, but there are many from that era who are still around. Ivan is one of those men, so be careful what you say around him. We're not immortal, but some Shifters are hundreds of years old." His voice softened, and he tucked a loose strand of hair behind my ear.

"I'm sorry, Austin. You know I'd never be disrespectful if I knew all of that. I've just been having a hard time dealing with this and I didn't think it was off-limits to make a few jokes."

A grin slid up one cheek. "We joke all the time, Lexi. I just want you to keep your nose out of trouble when we're around other packs," he said, tapping my nose.

The engine growled to life and by the time we hit the highway, I'd put away three sticks of beef jerky.

⌒∘⌒⊂⊃∘⌒

After a quick breakfast detour for sausage biscuits and black coffee, we pulled up to a majestic ranch house. Ten acres of cleared land surrounded the property, and there was a red riding mower off to the right.

"Ivan's living it up," I said, admiring two bright red sports cars on the left side of the house.

Austin parked behind them and cut off the engine.

"How long is this going to take? I can wait out here."

"No, you're coming inside with me. You're also going to hold my hand, and not because we're dating, but because I don't want you out of my sight for a minute. I trust Ivan; he's been around a long time. But I don't know his pack and in your condition…"

"Someone please explain what my condition is, because I feel perfectly normal. I thought only alphas could smell me?"

"We can pick up the scent when you first change over, but going into heat is something entirely different. It's like a pheromone. It draws the males to you before it starts and once it does, the weak ones aren't able to control themselves."

"Maybe it's my perfume."

He clicked open his door. "Come on, smartass."

Austin held my right hand and we walked up the steps to a winding porch. A small set of wind chimes tinkled in the breeze as we clomped across the hollow wood floor, announcing our arrival before any doorbell was ever rung. The door swung open, replaced by two men. One had a handlebar mustache and looked like he was short a Harley while the other was missing a surfboard and needed another bottle of bleach to touch up his roots.

"Ivan here?"

"Who's asking?" Harley demanded, folding his hairy arms.

"Tell him Austin Cole is here. He's expecting me."

"Austin Cole," a voice boomed. "Been a few years."

Harley and the surfer parted like two lovers who were just not that into each other anymore.

Ivan's presence made me grab Austin's arm and curl up against him. The man had salt-and-pepper hair with about two inches of beard, but he sure as hell didn't look like Santa Claus. More like the guy who slips into your house in the middle of the night, strings you up by your ankles, and cuts off your ears while telling a story about

SEVEN YEARS   165

his time in a Mexican jail.

Austin stood his ground and made no move to coddle me in any way.

"You've sprouted up, Cole. Not quite the young pup I remember," Ivan said in a gravelly, southern drawl. Not the good kind of southern drawl, but the kind you hear whenever you're skating through those tiny towns and pull over into a truck stop to use the bathroom as fast as humanly possible.

"I've formed my own pack, Ivan. The Weston pack."

"You don't say?" Ivan put his hands on his waist and tapped his snakeskin boots against the floor. "Boys, leave us alone. Y'all come inside before the skeeters get you. Damn bloodsucking insects have been a nuisance around here since the last hard rain."

The two men obediently disappeared. Ivan led us to a quiet sitting room full of musty old books and bizarre artifacts such as animal skulls and a tarantula in a glass orb. There were only two chairs and after Ivan sat in the red one, he began packing a pipe with a pinch of tobacco.

Austin hesitated. He still had hold of my hand and our palms were sweating.

Ivan struck a match and waited a moment before he lit up his pipe. After a few puffs that clouded his face, he extinguished the match and grinned slowly as he looked me up and down.

"Someone's about to make you feel real good, Cole," he said with a knowing chuckle. "Ever had one in heat? Ain't nothing like it. Nothing in the world." He took a few short puffs from the pipe and blew out the smoke, shifting his hips. "Have a seat."

It wasn't a suggestion.

Austin sat down in the chair and I jerked my hand free, wiping my sweaty palm on my shirt. He burned me with his glacier eyes, so I leaned on the back of his chair and that seemed to satisfy him.

"What brings you out here?" Ivan asked.

Austin sat forward with his elbows on his thighs. "You've got connections, Ivan, and I've got a situation. We have a woman missing—kidnapped—and I know you got men who can find her."

Ivan listened to the details, including the fact my mother was human, which rubbed him the wrong way. Then Austin said he would be indebted to him and Ivan's cloudy eyes lit up with interest.

He took another small puff from his pipe and set it down in a holder. "As it so happens, you can even out that debt today. I got a female I need you to take off my hands, and I've been knowing your family long enough that I trust she'll be in good care with you. If she chooses to go with another pack, then you let her, but I want you to look out for her as one of your own."

Austin rubbed his jaw and I listened to the bristly sound of his whiskers. "Who is she?"

"My daughter."

I gasped. Just a little bit. Ivan looked up at me and I dropped my eyes to the floor.

"She's going through the change soon and I need fresh blood in the pack. I can't have my own flesh and blood mating with any of these sons of bitches. You know pack rules—can't keep our girls, and she hasn't met anyone to take her off my hands."

"Why not one of the local packs?"

Ivan shrugged and tapped his boot heel on the floor with an outstretched leg. "I made a promise to her mother before she died I'd get her the hell out of Oklahoma. She never was fond of the packs in this territory and I guess I can't blame her. We're not like you city boys," he said, scraping Austin up and down with his eyes.

"Do you have a bathroom?" I interrupted, doing the embarrassing dance on my tiptoes.

"Lexi, no," Austin said.

"Tight little leash he's got on you, honey. 'Round the corner to the right."

Austin caught my hand and I jerked it free. "Sorry, Austin. I refuse to stand in here like a three-year-old holding it in. My bladder has needs."

Ivan rocked with laughter, but it was a silent laugh with a bit of a wheeze. His chest shook merrily until he wrapped it up with a long snarl and snort. "She's a keeper, that one. I think she'll get along well with my little girl."

I sprinted down the hall and opened three doors before I found the bathroom. It took a good five minutes before I was ready to come out. When I finished drying off my hands and opened the door, three men blocked my exit.

Their pupils were dilated and their nostrils flared. They shared the same look men possessed who watched Naya dancing on stage in her leather thong.

"Beep, beep," I said in a panicked moment as I tried to cut through the wall of muscle.

They weren't yielding, reversing, or allowing me to merge into traffic. Their bodies formed a roadblock and began walking me back into the bathroom. I stepped to the side nervously and one of them shut the door.

A hand slid across my thigh and I slapped it away.

"Don't touch me," I ground out through my clenched jaw. I'd had enough and snatched a bottle of shampoo and lathered it in my hands. Had there been a razor within sight I might have grabbed it, but Prell seemed good enough. If I didn't blind them, they'd at least have fresh-smelling hair.

When the tall guy in front of me yanked my shirt down so hard my boob popped free, I Prelled him in the eyes.

And then I blacked out.

CHAPTER 17

COLD TILE NUMBED MY ASS and when my surroundings became clear, I was sitting in the center of Ivan's bathroom with a black robe draped over my back.

"Jesus, Lexi," I heard Austin gripe. "Feeling better?"

The door was closed and he was sitting on the toilet with the lid down. I tightened the front of the robe and glanced around at a torn curtain, bottles strewn across the floor and bathtub, a flipped over bathmat, and tiny blood spatters across the mirror, cabinet, and floor.

"What happened?"

He sighed. "I'm not letting you out of my sight. If you gotta pee again, I'm going with you."

"Over my dead body. Where did those guys go?"

Austin straightened up and stretched out his legs, crossing them at the ankle. "Two of them are shifting to heal; I've never seen anything like it. A female taking down three men—that's just fucking wild," he almost said to himself. "Your wolf can hold her own, that's for sure." Then his chuckle evolved into a laugh. "One of them came running out with shampoo in his eyes and the ass-end of his jeans hanging open like a flap." He palmed away the tears and I sat up, staring at my clothes piled on the floor.

"You have a twisted sense of humor, Austin Cole. Get out so I can get dressed. God, this is so embarrassing."

Embarrassing because I felt no fear. Nor was there a sense I'd been a victim in this situation. In fact, I felt a lot like a prizefighter might after a boxing match. I had no idea what had happened, but my wolf was strutting her stuff and trotting around like nobody's business.

After I put my clothes back on and brushed off the fur and blood,

I rejoined the merry little group in the study. Ivan folded his arms, unable to look away from the drop of blood on my white sneaker.

"This is why you're taking my daughter," he said to Austin without lifting his eyes. "If your boys ever try something like that, I'm going to know about it. You hear?"

"Why don't you think about it before—"

"You backin' out on me? I'll back out on you," he threatened. "Think about it, Cole. I got men in five states who can solve your problems. They got connections in law enforcement and work directly with some of our own internal organizations. We can track a flea in a desert. What do you want me to do with the man who took her?"

It was the kind of question that suggested he had a few things in mind involving cattle prods.

"Austin, no," I whispered, tugging at his faded red shirt.

"Bring him to us."

"Unharmed," I cut in. Austin gave me a sideways glance. "He might be an asshole, but he's still my dad."

"Tough girl you got there, Cole. Feel like doing some trading?"

"I'm not a baseball card," I barked out.

Ivan shook with laughter and released a snarly snort at the end. "I like her. If you change your mind, give me a ring. I got a few bitches you can choose from, unless you want cash."

"She's not part of the deal," he said in slow, threatening words. When he took a step forward, I had to pull him back by the waistband of his jeans. His shoulders were stiff, his back straight, and his jaw was clenched so tightly it created a sharp shadow along his unshaven cheek.

"Fair enough," Ivan said. "I'll give you a ring tonight and I should have them in your custody in no more than forty-eight hours. How's that sound?"

"Like a deal."

They didn't shake on it. In fact, I had yet to see a Shifter shake hands.

Ivan patted Austin on the shoulder and led us to the door. Austin held my hand, except now I looked like a hot mess with my hair in tangles. One of the men in the room flew down the hall and slammed a door so hard a picture fell off the wall.

"She's in the car," Ivan said in a private voice. "Didn't want to make a production out of it because some of the men have had their eye on her. She's a good girl, Austin. But she has an effect like poison in this house because of her beauty. I'll be in touch to make sure you're looking after her."

We reached the car and a young woman peered through the window from the back seat. She appeared to be a little bit younger than me, but not by much. Her hair was pulled back in an untidy braid that fell past her shoulders. It was a beautiful shade of mahogany with a few faded highlights. Her lashes were dark, a soft glow warmed her skin, and she wore a long brown dress that tied around her neck. Very earthy, and Ivan was spot-on about her being beautiful.

"Hi," I greeted her, sliding into the front seat. I twisted around and she didn't lift her eyes. "I'm Lexi. This is weird and I'm sure you're as freaked out as I am about it," I babbled as Austin walked around the front of the car, glaring through the windshield. "Austin's not a bad guy and… Good God, this is *awkward*. What's your name?"

She lifted her warm brown eyes. "Ivy. My father likes to call me Poison Ivy, but don't tell anyone. I'd rather no one call me that name again."

"Did you want to come with us?"

Austin opened his door and got in. The car rocked a little and he sighed, turning around. "I'm Austin Cole. I run a small pack and they're all good men. You have nothing to worry about in my group; they're just a little rough around the edges because they've been on their own for a number of years. I'm very selective, and so far, it's just my brothers and me. What do they call you?"

She clammed up.

"Her name is Ivy," I said softly.

Then I turned around in my seat and wondered exactly what had changed regarding slavery. We had essentially just traded my mother's life for a man's daughter. No one was fighting it, which evidently meant these people played by rules, even though they still had free will. Austin had explained that women preferred to stay in packs because it offered them the protection they needed. Shifters who were panthers or other animal types didn't have to be concerned with these things as much as the wolves because of our inherent instincts. After seeing how those men had behaved in the bathroom, I could see his point.

"Jerky?"

She glanced at the overflowing plastic bag in the floor and reached in to pull out a stick. "Love these," she said. "Got any of the spicy peppered flavor? Something with a kick?"

I leaned around and rifled through the bag, then I glanced at her hands. "Ooo, I love that color polish," I said. "Turquoise or green?"

"It has an iridescent quality, so it's a little of both. I brought it with me if you want to borrow it later."

Austin clucked his tongue and revved up the engine. "Women," he murmured.

"Everlong" by the Foo Fighters blasted on the radio and we headed back home. Austin kept the air conditioner frosty and I reclined my seat back, kicked off my shoes, and put my feet on the dash. Austin sang under his breath and although the music was loud, he still outsang the shit out of that band.

⟶∘⟨✺⟩∘⟶

Austin had Ivy's bags slung over his shoulder when he unlocked the front door to his house.

"How many brothers do you have?" Ivy asked timidly.

"I got five in my pack. And do me a favor," he said, twisting his body halfway around. "Stay away from Jericho."

"Which one is he?" Ivy tugged the end of her long braid, which was wrapped around her right shoulder.

"The one with the hickeys all over him."

I didn't know what to make of Jericho, but he seemed like kind of guy you wouldn't want your little sister hanging around. Although I still wasn't certain how Austin felt about Ivy. She sure didn't look like a little sister, and he wasn't blind. I saw the way he appraised her when she got out of the car.

The door swung open and the sound of men filled the house.

Austin tucked his arm around Ivy and escorted her through the main entrance. She slipped out of her flip-flops and leaned into him.

I shut the door and felt a burning coal sitting in the pit of my stomach, and it wasn't hunger. We'd made a four-hour detour on the way home to eat lunch and pick up a few things at the store for Ivy. Her father hadn't allowed her to pack very much—just a couple of bags of clothes.

The sun hung low in the sky and the smell of barbecue made my mouth water.

Maizy was sitting outside in the atrium on a bench, blowing bubbles from a wire she dipped in a tall glass. I walked past Austin and Ivy and slid open the door.

Denver turned around, wearing an apron of a nude woman's body.

"In front of her?" I scolded.

He sniffed and rubbed his nose as a plume of smoke poured out of the grill and into his face. "What's the big deal? She's a chick."

"And why is she holding a wire? She's *six*."

"Beer bubbles. Damn, where have you been? You didn't play with those as a kid?"

I took the glass from her along with the sharp metal object. "No, we bought bubbles at the store for a dollar."

"You wasted a dollar."

"And you wasted a beer."

Denver waltzed over and snatched the glass from my hand, chugging down the warm yellow beverage that had a tiny piece of grass floating on top. Then he belched, winking his eye. "Nothing's wasted around here, honeypie."

Who would have thought such a pretty boy with his golden locks and dashing smile—despite the scar, which wasn't that severe—could be such a child himself?

"Did you have fun, Maizy? Come with me and tell me all about it," I said, taking her hand.

"Uncle Denny let me play video games and we shot the bad guys!"

"Oh, goodie. How about you take this and ask Uncle Reno if

he'll put it on?"

I pulled a DVD out of the back of my jeans and handed it to her. Her face brightened with excitement and she went bounding into the living room with the *Beauty and the Beast* cartoon.

Then I heard her crying.

"Dammit, Wheeler," I heard Reno bark out in his gravelly voice. He sounded like Stallone without the accent. "Let her watch it."

Austin escorted Ivy into the living room in the same fashion as he had me the first time.

"Lexi, come meet the rest of the pack," he said with a wave of his hand.

"Maizy, go put on your nightgown and brush your teeth," I said. She smiled and I tried to contain my laugh due to her missing tooth.

"It's fine," Austin cut in. "We shouldn't keep her in the dark."

I glanced at the twins on the couch. Their dusty brown hair was lighter than the others—choppy and styled a little messy. Their eyebrows were dark and pronounced with a little arch to them, making their eyes stand out. They definitely inherited the Cole looks because despite their more narrow features, they were handsome men in a very stern and mischievous way—I wasn't quite sure which. Liquid brown eyes sparkled like amber, bright and illuminating. They shared the same medium build with toned arms and lean torsos.

But here is where they differed. The one on the left wore tattoos like sleeves. One shoulder had a wolf, then I saw a dagger, some tribal, and they blended like one fantastic design. He also had a circle beard closely trimmed that he seemed to like stroking with his fingers.

"These are my brothers, Wheeler and Ben."

I turned my mouth to the side. "Where's that located?"

Simultaneously, they replied, "Ben Wheeler, Texas."

"At least it wasn't Beaver Dam."

"Ah shit," Ben said. He was the guy on the right who seemed to have a friendlier personality than his inked brother, and his smile was wider. "Don't mention that around Denver; he'll have a field day. The jokes never end with him."

"At least it'll get the attention off of me," Jericho said from behind. I turned around and Jericho greeted us in nothing but a pair of black jeans. He stretched his long arms up and held onto the frame above the hallway entrance. It looked like a vacuum hose had made out with him.

Austin went on with introductions. "This is Lexi, Wes's little sister."

I held my tongue and mentally rolled my eyes. I would never be more than Wes's little sister to these guys.

Ben and Wheeler didn't talk much. They resumed watching Reno putting the movie in while Maizy plopped down on the round carpet in front of the TV. She was eating up the attention because they didn't quite know what to do with a little girl around the house. Therefore, they spoiled her with whatever she wanted. Hopefully she didn't pick up on some of those fun four-letter words they enjoyed using. Regardless, I got a good vibe with the pack. Despite their differences, they were unified.

"Who's she?" Wheeler (the one with the tats) asked apprehensively.

"Our new packmate," Austin replied without blinking an eye.

"Since when are we taking in bitches?" Wheeler protested. I was surprised he didn't like the idea; you'd think a woman would be just the thing they'd want around here. While identical, Wheeler had a little darkness in his eyes that I didn't see in Ben. Maybe that's why he covered himself up with ink.

Ivy had attached herself to Austin like a wild vine. "Since today. Ivan is taking over the hunt for Lexi's mom and to return the favor, he asked that I bring one of his daughters into our pack because she's nearing the change. We're growing, and y'all know I make the decisions on who we take in. You'll get more say-so when it comes to men because I don't need you guys killing each other, but we need women to balance things out. Since Ivy doesn't have a mate, as a rule, it's hands off."

Denver wandered into the house and lingered in the hall to the right of the recliner. "Did you meet Wheeler and Dealer?" he asked with a smirk.

I couldn't help but notice that while Ben hardly paid attention, Wheeler's eyes slid over to Denver and looked volcanic. Odd reaction since the nickname seemed more of a jab at Ben.

Austin made sure to look all of them square in the eye. "Any funny business and I'll find out. Treat her like a sister, because from this day forward, that's exactly what she is to you. You know damn well what some of these packs are like, and I'm going to put in my claim officially so we don't have to worry about anyone closing in on our turf."

"You claiming Wes's sister?" Denver asked.

"Will everyone stop calling me that!"

I stormed past Jericho into his bedroom and slammed the door behind me. Where else could I go? I might have been overreacting just a hair, but I couldn't get my mom off my mind and what could possibly be going on with her. I'd never felt so helpless and lost—so uncertain of what I should do, and here these guys were, having a meet and greet.

I grabbed my bag and went across the hall into Austin's room, glancing around for anything that belonged to Maizy. I stuffed her wand into my bag and walked with a determined pace to the living room.

"Come on, Maizy. We're leaving."

"But my movie just came on," she whined.

"Lexi, what do you think you're doing?" Austin said, attempting to be calm but not doing a very good job of it. Ivy stepped around us and found the bathroom in the hall.

I snapped my fingers impatiently. "Come on, Maizy. I've got movies at the house and Auntie Naya bought you a new one as a surprise."

She got up and pouted, coming over to stand at my side, her blond hair in tangles. I didn't have time to look for her shoes, so I lifted her up and grunted from her weight. "Sorry, Austin, it's time for us to return to our lives."

"I can't let you go," he said firmly. The words lingered in the air and he lowered his eyes.

"Let's not do this here, okay? It'll get ugly. I really appreciate everything, and I'm going to come back over tomorrow so we can find my mom. I just need to be home, and it's totally safe. My dad has no idea where I live and just let him try. I think my mom went willingly with him because she still loves him. I don't know. I have Naya next door to watch Maizy when I'm out, but I can't keep crashing on your brother's bed."

I ignored his hostile stare and brows sloped at a disagreeable angle.

We breezed past the men and into the hall when Maizy cried out. "Wait!"

"What is it?"

"I want to give Uncle Denny a hug," she whimpered in a small voice.

Denver attempted to suppress his handsome grin, but I could see how such a small request touched him. She gave him a tight squeeze while still in my arms, and I heard the rattle of a plastic candy wrapper and decided to let it go and allow her to have it. Denver's lips pressed tightly as he turned away and folded his arms.

My car keys were on the same ring as Austin's—a little red flashlight dangled from the ring, so I spotted them easily. I had Maizy grab them since my arms were occupied holding her along with the bag. Austin followed me outside but seemed reluctant to make a scene in front of my sister.

After I buckled her in the car, I crossed around the front and Austin caught my arm. "Wait," he said in a softened voice. That sexy, growly, just got out of bed voice. "Don't go. Stay with us until we find Lynn."

"I have to go, Austin. I need to check on things at work and take care of personal matters. There could also be a message on my machine."

"We got that covered," he said.

"You don't have my life covered. I know you mean well, but maybe it's better that I'm not in the house if I'm about to have a pheromone party in a few days. I'm sure you can agree."

He stuffed his hands in his jean pockets and I could see every line of his body through the thin shirt he wore. Shirts shouldn't be that tight on a man; there should be some kind of a law against it. And then there was that lazy smile of his that nearly made me change my mind.

I stepped forward and slid my arms around his waist, leaning into his chest. His heart beat heavily against my ear where I rested my head. It felt so good to have him back in my life again, and despite all my anger I'd carried through the years, I could never hate Austin Cole.

"Thanks," I murmured. "Not just for helping with everything, but for coming back. I missed you."

His hands cupped the top of my head and he whispered into my hair. "Be careful, Ladybug."

CHAPTER 18

A FTER CLEANING UP FEATHERS AND hanging the curtains in my bedroom, I tucked Maizy in the bed and covered her with a fuzzy blue blanket. The door remained closed so that I could grill a cheese sandwich and not wake her up with the cacophony of pans rattling around. I relaxed on the sofa and noticed my apartment had that weird smell it gets when it's been left alone for too long.

The door handle jiggled and I shot up with half a sandwich in my mouth. I tossed the plate on the coffee table and hurried to the door. Naya waved through the peephole and I stepped outside, closing the door behind me.

"Everything okay? I was about to go to work and saw your lights on," she said.

"Yeah. Maizy's sleeping in the other room."

"I'm so glad the little baby's okay." She breathed a sigh of relief. "Does Auntie Naya get to see her? I bought her the prettiest dress the other week and—"

"I really don't know why you do that, Naya. You spoil her way too much." I chuckled and we sat on the steps together. Her makeup looked like spackle with a heavy coat of foundation and glossed-up lips. She had on a pair of shorts and a button-up blouse, but her real work clothes were underneath. I never understood why men liked that look, because she was prettier without it in her normal clothes. But I guess she had to project an image on stage.

"The dress is adorable," she answered. "You're going to flip out when you see it. I picked it up at a thrift store, but it looks exactly like a dress a princess should be wearing."

"You're just feeding her obsession," I said with a distant sigh, staring across the street at the shadow of a man as it disappeared behind one of the buildings.

"I don't have kids; let me live vicariously through you. Someday, she'll find out all that fairy-tale stuff about love is just a lie, so let her enjoy it while she can. Did you find your mama?"

That's when the waterworks came on. Naya hugged my shoulders and I cried against her shimmery white blouse.

"Don't cry, chickypoo. It's going to be okay, you just wait and see. I really hate to leave you," she said guiltily.

"No, it's fine. I know you're late. Maybe we can talk tomorrow, but I'm going to be in and out all day."

"That's what *he* said," she purred.

Naya knew how to snap me out of my funk and make me laugh. She blew a kiss and dashed off, leaving me alone on the steps. I had just wiped a crumb from the corner of my mouth when the sound of heavy footsteps approached from below. A long shadow emerged on the walkway and a man came into view. He slowly ascended the stairs and I leaned to the left to see if it was one of Naya's lovesick puppies who often swung by when she was at work.

Officer McNeal rounded the corner and smiled.

"Alexia Knight," he said from the landing below. "Have you been dodging me?"

"How come you're never in uniform?" I asked skeptically, looking at his black pants and shirt. McNeal looked like a cop, but it didn't feel legit, if that makes any sense. He looked forty, but something about his grey eyes seemed much older.

"I'm a detective—we're not required to wear uniforms."

"So why did you introduce yourself as an officer?"

He threw his left foot up on the step and leaned on the railing. "Your father is in some serious trouble and we need to locate him."

"You know about the kidnapping?"

His brow arched. *Apparently he didn't.* "Nelson stole something that's extremely valuable, and now the owner wants it back. He threatened to hunt down Nelson's family, and we're just looking to track your father down before this escalates out of hand."

Then a light bulb switched on. "You're not a cop, are you?" I rose to my feet with each foot on a different step. "*You're* working with the man my dad owes, aren't you? What did he do? Because he kidnapped my mother."

McNeal looked me over and cocked his head to the side. "It doesn't seem like he took *everything* of value."

The remark confused me, but I quickly realized McNeal might see me as a way to bait my father.

"You think he cares about me?" I laughed but the sound quickly died as I narrowed my eyes at him. "I'm not even his real daughter. He left us years ago and doesn't give a damn about my life."

McNeal drummed his fingers impatiently on the railing. "Your father is a thief."

"What did he steal, a few grand? Write it off."

"Fifty million in diamonds."

Holy shit.

"My dad worked in a warehouse," I said in a voice of denial.

"Is that what he told you?" McNeal huffed out a laugh and glanced upward. "He was a runner who completed payment transactions."

"What does that mean?"

"If someone didn't pay their debt, your father finished the transaction," he said with his fingers shaped like a gun.

Oh my God.

"You're lying."

"Am I?" He took a step up and I took a step back.

"I'm going to find him, and the longer I'm forced to wait, the more dangerous I become. Your family has been nothing but trouble; I should have washed my hands of you years ago by taking him out too."

"Too?" This time I stepped forward. "What do you mean… too?"

"I can sense by your energy you're not human," he said. "And I'd be curious to know more about how that came to be. Your brother was a fool. At least your father wasn't begging for immortality; he just wanted a fat paycheck. Humans should know their place."

I was three seconds from lunging at him. "What do you know about Wes? How could you know him?"

"Nelson wanted to bring him into the business." McNeal

shrugged. "Only, your brother didn't want monetary gain, that stupid human wanted immortality. Some of your kind get fixated on living forever and are willing to do anything, give up anything. Like a Mage is just going to give away that kind of power for a job? Fuck no. You got to earn your keep with us and show us your worth. It might take a lifetime to earn, but I didn't tell *him* that. Just gave him his assignment and he chickened out."

"What assignment?" I breathed. My heart raced like a hummingbird and my legs trembled.

"To kill a young Shifter—an alpha. We got a population problem around here with some of those wolves eating up land, and I'm trying to solve it. You take out the young alphas, and they can't form packs. Packs are stronger, so creating more rogue Shifters by circumstance makes them easier to pick off—it's a numbers game. Plus, no female wolf is going to pair up with a man who isn't part of a pack. He had a problem with the assignment; some shit about the guy being his friend."

It felt like a sheet of ice slid over my skin. McNeal was talking about Austin. Wes was trying to become immortal and his first assignment was to kill his best friend.

"You killed my brother?"

"Not personally," he corrected. "I keep my hands clean and outsource all the dirty work. Keeps me out of Breed jail."

"You aren't afraid I'll turn you in?"

He smirked. "You know what they call an accusation without proof in our world? Slander. And there are heavy consequences for ruining an immortal's good name."

A loud motor purred in the parking lot and abruptly cut off. When the door slammed, McNeal whipped his head around.

"We'll deal with this later. You better think real hard about where your father is, because things could get messy."

Faster than I could track, McNeal ran off. Just a blur of movement down the stairs and across the lawn. I felt dizzy and gripped the railing.

"Alexia!" a man shouted, footsteps climbing up the stairs.

It was Lorenzo.

He cupped my chin in his hand and tilted my head up. "Are you unharmed?" Then he looked over his shoulder. "I saw the Mage; do you know him?" His eyes narrowed to slivers and I shook my head. "Sit," he said, coaxing me down on the step.

"He's after my father." My hands wouldn't stop shaking and my cheeks felt flushed. "What are you doing here?"

"I got a man on your house and he gave me a call to let me know you were back. I heard you went to negotiate with Ivan. If that's the case, he'll have your mother back faster than we will. Cole must have paid him a fine penny for that favor. My men got as far as a gas station outside of El Paso but lost the trail. He's been stealing cars and changing directions—giving us a run for our money." Lorenzo's voice softened and he caressed my right cheek. He drew in a deep breath and his eyes hooded. "You're okay?"

"I don't know *what* I am anymore," I replied in a distant voice.

"Beautiful?" he murmured against my cheek.

Lorenzo sat to my left with his right elbow propped on one of the steps. With his left hand, he tenderly caressed my cheek, then my neck, and suddenly his fingers were traveling much, much lower. Over the curve of my breast, down the slope of my flat stomach, and then he brazenly cupped his warm hand between my legs.

"Nothing is more damaging to my willpower than seeing a woman in her prime. This'll be your first time in heat, won't it?"

All I could feel was the warmth from his hand, and my body quivered from his touch. Sparks shot through me and I closed my eyes, listening to the sound of his hypnotic words. The inflection in his voice had power and reminded me of how Austin spoke. It made the wolf inside me want to submit.

Over my sweatpants, his thumb slowly began to stroke in tight, small circles. I arched my back in response, unable to control the effect Lorenzo had on my body. The craving was beyond what I'd ever experienced before, and all he was doing was touching me.

Barely.

"I can make it feel so good your first time," he said in a low, rough voice in my ear. "You're going to want to bend over for me, because the instinct will be strong to be taken from behind. It's deeper that way."

My breathing grew heavy while his thumb continued circling. Images of bending over for Lorenzo flooded my mind, him slowly stripping down my sweats to my ankles and, oh God. His mouth was against my ear and I was getting close… *too* close.

"I'm an experienced alpha, Alexia. I know how to handle you properly. I know what will make you feel good and ease your discomfort. I know how to draw out the pleasure." Then he breathed in deeply. "*You're so close,*" he said in a broken whisper. One that barely maintained control. "Come with me, Nashoba. Come into my pack. Come into my bed. And then just come for me."

His thumb changed direction and I muffled a cry, my body trembling as I gripped the railing with my right hand. His fingers didn't stop, his knuckles putting pressure against my core while his thumb rolled in mind-blowing circles.

"That's it," he said, softly kissing my jaw. "Stretch out and let me take care of everything."

It was too much and then I panicked. What the hell was I doing on the stairwell letting a guy I barely knew bring me to orgasm? Even worse, I was on the verge of experiencing one that was so intense that I was liable to scream. Imagine explaining *that* to the cops.

I flew forward and ran down the stairs. I staggered across the grassy lawn, panting as he strode up behind me. My heart thumped against my chest with such intensity that I could barely hear myself talking.

"What are you doing to me?" I said in quickened breaths.

He held his arms out, palms up. "Showing you what I have to offer."

"Why me?"

"You're different, Alexia. You don't act like the other bitches."

My face tightened. "Don't call me a bitch."

His brows pinched together as an indulgent look crossed his face. Lorenzo closed in and threaded his fingers through my hair on one side. "If you don't like the word, I'll stop using it," he said with a heated breath against my ear. "But you're still the only bitch I want coming in my bed."

Two seconds later, all hell was about to break loose when Austin's car roared around the corner.

He didn't bother to shut his door, just ate up the lawn with one hell of a stride. Made me want to curl up beside him.

I knew that look on Austin's face and he wasn't about to have words with Church. He was about to break bones.

These were two alphas, and I didn't know the rules when it came to fistfights.

"Evening, Cole," Lorenzo greeted him. "Still mad about Winnie, I see. She made a great bitch, but I had to pass her off to one of my packmates. Turns out she wasn't up to my speed."

So that's what it was about. Bad blood my ass; Cole hated Lorenzo because of girl trouble.

Austin took my left hand and held it tight as Lorenzo posed a question.

"You have no official claim on her, Cole. So tell me what your intention is?"

I looked up expectantly.

"She's *always* been my pack," Austin said in slow, threatening words. He surprised me. I thought he'd pull a Beckett and go at Lorenzo with fists flying. But he maintained his composure and stayed in control, which made him even scarier.

Lorenzo brushed his long, straight hair away from his eyes. "Tell me why a Shifter was living with a human family."

"That's why I'd like to find my father," I interrupted. "Only he knows where I came from."

Some of that fire extinguished from Lorenzo's eyes and they skimmed over me. "You don't know your real parents?"

I shook my head. Austin inched so close I could feel his body heat.

"How old are you?" Lorenzo asked.

"Twenty-seven."

Lorenzo reached in his shirt pocket and lifted a box of cigarettes, pulling one out and lighting the end with a red plastic lighter. "That's interesting."

Austin picked up on it too. The way Lorenzo said it wasn't

conversational; it was the way you sound when you know something.

"What's interesting, Church? She's not yours."

He chuckled and savored another drag of his smoke. "Perhaps she is, more than you know."

I yanked my hand free and stepped forward, feeling Austin hook his arm around my waist. "What do you mean by that?"

Lorenzo nodded, staring at the stars with a contemplative look on his face. "My uncle was a Packmaster years ago. There's a family secret we kept for a long time, but he's dead now so it doesn't matter. My aunt had a baby and then a few weeks later, she was murdered and the baby went missing. There were territorial disputes over a large piece of property at the time and two names were on the deed—my uncle's and an old friend of his. We were told the baby was found dead and my uncle buried her on that property, where our pack belonged." Lorenzo drew in a deep breath and sighed, tossing the cigarette in the grass. "One night, I overheard my father talking and found out that my aunt had been cheating on her husband—the Packmaster. The baby was not his. To add further insult, the father was a drifter from up north—not one of our people."

"What does this have to do with anything?" I said, hoping he'd get to the point.

"My father suspected he had hired someone to take out his wife and baby, then pinned it on the neighboring pack. Two problems solved. No more cheating wife and no infant to remind him of the affair, and an end to a dispute which had been going on for decades. My uncle challenged and killed that Packmaster, reclaiming his property. We sniffed around that land over the years. Never picked up the scent of a dead baby."

His eyes lowered and memorized me on the way back up.

"Uh-uh," I said, shaking my head. "You think that was me?"

"Little Talulah, all grown up."

I gasped, and Austin pulled me tight against his chest.

"She's a grown woman. I don't need to remind you of that," Austin warned.

"Alexia is ours."

"You mean… you're my *cousin*?"

The horror. Oh, God. I'd been felt up by my cousin.

Lorenzo laughed. "By family and pack, but not by blood. My father and uncle were blood relations. My aunt—your mother—was married in from another pack. She had a baby by a nobody, which makes us related, but not related."

My face heated and I looked away. Maybe we weren't really related by blood, but it still felt wrong in all kinds of daytime-talk-show ways.

"Hang on to her as tight as you want, Cole, but just remember she's a Shifter of free will until she signs with a pack. If she wants to come to my bed… then I'm not going to stop her. Goodnight, Alexia," he said with a soft growl.

I turned to Austin. "What's a Mage?"

CHAPTER 19

WHEN AUSTIN FOUND OUT ABOUT the Mage who had threatened me, he crashed on my couch. I received a brief education on some of the Breeds that lived in our world, and the Mage that was after my father had the ability to manipulate energy. Dangerous didn't even begin to describe their kind. All this was difficult to process and sometimes when you become so overwhelmed, you just learn to accept truth without explanation. What other choice is there?

Austin called Reno to review the video and apparently, he knew a guy who could do a facial-recognition scan.

Whatever that meant.

Needless to say, Austin wasn't happy when I told him I wanted the cameras out of my apartment because it was invasive. The last thing I needed was for Austin to get a call while he was having a beer, detailing how I was making out with someone. That was the downside, because thinking about a houseful of men sitting around a computer and watching me dry hump someone on the sofa was too much.

Not that I dry humped my dates, but a girl has to put her foot down when it comes to her privacy.

I woke up on the bathroom floor because I'd been afraid to sleep in the same room with Maizy. I was certain my wolf wouldn't materialize, but Austin had me paranoid about it.

"Why do you got all those marks on your arms?" I heard Maizy ask.

I rubbed the sleep from my eyes and dragged myself into the kitchen, where I poured a short glass of cranberry juice and greeted my guests with a sizeable yawn. Maizy sat on the cabinet wearing her pink unicorn nightgown, watching Austin make pancakes.

"Because I like to doodle," Austin said in a teasing voice.

Maizy giggled and I leaned over the stove. "What is that?" I glared at the misshapen batter.

"These," he said, flipping one over carefully, "are my specialty flapjacks."

"He's making me a kitty," Maizy explained excitedly.

I glanced at the batter again and noticed the tail. "Very sweet."

"Looks better than your dragon."

I narrowed my eyes and shoved his arm. "Austin Cole, you leave my dragon alone. I was five when I made that cup and you're how old? I think my artistic abilities excel in comparison." I leaned over the pan and touched the ear. "It's all crooked."

He snatched my wrist. "It's a work of art. Why don't you put on some clothes?"

There it was again—that husky morning voice oozing with sex. It made me want to snuggle against him. Sometimes I wondered if there was a power in his voice because he was an alpha.

"It's my house," I argued. "If I want to prance around in my underwear, I will."

Maizy giggled and when she started humming the kissing in a tree song, I lifted her off the counter. "Go watch cartoons, sweetie."

She jogged into the living room clutching a little stuffed dog I kept around for her. Maizy also had her own drawer of clothes for her visits, although Auntie Naya had a whole wardrobe for that child. Naya treated her like a girly girl and Maizy adored her. The last time they went swimming, Naya bought her a pair of pink sunglasses shaped like two hearts. Maizy wore them for two weeks until they finally broke when she fell asleep with them on.

Austin scooped up the pancake and put it onto a plate. "You want me to make you one?"

I cracked a smile. "You want to cook me breakfast?"

While wearing no shirt *and* doing his infamous lean against the wall, holding a spatula in his right hand. He had great arms. Cords of muscle that roped around, but not the kind my meathead ex had with the bulging veins. Austin was built like a man should be, all the way down to the V-cut that peeked out of his jeans, which were slung low on his waist.

Damn, that lean.

I grabbed the pitcher of batter and made an attempt to do something creative in the pan.

Austin came up behind me and peered over my shoulder. He took my hand and guided the drizzle that shaped into a snake. Then I realized he was trying to do his own rendition of my version of a dragon.

"Cut it out," I said with a soft laugh. He used a knife to shape the legs. His left hand slid around to my stomach as his chin rested on my right shoulder. Then his breath grew heavy and he suddenly stepped back.

Austin tossed the knife into the sink and raked his hands through his hair. "You're right," he said. "You can't stay at my house. Not right now."

I turned off the burner and moved the pan. "I'm glad we see eye to eye. What's really bothering me this morning is what Lorenzo said. I don't know anything about pack rules, but why would his uncle have murdered his wife?" Then I thought about it. "My *mom*."

Austin had a pensive stare that made me uneasy. "The greatest shame on an alpha is for his woman to go to another man's bed. Having his baby? Even worse."

"Divorce?"

"It's not the same with us as it is humans. When we choose a mate, we mate for life. Some alphas have more than one mate, and that's their prerogative, but loyalty is expected on both ends."

"He's hardly loyal if he has more than one wife."

"If it's consensual, it's loyalty. If he strays outside of his females, it's infidelity. His pack won't respect him if his woman doesn't."

"That's really scary, Austin."

"It goes on in the human world," he said indifferently. "It's not commonplace, but I see his motive. Had it been proved, he would have been put to death. That would have shamed his entire pack, so maybe that's why they covered for him and kept it a secret."

I stared at his abs and began daydreaming about how close

Lorenzo was to having his way with me. My mind drifted back to what the Mage said about Wes. Austin had taken care of the killer years ago, but not the man who put a hit on him. And if my father stole diamonds, why did he come back? My head was swimming.

"Did you hear me?"

"Huh?" I glanced up at Austin's messy bedhead as he was raking his fingers through it. He yawned and casually leaned against the sink.

"I was just asking if I could take you to The Pit for dinner. It's been a while since I've gone there and I'd like to take your mind off all this. You got nothing to worry about with your mom; I trust Ivan will keep to his end of the deal. We can talk about old times."

Then I got nostalgic. Me tagging along with Wes, Austin, and two more of their friends one Friday night at The Pit. I felt like I was part of the cool crowd. Wes had this thing about keeping his cigarettes under his shirtsleeve and when we sat at the table, I snatched the box and pulled out a cigarette. It broke when Wes grabbed it from my hand. His friend Randy complained, "What are you, her dad? Let her have it. She's a big girl."

So Wes let me have my first cigarette. He admitted later on he wanted me to get sick smoking it so I'd never pick another one up again, which is why he kept telling me to take another long puff. It worked. Fifteen minutes later, I ran outside and threw up by a newspaper stand. Then I started to cry. I was only fourteen at the time, but I felt humiliated in front of his friends.

I crouched down on the curb, hugging the yellow stand and crying relentless tears. I was too embarrassed to go back inside and I had no other way home. All I could think about was hearing them laugh as I bolted from the table, and it burned me because for a split second, I thought they had accepted me. Stuff like that's a big deal when you're a teenager—it's your whole world.

There was one person who didn't laugh.

I'd made it two blocks when Austin pulled up in his Camaro. He helped me inside the car without saying a word and drove me home. I'd always assumed Wes had sent him after me, but now I wasn't so sure. In retrospect, there were a number of memories I had of Austin looking out for me, I just never thought of it that way at the time.

"Well?" Austin asked, setting the spatula on the counter and wiping up a splatter of pancake mix. "Unless you'd rather go somewhere else."

"I need to find out if Naya can watch Maizy for a few hours."

"Bring her," he suggested. "If they still have crayons at the table, she'll have something to do."

"No, I'd rather her stay with Naya. I won't be able to talk to you about certain things with her there. She's been asking where her mommy is and I don't have an answer. I just don't know what to say."

Maizy suddenly ran into the kitchen half-dressed with her blond hair in wavy tangles. Her pea-green summer dress was open in the back due to a stubborn zipper.

"Lexi, can you fix me?"

"Sure, sweetie. Turn around."

"Can we go to the pool?" she asked hopefully.

"No, not today. You don't have a bathing suit."

I knelt down and straightened out the fabric. "What time did you want to go out?"

"Where are we going?" Maizy asked.

"Not you. You're going to stay with Auntie Naya tonight while me and um…" I started thinking about all these aunts and uncles and how confusing that was going to be for her. "Mr. Cole and I are going to go out and talk about grown-up things."

The zipper got stuck and I tugged it a few times, but a stubborn thread was wrapped around it.

"Here, let me try," Austin said. He knelt down and as he grabbed the zipper, he froze.

"I like Auntie Naya," Maizy went on. "She's pretty, and so is Misha even though she hides from me."

"What's wrong, Austin?"

He was staring at her back. "What's this?" he asked in a whisper, pointing to a mark on her shoulder blade.

"It's a birthmark, silly."

He leaned in and looked closer, rubbing the pad of his thumb over it. "I've seen that pattern before. That's no birthmark." Austin yanked up the zipper and Maizy took off.

"What was that about?"

Austin stood up and covered his mouth. His eyes were sharp and wide.

I shoved his chest, coaxing him to talk.

"I met an old woman when I was up in Wyoming. She was one of the ancients—a Chitah."

"What the hell is a Chitah?"

"It's not just Shifters out there, Lexi. Chitahs live much longer than we do and while they don't shift, they have an animal spirit within them. The woman had the same exact mark on her wrist."

"So?"

"Some are born into the Breed, but not everyone. Humans can be transformed into a Mage or a Vampire if chosen, but the rules are pretty cut and dry. Breed can't have babies with humans. She told me she was once a human, which is impossible because a Chitah is *born* into their race. She said there are a rare group of humans called Potentials, and there's something special about their DNA. She didn't seem to know much more than that, other than they all carry the same exact mark."

"I don't get it; so she shares the same mark."

"This changes everything," he murmured.

Now he was really freaking me out. I stepped closer until we were just an inch apart. "Changes what? Don't scare me with some old wives' tale."

"Maizy has the ability to absorb Breed DNA and fuse it to her own." He looked down at me and I still wasn't getting it. "When she's a woman of age and beds a man, the first Breed male she takes in, she'll *become* that Breed. No take-backs. If she stays with human men her whole life, she'll be nothing more than a human herself. What that means, Lexi, is if Maizy sleeps with a Mage, she's going to become a Mage. If she sleeps with a Shifter, she'll become a Shifter."

Now we were both pacing in small circles and cursing under our breath. "Why isn't this common knowledge?" I asked.

"I'd never heard of it until I met the old woman, but some of the ancient ones know about it. There's always rumors floating around and half of them are bullshit. Or so I thought. The old woman said Potentials come from human parents, and she thought somewhere way up in the line, there must have been a crossover of some extinct species. She was a little batty, so she had a lot of theories I had to listen to."

"Then maybe she was crazy and—"

"It's the *same* mark. It can't be a coincidence. Do you want to take that chance?"

My stomach turned and I stepped back, gripping the handle to the oven door.

"You'll have to tell her what she is when she's older, Lexi. It wouldn't be fair to her not knowing what she could become, but it has to remain a secret." Austin placed his hands firmly on my shoulders and backed me against the wall. "*No one* can know. Not even your mother. There are Breeds that can't have or make one of their own. She would even be appealing among Shifters or Chitahs because she doesn't know the rules or how women of that Breed behave, so a deviant man would find her… trainable," he almost growled.

"I won't say anything," I promised. "But can you do me a favor and stop springing all this *life-altering shit on me, Austin!*" I shrieked.

That was it. I'd finally had more than I could take and flew out of the room to take a shower and curse as I gave myself an angry shampoo.

◦◦⌖◦◦

Naya was a gem and agreed to watch Maizy for the day. I actually felt more safe with her over there than in my apartment; McNeal didn't seem to know about Maizy, so it kept her out of danger. Naya had a day planned of movies, pizza, and shopping.

I drove to Sweet Treats to check on April and see how she was holding out on her own. It was over a hundred degrees outside and I dressed for it in my jean shorts, long T-shirt, and a pair of flip-flops. When I opened the door, a cool breeze didn't smack me in the face like it usually did. It was sweltering, and April was on her knees with her hands in a canister, lifting a gooey mess and chucking it into a trash can.

As her eyes floated up, she wiped her brow with her forearm and her lip quivered.

"What happened?" I scanned the room and couldn't believe the disaster before me. Half the canisters were empty with smears of melted candy on the plastic as well as the floor.

And April, for that matter.

"Charlie didn't pay the electric bill and they shut it off."

"What?" I gasped. "Can they even do that?"

"Apparently, they can." She glanced around and wiped her hand on the apron. "I managed to move some of the candy, but I didn't have any place to take it. The pizza shop next door didn't have any cooler space and I couldn't put them in the car," she said, throwing her hands up in surrender. April's stylish hair was streaked with pink and chocolate. It was sticking out on one side and her face was red with sweat dripping down her temple. "Now it's just a race to get them out of the canisters before they make an even bigger mess for me to clean up."

"Did you call Charlie?"

"He's not answering."

"When did this start?"

April shrugged. "I don't know. Bridget called in sick, so I came in around noon to open up shop. The store felt like the freaking jungle, so maybe it went out last night?"

I reached around to my back pocket and pulled out a band, tying my hair up in a ponytail. I was going into crisis mode. We had a candy war on our hands and time was of the essence.

"The candy can't be salvaged," I said. "He'll have to take the loss. What you need to do is start ordering more inventory. Tally up how much we need, because we're going to want to make sure we can quickly restock our supply when the power comes back on. I can't afford to cover the bill for Charlie, so I'm going to drive to his house and see what's going on. Leave the candy. Once the air comes back on, we'll drop the temperature so the candy re-hardens. It'll be easier to pull it out instead of you contending with ten gallons of taffy."

April had a bright laugh—like wind chimes—but she was a

control-freak and didn't handle chaos very well. One of the canisters tipped over as she stood up.

"I'll put a sign on the door and cancel our orders," she said. "Maybe some of them will reschedule, but I seriously doubt it."

"I wonder how much those canisters cost," I murmured, deciding they were probably ruined. "Do me a favor and open up the doors. Put the sign up that we're closed. Call the girls and tell them we need them on standby. I really don't want everyone in here dying of a heatstroke, but if it cools down later tonight, we can start cleaning up."

April got out her phone and a list of contacts she kept under the counter.

"Uh-uh," I said, taking her wrist. "Change of plans. Lock up the store and go cool down at the pizza place while you make your calls. Order a few glasses of water and *do not* overwork yourself. Your health is more important than all this."

After she washed her hands in the bathroom, April closed Sweet Treats and I stood out front and called Austin to inform him of what was going on. He wanted me to keep in touch and let him know where I was because he expected to hear news from Ivan today.

April staggered up the hot sidewalk like a zombie, and I hopped in my car and headed over to Charlie's house. I'd been there a couple of times for barbecues and had once picked up his mail when he traveled out of town. He lived fifteen minutes away from the shop and when I pulled up to his small, two-bedroom house, something immediately caught my attention.

Several newspapers were scattered across the brown grass.

I picked one up and noticed the date. I began tossing them onto his porch and rang the bell. After a third ring, I walked around the house and peered into the windows, but the drapes were all closed and it was hard to see anything. The garage door was down, so I couldn't tell if he had gone out of town.

"You lookin' for Charles?"

A woman in her sixties stood on the edge of the driveway, watering her grass with a green water hose in an attempt to save her dried-up lawn. She had a southern drawl and a scratchy voice that sounded like a cat squalling.

"Yes, ma'am. He's my boss. Have you seen him?"

A ring of sweat circled beneath the armpits of her blue shirt. She was clearly a woman who didn't give a damn about water restrictions as she sprayed water on the dirty driveway. She scratched her curly hair, dyed a pale blond, and sprayed another patch of dead grass.

"He's been sick with cancer. I saw the ambulance here the other night and Lord knows what happened to that man. I don't think he's got any family that I know of, except an older woman who came by a few times. I think she's his sister because her license plate said Ohio. I don't know who else would drive all the way from Ohio to Hell, unless it was for family."

Cancer? I knew Charlie hadn't been feeling well lately, but I had no idea how serious his condition was. "Do you know what kind of cancer? How long has this been going on?"

She pursed her lips. "I reckon a year or two, maybe more. He mentioned it to Daryl once but didn't say what kind, just that he was getting those treatments. Charles told us his hair was thinning and he bought himself one of those rugs." She chuckled and sprayed a leaf into the grass. "Ugliest damned thing I ever saw."

"What hospital?"

"What do I look like, the news channel? I just saw the ambulance come in and drive off. Haven't seen him since."

When I got back to my car, I turned down an old Foreigner song and dropped my head against the steering wheel. "*Cancer*," I whispered. Had I known, I would have visited him, brought over dinner, and helped Charlie out with any errands he needed done. We were probably stressing him out with work-related calls when he needed someone to take care of him. Charlie didn't have a family to look after him, and was only in his late fifties.

The rest of the afternoon, I ran errands that were long overdue, including a visit to my mom's house to check her mail and make sure her bills were taken care of.

I shivered and slid the thermostat up to eighty. No sense in having cold air blowing in an empty house. I grabbed a small bag for Maizy and then stuffed a few of Mom's clothes into a separate bag.

I wasn't about to prepare for the worst, even though I sat quietly in her bedroom, staring at a picture of us on her dresser.

I packed her root touch-up because she dyed her hair blond and the last time I talked with her, she had mentioned her roots were showing her age again. I didn't know what she was talking about. She could let her hair go grey and she'd still be the prettiest woman I knew.

The only thing that had changed was I could no longer look forward to looking like her when I grew up.

CHAPTER 20

"JOURNEY? THEY'RE REALLY BREAKING OUT the oldies," I said with a nostalgic smile. Classic rock still dominated the playlist, and not much had been upgraded at The Pit since my last visit. Best barbecue joint in town and it hadn't changed in all these years. The walls were the color of the sauce and still decorated with wooden wagon wheels, knotted ropes, and antlers from a dead animal. I never liked staring at animal parts nailed on a wall because the last thing I wanted was to be reminded of what I was actually eating.

Austin lifted the yellow plates off the tray and set them on the wooden table. I had sent him on a mission to order my dinner because I was curious if he would remember what I liked.

"I don't know how you can eat that," he remarked, wrinkling his nose at my plate.

I popped the fried okra in my mouth and grinned. "Because okra is good for you."

"Deep fried?"

It was bustling in here. The families had already vacated and the atmosphere changed, becoming more rowdy. Several groups of single teenage girls sat in clusters while the guys spun around in their seats, whistling and flirting with them.

Some things never change.

I took a bite of my rib and wiped my hands on the paper towels they put on the table. I tapped my finger against the edge of my plate, looking around the room.

"Something wrong with your food?" he asked, eyeing my hand.

Austin had rolled his short sleeves over his shoulders because the ceiling fans did nothing to cool things down. A few of the women were gawking at him, and the tats were working in his favor.

"I hope you know all the women in here are sizing you up for dessert," I pointed out while sipping my draft.

Austin laced his fingers together with a lazy grin spreading across his face. "I hadn't noticed."

On cue, a woman's black heels clicked on the floor and stopped at our table, just to my left.

"Well, well, Austin Cole. Been a long time since I last saw you, honey. I hardly recognized you with all the tattoos."

There was a soft vibrato in her voice—the kind a woman uses for dirty talk, which must have been on her mind by the way she slowly twirled her necklace between her fingers. I didn't have a clue who she was, but I wondered if the two of them had been intimate, because his eyes slid up her body and met with hers as if he were remembering something.

"Life's treating you good, Bonnie. You still live around here?"

She jutted her hip in the painted-on jeans that threatened to rip apart if she bent over.

"Mmmhmm. Just up the road a ways. Where you been hiding all these years?"

I began to feel invisible, because Bonnie was hitting on Austin like I was nothing more than restaurant décor. It shouldn't have bothered me as much as it did, but I stopped eating and looked out the window.

"Had to get away and live a little," he answered.

"I'd love to hear all about it," she said with a lift in her voice. "I remember when you used to come in here with those troublemakers back in high school. Shoot, I can't even remember their names anymore."

And then, all of a sudden, Austin's hand slid across the table and rested on mine. He still kept his eyes on hers, engaged in conversation, but he held my hand and stroked my fingers with his thumb. A flush of heat touched my cheeks and I turned to look at Bonnie and caught her smoky eyes staring at our hands.

"Did you ever settle down?" he asked. "Kids?"

Which threw a wet towel on her parade of whoredom. "I married a few times, but I just got the one kid. He's with his grandma now. You got kids?"

"Seven," Austin replied with a straight face.

"Lord have mercy, you're kidding me!" She looked horrified.

"Always wanted a football team," he said with a wink. "Just divorced the wife, so I'm looking for someone to fill that spot and help me achieve my dream. Are you a team player, Bonnie?"

I spit out my beer and quickly set my glass down before I spilled it.

"Good running into you, Austin. I've heard of sacking the quarterback, but I think that's a little bit much for me. Good luck at the playoffs," she said, clearly not amused.

Bonnie sauntered off and the heat from Austin's hand was the only thing that registered in my brain. I don't even think I heard the music playing until Austin sat back in his seat, shaking his head at Bonnie as she strutted her stuff right out the door.

I chewed off a few bites of my rib and wiped my fingers with the paper towel again, deciding it was better not to ask him why he'd held my hand. Obviously, he wanted Bonnie to think he was taken so she'd clear out. Austin resumed devouring his rack of ribs. Except men didn't hold theirs daintily like women did, using their fingertips. He held them caveman style.

Maybe it was strategic so he could sexily turn up his hand and slowly suck off the sauce from his thumb.

Or maybe I had an overactive imagination and shouldn't have been noticing such a thing.

"Seven?" I asked.

His black lashes winked over his wolfish blue eyes. "Wishful thinking."

I was seconds away from bringing up the topic about my boss when I remembered April sitting in a pile of taffy. A laugh began to bubble. Then there was my mother and sister being kidnapped, staying in a house full of strange men, realizing I was a Shifter (and going into heat, no less), discovering my brother was a murder victim, and then my father being a criminal on the run for diamond theft.

My unbelievable life finally erupted into a burst of maniacal laughter. It graduated only briefly to the infamous Beaker laugh before tapering off into tears. Austin watched me with apprehension, because nothing was funny. He must have sensed it was one of those moments when a person has a very public display of a nervous breakdown. A few people turned to look, but he ignored them.

"You okay? Shit, I'm really sorry, Lexi. I haven't been the most sensitive person with everything going on." He set down his rib and wiped off his hands. "Ivan should be calling me tonight. He said if I didn't hear from him by midnight, then either he was dead, or Hell had finally frozen over."

"I hope so," I said.

"He'll find her," Austin reassured me. "And if he doesn't, I'll find her myself."

"I think my boss is sick," I finally said, taking a long sip of my glass of beer. "A neighbor said he has cancer and went to the hospital. That's why the bills haven't been paid on the store. I didn't know it was that bad."

He sighed, rubbing his clean-shaven jaw. The talisman around his neck was tucked inside his white shirt and he had styled his hair handsomely. He still looked like he could drag anyone in the parking lot and kick their ass, but I didn't see that side of him when I looked into his eyes. I just saw Austin.

I still wanted to mess up his hair with my fingers.

"Don't worry about the store. I sent the twins over to clean up."

"You what?"

"You shouldn't be doing all that work yourself." Austin glanced at his watch. "They'll be there until one o'clock and then head back to the house. I keep a tight watch on my pack." He turned his fork between his fingers and set it down. "Don't look at me that way, Lexi. Just accept my help."

And I did. I accepted it because at this point, my only support system was a bra. "Thanks. I hope April knows what's going on; she might have a problem with two strange men showing up to clean."

"Shouldn't be a problem," he said, eying my plate. "They took Ivy with them. Women are more trusting when another woman is around."

"Lovely. You sent Ivy into a sweatshop environment to scrub a dirty floor? She's really going to want to stay with you now," I said sarcastically.

The coleslaw was just as good as I remembered and I must have cleaned it off my plate in five scoops.

"Never did know where you put it all," he murmured, setting down his fork.

"Well, you can probably tell now. I've put on a few since you last saw me."

He snorted and stuffed a roll in his mouth. "In all the right places."

There was that tingle again.

I wrapped my lips around the prongs of my fork and looked up. Austin wasn't just watching me, his eyes were glued to my mouth, and I became self-conscious when a piece of cabbage stuck to my bottom lip. My hand flew up to cover my mouth and the awkward moment passed. The music changed over to a song by Pink ("Try," I think it was), and a paper wrapper from a straw sailed by us and landed on the floor.

Austin smiled nostalgically and rapped his knuckles on the table to the beat of the song, lost in his thoughts. "This is nice," he finally said.

"Yeah."

I think I knew what he meant. We were always linked by Wes, and it was getting easier to be together without his ghost hovering between us.

We talked about old times and I asked stupid things like if he still had his old leather jacket and why didn't he join a rock band with Jericho. Austin could carry a tune, but he said it wasn't his thing. Now that he was a Packmaster, his responsibility was maintaining stability within his family and the Shifter community. They would get jobs and help bring in money as well as assisting other packs as needed, but Austin had acquired a lot of money from his jobs over the years. Evidently, his work paid well. Money wouldn't last forever, so he encouraged them to find something they enjoyed doing. Jericho sang, Denver worked as a bartender four nights a week, and Reno... well, Austin didn't mention what exactly Reno did. Ben and

Wheeler were out of work and looking.

After another tall glass of beer and a few sips of Austin's root-beer float, I decided it was time for us to head home.

"Big girl's room," I declared with an impish grin.

Austin chuckled and stretched his arm across the seat, watching me get up. He might have been sly about stealing glances, but I noticed his eyes sliding down to my ass. As I walked by him, I bent over and squinted. My face was numb, one of the telltale signs I'd had too much to drink.

"You have something... right *here*," I said, tapping my chin with a lazy smile on my face.

A sexy smirk tugged at the corners of his mouth. "Then lick it off," he teased.

Never one to turn down a dare, I bent forward and sucked on his chin. In my defense, I was drunk. I would never have done anything like that in a sober state of mind, but the tingly feeling of beer slid through my body and made me lose those inhibitions. It also shocked the hell out of Austin because I felt his entire body tense up, which I noticed because my hands were resting on his hard biceps.

I moved my mouth slowly, swirling my tongue over the dab of sauce, and suddenly there was a moment, even if only a brief second, where something fired up between us. His bristly chin had the first hint of stubble, the tang of barbecue sauce awakened my taste buds, and his shallow breath heated my cheek.

Had a sharp wolf whistle across the room not snapped me out of it, I might have even slid my lips over to his... just to see what would happen.

Austin was real smooth about it, too. When I pulled back, he lifted his left arm and touched my nose, dabbing a dollop of sauce on it. Maybe he was being funny, or maybe it was a dare on his part, but I wiped it off and left the table before discovering what base I could get to with Austin and a bottle of barbecue sauce. He laughed and stretched back in his seat.

Damn. He still had a great laugh.

I went to the restroom for a very long pee and decided okra and beer got along. In fact, they were so in love they were doing the tango and making me queasy. The bathroom also served as a temporary hiding place since my slutty behavior planted serious doubts I could ever look him in the eye again. I never behaved that way with other men, but something about Austin drew out a sexually aggressive side that made me want to slap myself.

I'd never felt so conflicted with a man as I did with Austin. Part of that had to do with the fact our relationship was wrapped up in years of history, combined with years of separation.

Still, it *was* a fantastic dinner and had almost felt like a date. He took my mind away from all the worry and stress about my mother, and somehow I just knew he would make sure everything turned out okay. The strange part was how quickly my perception of Austin was beginning to change. He continued stepping up to help through every situation and never asked for anything in return.

Not a kiss, not a check, not a single favor.

He'd matured into the most selfless man I'd ever met.

I emerged from the restroom marked "Cowgirls" and stared at our empty booth. Then I spotted Marcy Robertson, the former head cheerleader at my old high school. I hid my face and dashed toward the front door before she noticed me. Those chance meetings were so uncomfortable because I had to explain what I did for a living. It was like a competition to see who had succeeded in life. Most of the girls knew who I was back in high school, even if I wasn't the most popular, because they all used to crush on Wes.

The balmy June air smelled clean compared to the heavy aroma of grilled meat from inside the restaurant. I glanced around and wondered where he parked the car, because when we got here, Austin had dropped me off at the door so I could get a good table.

I stepped down on the curb and took a seat—my beers had been served in tall glasses and I had always been a lightweight when it came to drinking. My eyes were losing focus and God, how embarrassing was that? Here was Austin, trying to show me a good time, and now I was sitting on the curb because I couldn't hold my liquor.

Still, I'd had fun. Hanging out and talking with Austin was so effortless now. He could spin a good yarn, and he attentively listened as I filled him in on some of the things I'd done in the past few years.

While we still felt like strangers, an indefinable intimacy existed between us—one that happens with those who have seen you at your worst and remember you before all the big events in life happened.

A car engine prowled closer from the street entrance, growing louder by the second. My eyelids drooped and I closed my eyes, deciding I was going to crash on the sofa when I got home.

And then I blacked out.

The minute Lexi closed the bathroom door behind her marked "Cowgirls," Austin slid down in his booth and rubbed his face.

Holy shit. He hadn't felt so alive by a woman's mouth on him since he kissed her seven years ago. All that time he wondered if he had built up their kiss in his mind to something it wasn't. Even the brief interlude in Jericho's bed didn't confirm anything because he'd just woken up and wasn't thinking straight.

No, now he knew it was more than the kiss. It was *her*.

Austin had thought it was going to be tough going back to The Pit—facing all the old memories of him and Wes bonding the way friends do. Losing Wes nearly broke him. But it felt good going back to their old hangout, like he was putting to bed all that anger he had carried with him over the years. Everyone has that one place from their youth that transports them back to an earlier time. The Pit was that place. It's where they'd scoped out girls, talked about muscle cars, and where they fell in love with old-school rock instead of the current stuff on the radio. It was a rustic joint with personality, ambiance, and initials with hearts surrounding them carved on the wooden tables. It was the kind of place you could smoke a cigarette and no one would say anything as long as you kept it hidden.

After cleaning their plates, he decided to bring the car around front and save Lexi the walk of drunken shame. Austin smiled, thinking about how she had asked him to order her dinner. "*I trust your choice,*" she'd said, which was code for, "*I want to see if you really remember a damn thing about me.*"

Of course he did. He even knew she liked a cup of sauce on

the side to dunk her roll in. Why he remembered stuff like that was crazy, but he'd thought about her a lot over the years.

Except in those thoughts, he'd imagined Lexi had already settled down with a man and had kids. Her being single made no sense to him. Then again, it was for the best considering she was a Shifter. He also noticed nothing had changed in regards to how men's eyes were all over her. Lexi had always possessed a natural beauty and he didn't think the Shifter allure was behind every roving eye.

When Lexi rose from the table and bent over to mess around with him, Austin's eyes skated to the left and caught a guy checking out her ass. That's when a possessive feeling took hold, but it didn't make him want to pound the guy's face in like he might have ten years ago. Austin wanted to grab her ass and claim her as his woman, just to rub it in.

Funny how being around her made him feel young and stupid again.

He even let her talk for five minutes with a piece of coleslaw stuck to her cheek because he thought she was too damn cute to spoil the mood by embarrassing her. He was afraid she'd eventually discover it and scold him for not telling her, so he'd cleverly pinched her cheeks in the middle of a conversation about how Wes used to call her chubby cheeks when she was a toddler. The topic was a diversion that allowed him to brush the coleslaw away without her knowing.

Austin wouldn't allow their night to be tainted with bad memories. He remembered all too well an incident when she was a young teenager that left her crying on the curb outside The Pit. Some of Wes's friends were real dicks and teased Lexi a lot, but what she didn't know was that they did it because they liked her. They just didn't want Wes to find out.

Austin twirled his keys around his finger as he walked out of The Pit. He thought about how amazing Lexi's slim legs looked in those Capri pants and liked that casualness about her. Not once during their talks did he think about Wes, and wasn't that a strange thing?

When Bonnie had come up to their table and hadn't mentioned Wes, it had become the elephant in the room. He knew damn well she remembered who Wes was because she dated him for about a month. It must have stung Lexi to hear that. *Everyone* knew those two were best friends. When he saw her gazing somberly out the window, he reached out and took her hand. Maybe she didn't understand why, but he wanted to console her. It felt instinctive.

When Austin walked outside after their meal, he closed a chapter of his life. It was time he found a new joint to create memories. Maybe the Dairy Queen where he first saw Lexi the day after he arrived in town, or the bar where Denver worked. It was time for change.

He lifted his chin and scoped the parking lot, jingling the coins in his pocket. Something felt off. An icy chill skated across his skin and the metallic tang of adrenaline settled on his tongue. Instead of walking directly to his car, he dodged around the back end of the building and approached it from behind.

That's when he saw Beckett standing by his Dodge Challenger, holding a wooden baseball bat in his hand.

⎯⎯⎯⎯⎯◦◦◦⎯⎯⎯⎯⎯

"Wake up, Nashoba."

I wrinkled my nose at an unfamiliar scent, rubbing my eyes and peering through my lashes. Animal fur covered me and I looked around to find myself in a stranger's bed. Lorenzo was standing beside me with his brown arms folded. Directly over the bed, a large mirror captured my stunned reaction.

I scrambled beneath the covers, fearing I had shifted and was lying naked beneath his silk sheets. Thankfully, my Capris and stretchy tank top were still accounted for.

A smile curved up one cheek and he lifted his brows. "You growl a little in your sleep."

I sat up, looking at my surroundings. "Where am I?"

"My home."

"And why am I in your bed?"

Then his face tightened so that his cheekbones appeared to be carved out of wood and his lips pressed into an angry line. "Because that alpha you were with left you alone—intoxicated and passed out in a parking lot. If you were in my pack, Alexia, I would never leave you unprotected. I make sure my women are properly looked after."

I ripped the blankets away and rubbed my eyes.

Wow. Lorenzo was loaded. The canopy bed had four posts with detailed designs carved into the wood. Native American artifacts and paintings decorated the spacious room. The ceilings stretched higher than fifteen feet, the floors were polished wood, and the window view made it seem like we were in the treetops.

His bedroom alone was a fully functional apartment, equipped with a small bar, a sitting area with cozy chairs, and a fancy bathroom farther down on the right. All I could make out was an oversized Jacuzzi with two steps to get in. But what really made the whole thing breathtaking were the windows that lined the walls in front of me, all the way down to the Jacuzzi. The golden light of sunrise shimmered on the glass.

Lorenzo played statue on my left by the door, watching my appraisal of his living accommodations with avid curiosity. Then I saw one of those fancy hotel carts with silver trays and food on it.

"Why did you bring me here?" I hopped out of bed, looking for my shoes.

"You would have rather I left you passed out in the gutter?"

"Austin was coming for me."

"And how do you know this?"

My hands rested on my hips and I carved him up with an intolerant glare. "Why are you trying to plant doubts in my head? I know Austin better than you do, and he was coming for me."

Lorenzo nodded and walked around the bed. "Ah, but I was *there* for you."

"To show off your swanky place? Sorry, it doesn't erase the fact you're my *cousin*," I murmured, lifting the covers and looking under the bed. "Where are my shoes?"

"If you keep saying that, I'm going to take you to my father and have him explain why we're not related by blood," he said in a clipped tone.

"No," I almost shouted. "I'm not meeting your family. Tell me what you did with my shoes because I have to go home."

"Home to what?"

I shoved his chest. "My baby sister, you idiot! I left her alone all night with my neighbor."

The humor melted away from his face. "Which neighbor? I'll bring her here. Why would you leave a child with someone who is not family?" he hissed.

"Because I was kidnapped?"

He lifted his phone and dialed a number. "It's Church. You know the young wolf's apartment you're watching? Her neighbor—"

I snatched the phone and hung up. "Don't you dare send one of your men to get my sister! You're having me watched?" I stuffed the phone in my back pocket. "Take me home, *right now*," I said in slow words.

He chewed on his lip for a moment, considering my request. "I've had my men on you since one of them first spotted you at the cemetery. He sensed you were a Shifter and word spreads fast when it comes to rogue females."

That damn dog really *was* a wolf.

"Tell your friend the next time he chases me up a tree and tries to gnaw on my leg, he's going to end up tangling with the wrong wolf. I bite back."

Lorenzo moved forward and lowered his chin. A dark intensity flickered in his eyes. "He did *what?*"

"I guess your pack isn't so loyal, after all. If you don't give me my shoes, I'm walking home barefoot."

"Then you'll end up hiking over sticks, and I won't have that. If you insist, I will see that you're safely escorted home. But you will not be permitted to leave my house until you are well fed. There is breakfast on the tray. Use my phone to make any calls you need to." Lorenzo made no attempt to brush away the long strands of hair that fell in front of his right eye. "My home is always open to you," he said, inching closer so that our bodies bounced heat off each other. His mouth brushed against my ear. "And my bed is still open whenever your legs are open, my sweet Nashoba."

I drew in a sharp intake of air and stumbled back before he got me worked up again. There was no doubt that alphas had an undeniable magnetism that lured you under their spell.

I reached behind me, grabbed a croissant, and stuffed it into my mouth.

Lorenzo laughed heartily and cupped his hand against my cheek, patting lightly. "You are a wild little wolf. I think your spirit is what attracts me to you. Have all you want, and if there is anything you desire, let me know and I'll get it for you. When you are ready to go, I'll be downstairs."

Clever man. He brought me here to dazzle me with the luxuries he could offer. Money, a huge bathroom, and croissants. He seriously didn't know what kind of girl I was.

Although, the croissants *were* scrumptious. They had a flaky consistency with a sweet glaze, and…

"Alexia, I do hope you change your mind and consider joining my pack. You don't officially belong to anyone yet, so you are your own woman. Make the right decision. Cole lives in a shed and can offer you nothing." He slowly threaded his hair away from his face, steadily watching me. "I take very good care of my own."

I dropped the croissant on the plate and wiped the crumbs on my pants. "So tell me why you were trying to buy my junky old car?" I asked with a mouthful of pastry.

He lowered his head and crossed his arms. "To meet you. After my man spotted you, we tracked down your plates to find out who you were. We know all the Shifters in the area, and someone new stands out. I have a man who does thorough background checks, and your name showed up in the newspaper database online. You shouldn't put your full name in the paper like that."

"So I've been told," I said, licking my thumb.

It was difficult to hate Lorenzo, even though I gave it my best effort. He didn't go about any of this the right way, but deep down I could sense decency. He just had a serious issue with wanting to possess things. I didn't have a desire to be possessed by any man, only loved.

After Lorenzo left the room, the first person I called was Naya, who chewed my ear off. She had taken the night off to babysit Maizy. They'd made mini-burgers and sweet-potato fries for dinner before having a *Cinderella* movie party in the living room. I loved Naya to death. I just didn't care much for her psychotic cat. Since she had to go to work that evening, I promised I'd be over as soon as possible to pick up my Maizy.

Then the dreaded call to Austin. Maybe what Lorenzo said stuck in my head, but I was mad at Austin. But not as mad as *he* was when I used Lorenzo's phone to call him and it showed up on the caller ID.

"Where did you go?" I asked, pacing around in the room and glancing out the window at a clearing in the woods.

"I'm coming to get you."

"He's having someone drive me; it'll be quicker this way. I need to get Maizy."

"Denver is on his way to pick her up now."

"Why?"

Austin sighed. "We found your mother."

My stomach did a somersault and I sank into a brown chair. "Is she okay? Oh God, please tell me she's okay."

"She's fine. We brought her to the house and I'm not letting her go home."

"Why not?"

He paused and I could hear him rubbing his jaw. "Your father got away. He's clever; knows a lot about the Breed and how to evade us. Even has the right kinds of sprays to throw off his scent from trackers. We'll talk about it when you get home. Your mom was... not happy to see me."

"I'll be there as soon as I can."

CHAPTER 21

WHEN LORENZO FOUND OUT I was going straight to Austin's house, he insisted on personally delivering me to his doorstep. It was the first time I'd ever ridden in a Ferrari, and I might have enjoyed it under different circumstances. He said it was an Enzo and chuckled about it because that's what his friends called him for short. I thought it looked more like the Batmobile.

The car rolled to a stop in front of the house. Lorenzo exited the vehicle and walked around to open my door. He offered me his hand and I accepted it—all while Austin stood on the porch watching.

Nothing awkward about this at all, I thought.

Lorenzo corralled me against the car, but not forcefully. He cupped my cheek with his hand and brushed the pad of his thumb across my cheekbone. "Call me before the sun goes down, Nashoba. I don't like that you're in a house full of men and so close to going into heat. If Cole couldn't look out for you last night, I have little faith he can protect you with his own."

"Don't doubt Austin," I said, moving his hands away. "You don't know him. This is about a girl that you two had a thing over, but I'm not about to get caught in the middle of your testosterone war."

Austin's boots crunched across the gravel and he neared the front of the sleek black car.

The wind kicked up Lorenzo's hair and he clasped his hands behind his back.

"I want to speak to you alone," Austin demanded.

Lorenzo accepted his invitation with a simple shift of his body.

"I'd very much like to hear an explanation of why you left a female Shifter unconscious in a parking lot," Lorenzo said, lifting his chin. "You're not fit to take care of a woman, but given you have none in your pack, your inexperience comes as no surprise."

Austin flexed his jaw and straightened his shoulders just a fraction.

I stepped between the two men before declarations of love turned into declarations of war. "Where's my mom?"

"Take Alexia to her mother," Lorenzo said, backing down. "I do not wish to upset her as it is a happy day to see mother and daughter reunited. Another time, Cole."

Before Lorenzo could get inside his car, Austin captured my arms and looked me over with concerned eyes. "Did he hurt you?"

I shook my head, but secretly his words melted me just a little bit. They weren't the angry "I'm going to kick someone's ass" kind, but were spoken with sincerity. Which also made me a little mad.

"Where *were* you, Austin?"

The Enzo revved so loud I jumped, and Austin let go, glaring at Lorenzo as if he could incinerate him with his eyes. Then I noticed his bruised knuckles and pulled up his hand.

"What is this? Did you run off fighting again? And what happened to your eye?"

He was still looking me over as if he didn't believe I was unhurt. Without a word, he cupped the back of my head and pulled me to him, murmuring in my hair. "I thought I lost you. We were in public and I couldn't shift; I thought the Mage had taken you. Then thirty minutes later, Ivan called and said he had your mother. It was chaos. My brothers went to track you down and I picked up your mother to bring her home safe, as I promised. She's the one who clocked me in the eye."

I laughed against his chest. Why did I find that such a disturbingly funny mental image? My mom—of all people—punching Austin Cole.

"What happened to your hand?"

He stepped back and shook his head. "Your ex was in the parking lot when I went to get the car."

"Beckett?" I said in disbelief. "Why was *he* there? What did he say?"

"I want you to stay away from him, Lexi. He's not right in the head. We can talk about this later."

I hurried inside the house, my heart racing. The twins were in the atrium sitting in lawn chairs while a thin cloud of smoke escaped from the grill. I walked through the hallway until I reached a room with the door closed—one I hadn't been in before. I lightly knocked and pushed the door open.

"Mom?"

The walls were the color of cinderblock. Four packages of gum were lined up precisely on the black dresser to my left. Three pairs of polished boots sat against the wall, and I immediately recognized Reno's dark shades on the dresser. Tidy wouldn't be the word I'd used to describe the room, but immaculate. My mom slept with her back to me on a twin-sized bed to the right.

Without saying another word, I curled up behind her and hugged her shoulder. She shifted a little and glanced back at me.

"Lexi?" she said in a weary voice. But all I heard were my tears. Mom turned over and wrapped her arms around me.

Then everything was okay.

"Where's your sister? I need to see her; I need to make sure…"

"She's coming," I said with a sniff. "Austin sent someone to pick her up. She was staying with Naya. Are you okay? Did he hurt you, Mom?"

"No, honey." She sighed and sat up, sliding her legs off the bed. "Your father isn't the same man I once knew. He's in serious trouble and someone is after him. He said they threatened to hurt me. Your dad left us years ago because he didn't want a family after Wes died. He didn't want *me*." She rubbed away the tears with the back of her hand. "But deep down, he still loves me in his own way. He came down to protect me from whoever is chasing him. He didn't want that on his conscience."

My tone changed to restrained fury. "That man has no conscience. Why did he dump Maizy on the side of the road?"

Her blue eyes dulled and she looked down. "He doesn't think Maizy is his."

"But she is."

"Of *course* she is, but your dad always had doubts. He was in denial during those last years and didn't want anything else to tie him to this life like a new baby would. So he accused me of cheating on him. I'd never do anything like that."

"I know. You're okay?"

"After he left her on the road, I just—I completely lost it. I went into hysterics, screaming in the car and almost forcing him to wreck it. The farther away we got, the more numb I became. Oh, Lexi, I thought I'd never see her again." She held my hand and kissed the back of it. "I hit Austin in the face and broke my nail."

My mouth flew open and a burst of laughter escaped. "You never told me about your right hook. Did you see the shiner you gave him?"

She covered her face. "I can't believe I did something like that. I'm upset with him, but I didn't have any right to behave the way I did. He insisted on taking me here instead of my house and… That's just not the kind of person I am."

"Well, you're not going back home until we find the guy who's after him. It's too dangerous."

"I can't face Austin. Not after the way I behaved."

"Trust me, Mom, they've seen worse. I was just as mad, but life's too short to hold a grudge. Austin was young and we all make mistakes. You don't have anything to worry about with his brothers; they've been really good to me and Maizy."

It was a relief to have my mom back, but something was bothering me. It was the fact I was a Shifter. If my aging slowed down, she was going to eventually notice. Would she still love me if she knew what I was?

"Mommy! Mommy!" a little voice cried out from the other room. Mom hopped up and hurried out the door while I stayed behind, lost in my thoughts.

Austin came in and sat beside me, patting my leg. He kept his hand on my knee and I leaned against him, enjoying the subtle scent of his cologne.

"She'll still love you," he said, and my heart ached. "We'll have to tell her the rules about revealing our secrets, but I trust your mom. I've known her almost my entire life and I get good vibes from her." He blew out a breath and lowered his voice. "I put Ben and Wheeler to task finding a new house, or at the very least, some property we can build on. One's big and has an amazing view up high. It's modern, has a pool, and will cost me a fortune. The second one is older and used to be a hotel but was renovated years ago. The owners are old and don't have any kids to pass on their inheritance, but they haven't had any luck selling because of the location and condition of the house. It's just as big as the first one, but it needs work. It's rustic, doesn't have a pool..."

"That's the one you should take," I said decidedly.

He made a "huh" sound. "Why's that?"

I stood up and looked over my shoulder. "Because you're not Lorenzo. He would have bought the first house to show everyone up. Sometimes things that are worth having are worth fixing up. Not everything comes in perfect condition, but it doesn't mean it's not the right one for you."

When his eyes slid up to mine, my breath caught. Austin's next question had a deeper meaning we both understood.

"Which house would you choose?"

———————⊶◦⟪⟫◦⊷———————

Outside of our brief conversation, Mom had no insight as to why else my dad would have kidnapped her. Deep down, he must have loved her in some irrational way, but his reckless actions had put our lives in danger and it only fueled my hate for him even more. Now that I knew he wasn't my real father, it was easier to hate him. Because he was Maizy's, I didn't say anything out of respect, even though she didn't know him. I didn't want her to have memories of me slamming him, because one day she would find out for herself what kind of man he was.

I spent the entire afternoon with my mom, but I couldn't get the shop off my mind. Ben and Wheeler ate their hamburgers and headed out. When I asked where Ivy had gone, Austin explained he had begun the process of officially claiming her with one of the head

Packmasters in the territory, and the man's wife wanted to speak privately with Ivy.

It was sometimes customary for the women to open their door to one another, and perhaps she wanted to make sure there was nothing being forced on this young woman.

Just after sunset, I headed back home alone. Mom agreed to stay with Austin until they caught my father. While Ivan had retracted his offer to help us any further, Lorenzo hadn't ended his search. I knew because I'd kept my promise and called him earlier that day.

"How did everything go?" I asked April over Lorenzo's phone. I was beginning to think having one of these phones would come in handy. I ascended the stairs and twirled my keychain around, looking for the key.

"Um, you could have told me you were sending two hunks over."

I snorted. "Really? I didn't think they were your type."

"Well, kind of not. They're eye candy, but not really my kind of candy. One of them stared at my ass and the other guy didn't say much. The store is so clean you wouldn't believe it! Some of the canisters I'm not so sure they'll be salvageable. Have you heard from Charlie? What happened?"

I slid the key in the lock and glanced over my shoulder. "Cancer. I'm going to try calling around to see where he's at; his neighbor said they took him away in an ambulance a few days ago."

"Oh, no."

"Yeah." I sighed when I heard her sniffing over the phone. We really liked Charlie and were fortunate to have a boss like him, even though he had quirky ways about running his store. "Hopefully he's okay, but I need to get a hold of him so I can find out what to do about the power. Until then, just lock everything up and take off for a few days. There's nothing we can do at this point. We're not getting a paycheck this Friday, so you'll need to let the girls know. It's not going to hurt them as much as it will us."

"Gee, I didn't think of that. I need to be honest and tell you I might be able to let one paycheck slide, but that's it. I mean it, Alexia. And I'll need reimbursement for the missed week as soon as the funds are available."

I opened the door and flipped on the wall switch that connected to a lamp in the living room. Then I gasped.

"What happens if you can't find him? Alexia?"

"Um, April, let me call you back…" I hung up the phone.

My feet floated toward the dining room as I admired the most gorgeous flower display I'd ever laid eyes on. Seven clear vases of varying sizes were perfectly arranged in two rows, filled with red roses of such a lush shade that I drew in a deep breath and sighed. There was no baby's breath—instead, white lilies filled all the open gaps. A silver balloon hovered above the table, tied to a chair, with "Happy Birthday" written in elegant letters.

The closer I got, the more I began rubbing my eyes to make sure I wasn't hallucinating. A note was strategically placed in the center of the table, and while I should have been upset someone got into my apartment, I wasn't. My birthday was actually the next day, and the only men who knew were Austin and Beckett. This sure as hell didn't look like something Beckett would dream up.

My heart did a flutter, and I tore open the seal and pulled out the card.

Nashoba,
I could give you a garden and it would pale next to your beauty.
So let me give you the world.
Lorenzo

"Holy shit," I murmured.

No one had ever given me anything like this before, and then the note? Once the shock dissipated and I sat down, I realized that as beautiful as they were, the gift didn't floor me like it should have. Lorenzo didn't know a damn thing about me if he thought he could woo me with flowers. The note was the only thing that earned him brownie points, because you had to respect a man with a poetic heart.

Last year on my birthday, I drove with Maizy out to a diamond mine. They plowed up the dirt every so often, and you could rent a shovel and other supplies and dig in the dirt looking for treasure.

Supposedly, small diamonds were found all the time. The only thing we found were a few rocks that we brought home as souvenirs. It was the best time, and I packed a picnic lunch on the way home after picking up a few things at a local supermarket. Maizy had wanted to give me a diamond for my birthday and was upset. I reminded her that expensive things didn't make people happy, thoughtfulness did. And *she* was my diamond because I'd gotten to spend my entire birthday with her.

Still, the flowers *were* beautiful, and I wasn't about to be ungrateful for such an extravagant gift. I wondered how he managed to bypass the camera outside, but Lorenzo seemed like the kind of guy who could get away with anything. Probably had the flower delivery guy talk the landlord into letting him in.

I admired the delicate petals for a few minutes before changing clothes and pulling out the phonebook for a listing of hospitals. I made a few calls, but due to certain laws, I couldn't obtain any information since we weren't related. I collapsed on the sofa and nodded off for a few hours.

After I woke up, I tried calling a few more places. They would have admitted Charlie by now, so perhaps they'd moved him to another facility. His sister was from Ohio, but I had no idea if they shared the same last name. I had searched on the Internet but came up with too many listings. Without knowing her first name, it would have been a waste of time.

A light knock tapped on the door and it swung open. "How many times have I told you to lock your—" Naya gasped. "Honey! Who are the gorgeous flowers from?"

She practically squealed, running in short steps across my living room to the table. Naya had just gotten off work and hadn't taken off her impossibly high gold shoes.

"Someone adores you enough to send you all these? Oh, you need to marry him right this minute," she went on, burying her nose in a bouquet. After circling around the table to admire each one individually, she finally stood back and soaked it all in.

"I'm quite sure I'm not going to marry a man over a silly display of peacockery," I added.

"Pea-whatery?"

A grin slid up my cheek. "When guys think they can show you all their fancy feathers and you'll just fall at their feet."

"So he's thoughtful *and* rich?" She looked skeptical that I could reject the two things at the top of her checklist for the holy grail of a perfect man.

"He's got money."

Her eyes brightened. "How much money? I call dibs if you throw this one away, but don't you dare or I'll tie your shoelaces together and hang you from the nearest telephone wire."

She lifted the card and I tried to grab it from her.

"Lorenzo. Is he Spanish? I love Spanish men."

"You love *all* men."

"Italian?" she asked hopefully.

"No, I think he's Native American."

———◦◦❧◦◦———

It didn't sit well with Austin when Lexi went home alone. While there were still surveillance cameras, he couldn't get to her quick enough if something happened, and they weren't watching her twenty-four hours a day. Worry nestled in his head like a seed and began to take root until he finally told the boys he was heading out there for the night. He didn't plan on going up to her apartment, just sleeping in his car and keeping an eye on things.

During the drive, he thought about her situation at the store and located another candy shop in town. He talked with the owner about cost-related factors and inventory. Then he noticed an enormous display of suckers. They were Lexi's favorite—round and colorful with an assortment of flavors from watermelon to gourmet coffee. A mischievous grin surfaced because Wes had once revealed how he bribed his baby sister.

Her birthday was tomorrow and Austin had been thinking about getting her something special. He never bought birthday gifts for anyone; it's not something the Cole brothers did. But Lexi always loved her birthdays and he wanted to do something special to make up for lost time.

"Do you make arrangements?" Austin inquired. "I mean, can you take some of these and make it look like... hell, I don't know. Something girly?"

"Certainly," the man replied with confidence. "I have several containers in the back with foam, unless you want them tied in small bundles. I can do lots of creative things with these—you'd be surprised.

"What about a bouquet?"

"I designed one for a wedding two years ago, believe it or not," he admitted with a chuckle. "Let me know what you want, or how many, and I'll put something together."

He sure did.

When Austin arrived at Lexi's apartment, he was beaming with pride. He couldn't wait to see the look on her face when he gave them to her, not just because of the way they were arranged, but no one would have thought to get her something like this.

Austin walked quietly up Lexi's stairs with the heavy bouquet in his right hand. The man had done an excellent job, somehow attaching them to a ball in the center so that they stayed in place and gave it a handle that he could hold on to. It looked just as good as any flowers, and a delicate white ribbon wrapped around the bottom. The man urged him to fill out a card, but Austin found out he had more to say than what would fit on a small note card. He ended up writing his message on a sheet of paper that was folded up and burning a hole in his back pocket.

"Lexi, these are just the most beautiful things I've ever seen!" he heard a woman exclaim through the cracked door.

Austin eased up at the entrance, holding the bouquet behind his back. He peered in and his jaw slackened when he saw the obscene amount of roses all over her table. The woman in the tall shoes he recognized as her neighbor.

"Lorenzo," Naya said, holding a card. "Is he Spanish? I love Spanish men."

"You love all men."

"Italian?"

"No, I think he's Native American," Lexi replied with her back to the door. She touched one of the flowers. "They are pretty, aren't they?"

"Pretty penny," Naya agreed. "And the note! Totally swoonworthy. I can't imagine a man topping an offer like this, Lexi. You should take it. If he's good-looking, then that's just icing on the cake, but you already have my approval," she declared, placing her hands on her hips and jutting them out.

Lexi shouldered her and they both admired the roses. Austin's nose filled with the smell of defeat and he stepped back.

One of the suckers clacked on the concrete beneath him and Naya said, "What was that?"

"You left the door open," Lexi chastised. "Always lecturing me about locking up and you get all swept up by flowers and lose your mind." They giggled and Austin quickly backed away, hurrying down the stairs.

His chest actually hurt. Like someone had a grip on his heart and was strangling the breath from his lungs. It felt like the walk of shame across that lawn as he heard the door shut behind him. Austin squeezed the handle to the bouquet even tighter and wanted to throw it, but it would have scattered a hundred suckers across the lawn, leaving evidence he had been there.

Instead, he tossed the cheap bouquet in the passenger seat and moved his Dodge Challenger into a less obvious parking space. As he watched Naya leave her apartment, Austin glanced at the candy beside him and then back at her window. The lights eventually dimmed and he rolled down the car window, wishing he had a shot of something strong.

It was a stupid idea to give her cheap candy. They weren't kids anymore and she would have been insulted.

Lexi deserved to be taken care of. There was no rule that she had to be mated to the Packmaster or anyone else in a pack in order to be part of the family. It didn't stop how fiercely protective he felt of her. How when another man's eyes roamed across her body, Austin wanted to rip them from the guy's sockets. Lexi wasn't abrasive like many of the female Shifters, and that made her vulnerable. Growing up in a pack (and within the Shifter culture), a woman learned how to talk to men and get what she wanted. Ivy was an exception with her shyness, but he could sense a tough girl beneath her quiet exterior.

His father had warned him that a pack without balance turns on itself, and women provide the harmony necessary for a family to sustain itself over the years. Austin hadn't been raised in a pack environment. His parents had forbidden them from going rogue, and the only way to leave the family unit was to join a pack or become a bounty hunter. Too many bad things happened to rogue Shifters. When Austin stepped up in his alpha role, his parents made the decision to move on. It wasn't ideal for parents to be under the leadership of one of their children.

The idea of having Lexi's family living with them, even if they weren't Shifters, was appealing. Someone also needed to protect that little girl, and he didn't have a good feeling about leaving her and her mother alone. Bringing them into the pack was exactly what his men needed to shape up.

Damn Lorenzo. Even early on, he was always a man who did anything it took to get what he wanted. Now that he was advancing on Lexi, Austin was feeling more possessive and territorial.

He turned off his radio since the noise was distracting. The CD player was a nice addition to the car. The guy who sold it to him had a gift and could have converted a car into an airplane if you gave him enough money. He'd installed a CD player along with new speakers and did a little work restoring the body to maintain the vintage appeal.

Austin slid down in his seat when Lexi emerged from her apartment and noticed a piece of candy on her doormat. She glanced around before hurrying down the sidewalk that led to the mailboxes. While she checked her mail, Austin leaned down to read his text messages, not wanting the light from the phone to draw any attention to his car. He sent one to Reno to make sure they had everything under control at the house with Lynn. After several minutes, he sat up and rubbed his eyes.

A few fireflies lit up and Lexi paused on the way back, scooping her hand in the air to catch one. He laughed quietly, eyes sliding down to her hips as she jumped in the air and the bottom of her shirt came up just enough that he could see her belly button.

Then he shifted in his seat, because the thoughts racing in his head were sending blood to all the wrong places. He needed to stop thinking about her in a sexual way.

That's when he glanced to the right and saw something out of place. An expensive Jaguar blocked the fire hydrant—a car that had no business in this thirty-year-old complex. The driver appeared to be sleeping, and knowing a Mage was hunting her father, Austin launched himself out of the car to confront him.

CHAPTER 22

FTER NAYA LEFT, I WENT to check my mail and found a lollipop outside my door. She wasn't into eating candy, so it was an odd thing to find. I shrugged it off, but on the walk back to my apartment, I stepped on something hard and bent down to pick up another one. It was my favorite brand, and I looked around in bewilderment without knowing what I was really looking *for*.

Candy Claus? Sent to deliver all the good Shifters a bucket full of sweets in the middle of summer?

I laughed and swung open my door, stepping into the living room. My bedroom light cast a dim glow in the apartment and the smell of flowers filled my nose. When I turned the first lock, a shadow moved behind me. My heart did a flip-flop and I got that prickling sensation you get when you're not alone.

"I missed you," Beckett said, wrapping his arms tightly around my body from behind.

I squirmed, trying to break free, but his pythons were constricting. He loosened them just enough so I could turn to face him.

"You're drunk," I accused, smelling it all over his breath and seeing the glazed look in his bloodshot eyes. Not to mention his eyes were bruised; someone had finally given him a dose of his own medicine.

"Like what your boyfriend did to me? See what kind of man you got? What the fuck are *those*?" Without removing his eyes from mine, he pointed his heavy arm at the roses.

My mouth wasn't working and all I could do was open it and shake my head.

"You belong to *me*, Lex. Not some pussy fucking roses man," he slurred. "You got flowers and I got eighteen stitches in the back of my head," he spat angrily.

"Those flowers aren't from him, Beckett. Please, go home and calm down. You're worked up and I don't want to fight."

His slobbery mouth kissed my cheek and his broad chest pinned me against the door so I couldn't move.

"You can't tell me what I fucking need, because I need *you*. I'll forgive your slutting around, but you tell that motherfucker you're coming home with me," he said against my cheek. "Pack up your shit; this game is over. I fucked *one* girl, big deal. I could have fucked a whole lot more if you want to know the truth. But you were always the one I wanted to come home to."

My chest tightened and the heat made it difficult to breathe, as if I'd been running a marathon. Beckett had never behaved this way toward me and I was scared, but still unsure of his intentions. I thought I knew this man. He'd never once raised a hand to me or threatened my life if I left him. Those were the Lifetime movies I'd catch on the weekend and thank my lucky stars that I wasn't with a psycho like that.

Beckett was barely lucid as his rough mouth moved across my jaw, whiskers scraping like sandpaper against my skin. His breath smelled of whiskey or something much stronger than the beers he usually preferred.

"Please," I begged, pushing against his solid chest. "Just go home and sleep it off and I promise we'll talk."

But his lips began mashing against mine in another sloppy kiss and I turned my head again—my heart pounding wildly as he pressed even tighter against me.

"Stop," I mumbled. I could feel my wolf pacing anxiously, but I shut her out because of fear.

Fear I would shift and lose control, and who knows what I'd do to him. My heart hammered against my chest so rapidly I could feel it in my throat.

"I can't breathe, Beckett. Let's not do this. We can sit down and talk it over," I offered, trying to rationalize with him.

When he didn't move, I got scared. Real scared. The kind of fear you only experience in moments when something is about to happen.

Something bad.

"You're mine, Lex. *Mine.*" His hand slid up my shirt and gripped my side, short nails digging in deep.

"No, Beckett, stop!" I pushed against him and twisted the skin on his bicep.

His hand cupped the back of my neck and he stepped to the side. With brutal force, he threw me forward as hard as he could.

I flew across the dining table and shattered two vases, sending flowers and water all over the place.

"You like your flowers now, you *bitch*?"

A vase toppled onto the floor when I turned over. I was lying in a bed of soft rose petals and shards of glass, water soaking through the back of my shirt. Beckett yanked me by my hair and slammed my head against the table. Then he grabbed my ankles and tried to drag me to the floor. I kicked so wildly he stumbled backward when my foot struck him in the groin. I didn't even think to scream; I was too busy fighting for my life.

I rolled off the table to run to the door when he swung me by the arm and I slammed against the corner of the wall. Pain sliced through my shoulder and I cried out.

The violence pouring out of him stunned me. Beckett seized my upper arms and shoved my back against the wall.

His voice broke when he kissed my cheek again. "You're my girl, Lex. We go together. You put up with my shit, and I know we could have worked it out."

Then he was crying against my face. Actual tears, and it made my legs tremble so fiercely that I came close to fainting.

Beckett had never once cried in my presence.

It wasn't the kind of tears you shed for a love lost; it was a raw emotion I'd never seen in him before.

Ominous.

When his large hands wrapped around my throat and constricted my breathing, I suddenly knew why he was crying.

"*Can't breathe, stop,*" I mouthed, trying to pull away and hit his arms. I was too weak—too dizzy. He squeezed harder and tightened his grip.

Then he let go and I gasped for sweet oxygen, falling to the floor.

"Why did you do this to us? We had a good thing and you go and date a piece of shit who gives you fucking roses! You think I couldn't have given you roses? You never *wanted* me to buy you flowers!"

He scooped up a handful of stems from the floor and hurled them across the room. I coughed, still gasping for air, feeling like I might vomit. "No… *please.*"

An obtrusive noise filled my head, but I couldn't be sure if it was my heart beating against my eardrums or something else.

Beckett fell over me and kissed my mouth so sweetly I almost didn't realize his fingers were wrapped around my throat.

"You made me do this," he whispered.

Something switched off in his eyes. The emotion evaporated, replaced by a vacant, soulless stare. I clawed at his face and the pounding at the door grew louder until I heard the crack of wood.

The last thing I saw was Austin Cole, standing in the doorway looking as handsome as ever. He'd never know how beautiful his eyes were to me—like glaciers on a cloudy day. His dark hair was wild and messed up, just the way I liked it.

But his expression was savage.

Bright flashes of light filled my vision and darkness closed in, but I knew the Grim Reaper would have nothing on the menace Austin carried in his pocket.

I let go of Beckett's face and reached out to a beautiful black wolf with my trembling arms.

And then it went dark.

Austin approached the suspicious car in Lexi's parking lot and confronted the sleeping man, ignoring his ringing phone. It was Reno's ringtone—"Thunderstruck" by AC/DC.

That's when he recognized one of Lorenzo's men, probably sent to watch Lexi. Some fucking joke as the guy was asleep on the job. They got into a heated argument and Austin abruptly stepped back and looked around. Something felt off. The hairs on the back of his neck rose up and he looked toward Lexi's apartment window.

Austin lifted his nose in the air—an alpha could pick up scents a regular wolf could not. It was nowhere near the capacity a Chitah had, but sometimes intense emotions bled into the air. Austin could taste the sting of adrenaline in the wind, blowing from the direction of her apartment.

The Shifter became a memory as Austin ran toward the stairwell. The closer he got, the more intense the feeling. Alarm ran up his spine and he leapt up three steps at a time.

That's when he heard a man shouting from inside her apartment.

Naya peered out of her door with earbuds in her ears. "What's going on?"

"Back inside!" he snapped, summoning all his alpha energy. Naya slammed the door and Austin turned the knob to Lexi's apartment, but it was locked.

One singular word almost triggered him to shift involuntarily, but he had to maintain control of his wolf or he'd never get inside.

The word was "no." Then he heard Lexi say another word that made his animal thirst for blood.

"Please."

He turned around and back-kicked the door twice, but it wasn't enough. He almost rammed it in with his shoulder but gave it another solid kick instead.

The door crashed in and the first thing he saw was red petals strewn all over the beige carpet. Then everything in his peripheral became fuzzy when he spotted Lexi lying on her back with the human on top of her, his hands squeezing her slender throat.

The throat he once tenderly caressed with his knuckles on the night Wes died. Austin had wanted to kiss Lexi at least once in his lifetime before he left town. He had dropped by to pick up Wes and when he found out he wasn't there, Lexi followed him out to his car. Maybe it was the way the warm evening wind picked up a lock of her soft brown hair, or the gentle way that she laughed when he pinched her side to make her smile. Austin knew he might never see her again. He cupped her face with his large hands and tasted her lips for the first time. She barely kissed him back, but there was something between them that felt so right. Years went by and no kiss compared.

"*You did this*," Beckett growled, oblivious that Austin had broken into the room.

Austin erupted with fury and dove forward. A shadow of black fur streaked across the air and it was a vicious attack. He gave himself up completely to the nature of his wolf, relinquishing all control.

The human never stood a chance. Austin's wolf savagely sank his sharp teeth into Beckett's throat and ripped it out. Flesh peeled back and blood poured free.

It was over in seconds.

Austin shifted back to human form and immediately crawled naked to Lexi, checking for a pulse. He wiped the blood from his face and blew a few breaths into her mouth, just to make sure she was still breathing on her own. She was, thank Christ, and the coloring in her face slowly returned.

"Still alive," he whispered, throwing on his clothes. Then he landed on his knees in front of her and cradled her head. "Lexi, I need you to shift," he said insistently. "Can you hear me?"

She was barely conscious. Alphas could force a Shifter to change into their animal, but not so much the other way around as that would require cooperation from their human. Austin summoned the Breed magic within him and whispered in her ear, "*Shift.*"

In a flash, her wolf materialized.

"I'm so fucking sorry," he said, gritting his teeth. The pain in his chest was insurmountable. So much rage that he wanted to bring Beckett back from the dead just to kill him all over again. Choke the bastard and let him get a taste of his own wickedness.

Austin scooped the wolf up in his strong arms. Her breathing was labored, but the shifting had healed her to some degree. He hustled down the stairs to his car and carefully placed her in the back seat, leaving behind Beckett's body in the destroyed apartment.

Lorenzo's man spoke frantically on his cell, shouting a few curse words. After closing the car door, Austin fired off a growl that sent him hauling ass.

Austin barely remembered the drive home. A firestorm of emotions overwhelmed him, from shame to rage, and then complete and utter devotion to this woman. In that moment, he knew with absolute certainty he wanted to protect her for the rest of his life. Whether she decided to take a spot in his pack or as his mate, it didn't matter. He was willing to die for her. If Lexi didn't make it through this, Austin would never be able to forgive himself.

His stomach twisted into a nervous knot as the wind from the open windows created a vortex within the car.

The tires skidded across the driveway of his house and Austin hopped out, opening the back door.

"What the hell is going on?" Reno shouted out.

Austin gently lifted her out and growled a warning at Reno when he stepped forward and got an eyeful.

Austin actually bared his teeth. "Get away from her," he said darkly.

"Bring her inside."

Lexi's head flopped down and she began to twist her body. "Easy, girl," he soothed in his alpha voice. She relaxed and Austin stalked toward the house with Reno following close behind.

Denver strolled along the edge of the woods with Maizy up on his shoulders. She had a jar full of lightning bugs sitting on top of his head. "Lookie, Mr. Cole! I got a bunch of 'em!"

"Denver, you two stay outside," Reno demanded before turning his attention to Austin. "What happened? I tried calling your ass and you didn't answer. I happened to check the monitor and caught a man entering her apartment, but we don't have cameras set up inside."

"Someone tried to strangle her," Austin replied through clenched teeth.

"Hope that someone is taken care of," Reno said in a chilling voice.

Lynn shrieked at first sight of the wolf. "What are you doing bringing *that* in the house?"

"Red alert, boys. We got a situation," Reno announced.

Austin gently placed the silver animal on the brown carpet spread across the center of the living room. Ben and Wheeler stepped back, and Ivy cautiously lingered in the hallway, tugging the end of her braid.

Austin searched Lexi's body to see the extent of her injuries; she needed to shift once more in order to heal. He had already tried in the car, but her wolf refused.

"Hold her back," he ordered the twins without looking up. They hooked their arms around Lynn to keep her from running—the worst thing you can do around a wolf.

Silken fur tickled his palm as he grazed his hand around her graceful neck. She whined, and it felt like a pitchfork pierced his heart.

"Lexi, *shift*," he demanded.

Three more times proved unsuccessful.

"That's not going to work," Ivy informed him. Her loose braid draped over her shoulder and the ends of her long gown swished as she took a step forward. "Do you think a woman wants a man yelling at her when she's hurt and afraid? She won't listen unless she trusts you."

"And what do you suggest I do?" He lifted his eyes to meet hers. What Austin didn't say was that he was willing to do anything.

Ivy knelt down and wrapped her arms around her knees. "Kiss her nose. Tell her she's safe. Whisper you need her back. Don't demand it, Austin. *Ask* her. Let her wolf know she's more than just another Shifter of a lower rank; make her trust you because you care about what happens to her."

In front of all his pack, Austin laid down on the floor without a second thought. He stroked her white face and nuzzled against her snout, close enough to her canines that her wolf could have taken a chunk of his face off if she wanted.

"You need to shift to heal," he whispered, stroking her soft ears back. "No one here will hurt you; I won't allow it. No one will ever touch you again."

Her glittery eyes partially opened and she whined, her tail flapping once.

Austin smiled and kissed her nose. "There's my Ladybug."

And just like that, Lexi's wolf shifted.

Nudity was not a huge deal because it was part of their lifestyle with the shifting. Austin still pulled his shirt over his head and draped it across her hips to protect her modesty. The cuts healed and the bruises on her windpipe were faded, but not completely gone.

"I don't understand. What's going on?" Lynn gasped, barely holding on to her sanity.

Austin lifted his chin. "Your daughter is a Shifter. Your husband stole her from a pack years ago after killing her mother. We can discuss this later, but right now, I need to save her life."

He turned his focus back on Lexi and she moaned, her hands beginning to slide up to touch her throat.

"No," he said, gently holding her wrists. His mouth grazed against her ear and he asked her to shift. In another split second, Lexi switched back to her wolf. Relief swelled through him, as he knew this process would work the healing magic.

Most guys didn't care about scars, so they didn't bother shifting to heal the little things. Serious injuries could be taken care of by shifting, allowing the magic to work its way through the body, as long as it was done as soon as possible. The more time that elapsed, the less likely a wound would heal through shifting. Breed magic was something remarkable without explanation.

Austin rose to his feet and confronted Lynn with the truth about her daughter. "It's imperative you never speak of this to anyone. There are consequences for revealing our secrets. This is who I am, who I've always been. This is why I couldn't stay here after Wes died, because I belong with my own kind. Lexi loves you as a mother, and I hope you can still love her as a child. But know she's a dangerous animal, and the only reason I can get so close is because she's barely conscious. Our animals are nothing to mess around with."

When he twisted around to kneel by Lexi's side, Lynn broke free from the twins and flung herself on top of the wolf.

"Don't you touch my daughter!"

CHAPTER 23

I OPENED MY EYES AND FOUND my face nuzzled in silken fur. "Oh no," I murmured. Lorenzo had somehow found me again and wrapped me up in fur blankets. Although, they *were* warm blankets. I lifted my heavy head and glanced around.

No penthouse view. I noticed a poster of Led Zeppelin on the wall and my left arm was tucked around something soft, furry, and warm. When his head popped up and he growled, I was eye to eye with a wolf.

My heart skipped and I slowly retracted my arm. The wolf flipped onto his feet and stood over me, yawning. I curled my arms, instinctively covering my neck, and then it all came back.

Beckett choking me.

I threw my arms out and slapped at the wolf's chest and head. In that moment, I didn't see a wolf—I saw Beckett. My breath quickened, my legs kicked. He merely turned his head to the side and made a grunt, taking the full beating. My panic attack subsided and I threw my arms over my face, trying to catch my breath.

He was an impressive creature. Sable black fur with the iciest blue eyes I'd ever seen, rimmed in black and staring down like two glaciers. He stood astride me with his legs on either side, sniffing my nose. I would have been willing to bet he weighed more than I did.

"I have to pee."

He seemed unconcerned with the current state of my bladder. The wolf lapped my cheek with his pink tongue. When I tried to push myself up, my weakened body refused. It was similar to the gravity you feel when you try to get out of a swimming pool after having spent over an hour in the water. I tried again and sighed in frustration.

The wolf rested his chin on my shoulder and snorted, making an impatient sound. Instinct took over and I did what might have been one of the dumbest things I'd ever done, and that was wrap my arms around a wolf's neck.

He backed up, pulling me to a sitting position. There wasn't much room on the bed, so he hopped on the floor and sat down. Thankfully, someone had dressed me in a long nightgown.

"Austin!" I called out.

The wolf barked.

"Austin!"

Then he howled. The door cracked open and Denver peered in. "What the fuck is going on in here?"

The wolf reared around and snapped at him, causing Denver to swing the door closed to just a crack.

"Denver, where's Austin? Why am I locked up in here with a wolf?"

The animal delivered a death threat with a low, thrumming growl.

"Damn, girl. You really were knocked in the head. Austin won't let anyone near you."

"Where is he?"

"In front of you."

The door slammed and my mouth opened. Austin had warned me about his wolf—how dangerous he was. I didn't doubt it, either. He was always a tough guy growing up, but the past seven years had changed him from the person I once knew. He had a fierce animal with thick shoulders, sharp canines, and savage eyes.

"Uh, Austin?"

He lifted his eyes to mine and I blinked, looking away. Raw power emanated from his gaze, and while I'd never felt submissive in Austin's presence before, I now understood why his brothers were so obedient. He truly was born to lead, in all forms.

I touched my throat and felt the back of my head. There wasn't any bruising or pain, so I must have shifted to heal. I couldn't remember.

A series of knocks sounded at the door and it swung open. "Lexi, honey, Denver told me you were awake," Mom said, squeezing inside.

"Mom, no!"

She held a small plate of food and my eyes went wide.

"Oh, it's okay, honey."

Mom reached down and patted Austin on the head and I almost rolled right out of the bed when she walked past him and set the plate on my lap.

"Mom?" I asked in disbelief, having expected her to get mauled due to her careless behavior.

She smiled and kissed my forehead. "I don't believe it, I don't really understand it, but you're still my daughter. It took them a while to pull me off you and then I had a long talk with Austin. Ivy made the most sense and I really like that young lady; she has a good head on her shoulders. I've seen it with my own eyes, so I can't deny who you are."

"You got near my wolf?"

My mother was truly a fearless woman.

She sighed and patted my leg, as if I had just asked the dumbest question on the planet. "Eat up and if you don't feel like getting out of bed, then you stay here all day." Her face tightened and she looked down. "I actually liked Beckett; I thought he was a nice young man. Obviously I have no sense when it comes to men."

"It's not your fault, Mom."

Jericho slipped into the room and looked down at the wolf. "Austin, you need to come see this. Someone brought you a present."

The way he said it rattled me, but Austin didn't shift. I followed Jericho down the hall, the black wolf never leaving my side. He walked with the same stride, keeping his body pressed against mine.

Jericho and Denver were in the hall by the front door with their arms folded. I walked around them and to my left, two dead wolves lay side by side on the front porch.

"It's a message," Denver said. "A warning."

Parked out front was Lorenzo, leaning against the grill of his truck with one hand tucked in his pocket and the other holding a cigarette. He took a long drag, watching me as I stood there in an ankle-length gown that belonged to my mom.

Austin growled when I got too close, but I knelt down and got a good look at one of the wolves. "It's not a warning," I said. "It's an offering." I didn't know if Austin could understand me or not, but I turned and looked at him as if he could. "This was the dog that treed me in the cemetery. I don't know who the other one is though. The warning is for Lorenzo's pack, not yours. But this is a gift… for me."

The message being that anyone who thought about hurting me would answer to him. I wondered who the second wolf was—maybe the one who was supposed to have been watching me that night. Lorenzo said he had a man following me at all times.

Somehow, a dead body was not a romantic gesture.

"Come away from there, Lexi," Jericho said, stepping forward with his arm outstretched.

Austin snapped at him. Jericho turned his head and sighed through his nose in frustration. "Is he ever going to shift back?" he asked Denver. "'Cause that biting shit is starting to piss me off."

"How long was I out? What time is it?"

"Two days," Denver said. "Ivy and your mom took care of you; they were the only ones who could get near Austin."

"He hasn't shifted back?"

Denver strolled out of the room, hiking up his sweats. The motor fired up on Lorenzo's truck and he slowly backed out.

"He's been that way since he brought you in," Jericho said, putting an unlit cigarette into his mouth. "All hell broke loose when your mom jumped on top of you. We tried to get her off and Austin suddenly shifted and guarded you two like his life depended on it. Between you and me, Austin's wolf is one *badass* alpha."

"Where's Ivy?"

Jericho stuffed his hands in the pockets of his black jeans, shredded from thigh to knee, biting down on the cigarette as if he hadn't decided whether to light it or not. "Helping your friend at the store."

"Do what?"

"The power is on and the shipments are due to arrive today. The twins are unloading while the girls set up."

I tucked my hands under my arms. "Lorenzo paid for all that?"

His brows knitted and he tucked the smoke behind his ear. "No. Austin did."

I took a moment to process that, because I had never asked him for any help in that regard. It wasn't even his problem, and yet he took money out of his own pocket to keep the store running. A store that only paid me a mediocre salary.

"I can't believe it," I whispered. Jericho shook his head a little to get his hair out of his eyes and I lowered my voice. "What happened to Beckett?"

Jericho made a slicing motion across his throat and I shuddered. "Austin took care of that problem, and your friend took care of his."

"Which friend?"

The wolf's toenails clicked on the tile as he turned in circles and sat in front of me.

Jericho combed his fingers through his hair. "Your neighbor. I guess she knows some cleaners and instead of waiting for the cops, she had the body removed like nothing had happened."

"Are you sure you don't mean Lorenzo?"

"Nope," he said, shaking his head. "Shifters have connections, and I guess she's got the hookup for taking care of dead bodies."

"Naya is a Shifter?"

My legs weakened and I closed the door.

"Mmm. We went to check on things and she was in there picking up roses. Nice tits on that one." Then he looked at the shock plastered across my face. "You didn't know she was a Shifter? Our kind tends to gravitate toward one another, even if we don't know it. We also look out for those we bond with, so if you two were tight, then that explains why she went the extra mile. Believe it or not, this city is teeming with Shifters. Not sure what her animal is, but I'd be willing to bet it's a cat," he said, rolling his tongue over his bottom lip. "Afraid I'm not into cats; too much maintenance. But they're prettylicious to look at."

"I think I'm going to throw up now," I declared, walking around him and into the living room. *Naya was a Shifter?* It made sense, but I still couldn't believe it. "Where's Maizy?"

"Denver's keeping an eye on her in the study across from the atrium. When I last checked, she was looking at the pictures in some old *World Almanac* we've had around for about fifty years. He took her outside to play 'slay the dragon' this morning. They were trying to kill the snake Reno saw under the house."

"*What?*" My question was more of a declaration I would kill him if he was serious. "Can you trust him with her?"

I was beginning to have second thoughts about Denver if snake hunting was on his daily agenda.

Jericho waltzed by me and lifted a box of matches from the bar. "Emphatically. It's his wolf I don't trust. Denver has control over his animal and doesn't shift on emotions, so she's safe with him. But don't ever let that child near his wolf. He's loco."

I decompressed in the shower and allowed the hot water to rinse away my salty tears. While I had no physical marks from the attack, the emotional ones left behind became fingerprints that would never wash away.

I'd never seen it coming.

I kept analyzing our relationship to see if there were any signs that Beckett was capable of that level of violence, but he'd only been aggressive with other men. He obsessed over professional wrestling, and sometimes I wondered if he took the job as a bouncer just to push people around and feel superior. Off the clock is when he got in the most fights, and usually it was after a few beers if he spotted some guy talking to me. But he never actually pushed *me* around, quite the opposite, in fact. Outside of his infidelity, I thought Beckett loved me.

Maybe too much.

His behavior had started to change after we split, with phone calls and confrontations. Losing me didn't seem to push him over the edge as much as the thought of another man in my life. And being as drunk as he was…

Then the memory of his death slammed into me like a train. I shouldn't have felt guilty for someone who tried to choke me on a blanket of rose petals and glass, but I did. Then I got angry and threw a bottle of shampoo against the wall, hating him with every fiber of my being. Rage poured through me as I shut the water off and tore down the shower curtain—the rod clamoring on the tile. I growled, sobbed, and made guttural noises—gripping the edge of the tub and letting the pain consume me.

Denver called my name from outside the door and I heard Austin's wolf viciously snarl.

"You okay in there?" he yelled.

Was I?

Had Austin not showed up and forced me to shift, I would have died. My mother would have had to bury another child.

I kept to myself for the rest of the morning before talking with my mom. She seemed to accept the facts more easily than I did on what I was. Later that afternoon, she put on a brisket, preparing to floor these men with her world-class cooking. I stirred the potato salad while sitting at the table, but I was in no mood to cook. It was also hard maneuvering around the kitchen with Austin's wolf at my feet.

He never once left my side from the moment I woke up.

Denver said Austin had showed up at my apartment to keep an eye on me. I wondered if he felt guilty and that's why he wouldn't shift back. When I asked Denver why he thought I didn't shift during the attack, he shrugged. Said it happens sometimes with the new ones, especially when mixed signals are sent to the wolf.

Once the brisket was in the oven, Mom went to take a nap with Maizy. It was hot that day, and the cicadas were singing in rhythm as the afternoon sun baked everything in sight. I sat in a lawn chair in the front yard with my legs browning in the sun, trying to shake off the attack. I noticed someone had parked my car next to Denver's yellow truck and had given it a wax and shine.

It was then I decided my mom would have to stay with Austin. Until my father was caught and this whole thing was resolved, she wouldn't be safe living by herself. Judging by the way he had treated Maizy, my dad wanted nothing to do with his kids.

At the end of the road, a white car approached and Austin's wolf trotted off the porch with his head low. The car parked on the right side of the driveway and a man who looked to be in his fifties waited inside, staring at the wolf apprehensively.

"Austin," I called out. "Let him out so we can see who it is."

His black wolf hopped on the porch and sat beside me. Denver was the only other pack member on the property, and he was snoozing in the atrium with his earbuds on.

A stocky man wearing a pale blue dress shirt and red tie stepped out of the car. "I'm looking for Alexia Knight."

"Who wants to know?"

He shut the door, leaning against the hood as he stared at the wolf. "My name is Tom Gardner and I'm Charles Langston's attorney," he said with a southern drawl. His refined accent that told me he was from money. "I spoke with your neighbor, Miss James, after talking with one of your coworkers. It took a little convincing, but she gave me this address. I need to speak with you on legal matters. Do you mind locking your dog away?"

"He won't hurt you," I promised, grabbing a tuft of Austin's fur. I should have reconsidered handling an alpha, but I needed to communicate to him that he had to behave. This guy didn't seem like a threat. "Come up on the porch and have a seat," I said, squinting at the afternoon sun.

He tucked a brown satchel that looked a million years old beneath his arm and cautiously approached, not showing fear in front of the black wolf. But I could tell the sweat on his brow wasn't from the sun. He took the farthest seat on the left and Austin's wolf sat down in front of my chair.

"It's with great regret that I must inform you Mr. Langston is deceased."

My heart stammered and I covered my mouth. "What? Oh my God."

He gave me a moment to digest the news and I took a seat beside him, staring at my shoes, my forearms on my knees. "I just can't believe it."

"He's been ill for some time, and we've discussed his future at great length. I do apologize you had to hear it from me, but I seem to be the bearer of bad news today as I had to call up his sister this morning. Not the standard protocol, but we became friends and I was there in the end. Charles was a very well-liked guy around my office. He always brought the girls a little something from his store." Mr. Gardner put the satchel on his lap and pulled out a short stack of clipped papers. "His only family is an estranged sister who lives out of state, and he's expressed no desire to pass on any inheritance to her. Mr. Langston drew up a detailed last will and testament, which he wanted me to bring to your attention immediately upon his death. His fear was that you'd quit the shop and time is of the essence due to the nature of the company."

"What do you mean?" None of this was registering for me, because while I'd known Charlie for seven years, we'd never discussed anything beyond my paycheck when it came to the business.

"I'm not here to gussy this up, ma'am. Mr. Langston signed over the business and most of his money to you. His house will go to a young family he met a year ago when donating to a homeless charity, along with enough money to pay bills and taxes for a year. After that, they can sell it for the money if they choose."

My jaw hung open and I barely heard the last words he said. "He left it all to *me*? I think you made a mistake."

"No," he countered. "It's all in these signed documents. He has quite a list of instructions and advice he left behind in print and on a flash drive." Mr. Gardner reached in his back pocket and fished out a small plastic flash drive and placed it in my hand. Austin growled but made no attempt to move. "He wasn't a rich man, so the money in his account won't get you far with the business if you're not pulling in a profit. Have you ever managed a company before?" he asked in a curious tone.

I shook my head. And then the tears started to come. Charlie was the kind of guy I could have envisioned as my dad. We weren't close, but he always gave me good advice and made sure I'd enjoyed working for him. He used to be in the shop four days a week, but in the last couple of years, Charlie felt it was time he allow us to manage things on our own so he could focus on other business matters.

Little did I know that matter was cancer.

Mr. Gardner continued. "He said there's a bright young lady working in the shop who has a head for business that he suggested you keep around. He was concerned about you getting in a financial pitfall, which is why it's imperative you read over his instructions. He was fairly confident the shop would stay afloat and was pulling in a decent profit. I have papers I need you to read carefully and sign. I'll leave them with you and you can schedule a meeting with me when you're ready to discuss this further."

The sound of wind chimes in the distance floated in the breeze. A fly landed on his hand briefly before he shooed it away with a wave of his arm.

I tried to swallow but my throat was dry. "Did they bury him already?"

"He asked to be cremated; didn't want anyone fussing over him and he didn't think anyone would have come to the funeral."

I covered my face with my hands and quietly wept. Mr. Gardner's voice couldn't have been less somber, which made delivering the news even sharper against my heart. Austin's wolf licked my fingers and I finally wiped my cheeks and pulled a strand of long hair away from my wet lashes.

"He wanted his ashes to be spread across the Grand Canyon." Mr. Gardner stretched his legs out and watched a lone cloud painted against the blue sky. "He talked about how that river carved away the land and he wanted to be a part of something that's everlasting."

After wiping my nose and regaining my composure, I looked apprehensively at the balding attorney. "I need time to look this over. I'm just not sure Charlie was in his right frame of mind when he made this decision."

"Well, if it's any consolation, he thought highly of you. It wasn't like he was forced to pass off the business; he had other options. But that was his first request and he wanted to make it happen. He said you had a..." Mr. Gardner reached for the right words. "He said you had a *nose* for business. Mr. Langston felt you could take it wherever it needed to go, and only wished he could have stuck around to see what you'll do with it. Well, I need to head out."

He glanced at his watch and stood up, eyeing the wolf. "My number is on the card clipped on the top. Regardless of what you decide, we'll have another meeting to discuss this in detail with any questions you might have. Oh, and something else," he began with a short chuckle. "He told me to tell you that you don't have to wear those fruity earrings anymore if you don't want to. I'm not sure what that means, but he wanted me to let you know."

Tom hesitated, waiting for the wolf to move and I motioned Austin with my eyes and he complied, allowing the lawyer to pass.

"Y'all have a good afternoon," he said, walking back to his car and wiping his sweaty forehead with a handkerchief.

My heart ached for Charlie, and I only wished I could have seen him one last time. I wondered if he knew how much he meant to me. But why did he do this? How could he leave something so important in my incapable hands? That got me scared, and I needed to talk to April. She would be able to keep me from going into a full-blown freak-out.

I leaned back and stared at Austin. He rested his chin on the arm of my chair and I got lost in his clear blue eyes.

"How long are you going to stay that way? Because I'm starting to feel like you're avoiding me." I patted his nose. "Anyone ever tell you that your breath stinks?" Nothing riled him up. "I could take you to the pet store and have them clip your toenails and paint them pink."

He snorted angrily and grunted, circling around the porch.

Then I suddenly felt a tingle between my legs and slid down in my chair a little bit. Maybe it was the hot afternoon sun, but damn if I didn't feel… turned on. Austin's wolf was making a peculiar sound of distress while pacing back and forth, as if he were guarding me from invisible predators.

When it passed, I took the papers inside and laid down for a nap.

CHAPTER 24

E VERYONE GATHERED IN THE KITCHEN to devour Mom's succulent homemade brisket. The small table only seated six, so Ben and Wheeler ate at the counter while the rest of us sat down. Austin's wolf trotted out of the room.

Mom was still shaken up about Maizy having been left on the side of the road and every so often, I caught that look in her eyes a mother gets when they've come close to losing the most precious thing to them. I admired her courage and resilience for all she had been through in the last week, and I guess like me, she valued family even more because of it.

During dinner, I noticed Maizy hiding her meat beneath her mashed potatoes. Denver waltzed over to the microwave and heated up a hot dog. Her eyes brightened when he dropped it on her plate and she hunched over with a big smile on her face, looking like she had just gotten away with something. Maybe she had. He appeared satisfied with himself, although he tried to hide it from the guys. Maybe it wasn't a "cool guy" thing to have a little girl think you were the best thing since peanut butter and jelly. Despite his idiotic methods, I trusted Denver with her more than I did the others. Reno was too rough around the edges and I still didn't know what to make of the twins. Wheeler was the smarter of the two, though you'd never know it by all the tattoos, not to mention he seemed to be a moodier guy than his brother.

Jericho mentioned getting another tattoo and my mom told him he already had one too many.

"Boys, we're going to be staying the night out," Austin announced, walking into the room with a swagger I couldn't help but admire. His dark jeans were loose (in a good way) and his tight black shirt was tucked in, showing off a nice leather belt with a silver buckle.

Jericho whistled mockingly.

"Who's *we*?" I asked.

"Me and you. Let's go." He flicked an icy glare at Jericho, who had scooted his chair right beside me—so close our arms touched. Reno took the spot on my left and everyone else looked spread out. I guess I didn't think about how it might look to be sandwiched between his brothers until Austin came in and made me aware of it.

The extra space at the table allowed them room to move down, but they chose to sit right beside me. I just thought they were being consolatory because of the recent attack.

"Why should I go?" I looked at Austin and he gave me *the look*. I didn't really need an answer because I knew where he was going with this. The tingling had been coming and going with more frequency over the past few hours. Maybe I was just hormonal, but either way, I didn't want to stick around and find out.

I got up from the table. "Going out, Mom. There're a few movies in my bag if Maizy gets bored."

We had spent the past hour talking about my dad. She didn't think he'd come back for her and even if he did, I doubted he stood a chance against the Cole brothers. Anyhow, he had no idea Austin was back in town, nor would he think to show up here.

Damn, Austin was doing his lean on the frame of the kitchen doorway and I got the shivers again just looking at how snug his shirt was. I could almost see his abs through the thin fabric, and the bold ink patterns on his upper arms were so striking I wondered if it had hurt to get them.

Jericho snaked his arm around my upper leg and nestled against me. "Stay with us," he said in sweet, syrupy words, nuzzling into my shirt. "I'll play my guitar and sing a song for you."

Austin crossed the room before I could reply. He gripped the back of Jericho's chair and pulled it out, dumping him on the floor. "I think we all know what's up, boys. You need to learn to put that in check, because our numbers will grow. And now that we have another female in the house, let me reiterate to you all that respect is something we live and die by when it comes to one of our own."

He meant Ivy. She'd passed on dinner and gone to lie down in one of the twin's rooms. I had a feeling she was having adjustment problems and needed time to herself. The house really closed in on you after a while with all these men.

"Come on, Lexi. Let's go," he said, holding out his hand.

Something restrained flickered in his eyes—something hot. When I took his hand, I gasped at the warmth and saw a muscle twitch in his cheek. He had already packed an overnight bag for me and loaded up the car.

When we drove off, I finally asked, "Where are you taking me?"

"It's a surprise." Austin flipped on the radio and we listened to Bush singing about breathing in and breathing out. Which was exactly what I was doing. I rolled the window down, hoping if I was leaking any kind of sex perfume, the outside air would keep Austin from having to put up with it.

He pulled up to a stretch of property that reminded me of how Ivan's house was set up, with a generous amount of cleared land in front and a thicket of woods around the back. It looked like a mansion, but not pretentious. The square windows were fogged over and needed replacing. They showed signs of wear, as shutters were broken and pulled away by time. A covered porch ran along the front and around the sides with a balcony off one of the rooms on the second floor. It looked like there was an attic, but I couldn't tell from the front. I could imagine how beautiful impatiens and roses would look on the top balcony in the springtime. It must have been a grand place in its prime.

"Is this the house you were talking about buying?"

"I bought it," he confirmed, switching off the radio. He brushed a strand of hair away from my face and melted me with his pale eyes. "Are you okay? You know what I mean. We haven't really talked about what happened with Beckett."

It wasn't cold but I shivered. "I'm still trying to process it. I'm not sure I want to deal with it right now."

"Well, stuff like that messes with your head. So whenever you're ready to talk, I'm here. Doesn't matter if we can heal or not; some scars are beneath the skin and mark us in ways we least expect."

"Thanks."

He shut off the engine while I gaped at the house. "This is our new home," he said. "You were right; the other place wasn't me."

"Why were you at my apartment the night Beckett came over?"

His fingers tightened around the steering wheel. "Just wanted to check up on you. Make sure you didn't need anything."

"Is that all?" I glared at him because it sure didn't feel like all. He clammed up and I got mad. "Tell me lies, Austin," I said, mimicking the song we had listened to on the way over. I slammed the door and stormed up the steps.

"Lexi, wait," I heard him call out from behind. "Don't run off before I explain."

I turned on my heel and watched him slowly walk up the steps. We lingered on the porch, lit by a half-moon that kept peering out from behind a gathering of brooding clouds. A cool wind brought the sweet smell of rain, and a cricket chirped from beneath the porch.

"Well?" I tapped my fingers on the wall behind me and a smiled tugged at the corner of his mouth.

"I showed up at your apartment to bring you a birthday present, but I saw the flowers from Church and clearly I'm out of my league when it comes to that kind of thing."

"What present?" I stopped drumming my fingers and cleared my throat. *Austin bought me a gift?*

After a few seconds of clenching his jaw, he finally swung his left arm around from behind his back.

I sucked in a sharp breath. "Oh. My. God."

Lollipops. My absolute all-time favorite candy and he'd made them into a *bouquet*. When my face began to hurt, I realized it was because I was smiling so hard the corners of my mouth were getting introduced to my ears. Austin didn't lift his eyes but had a defeated look on his face as he turned the candy in his hand and stared at it.

"I wanted to surprise you and… it was obviously a dumb idea. You're not twelve anymore and I should have gotten you something better. Perfume, or real flowers."

"Are you kidding me, Austin Cole?" I snatched the bouquet and dipped my nose in, smelling the sweet bliss of sugar. "This is the most beautiful thing I think I've ever seen."

Then my lip quivered and I felt like a fool. "Wes used to give these to me whenever he wanted to shut me up about something."

"I know," he admitted. "He told me about your addiction years ago. No need to make a big thing of it. I'll get you something better."

Austin wanted to get me something better? *Impossible.* Just the fact he wanted to do something for me made my knees shake a little bit and my heart flap around like a nervous hummingbird. There wasn't a chance in hell he was going to walk away thinking he didn't just blow my mind.

I threw my arms around his neck and squeezed him tight. "I love that you know me so well," I said. "This is better than roses by a mile." Then I smelled him and he wasn't wearing cologne. What's more, I noticed he was smelling me when I felt his nose tickle against the crook of my neck.

When I stepped back, I plucked one of the candies from the cluster and ripped away the wrapper with my teeth. Immediately, I sucked on it and then held out my tongue, spinning the candy in circles.

Austin's eyes were following every movement as he watched the whole affair. His lips parted as he eyed my mouth. "Keep doing that," he said in a hoarse whisper.

Then he shocked the hell out of me when he leaned down and licked the other side. I felt his tongue slide against mine and I froze. Then he did it again, only this time more slowly until he pulled the candy away and began sucking on my candy-coated tongue as he cupped my face in his warm hands.

The tingles were roaring.

Suckers fell to the floor with a *whack!* My right leg wrapped around his waist as he lifted me up by my thighs.

The kiss was deep, wet, and salacious. My chin burned from how rough he was with his whiskers as we angled our heads to the left, then the right, and nibbled each other's lips while discovering our groove. That comfortable groove you get into once you learn someone through their kiss—their moves, their rhythm, the intensity of how they use their tongue, even where on your mouth they linger during the kiss. Upper lip, lower lip, left side kisser, or all over the place.

Our kiss became so expert it was as if we had been lovers in another lifetime. His hand turned the knob and he stumbled forward, almost falling before he regained his balance and walked into the dark house. The wood creaked beneath his feet as he kicked the door shut behind him—my legs still wrapped around his waist and my fingers disappearing in his dark hair.

The kiss never stopped.

It echoed in the empty house as every sound we made was amplified. Sucking and licking—the wet sounds of our lips greedily giving in to the raw nature of passion.

Decades in the making.

At least on my end.

I moaned into his mouth and a growl rose from his chest—the deep, throaty kind that made me squeeze my legs a little tighter. He was walking me somewhere, and that somewhere was a room with a mattress and sheets.

Austin lowered me onto my back and the aroused look in his eyes caused me to fist the sheets. Moonlight trickled through the tall window when it wasn't hiding behind the clouds, and I could make out the contours of his body through shadows and light.

Then an ache like I'd never felt before struck me so hard I curled my knees up and cried out. Austin moved on top of me like it was affecting him in the same way—clawing at my shorts as he kissed my legs hungrily, coveting me with every stroke of his tongue. Austin had a beautiful mouth—the kind of lips a woman wanted all over her body.

"We can't do this," he panted.

Confused, I swallowed hard and looked down at him. "Why not?"

I shivered when he lifted his eyes to mine. "You want a baby?"

That killed a little of the fire. I wasn't exactly ready for kids, at least, not that very second. Kids were the kind of thing you discussed and decided on. Well, most of the time.

"You're extremely fertile when you're in heat; that's how it works with Shifters. It comes around once a year, maybe less, and it can last hours or days," he said, his breath warming my skin. While he was talking, his nose pushed up the hem of my shirt so he could taste my stomach. "If I take you, then you'll get pregnant."

"Condoms?"

Austin chuckled. "Wouldn't work with Shifter sperm. We don't just have an army; we have a legion of—"

I touched his lips with my fingers. "Austin, please don't kill the moment talking about your sperm."

Then he sucked on my finger and the tingles roared through my core and melted down my thighs. *Oh God*, I wanted this.

"Complain all you want," he murmured against my stomach. "But you're going to learn tonight the only way…" He pressed his face against my belly and I felt how enflamed his cheeks were.

I grabbed a fistful of his hair. "Finish what you were about to say."

His bristly jaw scratched my skin as he looked up. "The only way to taper it down and get you out of heat is to give you orgasms." *Plural.*

A smirk turned up the corner of my mouth. "No complaints here."

"No sex."

"Okay, I have a complaint," I said, propping up on my elbows. "Exactly *what* are we doing here?"

An intense, dark look swirled in his eyes that I couldn't read— one with hidden secrets and meanings that drove me nuts. "Do you really want to ruin our friendship with sex? I don't want our first time to be because of raging hormones," he said, curling his fingertips inside the hem of my shorts and sliding them away from my hips, down to my knees, and finally my ankles. I felt every second of their slow journey and it drove me wild. "It's going to be without all the biology bullshit. Just me and you and no regrets."

I knew he was talking, but my ears were starting to hear that wah-wah sound Charlie Brown's teacher always makes in the cartoons. Maybe it was the fact that the only thing between Austin and me was a pair of black bikini bottoms.

His thumb hooked beneath one of the strings, inching closer to the center. My heart could have gotten a speeding ticket, as it refused to slow down no matter how much I concentrated.

"What are you going to do then?"

His eyes answered me before his mouth did. They were hooded and dripping with heat. "I'm going to make you come."

Which almost did. Just the words rolling off his tongue and the way he was looking at me made every muscle in my body tense.

"As many times as it takes until you're over this, because that's how an alpha looks after his women. But over my dead body are we going back home so I can sit and watch my brothers look at you the way they were doing at dinner." A palpable flicker of jealousy sparked in his eyes. "I don't run the kind of pack where we *share.*"

Which implied packs existed that did. Austin had promised me independence with no strings attached. Most women went into a pack mated because sometimes the men would get possessive and fights would break out. That's why he was adamant about his brothers treating Ivy as a sister and had planted the suggestion in their head so they would be more inclined to protect her than mount her.

Then he got right back to business and put his mouth on my sex, moving his lips over my panties as if he were making out with me. I moaned unabashedly and abruptly pushed his head away.

"What's wrong?"

I blushed. Hard. Then my knees pulled up and I flipped over to my side, staring at an outlet on the wall.

"Lexi?" His hand brushed over my hip and Austin laid behind me, propped up on his elbow so he could stare at my shadowy profile. "Did I do something to upset you? Don't lie to me."

I couldn't. The simple fact was no man had ever gone down on me. Even Beckett was more of a receiver than a giver when it came to sex. How embarrassing was that?

"I'm sleepy," I lied.

"Bullshit. Turn over and look at me before I tickle the crap out of you, and don't think I won't do it."

He totally would. I once stole his car keys and stuffed them into my bra when I was nineteen and the designated driver. Austin had chased me to the car, which made me run even harder. I dove into the front seat knowing Austin would never dig in my bra. Instead, he pulled off my shoes and tickled my feet until I screamed bloody murder. That was the only time I'd ever seen Wes turn on Austin. He yanked him out by the collar and coldcocked him. I guess from a distance, it looked kind of bad with me on my back in the front seat screaming while Austin was holding my legs.

"Since when did you get all shy on me?" he asked, thunder rumbling in the distance.

Austin's fingers tickled my skin as they slid down to my hips. I elbowed him away. "Don't."

"Then tell me what's wrong, because you're not going anywhere, and I sure as hell ain't going anywhere. Whatever it is won't leave this room. You can trust me."

A few taps of rain touched the windows and flashes of lightning illuminated the room. "I've never had a man do that to me."

The air was so quiet I actually heard the high-pitched whine of a mosquito buzzing around my ear. I waved my hand around to shoo the insect away and ended up smacking Austin in the mouth. "Oh, shit. I'm sorry; I didn't mean to do that," I said, rolling onto my back.

He was grinning, but not because I slapped him.

Then I blushed again, and I wasn't a big blusher, but I'd just revealed something very personal and his first reaction was to laugh? I was about to run out of the room in T-minus 3... 2...

"I'm not going to even ask why, because it doesn't matter. I'm only going to guess the men you've dated didn't know a damn thing about the most erotic thing you can experience with a woman. To run your tongue over that secret place, to slide it in and taste her as you suck and stroke her until she screams out your name."

His fingers had wandered down between my legs while he spoke, expertly caressing me.

"I'm not one of those boys," he said softly in my ear. "I'm a man who knows how to take a woman and give her what her body needs." His fingers slid between my folds and by then, he knew with absolute certainty I wanted him.

"I can't do it," I admitted. "It's too... I don't know. Personal."

"You need to let go of all your inhibitions and just feel it. Can you feel it?" He worked his fingers into my panties and made me suck in a sharp breath and hold it. "Feel it, Lexi. Before the night is over, I'm going to have your legs wrapped around my shoulders as you beg for more." Then his moist lips touched my cheek and he whispered one hot word. "Beg."

"*Please.*"

He knew what game we were playing.

Except I was the one who didn't. Austin abruptly stopped and grabbed my wrist, guiding my hand down. "Finish."

"What?"

His lips met mine with a warm press and he spoke against my mouth. "I need to know how you like it so I can make this experience easier for you. If this goes on for days, then I'm not going to tease you. I'm going to make you come. Now show me how you like to be touched. Don't be afraid to take what your body needs. Do it once and I'll take care of you from here on out."

That was something I'd never done in front of a man either. But not wanting to seem prudish, I played his little game and cupped myself, widening my legs so I could fall into that imaginary fantasy of mine.

The one he didn't know about where we were having sex. The fantasy was even hotter knowing he was in the room watching me, and it didn't take long before I closed my eyes and forgot he was there. My back arched and I suddenly felt his hands brush over my nipples. That snapped me back into reality. Austin was ruining the dream where he falls asleep beside me on the sofa and I slowly unzip his pants and pleasure him. That had been the running fantasy for the last nine years, closely followed by sex on a pool table.

"Please, Austin," I begged again. "Make love to me."

He laid down beside me on the left and slipped his hand beneath my shirt, pushing up my bra so he could tease me with his fingers.

"I want to do more than that, Lexi. I want to fuck you on the hood of my car."

Okay, so I gasped a little.

"You don't talk like that," I said in a confused voice. Not sure why I thought Austin would be the kind for romantic words, but I'd never imagined him saying those things to me. It wasn't just hot, but *completely* unexpected.

"Correction. I've never talked to *you* like that. I might fall short in the romance department, but I more than make up for it in other ways. I want to slide my hand down your body, rip off those panties, and take you all over every inch of this house, but it doesn't mean I don't respect the fuck out of you," he said, as if the last bit meant something. "So do me a favor and spread yourself over the hood of my black car, arms wide as I slide down your shorts *very* slowly. All the way to your ankles."

Tingles returned as I got the full visual of what Austin was mentally doing to me. I'd had men dirty-talk in the bedroom, but this was completely different.

"Then your panties go next, but you keep a long T-shirt on so I can just make out the cups of your fine ass. Yeah, Lexi, you have one *fine* ass."

My fingers were going for gold, touching all the right places as he set me on fire with his words. Every so often, I opened my eyes to discover him closely watching everything I did with my hands. The rhythmic way my fingers stroked and circled and how my other hand massaged the inside of my thigh as if it were his hand.

Then he kept talking in that sexy, assertive voice of his.

"My engine is still warm against your stomach, and someone could be watching us because we're not so far away from the main road. That's okay, because I don't care who the hell sees us. I spread your legs wide and kneel down so I can run my tongue between your legs, and you like it. You're crying out for more as I make you even wetter. Do you like that?"

"Uh huh," I moaned and cried out all at once. My knees pulled up as I kept the fantasy alive in my head. "*Don't stop*," I said.

"Yeah, you'll say a lot of that too. Don't stop. Don't stop. Don't stop."

My breathing was out of control and warmth licked over my skin. A dull ache grew sharper with each second, swelling and tightening beneath my fingertips. *Almost there. So close.*

"You want me," he said in a husky voice. "So then what?"

"You…"

"Yeah? Say it," he growled in my ear, sucking on the lobe. "*Say what you want me to do to you next while I'm stretched across your back and widening your legs.*"

Then I felt his tongue glide across my neck as his warm hand smoothed over my breast and massaged.

"You can hear my belt unbuckling and sliding out of the loops. Tell me what you want me to do to you as you hear the sound of my zipper coming undone. Can you feel that thick press between your legs? That's how much I want you. Christ, I *need* to hear you say it. What am I going to do to you on the hood of my car, Lexi? *Tell me*," he urged in his alpha voice.

Austin nipped my ear and the sweet sting of pain caused me to answer.

"You fuck me. God, Austin… *fuck me!*" I cried out and arched my back as he quickly placed his hand on top of mine, nuzzling against my neck.

Bursts of energy rolled through me as I came so hard my entire body tensed up. Being in heat intensified everything like I'd never experienced. I barely noticed Austin's lips melting against my shoulder.

He twirled my nipple between his fingers and tugged, bringing another jolt of pleasure through my belly. My legs straightened out like useless timber and I panted, slowly becoming aware I'd just pleasured myself in front of Austin Cole, who was still fully clothed.

His lips kissed mine softly, in a different way than they had before. "Thank you," he whispered.

This threw me, because it should have been me thanking him. So I played it cool. "Anytime."

Austin laughed warmly and rolled onto his back, locking his hands behind his head. "Feel better? I have a short fridge with some food in the other room if you get hungry. You should eat before the next wave hits. The house needs work, but I got the power turned on last night. I thought we could sleep with the windows open tonight since the rain should cool things down."

Rain? Oh yeah, that hammering noise going on outside that I hadn't even noticed over the sound of my pounding heart. This was too weird. Here I was, coming down from the throes of a mind-blowing orgasm, and Austin was discussing the weather and the electric company. I was looking around for my shorts when he yanked me back down.

"Let me go," I protested.

"Nope. Not letting you leave, Ladybug. If you're chilly, you can wrap up in the sheet. But the shorts stay off for the rest of the night."

"What about yours?" I pointed out, wrinkling my mouth.

He smirked and shifted over so he was propped up on one elbow and lying on his right side. "That's not going to happen. You have to be careful with loaded weapons."

I rolled my eyes. "Give me a break."

"I'm just here to give Mother Nature a hand."

My legs crossed at the ankle and I stared at the ceiling. "You were always so bad with jokes," I groaned.

"Did you really like the candy or were you just being polite? Be honest; my feelings won't be hurt and I swear I won't be crying over a gallon of ice cream at two in the morning with Denver, talking about my feelings and shit."

A burst of laughter flew out of my mouth and I curled on my side. Austin's look was so serious my Beaker laugh slipped out and then he quickly kissed my neck. "There it is," he said. "That's the Lexi I know and love."

My smile was erased like a mistake on a chalkboard. I sat up and covered my bare legs with the sheet. "Don't say flippant things like that if you don't mean them."

An ordinary remark hit the psycho switch in my brain and turned me into one of those... sensitive girls. Normally, I just rolled with the punches and dished what I got, rarely taking what people said to heart. But for whatever reason, hearing "love" come out of his mouth in the same sentence with my name provoked a new feeling I didn't have a grasp on.

An uncomfortable moment passed between us and vanished

when thunder cracked outside and I screamed, flying against Austin's chest. He rocked with laughter and threaded his fingers through my long, silky hair.

"Why didn't you bring a blanket?"

"I did. I brought the Austin special," he said, running his hand teasingly down his chest.

A snort escaped. "Very funny." I was too afraid to ask what any of this meant—if anything—so I just let go of all the questions and lived in the moment. "Did you kill a lot of men?"

"Yeah," he admitted. "Bounty hunters track down outlaws and it's dead or alive. Outlaws in the Breed world are the worst kinds of criminals, so we do whatever it takes to bring them in. Hunting is a legal, respectable position that pays well. I needed to build up my finances before starting my own pack. Our parents didn't leave us with much money because they'd never established a pack of their own, which is how you get that kind of security. Most of the men were turned in alive, if that makes it any easier for you to think about."

"That business card you gave me, was that your old job?"

"I still have a few of those left," he said. "It was my calling card. The bow and arrow is the symbol of a bounty hunter. You'll see that a lot among Breed in certain professions; we use symbols instead of titles. That's the life I'm leaving behind."

The room lit up with strobe lights and we quietly waited for the crash of thunder. Instead, it was a heavy roll, like a bowling ball traveling down a wooden lane. I felt like I was supposed to say something profound, or funny—something to kill the silence. But there was a sweetness in the quiet moments we shared that I enjoyed too much.

The rain. The rumbling thunder. The flashes of light and catching glimpses of his pale eyes watching me. His fingers threading through my hair. And when I began to drift off to sleep, his soft lips kissed my eyelids.

I wanted to ask what I meant to him. I wanted to hear it from his lips, even if they were words of denial. But all I felt was his warm body against mine as I fell asleep, wrapped up in his embrace.

CHAPTER 25

HE PREVIOUS NIGHT WAS ONE sexual blur. I'd love to say I slept in Austin's arms for the rest of the night, but that heat thing ain't no joke. I had four more episodes, and he was right there, taking care of me like he'd promised. I loved that at twenty-eight, Austin could give me a first-time experience. Honestly, it meant more *because* it was with him. He wasn't exactly a perfect gentleman, but he kept his word that it wasn't about reciprocating the favor (not that I would've objected).

Yeah, I was a little disappointed. But in retrospect, I knew he was right. It would have been weird between us. This was weird enough, but sex kind of solidified it in a more irreversible way. Not to mention if I'd become pregnant, it would have complicated my life in a way I wasn't prepared for.

Still, it was one of the most erotic nights of my life. Strange to think it was possible to feel that way when we didn't even have traditional sex. I'd probably need a cold shower for the next five years whenever I thought about what he did to me. What I didn't realize was that Austin had inadvertently planted a permanent fantasy in my head where every time I'd touch myself, I would think of him.

Looking at the hood of his Dodge Challenger without getting aroused would also prove to be impossible.

I stretched my toes and buried my face in the soft pillow. Austin smacked my ass. "Get up, lazybones."

"Get out."

"Why?"

"I don't want you to see me."

Without a doubt, I knew I looked like a hot mess. Dried sweat and matted hair, smeared eyeliner, and probably marks on my face from having slept on wrinkled sheets.

"Don't tell me you're one of those girls," he said, laughing heartily. "Jesus, Lexi. I've seen what you look like in the morning, and you've got nothing to hide about."

"Yes I do," I mumbled.

"Maybe you're right. Your breath does tend to smell like sweaty socks when you wake up."

I waved my arm out to slap him but missed. "That's not funny."

"Fine. I'll just sit here staring at your lovely rear end for the rest of the morning. On a side note, I like these panties with the strings on the side." He pulled the elastic and let it snap against my hip. "But I think the ones that ride up in the back are sexier. What do you call those?"

"Slut shorts."

He chuckled warmly and fell against the mattress. I gathered up the sheets and covered my waist, sitting up with my back to him. A clump of hair fell in front of my face and I hiccupped, looking around for my clothes. It was so bright and sunny in the room that the memory of the night before was almost erased.

Almost, but not a chance in hell.

"Do you have any coffee?"

"Yeah," he said, getting up and stretching out his back.

I tried not to peek at him through an opening in my hair, but damn, he looked good. Tight abs, his jeans slung low on his hips because the belt was off, barefoot, and shirtless. Austin had a nice tan all over, not to mention he was sporting the messy hair I found wildly attractive. When he rubbed his hand over his pec, pushing the skin around, I slammed my eyes shut. "Um, the coffee?"

"On it," he said, bare feet sliding across the wooden floor. "The bathroom is down the hall and I left a few things in there for you like towels and a robe. I wasn't sure how long we'd be here, but it ended sooner than I thought it would. Christ, I don't think I could have taken much more of that." His voice was strained, the words meant for his ears and not mine.

Austin disappeared and I ran in quick steps across the house with my clothes in my arms, looking for the bathroom. It was a beautiful house with a large staircase in front that led up to a second landing before turning right and going up another flight. The floors were an unfinished wood, and the white paint on the walls had begun to age. I didn't have time to look at all the details, but I did notice a hole in the wall next to the staircase.

After a quick shower, I brushed my teeth and put on some fresh clothes Austin had packed. Jean shorts and a thin white shirt. Men didn't really think about such things, but all he'd packed were black bras. I sighed and put one on anyhow. On hot days like these, I preferred wearing a thin shirt to a tight tank top. Just not with the faux pas of my bra being visible.

I walked barefoot through the beautiful house, my long hair tied up in a wet ponytail. Sunshine poured in through the front windows and I could see tiny dust particles floating in the air.

"Austin?"

"Out here," he called from the front.

The house faced east and sunlight splashed across the wooden porch. Austin was sitting on the steps with a steaming cup of coffee in one hand and a small plate on his knees. I sat beside him and lifted my red mug from the step. "*Hola*. What's that you're eating?"

He held the plate in front of me. "Bananas, granola, and dried cherries."

"How did you get so fit eating birdseed?"

Austin held out his right arm and flexed a little. "You think I'm fit? I could probably use a little more muscle. I've been slacking these past few months."

He had to be kidding. If he had been any more toned, I might have dry humped his leg when I first saw him at Dairy Queen. Maybe that was extreme, but it made me laugh and I took a bite of the banana.

"Want to share?"

"Not really," I said, knowing he was asking about my thoughts, not breakfast. "Are there any neighbors nearby?"

"No." He quietly sipped his coffee and made an audible swallow. "I bought a hundred acres, so we're pretty spaced apart."

"How much did that cost?"

Austin didn't answer. I guess at this point, it didn't matter. Finally, he pointed to the left by a pear tree. "What do you think about putting a garden over there? I could make some wind chimes and hang them from the branch."

"You know how to whittle?"

He gave a handsome smirk and his dark brows sank over his sparkling eyes. "Don't look so surprised. A Shifter once showed me how to make them out of wood. It's not difficult."

It was such a little thing, but it gave me insight to a side of Austin I'd never seen. Suddenly I wanted to know everything he'd been through in the past seven years—even the bad stuff.

"Can you remember things when you're in wolf form? I mean, everything in detail?"

After taking another sip, Austin set the coffee down and stretched out his legs, crossing them at the ankle. He'd put on a pair of brown hiking boots.

"Most of it. I can't remember details of conversation too well, but I get the gist of emotions and things that I pick up through my wolf. Depends on the situation. Why?"

"Do you remember the lawyer coming by?"

"Ah, so that's who that was."

"My boss died."

A blue jay squawked and flapped into a nearby oak tree.

"Sorry to hear that."

After another bite of banana, I set down the plate. "He willed me his shop and I don't know what to do. I've never run a business before; I'll screw it up."

Austin chewed on his lip for a moment, staring at the open stretch of land. "Do it. You've got my support, Lexi. Just don't run yourself into a hole, and if it comes to that, then sell it or quit. You'll regret it if you don't try."

"I know," I said, resting my chin on my knee. "I just don't know how to feel about it. Charlie's gone, and it hardly seems like it's the same without him."

"But you knew how he ran the store and what it took to make money. You're a smart girl, Lexi. I know you've picked up some business sense over the years working there. I'll help if you need it. Maybe put Ben and Wheeler's sorry asses in there to work for you."

"Uh, no thanks. They'd scare the children."

He laughed and leaned forward, chewing the granola and wiping his hand on his jeans. "When I was younger, they were more like Denver, personality wise. No tattoos, no morose expressions, and Ben worked with Wheeler for a while before he decided to play cards professionally. Something happened between them, and if I had to guess, it has to do with money or a woman. They still get along, but it seems more like they're doing it because of rank or something."

"How many more will you add to your pack?"

"Hard to say," he mumbled, chewing the last bite of granola. I watched his strong jaw working hard and noticed he had shaved, although he'd missed a patchy spot on the side. "This house was renovated and has about fifteen bedrooms. If anyone brings in a mate, then that could double the occupancy without using up all the rooms. That's why I bought the additional land. I'd rather not have everyone living in separate houses; that never works well with Shifters. But I can always build onto this one, or have a house just over there," he said, waving his hand to the left. "We could connect them with a walkway or something."

"What happens when the women go into heat?"

"They stay locked up in their bedrooms."

I frowned. "That's not practical. Maybe if you build an extra house, it could be the heat house." I laughed so hard at my joke that Beaker made an appearance and I plugged my nose to make him go away. I hated my laugh when I got riled up because people used to make fun of me. It wasn't any weirder than Pamela Jones, who used to snort with each breath. Or Danny (one of Wes's friends) who would scream out his laugh like some old drunkard.

Austin pulled my hand away. "Don't cover up your laugh," he scolded. "Now finish up your coffee and we'll head out. I'm anxious to start moving in and the boys have a lot of work to do before that can happen."

"What kind of work?"

He stood up and locked his fingers behind his head, stretching in the morning light. "Marking territory. One hundred acres. We're going to have to stop off and buy a few cases of Gatorade. Denver's going to hate my ass."

─────────────⊷∘⊂⊘∘⊂─────────────

I called April and she confirmed that thanks to Austin, things were running smoothly again. I was a little too embarrassed to go straight to Austin's house and face the music (and the stares), so Austin dropped me off at Sweet Treats. Now that I was out of heat, he was okay with taking off, which I was thankful for. I didn't need someone in my life that was so possessive I couldn't walk five yards without feeling a tug at my leash.

April didn't take the news about Charlie's death very well. She might have a nose for business, but her sensitive side still ran deep. After fifteen minutes of crying in the bathroom, she emerged with a puffy nose and smudged eyeliner. She had also changed out of her work clothes, so I guessed she needed the rest of the day off to grieve. Girls like April looked even prettier at their worst; she just exuded a natural beauty I envied. I heard guys whispering about how she looked like a younger Keira Knightley, only blond with a punk-rock hairstyle like Pink. April had a unique look that made me wonder why she'd never tried modeling. Beckett once told me I looked like Megan Fox, but that's when he was going through his *Transformers* movie phase. Plus, boyfriends were supposed to say stuff like that. I had lied myself and told him once he looked like Matt Damon on steroids.

"You okay?" I asked as she sat in the chair behind the counter and blew her nose. "I'm serious about you taking over as manager. I don't know what I'll be able to pay you until I figure out the finances, but nobody knows how to run a business like you do. April Frost, you were born for this."

A little spark glittered in her eyes and I glanced at the streak of black dye in her platinum-blond hair. Her long bangs swooped over her face stylishly, and the streak ran diagonal. Last month, she tried a light blue color.

"Let me think about it. *Of course* I will," she said, as if there was never a doubt.

I walked around and hugged April so tight she let out a small fart. The both of us cracked up and I fell on the floor in hysterics. I needed that laugh; sometimes unexpected moments of childish humor made you realize how simplistically wonderful life was.

"Did you read over the information he left you?" she asked, twisting her bracelets around her wrist.

"Not yet," I said, pulling myself up. "I was busy last night and didn't get around to it."

That's when her eyes slid up and down my body. "With Beckett?"

I flushed and looked away because April had no idea Beckett was dead. The only person who would have reported him missing was his boss, but I had serious doubts he'd bother since they didn't get along. Beckett's only family was a drunk father serving time in the state pen. It simplified my holidays, which were always spent with my mom.

"No," I replied, unwrapping one of the colored candy canes and nibbling on the end. "I went out with an old friend."

"I don't think I've ever seen you wear your hair up," she noted. "Knocks five years off your age, but I guess you already know that."

No, I sure didn't realize a simple ponytail made me look younger, but a girl could always use a boost to her ego, so I spun around with a wide grin. "Think so?"

April wasn't paying attention as she thumbed through the ledger. "If you don't mind, could I close up the shop for the day to do some work? I'd also like to see the papers he gave you. Don't worry about the store—I'll work out shifts with the girls until you come back. Say, when *are* you coming back?"

Good question. As the owner, would it be appropriate for me to be stocking candy? "Umm, as soon as I can. You call me if you need anything. I'm serious, April. I'll give you the number where I'm staying and I'm going to get a cell phone."

"Holy smokes!" she exclaimed. "You? A phone?"

"All right, that's enough, Miss Sassypants. I'm having some family issues I need to resolve and you know I'm not someone who takes off work unless it's important. I have a lot of time built up and—"

She lifted a hand. "You don't have to explain it to me, boss."

We both smiled at each other. There we were, running our own place, and that was probably the first moment it really sank in. *Thanks, Charlie. Not just for dumping one hell of a responsibility on me, but for trusting and believing in me.*

"I'll drive you home and that way I can go over some of the books and look up a few things. Do you know where the money is all going now?"

"I'll have access to the business account, and he provided a list of all the companies he receives bills from or does business with so I can contact them with the changes. His savings is going into the account and I'll receive half of his life insurance."

"I can help you with some of that if you need me," she offered. "Where are you staying? You said you would give me the number but didn't say where that was."

"Um, that friend's house."

"Serious, huh? You always luck out with guys."

I frowned as she grabbed her oversized brown purse from beneath the shelf and wrapped the ridiculously long strap across her shoulders.

"I wouldn't say some of the losers I ended up with were a lucky streak, April. Just because I've had a few boyfriends doesn't mean I'm fortunate by any means. I know you don't talk about your personal life that much with me, but you could get any guy you wanted to. You're smart, beautiful, and know how to handle some of these kids like a pro. What's not to love?"

Her jeweled flip-flops clicked on the floor as she jingled the keys between her fingers. "I got that shy-girl problem. I don't know how to talk to guys. You've seen me in action whenever a hot guy comes into our shop. I totally clam up and either can't think of a thing to say, or I end up putting my foot in my mouth." She locked the doors and a kid on a skateboard whirred by.

"You just need to relax and be yourself like you are with me. You're over-thinking it too much, April. Just pretend the next hot guy you see is me."

"No offense, Alexia, but I'd never have sex with him if my imagination worked *that* well." She gave me a look and I shrugged. "I had a boyfriend once."

Once? I thought. April wasn't exactly a teenager; she was just out of college.

"And?"

"He cheated on me. With three other girls. I forgave him for the first two, but the third one was my best friend. All guys cheat; I guess I just didn't know how to keep him from going through them like potato chips. One is never enough."

"You are kidding me, right?"

Her VW felt like an oven and I cracked the window after she started up the engine.

April glared at the colored candy cane in my hand. "I don't want to talk about it anymore. Can you throw your candy out? This is my sister's car. Mine's not running right now, so she let me borrow it."

"Is this going to be a problem with you coming to work? I can lend you mine."

"The cootiemobile?"

"Stop calling it that," I grumbled. Yes, I wanted the car to burn, but I hated to be reminded of the events that earned it its new nickname. "If you need the car, it's yours. I don't want to worry about you taking the bus, walking, or hitchhiking."

"Sure," she said with a laugh. "Like I'd hitchhike wearing an apron and skintight shirt with Sweet Treats written on it."

We both laughed as the car sputtered down the road.

"Maybe you should change it up," she suggested. "It's your baby now."

Yeah, but there was something nostalgic about Charlie's magic touch, and a part of me wanted to put on those cheesy earrings in his honor. "I'll think about it, but keep enforcing the work gear. I want everything running the same until I determine what changes need to be implemented."

"Yes, sir."

April pulled up the driveway to Austin's house and Reno was

out front throwing horseshoes. The recent rain had cooled things down just a little, but not enough, apparently, since the heat had driven Reno to strip out of his shirt. I'd only seen him wearing long sleeves, but without the shirt, he looked even tougher. Like he'd been chopping wood for three hours a day.

A dark blue baseball cap and mirrored sunglasses obscured his face.

"Who's that?" she asked in a short breath.

"Reno. Austin's older brother. I think he's the eldest in the family."

"Was he in the military?"

Good question. Reno kind of gave off a military vibe. It wasn't just the short hair, but something about the assertive way he held his shoulders back and carried himself. Maybe it was the combat boots that made him stand an inch taller than Austin, and I wondered if he had a complex about his baby brother being the leader of the pack.

I scribbled down a few numbers on a scratch piece of paper while April turned on the windshield wipers. It didn't help, because the unpaved road had kicked up dirt all over the car.

"My sister's going to kill me," she said, staring at the hood. "She just took the car to the wash this morning and now I bet the tires are caked in mud."

"Who washes their car in the morning?"

April shrugged and turned on the radio. "My OCD sister who is going to have a fit. I may need to borrow your car after all."

"Not a problem," I said, barely paying attention as I dropped the pen in my purse. When I looked up, Reno was facing the car, staring at us with a horseshoe in his right hand.

Then I looked at April and saw her cheeks turn blazing red. She looked at the radio again and started fidgeting with it.

I smiled. "Want to meet him?"

"No!" she almost shouted.

I took that as an invitation and pulled the keys out of the ignition and quickly got out.

"Alexia, give me those!"

I walked toward Reno and heard her feet crunching on the dirt behind me.

"Give me the keys, Lexi. I have to go!"

"Reno, isn't it a little hot out here for horseshoes? Where's Austin?"

"Inside."

Panic was coming up the rear and she snatched the back of my shirt.

"I'd like you to meet my friend, April Frost," I said with a wide smile.

I stepped to the side so he could see her hiding behind me and April froze up like a statue, staring at the ground. She wasn't overly tan, so the blush on her creamy cheeks was noticeable, but it could have been the heat.

"April, this is Reno Cole."

God, that name really sounded horrible together. My brain was saying it ten times fast and it ended up sounding like a drug medication. I snickered and waited for them to start talking. But Reno folded his arms and kept intimidating her with his stare. The mirrored sunglasses weren't helping.

"Hi," she said in a small voice, kicking a pebble around with her jeweled flip-flop masquerading as a sandal. Her fingers twined around a frayed piece of her cutoff jean shorts and it was then I noticed her Billy Joel shirt. Maybe introducing her to Reno was a bad idea; he didn't look like that type that jammed out to soft 80s piano rock.

"It's pretty hot out here," she said.

A lone drop of sweat rolled down his cheek and agreed with her assessment.

"Alexia, I really need to go. Can I have the keys?"

April—who could sell a condom to a nun—couldn't talk to a man. I'd seen her work her magic in the shop buttering up customers, but it was always business related. She never had personal conversations with male customers, so I guess I just didn't notice how uncomfortable she really was around them. But why? Something else was going on with her, but I decided to let her off the hook and tossed her the keys.

"Thanks for driving me home," I said. "I'll call you later when I get a chance to look over the documents."

"Sounds good." Her eyes skidded to Reno for a second before she walked backward and stumbled, almost falling on her ass. "I'll talk to you later."

April jogged back to the car and Reno didn't stop staring.

"Could you look a little bit less intimidating?" I asked him. "You're traumatizing my friend with your scowl."

The engine revved and then April made a half-assed attempt to back up and circle around, but she wasn't masterful with the clutch. She backed into a deep pothole and the rear tire got stuck.

That's when Reno stalked forward with his heavy arms swinging at his side and I could see April inside the car, gripping the wheel and watching him with wide eyes. He moved to the rear of the car, bent over, and lifted it.

Actually *lifted* the car and pushed it out of the pothole. Now, I knew VW's weren't very heavy compared to some cars, but I was pretty damn impressed. She zoomed away and he lingered in the road, staring at the hole.

Austin emerged from the house with Maizy holding his hand. It warmed my heart to see that image, and then she sleepily waved at me.

"Everything okay?" he asked.

Reno lifted a shovel from the side of the house and was stalking toward the hole when something in the dirt snagged his attention. He bent over to pick it up and looked at the object in his hand.

"April's in on the plan. She just dropped me off, but she agreed to take the promotion without a raise increase—for now. We're going to work out the details later on."

"That's good news," he said, looking down at Maizy. She was swinging their hands a little bit and her eyelids kept drooping.

"Has she had her nap?"

Austin glanced down. "No, should she?"

I walked toward him and smiled. She napped in school and it was hard to break the habit over the summer because she'd get cranky and drive Mom nuts. But our family was always big on naps; it gave everyone a chance to go to their respective corners and relax for a little while. "Yeah. Afternoon naps are a must."

Without hesitation, Austin bent down and picked her up. She wrapped her tired arms around his neck and rested her cheek on his shoulder—eyes closed. Seeing that image of Austin being so paternal really did a number on me, and I swear my ovaries sighed. I followed him inside as he carried her to his bedroom and tucked her in. After closing the drapes, he turned the window unit on low.

"Are your brothers at the new house?" I whispered as he closed the door.

We stood in the narrow hallway and he nodded. "Reno stayed behind to watch over your family. I can't give you a personal guard like Lorenzo, but I don't think that's what you really want—to be followed around by someone for the rest of your life. That's not how I run my pack. I trust you, and yeah, shit happens. But everyone in the territory will know you and your family are protected by my pack, and nobody fucks with my pack," he warned. That was the dark moment when I could see a flicker of the dangerous man Austin truly was.

Austin folded his arms and pushed out his biceps, temporarily distracting me. "I want you to make a decision before we move, which is soon. Shifters live alone all the time, but it's too dangerous for a female wolf to turn rogue. Your mom is human and if she wants to go back to her old life, fine. But if she wants to stay here with us, then they're part of our pack and we treat them the same." He lowered his chin and looked serious. "That's an open invitation, Lexi. I mean it. I've brought it up with Lynn and she's thinking it over. Raising a child alone is stressful on her."

I leaned against the wall and cupped my elbows. "How permanent is this? It sounds like a big decision and I just want to be sure." I turned my head, listening to Ivy and my mom in the kitchen humming a song. Well, mom was humming and Ivy was singing. Couldn't make out the song, but it sounded like an oldie. A few pots clamored and the fridge door opened and closed.

"You're not signing your life away in blood. There's always a choice to switch packs if your needs aren't filled or you're unhappy."

Deep down, I knew my mom would only stay if I did. Being alone was wearing on her, which is why I visited so much. Having a houseful of men and women gave her people to look out for who, in turn, would offer her protection. I hadn't seen her look so energized in years.

"Just give me a little time to think about it, Austin. It's a lot to take in."

He stuffed his hands in his pockets. "Is it him? Church? Are you thinking about going to his pack? He's got a lot to offer a woman like you."

I sighed, unable to look him in the eye. I didn't really want to go with Church, but I wanted to know more about my real parents. Would moving in with Austin be a good idea? How would it change our relationship? Maybe he felt an obligation to Wes to look after his family; Austin was loyal like that. He would have jumped in front of a train for Wes. But did he see us as a burden on his pack?

"I just need to think about what's best for everyone," I finally said. "There are just way too many decisions being dumped on me at once and I need a little time to think them through. I've got this thing with the business, and then I've been contemplating calling the cops about my dad. Of course, I don't know how to explain that one, but I feel like someone should be looking for him."

"Someone is."

His statement rattled me. "Who? Ivan? I don't want you owing a man like him."

He took a deep breath through his nose and spoke on the exhale. "No, it's not Ivan."

"Then who?"

"Prince."

"Huh?"

He leaned against the wall across from me, planting his feet beside mine. "Prince called me up; I don't think the idea of what happened to Maizy, her being left on the side of the road, sat with him too well. He's a man who looks after his own, and while he doesn't have a mate or any kids I'm aware of, I guess it hit a sore spot with him. Prince is doing it on his own, no strings attached."

"He isn't going to hurt my father, is he?"

Austin tilted his head. "That man is *not* your father."

"Doesn't matter. I don't know what your rules are, but he's still Maizy's father. I'm more concerned about the man who's after him."

Austin scratched his chin, deep in thought. "I'll have a talk with Prince and see where his head is. Why don't you go in there and help your mom? Rumor has it she's making prime rib, and Denver is coming out of his skin waiting for dinner. I've caught that idiot in there three times stealing bites of what they're cooking on the stove."

I smiled. "Maybe you need to put him outside in the doghouse."

CHAPTER 26

————◦◦⟨⟨⟨✦⟩⟩⟩◦◦————

L ATER THAT EVENING, WE GATHERED in the kitchen at the small oval table. Only this time, Austin sat to my immediate left.

"We need a bigger table," Mom declared, setting the prime rib in the center. Denver sliced into the succulent meat with a carving knife, devouring the visual display with his indigo eyes. He had a fit body—trim, but not svelte like Jericho. By the time my mom was finished with him, he was going to need to upgrade his shirt size.

No one dressed up for dinner. Denver sported an orange Atari T-shirt and Reno wore long sleeves. It was thin, breathable material, but I couldn't figure out why he'd dress like that in summer. I hadn't noticed any scars or tattoos, but it did give him a more serious air of authority. Austin had mentioned Reno was the most obedient wolf in the pack, and I wondered how the family dynamic affected the oldest brother who was used to being in charge and looking after his younger siblings.

Maizy sat beside Ivy, who placed a spoonful of cucumber salad onto her plate. Maizy loved vegetables, but she didn't look crazy about the meat. We also had homemade mashed potatoes, and Austin looked like he was in heaven as he devoured my mom's home cooking. He used to eat dinner with us at least three times a week, and I could tell each bite took him down memory lane.

Mom periodically described how she seasoned the asparagus, or the technique she used to grill the French bread, just so everyone would compliment her cooking all over again.

Totally eating up all the attention.

"You going back to work?" I asked, sipping my tea.

"I'm not sure what to do," she said with a click of her tongue.

"The house is paid off and I've been thinking about selling. Too many memories."

"You're living with us," Wheeler said. "No arguments. If I can eat like this for the rest of my life, then I'm going to die a happy man."

Mom beamed and tried to refocus on my question. "I'm too young for social security, but I do have a little money tucked away to live on. Not enough to keep up with the bills, so I guess I have no choice but to work."

Jericho quickly wiped a napkin across his mouth and pushed away from the cabinet where he'd been eating. "I have to head out. I've got a gig tonight and I'm already running late for sound check."

His brown hair had been gelled and styled in that sexy "I don't give a shit" way, with strands of at least two shades of brown. His jeans were loose and black with a few chains going around the back, and his sleeveless shirt had the name of some band I'd never heard of before. Not to mention he wore a smudge of black liner that made his green eyes pop.

Jericho leaned around to kiss my mom appreciatively on the cheek before heading out the door. "Thanks, Miss Knight." He strutted out the door and Mom looked wistfully at her plate.

Miss Knight. I knew what she was thinking. She had been called Mrs. Knight for years, and even after my dad left, she never corrected people. That's just what women her age were assumed to be. It had taken three years before she stopped wearing her wedding ring.

Reno stood up and filled his empty plate with seconds. "The new house needs a paint job," he informed Austin. "We can hire someone to do the exterior, but you need to figure out if you also want them to paint the inside. We patched up some of the holes in the wall. I don't know what the fuck happened in there, but it looked like a barroom brawl."

"I can help," Mom volunteered. "Ivy can come along and we girls will see what needs to be done. I've laid my own flooring, installed crown molding, and even wallpapered three rooms."

"True story," I said, chewing a piece of bread. "Don't even get her started on landscaping. You have no idea who you're messing with; my mom can wallpaper Alcatraz and you'd think it was a bed and breakfast."

She slapped my hand jokingly and I smirked, sipping on my glass of sweet tea.

"I'd appreciate that, Lynn," Austin said.

Awkward.

Austin had always called her Mom. *Always*. It was never Mrs. Knight or even by her first name. That's just how he saw her. Maybe he felt like he had disappointed her and his privileges were revoked.

Mom tapped her fork on her plate, pushing around the cucumbers. I don't think she knew how to go about addressing the topic, but I could tell it was on her mind.

"Damn, this is fucking good," Wheeler exclaimed from the counter he sat on. "If you don't go back to work, then I'll hire you as our personal chef," he offered, wiping the back of his wrist across his mouth. Good thing he kept his circle beard short; the idea of men getting food in their facial hair repulsed me.

"Maybe I'll take you up on that," she replied.

"Dead serious," he said, lifting his light brown eyes to hers.

"You need a job to be able to pay her," Austin suggested, chewing off a bite of bread.

Wheeler's posture stiffened and his lips thinned. "How about we take this conversation offline? 'Preciate ya," he said in low words.

I lightly stepped on Austin's foot beneath the table and got the weirdest vibe from him when he looked at me. The alpha didn't know how to react with a woman silently telling him to shut up.

"What kind of experience do you have in finance, Wheeler?" I asked.

His brows popped up and he leaned forward on his elbows, pushing something around on his plate. Wheeler's mouth curved up at the corners and my, didn't he look like a slick fella? "I have a CPA license. I've also done taxes, accounting, and worked as a financial advisor. Lots of rich assholes out there who don't know how to manage their money. But I've dabbled in other things."

I looked at Austin and we had a mental conversation.

"I may need your advice on something if you have the time. We can talk about it later."

He licked the prongs of his fork, watching me carefully. "Maybe."

"No maybes," Austin said in a thick voice. "If Lexi needs your help, then you're going to give it to her."

"*I'll* give it to her," Ben said suggestively, and he wasn't talking about accounting.

"Keep it up," Wheeler warned Ben. "See what happens."

Austin's chair scraped against the floor as he rose from the table and delivered a palpable glare at Ben. There was no attempt to charge after him, and somehow it made him more menacing. Ben submissively walked across the kitchen and ate in the corner alone. Austin sat back down and my mom was the only one who didn't notice what had just transpired between the men.

Everyone else did. Ivy stared at her plate, shoulders hunched, spreading her mashed potatoes around with a fork.

Mom sprinkled a dash of pepper on her steak. "I'll go with you in the morning and see what you boys are dealing with. As a homeowner, I know a thing or two you wouldn't think to check. I just hope you had an inspector come out and look at the foundation. Lexi, do you mind watching Maizy for the day? I won't be able to keep an eye on her and I don't think that's the kind of place she should be running around in. There might be nails or loose wires."

"Sure. No problem." Mom didn't bother asking me to go because she knew my stance on manual labor. Especially after the paint-thinner fiasco.

"Good. We'll stop by the hardware store and pick up several gallons of white paint. Something always needs a fresh coat of paint and we might as well get started right away."

"Mom, do you really want to be painting in this heat?" I argued.

Yeah, she did. That woman was born to redecorate. She just never had much room to do it in her small house. But the idea of a large home that was big enough to have once been a hotel? I knew she was about to die a little bit and go to heaven. I wouldn't be surprised if she had them laying down wood flooring by sunset.

I leaned into Austin and spoke privately. "Did you clean up everything?"

The first thing my mom would see when she walked into the

house was a mattress with tangled sheets, and I was sure I had left some of my things there. I didn't want to give her the wrong idea of what kind of daughter she had raised.

Austin grinned, telling me visually that *hell no,* he hadn't moved a damn thing.

Ivy finally piped in. "I can help furnish the rooms. I'm good with finding cheap or free furniture and fixing it up; just give me some money and I'll work with a budget. People wait for trash day and put it on their curb, so if one of you can come along with me on those days, we can scope out some of the neighborhoods and load them onto a truck. Garage sales will get you bargains if you go late."

"Why late?" I asked. "Early bird gets the worm."

She pushed her braid off her shoulder and a strand of hair slipped in front of her nose. "Early bird also pays a fortune. The late bird gets the deal on leftovers, because the owners just want to get rid of it for any price at that point. People can't see the potential in some pieces that look ugly or broken. I can. I see beneath all the glossy paint at the raw beauty below the surface."

Hand to God, every man in the room was watching her like she was a prophet. Ivy had such a beautiful voice and the manner in which she spoke drew you to her words, as if everything had a deeper meaning. She could be talking about scrubbing a toilet and make it sound like she was teaching you a lesson about humility.

I smiled and took a bite of cucumber. Ivy was going to fit in well; she was exactly what this pack needed. They had somehow accepted her as a sister, even though she was insanely beautiful in an earthy way, with lush lips and delicate features. I had so much to learn about Shifters.

"You going to be okay by yourself?" Austin asked hesitantly.

"Sure. I'll have to plan something fun with Maizy," I said in an animated voice, grabbing her attention. I winked at her and she giggled while nibbling on a tomato wedge. "Maybe we'll do Pretty Pigtail Day and make some homemade pizza. Would you like that, Maze?"

She gave it the weighty consideration only a six-year-old can. "Umm, okay. Can we play games like at the pizza place?"

I glanced at Austin, not wanting to let her play on Denver's game system. "You got any kid games around here?"

He frowned a little and thought about it. "Cards?"

"Then I'm just going to have to kick it old school and show her how to play hopscotch."

"Hide and seek!" she replied.

"I don't think we have the stuff to make a pizza," Austin murmured in a deep voice.

"Trust me, you do. I know how to make homemade dough. Heck, I can make a pizza using toast if I really need to."

"She can," Mom agreed. "And it's appalling."

"You have tomato sauce in the cabinet and there's provolone cheese slices in the fridge, so it's all good. Call me if you want lunch later on. Maybe you can lend me the keys to one of your cars and I can swing by."

"What's wrong with yours?"

I gave him *the look*. His brows relaxed as he remembered. I'd once hated that car because it was a symbol of Beckett's infidelity, but now it was a reminder of the man who tried to take my life.

"The wolves will stay off the property," he stated as fact. "I've marked a warning and the Packmasters in the area know about our situation. If you have any trouble, you can call Prince. His number is on my phone and I'll leave it with you."

"Prince?" my mom suddenly piped in. "The guy in the sparkly pants who sang 'Purple Rain'?"

I did a facepalm, trying not to laugh, because it *was* funny. I'd actually gotten used to his name and didn't find it unusual until she brought it up.

"I like Prince," Maizy declared, putting a giant forkful of mashed potatoes into her mouth. Ivy pointed to the napkin on her lap and silently coaxed her to wipe her face. "He's my hero and got me from the road with all those cars. I was really scared that no one would find me."

Denver stretched his arm behind Maizy's chair and angrily tossed his fork on his plate with a clang.

Mom looked at Austin. "He was the one who found her?"

Austin nodded and sliced up more of his meat. "He's sent a few of his men to look for your ex. I don't think he liked finding a little girl abandoned on the side of the freeway because her father decided to drop her off like a bag of garbage."

"What are you going to do with this house?" I asked, changing the subject.

"Keep it," Austin said with a mouthful. "It belongs to my parents and I don't plan on selling. Maybe I can pass it on someday."

Then he got real quiet and cut his meat into sizeable pieces.

"The house will fall apart," I pointed out.

"Land doesn't fall apart. The house can go for all I care," he said, waving his fork around. "It's the property that holds value. We can use it for a getaway whenever someone in the pack wants some time alone with their woman, or their wolf wants a private run."

Ivy's eyes brightened and she glanced around, as if she were thinking the same thing I was. *What woman?* These men didn't seem like they were ever going to settle down.

Austin held the fork to his mouth and slowly pulled the meat from the prongs. He had a look on his face that only an inside joke could deliver. "You *did* mention something about a heat house."

Oh God. I blushed so hard I had to pretend to drop my napkin on the floor and then bent over to pick it up. Someone in the room snorted with laughter and I was tempted to crawl all the way underneath the table.

"I want the key to *that* house," Ben said from across the room.

"A place like that would be useful," Ivy remarked. "I'd be interested in something like that."

"What are you all talking about?" my mom finally chimed in.

I swear, I couldn't get up. I kept staring at the floor, three seconds from bolting out of the room. Then I felt Austin hook his fingers around the waistband of my shorts as if he could read my mind.

"Females go into heat," Austin said matter-of-factly.

Oh God, just shoot me now.

"Heat?" Mom asked, setting her fork down.

"It means they go into freak-mode," Ben replied in a humorous tone from the other side of the room. "Ever seen a cat in heat?"

I tried to get up but Austin's grip on my shorts tightened. I remained under the table, holding the napkin between my fingers and staring at my mom's black shoes. She was probably wondering what the hell was wrong with me.

"It's when they're ovulating and their body wants someone to give them babies," Maizy suddenly blurted out.

I sat straight up like a lightning rod and glared at her. "Who told you that?"

She tucked a large cucumber in her mouth and smiled. "I saw it on TV. That's how kittens are born. Can we have a kitten?"

"No," Wheeler cut in, tearing off a piece of his bread and stuffing it into his mouth. "We don't like cats around here."

"That's all you," Ben said. "I don't give a shit about cats."

"Watch your language around Maizy," Mom scolded.

"Well," Wheeler replied, "*I* don't like cats. I don't want them anywhere near me."

Ben smirked. "What's the matter, Wheeler? Afraid of a little pus—"

Austin slapped his hand down on the table and everyone shut up. "We'll head out before sunrise so we can get as much done as possible before it gets hot. I don't want to hang around here any longer than we need to, so the sooner we move, the better. I'm going to close out the bills on this place by month's end."

After the table was cleared, everyone fell out of their chair when Mom surprised them with peach cobbler and vanilla ice cream.

Yeah, she was definitely worth her weight in gold around this place.

◦•◦◦◦◦◦◦•◦◦

A few hours after dinner, Austin was sleeping in Jericho's room with Lexi beside him. Only this time, there was no touching. It was weird since he had spent the previous night pleasuring her for hours. But Austin didn't want to throw mixed signals by showing her affection that would make her question their nonexistent relationship. Lexi didn't know the rules of pack life, especially not the dynamic of a single woman in the mix.

As an unmated Packmaster, it was his duty to make sure his women were taken care of. That meant abating Lexi's discomfort while she was in heat. Single women in packs didn't sleep around with the men because of the friction it created, so it wasn't uncommon for them to seek out the alpha for relief. An alpha had more self-control, which would allow him to satisfy her without it resulting in an unwanted pregnancy. Most Shifters had no restraint around a female in heat and couldn't resist the urge to have sex. He *could* have left Lexi alone to take care of business.

But damn, the idea of having his hands on her was an opportunity he couldn't pass up. Her luscious scent was floral, like roses after a thunderstorm, awaking the male within who desired nothing more than to please her. It was an epic internal battle raging, because he wanted to take it a step further. But sex might have pushed her away and left all kinds of question marks about his intentions. It wasn't like that among Shifters, but he knew how human women broke it all down. Lexi was a complicated woman and too good for a one-night stand.

So when they crawled into the bed after a second round of peach cobbler, Austin turned his back to her and didn't say a word. He stole a glance over his shoulder and saw she had done the same thing.

Nothing had felt more awkward.

Sleep was an exercise in futility. All he could think about was wrapping his arm around her and smelling the leftover sunshine in her hair.

He remembered how beautiful she'd looked on the porch that night with a storm brewing in the sky and in her rich brown eyes. The way she looked up at him as the breeze lifted a few strands of her hair. He wondered if he fucked it up by staying with her and not sleeping in another room like originally planned.

Then he thought about Lorenzo, who was an attractive choice for a woman looking for money or status. Most women didn't hesitate to choose him, and Austin had learned that the hard way years ago when Lorenzo Church wooed Austin's first Shifter girlfriend away from him. Not exactly a way to build up an alpha's confidence.

Regardless of how he felt about the asshole, Lexi had a right to learn about her family. She possessed Native American features, now that he thought about it. High cheekbones, beautiful brown hair, and supple lips. Yeah, supple. The kind that he wanted his mouth all over the more he remembered their kiss on that porch and the sweet taste of sugar on her tongue.

She was no longer the girl he once remembered, but in a strange way, she was. The qualities he loved in her she had never lost, even though her body had blossomed into that of a stunning woman.

Sleeping beside Lexi without touching her was one of the hardest things Austin had ever done. The idea of her being with any other man, or in any other pack, made his wolf pace nervously.

When he had taken her out to The Pit on their date, Beckett had been waiting outside for them.

With a baseball bat.

Austin had picked up a strong scent of adrenaline and instead of walking straight to his car, he'd gone around the back of the building. That's when he confronted Beckett and they got into a brawl. It was against the law to kill a human, so all he could do was beat the shit out of him. By the time he got back to the restaurant, Lexi was nowhere to be found.

Twice he almost lost her, thanks to Beckett. He shouldn't have been distracted by his phone when Beckett had crept into her apartment, nor should he have confronted Lorenzo's guard while Beckett was attacking her. That split-second decision had almost cost Lexi her life. Austin didn't have any remorse over the murder. Even if they did find the body, he stood a good chance of justifying his actions.

If he didn't? Then fuck it. She was alive and that's all that mattered.

Thinking about it made him want to pull Lexi against him and feel her heartbeat, but he stayed where he was, content with listening to her breathe as he stared at the misshapen patterns on the wall. She made sexy little growling noises in her sleep that his wolf loved. He always liked watching her sleep, even when she was a kid. She looked so peaceful, as if nothing in the world was wrong, even when it was.

The next morning, Austin woke up before dawn and carefully

crawled out of bed. Lexi rolled over and threw her right arm across the sheets, nuzzling her face against the pillow. After getting dressed, he watched her for a few beats before waking up the rest of the crew. It gave him peace of mind to know Prince was tracking down her father—just one less thing he had to worry about.

One advantage of making allies among neighboring packs was that they looked out for one another, reported suspicious activity, and were more likely to lend a hand than a rogue was. Not many packs occupied the immediate territory, but Austin had spent time building a rapport with the Packmasters, making them aware of his situation with the human family. Something he would have to start all over again in the new house. There were three packs in his immediate area, and one of them belonged to Church.

Ain't that a bitch.

Austin tucked his shirt in his jeans and peered into his bedroom, lightly tapping his knuckles on the door. He flipped on the light and stared at an empty bed.

"What the… Reno!" he yelled out, storming down the hall to the living room. "Lynn!"

Denver was lying on the sofa with a bowl of cereal on his bare chest while Maizy sat in front of the TV watching cartoons.

"What the hell, Aus? Chill out. The chicks went to redecorate. They were so excited about buying curtains and shit that Reno drove them out to Walmart about a half hour ago. The twins went to the house to crank on the air, and I've just been waiting for you to get your ass out of bed so we can meet up with them."

"It's not nice to say bad words," Maizy reminded him without taking her eyes off the TV. She was already dressed as if she were going somewhere.

Denver's face turned a little red and he stretched his arms behind his head and set the bowl of cereal down on the end table. "You ready? And PS, the next time you want someone to mark a hundred acres of territory, that's *all you.*" Denver shot him a hostile glare before slinging his legs off the sofa and getting up, then walking barefoot toward the bedrooms. "Jericho said he might stop by, but I doubt it. You know how he gets after one of his shows; probably lying in bed drunk and stoned with two hot babes on each arm. Lucky bastard," he murmured.

The clock read 4:35 a.m. Ordinarily, the men would have slept in, but Lynn was already working her magic to whip some of these lazyasses into shape. Now *Austin* was starting to look like the slacker.

When Austin sat down to put on his shoes, he looked over at Maizy who leaned back on her hands. The mark on her shoulder blade concerned him as to what fate lay ahead of her. Most of the younger generations of Breed wouldn't know what it meant, but some would. Austin had never felt so fiercely protective of a child, and that's when he knew Lynn and Maizy had to stay with him, even if Lexi chose not to.

Human or not, they were his pack.

Maizy peered over her shoulder. "I like you."

His face softened and his chest tightened a little bit. She might not have looked like Wes, but damn if she didn't have his smile with the dimples.

Austin walked over, squatted down on one knee, and tied her loose shoelace. "I like you too."

CHAPTER 27

A FTER I FIXED A PLATE of scrambled eggs and maple bacon for Maizy's breakfast, I relaxed on the concrete porch step with a glass of orange juice, taking a moment to savor the early morning sunshine before the heat settled in.

In Texas, that meant around ten in the morning.

I had Austin's cell phone tucked in the back pocket of my shorts so he could get a hold of me if needed. I stressed that he not let my mother overwork herself, but I was glad she had something to keep her occupied after everything that had happened. When my father left us, it destroyed her, and I was worried she might slip into a state of depression like before.

Quite the opposite, in fact. Her ability to find strength through all this allowed me to focus on other matters.

After spending an hour reviewing the documents Charlie left for me, I uploaded the flash drive onto a computer in Austin's house and e-mailed a few files to April. I considered having Wheeler review some of the bookkeeping stuff if he had any expertise in this area, which I'm sure he did.

People never got why I liked working at the candy store, and maybe at the time, neither did I. But pieces were locking into place, and now I understood what I didn't then.

I loved the store, plain and simple. It felt like home. Charlie had been grooming April for the manager position—I could see that now.

Little did I know he had something bigger in store for me. It explained why he'd left me in charge to make decisions I shouldn't have been making.

My legs were quickly browning in the sun, so I finished my

coffee and went inside. Maizy wanted me to paint her nails shell pink. I braided a few strands of my hair, wishing I could wear it more like Ivy did. It suited her in an elegant and lovely way, whereas I would just look childish. I put a few braids in Maizy's hair because we were going to graduate from Pretty Pigtail Day to Salon Day. After our trip to the Salon of Lexi, we devoured a homemade cheese pizza for lunch.

Austin called to check on me and we chatted for a little while. I laughed when he told me my mom was running the show like a drill sergeant, giving orders on where to paint and what not to touch. She had put Denver in charge of scrubbing the floors.

Austin told me he'd been able to secure the new house so quickly because the couple had moved out a year ago. They hadn't gone through a realtor, so he'd bought it from them directly.

In cash.

That pretty much earned him the key on day one after signing a few papers and shaking hands.

A few minutes after Maizy went to her room with a book, I dozed off on the brown sofa. I missed lawnmowers, dogs barking, and passing cars—all the vibrant sound effects associated with living in the city.

The phone in my back pocket startled me and I answered in my sleepy voice. "Hello?"

"I hoped you would answer," Lorenzo replied.

"Hi, cousin," I grumbled, sitting up and rubbing my eyes. I walked into the atrium and closed the sliding glass door behind me so I wouldn't bother my sister with our conversation, in case she had fallen asleep. "Why are you calling Austin's number?"

"Because you returned my phone and I had no way to get in touch with you. I was going to give Cole a piece of my mind, but I'm glad it's you. Is he taking care of your needs?"

"I take care of myself," I said, crossing my ankles and leaning back in the lawn chair.

"I hope you took care of yourself when you were in heat. Is that over?"

I held the phone away from my ear and looked up at the sky

with my palms up. *Why me?* These guys thought my libido was appropriate table conversation to bring up while discussing their favorite beer or what's on TV.

"Alexia?" he called out.

"I'm here. All that's over with so, yeah. I don't really want to discuss it."

"Fair enough, but one day, you're going to tell me everything that happened. I hope Austin warned you that you shouldn't have sex while in heat unless you want to get pregnant. That's what your body is preparing for, and a baby will tie you to him permanently."

He was trying to get me to fess up either way on what happened. I decided to whistle instead.

A deep chuckle filled the other end of the line. "I get the point. Have you decided if you want to join a pack or are you stalling?"

"What do you have to offer?"

I was only kidding, but Lorenzo switched to his business voice and decided to give me his best sales pitch. "My property is five hundred acres and I own two more lots on the other side of the city. As I've told you before, I control a large pack. That means safety and protection for the females who live among us. My men follow orders or there are consequences. I left two of those consequences on your porch the other day." He paused so I could get his full meaning. "We have sixteen bitches in the pack and eleven are mated."

"To you?" I asked in an irritated tone.

"No one is mated to me, but three share my bed when they are willing. No other male can touch the ones I've claimed. There's a code we follow and no one is forced to do anything against their will."

"One isn't enough?"

I heard the clicking of his teeth. I'm sure he was figuring out how to answer that one without digging himself in a hole, because Lorenzo didn't really know my stance on such things. He'd never asked me out on a date or bothered to question what my favorite food was or what I enjoyed doing on the weekends.

"All I'm saying, Lorenzo, is that most women don't want to share any more than you men want to share. They may seem okay with it, but if you married one of them, I can guarantee you *she* wouldn't be okay with it. It's not in our nature to share our man."

"Which is why I haven't mated. I'm not asking you to be my life mate, Alexia. I want you to keep my bed warm."

"Not if someone else has kept it warm for me. And besides that—"

"If you bring up the cousin thing one more time, I'm going to come over there, throw you over my shoulder, and bring you home with me. We're not related by blood, so let's drop it. Are you wearing shorts?"

I glanced down. "Uh, yeah. Why?"

He laughed darkly. "I just wanted the mental image of what you'd be wearing while I was wearing you over my shoulder."

"Someday you're going to find a woman who doesn't like it when you talk like that."

"Suffice it to say I've never had any complaints from a woman when it comes to the private words I whisper in her ear."

I glanced up at a red-tailed hawk spreading his wings across the blue sky and piercing the silence with a scream.

"This is who I am," he continued. "I have yet to meet a woman who doesn't accept that I'm a feared and respected man."

"Oh? Is that the kind of man you think women desire? I guess you're not the same person who wrote that poetic message on the card that came with my roses."

"Touché," he replied. "We are all more than who we portray ourselves to be. So, Alexia Knight, who are *you*?"

Suddenly, I wanted to start singing an old classic rock song to those words. "I am a plethora of knowledge when it comes to rock and roll music. I love my family, rum makes me sick, my favorite sport to watch is soccer, and I'm a business owner."

Wow. It felt amazing to say that last part.

"Impressive. Business owner?"

"Sweet Treats. It's mine now. The owner recently died and left me the company."

He was quiet for a moment. "Wouldn't you prefer to sell it to someone with experience?"

"Not really." The comment needled me and I pulled at a frayed piece of material on the chair.

"That's more than a woman can handle. There's too much involved with operating a business, and I can speak from experience because being a Packmaster is not much different."

That peeved me. "What's the matter, don't like your women with a mind of their own? For your information, Austin supports me and thinks I should do it." I heard a car pull up out front and I glanced inside. "Listen, I need to go. Don't call me back on this phone because Austin will probably be the next person to answer, and he won't like that."

"Ah, but I will. If you need anything, you know how to reach me."

Something must have happened for Austin and his brothers to come back so soon. They had planned to stay until dark and when I last talked to him, he said Reno had left to pick up a sack of burgers and fries. That let me off the hook of having to drive across town to deliver their lunch.

The hawk cried out again before disappearing. While sitting in the atrium, I'd come to the decision I wanted to move in with Austin. I didn't know where it would lead, but I was absolutely certain of it now. My family needed protection and Austin had an accommodating house. It required enough work to keep my mom happy, right along with feeding five hungry men, who would eventually grow into a larger pack.

Then there was Maizy, who needed all kinds of protection if what Austin said was true. What if some pervert wanted to keep her as a little girl, like a Mage or something? I didn't know much about other Breeds, but there were some twisted people in this world. I was going to have to make sure she concealed the mark and didn't speak to anyone about it. Once she was old enough to understand, it wouldn't be a big concern.

I'd have to break the lease at my apartment, and hopefully any evidence of blood had been cleaned up. Even if I didn't remain with Austin, I'd never be able to go home again. I got chills just thinking about Beckett going savage and all those crimson rose petals scattered across the floor.

A high-pitched scream blared like a siren and I shot up out of my chair, flipping it over. My heart raced as I pulled open the sliding door and ran inside the house.

There was my father, holding Maizy under one arm like he was hauling a sack of potatoes out the door.

"Put her down!" I shouted.

Maizy's eyes were ripe with fear.

I couldn't believe it. After all these years, there was the man who had raised me, five seconds from kidnapping my sister.

The years had changed him and he had put on a little weight around the waist. But he still had the black mustache, bald head, and mean face. The kind of face that wasn't afraid to look his teenage daughter in the eye and whip her with his belt. Maybe that's why I didn't have an emotional meltdown over him leaving. The only tears I had shed were for the destruction he left behind of a family shattered to pieces.

"Alexia, go back outside."

"What are you doing here?"

"Your sister has something of mine," he said, shaking her a little bit.

I stepped forward calmly. "How did you know we were here?" I was stalling, trying to figure out what to do.

He eyed the front door and sharpened his glance. "I followed you here yesterday from your job. Can't believe you still work in that piece of shit kid store. Didn't you ever grow up? Then again, you were never one of mine, so I always knew you wouldn't amount to much."

That stung. More than I should have allowed it to. When Maizy whined and Dad shook her with a violent jerk, I redirected my focus on staying calm. I couldn't afford to shift and put her in danger.

"Maizy's a smart little girl. She's just the sweetest thing and has always been good about doing what she's told. She'll be going into first grade in the fall. You missed out on so much by leaving us, but don't do this to her."

"I know what you're trying to do," he ground out, rolling his eyes and shifting her in his arm again. "Save your breath."

"Why do you want her? Let's just sit down and figure it out."

"She's a thief," he said accusingly, giving her another jostle.

Maizy whimpered and I stepped forward again.

"*Please* don't do this." My heart sped out of control and my hands trembled. "I'll help you with whatever you want. I'll go with you if you just put her down."

"Now why the hell would I want you? Wes was the only child who was mine, and now he's dead."

"Because of you."

His eyes narrowed into thin slivers. "*What* did you say to me?"

"I know you did illegal stuff, but why would you want Wes to follow in your dishonorable footsteps? He knew about the Breed world and wanted to be immortal. Wes made a deal with a Mage for immortality and it cost him his life."

Maizy slipped down from his arm, but he held a tuft of her shirt with a strong fist. "What the hell do you think this is all about, little girl?"

Now I was dumbfounded, shaking my head.

"I got paid jack shit for the level of work I did. Thirty years of busting my ass for that man, and when I asked for a higher salary, he told me I was getting greedy. Said I'd better watch my step, or he'd put me under like he did Wes. That's when I knew it wasn't an accident, that he had killed my son. I took his fucking diamonds right out from under his nose."

"Great job, Dad. Now you've put your entire family in danger. Way to show him. McNeal stopped by to tell me the story. Wes was a hitman?"

"That was never the deal," he interrupted, the pitch in his voice higher. "Wes was just a messenger."

"No. The Mage hired him as a hitman in exchange for immortality that he'd never give him. But Wes didn't go through with it. He was a tough kid, but he was no killer. When he backed out, McNeal had one of his men take him out and stage the crime scene as an accident, probably so you would keep working for him."

My dad's face paled as the truth found residence in his dark soul. Dad knew Wes had died, but obviously didn't know the whole story.

"You always were a liar."

My eyes widened. "Do you think I'm making this up? You know

McCrazy killed him, but you didn't bother to ask why. Did you ever tell Wes about my world? You're an idiot to think he wouldn't have eventually figured it out."

He drew in a deep breath and his features tightened.

"That's right, Dad. *My* world. I don't think it's a secret any longer where I came from and what I am."

"Wes would have found out eventually. Comes with the territory."

"Why don't you tell me a little bit about what happened to my real mother when you murdered her?" My lips thinned and I balled up my fists.

"That's enough!" he roared, baring his teeth with a ferocious scowl. "Do you think I asked to take out a woman with a child? I never knew who my victims were until I arrived on their doorstep, and by then, it was too late to back out. I've never done a woman before or since. But don't press your luck, because I just might decide a reunion is in order."

I gasped.

Maizy's expression was stoic, and it terrified me to see her withdrawing from reality.

"Get outside," he said, pointing to the atrium.

"I'm going with you."

"The hell you are. I don't care if you are grown," he said, actually unbuckling his belt like he was about to let me have it.

When it slid out of the loopholes of his pants, he expertly folded it with one hand.

"Think you scare me?"

His brow arched. "Maybe not, but I'll sure scare the hell out of this one." He gave Maizy a shake and I tethered the wolf in me from lunging—afraid I would hurt her inadvertently.

"Your own daughter?"

"She isn't mine. No child of mine would ever steal from me."

"Wes stole your alcohol all the time."

Dad still got a facial tic when he was angry. "And my son isn't here to defend himself and call you a liar, now is he?"

"What is this about?"

"The diamonds."

I scratched the back of my neck and lowered my eyes to the floor. "Don't you have them?"

"I had them the night I took your mother. After I dropped the excess baggage on the curb, they were gone," he said, referring to Maizy. "By the time I noticed it the next day, I was too busy dodging a bunch of Shifters who were on my tail."

I dropped to my knees and softened my voice. "Sweetie, did you take any pretty rocks from this man? If so, you need to give them back. Please, Maze, listen to Lexi and give him what you took. I know you didn't mean it, and you're not in trouble."

Her lower lip poked out and I knew she'd taken them. At this point, I couldn't have cared less if he ran off a rich man; I just wanted him to get out and leave us alone.

"I don't got 'em anymore."

My dad swung her forward and backward, making her shriek as she was flung around like a rag doll. "Then what did you do with them?" he bellowed.

"Stop it! You're scaring her."

Dad dropped the belt and pulled something from the back of his pants. He aimed a gun at me, and Maizy started to cry. "Think she'll tell me if I put a hole in your leg?"

That's when I truly saw my dad for the man he was. As he stared down the barrel of the gun, it allowed me to see the very last thing his victims saw. How many? Were they innocent? I thought about my mother in hysterics, trying to protect her young baby from harm. Was he holding me at the time so I could watch?

"Why did you have to kill my mother?" Pain surfaced unexpectedly in my words, slicing across my tongue like razorblades as I felt sorrow for a woman I would never know.

His gun slightly lowered and a memory flickered in his eyes. "It was also supposed to be you. My orders were that no one be left alive. She twisted around to cover you up, so I shot her in the back. I thought the bullet went through and killed you too, but she just fell over you, bleeding. I rolled her off but didn't have it in me to kill an infant. You were covered in blood, and hell, your mother always wanted a girl."

Maizy's face was distraught and her words were barely a whine as they came through her tears. "Lexi, I want Mommy."

Dad's face cracked for a moment and he lowered his eyes, staring vacantly at the floor. I seized the opportunity and rushed forward.

He fired the gun.

Pain bit through my right arm and I clutched the wound with my other hand. The noise was so frightening that Maizy wriggled loose and ran out the front door. Warm liquid oozed between my fingers and snaked down my arm.

"Now do as I told you and get in there," he said, shaking the gun.

I never imagined I'd be in a position of deciding my sister's fate. He was unstable and likely to do something crazy if I didn't comply. But if I obeyed him, that meant he would take her. The shock of my father shooting me hadn't quite surfaced.

"If she hid the diamonds in the house and you leave, how do you think you're going to get them back? You seem to think Maizy went home with Mom, but that's not what happened. This is the only place she's been. The stones are here somewhere."

Which threw a giant wrench in his plans.

A loud engine cut off out front and I released a nervous breath. My dad picked up the belt and stalked toward the door with his gun in hand. I charged after him, fearing Austin or my mom would walk into the house, unsuspecting.

I tackled him in the hallway and we struggled, but the man was two inches taller and a hundred pounds stronger. He slammed me against the wall and I kicked him in the leg so hard he doubled over. Through the open door, a vision of horror consumed me.

McNeal patiently waited out front with Maizy in his arms. He was in uniform, except for the hat, and Maizy had her arms and legs wrapped around him. We used to tell Maizy if she ever got lost or separated from us to look for someone in uniform. I thought McNeal lied about working in law enforcement, covering up his real job. It sickened me to see he actually *did* work for them, and little did the humans know they had one of the most corrupt men masquerading as a good guy.

She had no idea she had just run into the arms of the enemy.

"Nice to see you again, Nelson Knight. Come on out and let's talk for a spell."

I dizzily leaned against a post, feeling close to throwing up. My dad aimed the gun at McNeal and my little sister.

"You killed my boy," he growled, holding the gun steady and straight.

"Think your gun is really going to do anything, Nelson? We both know you're just wasting your bullets on a Mage. Unless of course, you have another target," he said, gently twisting left and right, rocking my sister.

Maizy had on her pink princess skirt with the white tights. The shirt didn't match because it was yellow with cartoon characters on the front. She had spilled tomato sauce on her shirt and it was the only clean one I could find. I don't know why I noticed something so trivial, but my mind memorized every insignificant detail. The way the sunlight sifted through the trees and picked up the gold in her hair and the way her cheek rested on his shoulder as she sucked her thumb.

Maizy hadn't sucked her thumb since she was three years old and I bribed her with gum drops. Seeing that image disturbed me more than anything else.

I walked right past my father and stood between them, because I'd be damned if a shaky hand led to my sister getting shot. My dad spat curses at me, but I continued walking toward the Mage.

"Give me my sister," I demanded.

"I believe I'm owed a few sparklies for this one."

"Let me have her and I'll help you," I said. "Only Maizy knows where she put them, and she's not going to talk to either of you, especially with you scaring her the way you are. Please trust me."

"I don't trust Shifters," he said with a curl in his lip. "You're nothing but a bunch of breeding cockroaches that need to be exterminated."

Out of the corner of my eye, something moved behind the trees to my right. I kept my eyes locked on McNeal and my palms up. "I'll promise anything you want. You don't have to trust me, but I'll get her to talk. She'll listen, won't you, Maze?"

Her blue eyes turned in my direction, glistening with tears and innocence.

McNeal bent down and set her feet on the ground, slowly rising up with a devilish grin.

"She's all yours," he said, the words slow and enigmatic.

CHAPTER 28

⟶∘◦⟪⟫◦∘⟵

A USTIN TOSSED THE LAST CAN of empty paint into an oversized trash bag. The late afternoon sun smeared an orange trail of light on the porch, and all the windows on the lower floor were kept open after Ben inadvertently got high in the bathroom from the paint fumes. They couldn't have asked for better weather, but the manual labor made it miserable.

He'd gone outside to spray down the mud they'd tracked on the porch when Denver grabbed the hose and blasted a cold shot of water in his face.

"Jesus!" he yelled with a laugh. "Cut it out." Austin threw up his right arm to block, but he could hardly complain because it felt great. Denver aimed the nozzle straight up in the air and it showered them with water.

"You boys get away from the house. You're going to get spots all over the windows I just cleaned," Lynn yelled from inside.

"Damn," Denver breathed, clicking the nozzle off. "Our mom would really like that woman. Those two were probably separated at birth." He strolled to the end of the porch and sat down, taking off his sneakers and spraying his feet to cool them off. "Why is it women can never let a man have any fun? They just want to fuss about something."

"They're practical," Austin said, shaking off some of the water droplets from his hair. "We live in the moment and they think about what's coming. If they didn't keep us in check, we'd fuck up the planet."

"Yeah, well, I still think that cooling off and preventing a heatstroke is more practical than spots on the windows," he complained as a rainbow formed in the fine mist rising from the green hose.

Denver had always been the free spirit of the family—untamable. Truthfully, Austin didn't really want to break him. Not the way most Packmasters would. Denver loved people and that's why he worked as a bartender. His wolf was the only one who needed an attitude adjustment.

Jericho was the seducer in the family, although it never made sense because the man looked like he hardly showered. Denver was different. He could have any woman out there—he'd obviously hijacked all the best genes in the family. A masculine face combined with a mischievous smile won them over every time. But during their outings at the Shifter bar, he mostly hung out at the pool tables. He flirted like nobody's business, but was too damn selective to get serious. Who knows, maybe he didn't think they were good enough for him. Denver was only fifteen years older than Austin, although he looked younger.

"You wanna head back?" Denver asked.

"Yeah." Something was bothering Austin, so he picked up Reno's phone and dialed Lexi.

No answer.

Maybe she'd gone outside and left the phone on the counter, but Lexi had promised to keep it with her at all times. Something didn't *feel* right, and he couldn't put his finger on it. Everyone has intuition to some degree and most people blow it off.

Austin wasn't about to be most people.

"Heading out," he announced.

"I'll come with," Denver called out from behind, jogging across the dirt with wet feet.

"Why don't you stay behind and help clean up?"

Denver snagged a handful of Austin's shirt and yanked him back. "Because I feel that shit too. Something ain't right."

Austin tossed Reno's phone at Denver. "Call Wheeler and tell him what's up. I want them to sit tight, lock the doors, and watch the women."

Austin barely remembered getting in the car and starting the engine, but the next thing he knew, they were flying down the main road with rubber chewing up asphalt. The low afternoon sun splintered through the windshield and he squinted, having left his sunglasses at the house.

"Still no answer," Denver said after the fifth attempt at calling Lexi.

Who the hell could be on his property? "I want you to get Lorenzo Church on the phone." Austin recited the number while Denver handed him the phone.

"This is Church."

"Stay away from Lexi," Austin growled. "I want you and your men to back off."

"Hold on, is this Cole?" Laughter on the other end, and it only kindled the fire. "Good God, you *are* paranoid."

"You think I'm fucking with you? Try me." Austin gripped the steering wheel so hard it could have snapped. "Touch her and I'll break every finger on your hand. Take her, and I'll break your neck."

"What is this call about? You're wasting my time. I no longer have a man assigned to guard her, if that's what you're asking. That was her wish, and I will not force myself on any woman."

"It's not him," Austin said, glancing at Denver.

"Tell me what's going on," Church snapped, all humor erased from his voice.

Austin hung up and his foot became a cinderblock on the gas pedal. He dialed Prince, but it went to voicemail.

When they arrived at the turnoff, he slammed on the brakes and took off on foot. If someone was there, he didn't want to tip him off. Every muscle burned as adrenaline rocketed him up the road until the house came into view.

So did another scene.

A gun.

A wolf.

Blood.

A scream.

His heart almost stopped.

———————◦◦◦◦———————

Maizy remained motionless in front of McNeal, sucking her thumb with a vacant stare in her eyes. I kept my focus on the Mage, ignoring my father's shouts. They got into a heated argument and my arm was on fire from the gunshot, but the only thing that existed in my world was my little sister.

I knelt down and noticed her eyes were fixed on the blood trickling down my arm. "Come on, sweetie. It's okay. You're not in trouble. Come over here and let me give you a big squeeze, 'kay?"

"Maybe if I put a little shock into her, that'll wake her up." McNeal laughed, holding out his hands.

I had no idea what a Mage could do, but Austin had told me enough that it had me on my feet in less than a second. Before I could lunge, my father looped his belt around my neck and ran the strap through the buckle, yanking me back as if I were on a leash. The cold barrel of a gun pressed against my right temple.

That's when I saw the big picture. A large black-and-grey wolf bared its teeth at McNeal, stalking forward from the right. I could tell it was Prince from his unique multicolored eyes.

Austin and Denver looked like soldiers charging into battle as they sprinted up the driveway.

The Mage twisted around, and seeing the imminent danger coming at him from all sides, he reached for Maizy.

Prince's wolf lunged, driving his sharp teeth into McNeal's arm and thrashing about in violent motions. The Mage put his right hand on the wolf's head and he yelped, but didn't let go.

Maizy started to wail.

In a split second, Denver shifted mid-run. Clothes fell to the ground and in a blur of movement, his grey-and-white wolf charged toward Maizy.

I screamed, not able to comprehend seeing my little sister torn to pieces in front of me.

My father could barely maintain a grip as I struggled against him, reaching for my Maizy.

Oh God. *Please*, no.

My legs gave way, my father called me an ugly name, and that's when I witnessed the unimaginable.

Denver's wolf wrapped his body around Maizy, protecting her from the attack that ensued before her eyes between the Mage and Packmaster's wolf.

Austin approached at a steady pace and his blue eyes were electric.

"Get back or I'll shoot her," my dad warned. "All of you freaks get back."

At the edge of the woods, a pack of wolves stood like soldiers awaiting orders. They watched their Packmaster with the sapphire and brown eyes as he savagely attacked McNeal.

Dizzy and panting, I looked at Maizy and saw Denver's wolf taking slow steps, pushing her farther away from the violence. He faced the action and bared his teeth, but his sole purpose was to guard Maizy. I'd never seen anything like it. Austin had warned me Denver's wolf had a vicious and unpredictable nature, one that couldn't be trusted.

Except with a six-year-old little girl who adored him.

McNeal made a guttural moan as the wolf's canines pierced into his other arm, rendering them useless for harnessing energy as a weapon. His left arm had been jerked from the socket, and large chunks of flesh were stripped to the bone. The Mage kept reaching for slices of sunlight filtering through the tangled branches that would allow him to heal, but the trees were tall and the sun was low.

"Let her go, Nelson. Lexi's your daughter, whether she came from your body or not," Austin said in a steady voice, slowing his pace as he neared. "You raised her, fed her, and looked after her as one of your own. Don't do anything irrational because of greed or fear."

Austin's eyes flicked briefly to my bleeding arm and he flexed his jaw. Strange things drifted in my head. Like, why was he shirtless with wet pants? What was the story behind his tattoos? Had he ever thought about me in the years since Wes's death? Did he still like to eat Cheetos with cheese dip? Would I ever get to know these things, or was the gun against my head the last thing I'd experience in my life?

And when his frosty eyes lingered on me, I wanted to tell him I loved him. Loved him since I could remember, and now I knew without a doubt what I felt was more than a childhood crush or an attraction to my own kind. Austin didn't feel the same way, but it didn't erase how I felt. He had once vowed to kill the man responsible for ordering Wes's death, but Austin didn't flinch as a wolf took the honors and tore that man apart.

"I just want to get out of here," my father said. "Let me through and you can keep the fucking diamonds. I only wanted to get this guy off my ass. It's more trouble than it's worth. Now that you have him, feel free to take him out for me. That bastard killed my boy."

Austin inched forward. "I've spent the last seven years wanting to find the person responsible for killing Wes, and it led me to you. That Mage ordered his death, but *you* brought him into the dark corners of our world without a clue of how immortals perceive humans as disposable goods. You put your family in the line of fire by sending your *son* to work for a *Mage!*"

It was then I realized what Austin was doing. He was trying to get my father to turn the gun on him.

"Austin," I pleaded, trying to distract him. "No. Please don't do this. The Mage is the one you want. Wes wasn't given orders to kill just anyone, Austin. *You* were supposed to be his first hit."

He blanched as the words speared through him, and I had him for just a split second. The more Austin confronted my father, the more I feared for his life. My dad could shoot a cherry off a tin can, and Austin stood at point-blank range. But his eyes were resolute, and he never backed down.

Prince's wolf yelped as the Mage threw another burst of energy into him. They weren't sorcerers but powerful immortals who harnessed energy like a weapon. Blood was everywhere, and Denver's wolf was almost out of sight. Suddenly, Maizy wrapped her arms around his neck and I scarcely breathed. My heart skipped like a stone across the water until Denver's wolf slowly trotted out of sight with her safely on his back.

"Wes is in the ground because of you," Austin continued.

"You don't know jack shit," my dad shouted. "I should have known you were one of them. You think I wanted my boy growing up and struggling like I did for so long? The job paid well and he was willing."

"He didn't want money, Nelson. Wes wanted immortality. That's why he bartered with the Mage. He was star-struck with our world—wanted to be one of us. Let your daughter go; there have been enough casualties."

I'd never been in a situation like this before. I was just a girl who worked at a candy store and had a regular life.

Something flashed in Austin's eyes… something dark and bottomless. My dad must have seen it too, because he pulled me to the right side of the porch using the belt. He was going to make a run for it.

Out of nowhere, Lorenzo appeared from the side of the house and seized my father's wrist. He jerked his arm away and the gun went off. I stumbled forward and Austin caught me around the waist before I fell.

"So you are the human who killed my aunt?" Lorenzo said, holding my father by the throat. "You've caused us much grief over the years, and it's time to face the jury."

"Wait," I started to say.

Two men held my father while Lorenzo confiscated the gun and set it on a small table. I'd never seen him look so fierce. He had his hair tied back and wore the same black tank top with writing on it as he had when we first met.

Lorenzo's malevolent eyes darkened. "You may have some sentimental bond to this man, Alexia, but if he plays in our world, then he plays by our rules. This human committed a crime against my family by taking a life and stealing a child. He's going to face my family and serve his sentence. There's nothing you can say to convince me otherwise, so don't waste your breath."

He walked over and angrily removed the belt from my neck. "Shift, and heal yourself." His eyes flicked to Austin. "You have things under control here," he stated, more than asked. "I'll take my prize and go my own way."

"Just one minute," Austin demanded. He eased me into a chair and his heavy boots stomped across the porch until he stood in front of my father. Without warning, he threw a hard fist into his face, delivering two more brutal punches until blood poured from my father's broken nose.

Austin bent forward with a menacing scowl, speaking almost inaudibly. "*Nobody* fucks with my pack."

Lorenzo slid the loop of the belt over Nelson's head and tightened the strap around his neck. And just like that, Lorenzo took the man who raised me away. The man I no longer called my father and one I never wanted Maizy to understand was hers. A man who'd threatened her life, betrayed my family, and who held no value to the beautiful life that once belonged to my older brother.

I never saw Nelson Knight again.

Austin peered over his shoulder; Prince had the Mage under control. The next thing I knew, he leaned in and slid his arms behind me, helping me up. I held onto his neck as we traded places and he pulled me into his lap.

"Whatcha doin' here?" I said weakly, trying my best to smile.

Austin whispered something in my ear, a single word that made all my pain disappear.

"Shift."

CHAPTER 29

I DIDN'T THINK I'D EVER GET used to coming back into consciousness after shifting. It was disorienting, like a night after partying where I could only remember snippets of what happened.

But the sting in my arm had vanished and the only evidence remaining that I had been shot were smears of crimson across my flesh. I awoke on the front porch, naked, and Austin slid a knee-length T-shirt over my head. I robotically put my arms through the sleeves and turned around.

"You okay?" he asked.

But my mind was elsewhere. A sheet covered the body of the Mage, blood soaking through the white fibers, especially around the head. Prince stood before him, yanking up a pair of jeans I recognized as one of Austin's because of the hole in the knee.

His arms swung at his sides and he approached Denver's wolf, who was shielding Maizy. Prince wiped the blood from his face and chest with a wadded-up shirt as his pack looked on. In a commanding voice, he said, "Back away, and let me have the child."

I shivered at the authority in his voice. A feral growl rose from Denver and Prince shouted his order once again. This time, everyone in his pack lowered their heads submissively.

Prince bent down and lifted Maizy into his arms. He softly hummed a melody, taking a seat in the chair on the porch. She relaxed, coping as most little children do. She stopped sucking her thumb and patted her hand against her leg to the rhythm of his song.

Silent tears wet my cheeks.

Austin crouched on his knee and held one of my braids between his fingers. "How did you know to come here?" he asked Prince, but his crystal-blue eyes never looked away from me.

"I have a scout," Prince replied, pointing up at a red-tailed hawk perched in a tall tree. "That's not in violation of your territory; you don't have control of the sky."

"Why did you feel the need to have someone on my place?" Austin asked apprehensively, looking over his shoulder.

Prince considered this and stretched out his legs, crossing them at the ankles. "I made an agreement to help find the man who took her. We knew he was back in the city, but once again, lost his trail." Prince tipped Maizy forward and closed the rip in the back of her shirt. "You should take care to keep this mark covered," he said in a low voice. "They sell makeup which will camouflage it for a young child who doesn't understand the dangers."

He shared a private look with Austin and I crawled over and brushed my hands through her hair. "You okay, Maze? Bad guys are gone now and won't be coming back ever again."

"Why did he do that?" she asked in a sad voice. "He hurt you."

"No, honey. He missed. See?" I showed her my arm. "Don't you worry about me, little Maze. I've got that big-sister magic going on."

"Magic?" she asked.

"There are very bad men in this world, child," Prince began. He grasped her attention as she looked up into his pensive eyes—one sapphire and one brown. "But there are also men who will protect you. Always remember that, and surround yourself with only those you trust. You are but a fragile human, and there are things in this world you can't comprehend."

Maizy suddenly hopped off his lap and went inside the house. Austin finally sat down beside me, stroking my back.

"That advice goes for you too," Prince said, lowering his sharp eyes to mine. The hair he once had in a tight ponytail now fell free across his shoulders. "I hope whichever pack you choose, you keep the little one with you. She is a special child."

"I'm aware of that," Austin said. "She's staying with me. As long as her mother wants to remain with my pack, then she's welcome to, even if Lexi goes her own way."

Denver appeared, pulling a white T-shirt over his head as he walked barefoot across the hot gravel in a pair of jeans. He stopped, bent over, and brushed the soles of his dirty feet.

Prince stood up and slowly stepped off the porch. "My work is done here; the fiend has been brought to justice. I hear you're moving," he added, looking over his shoulder. "You still have my alliance. Let me know if you run into trouble with any of the packs out that way. I have pull."

He strode away with the confidence of a man who had been leading a pack for decades, if not longer. As he passed Denver, Prince showed respect for his bravery by touching his shoulder as he looked down at the corpse.

"My hero!" Maizy cried out, bounding toward the two men.

Denver grinned from ear to ear, but the light in his eyes dimmed when Maizy ran up to Prince and smothered him with a hug. Prince patted her head as she waved for him to squat down to her level. Denver stepped aside and turned his back, wiping the dirt off his jeans.

I went to say goodbye to the man who saved my sister's life.

"You all right?" I asked Denver.

He shrugged off my question and messed with his blond hair. I was about to hug him when he bent over and brushed a few pebbles from the bottom of his foot.

From the corner of my eye, I saw Maizy open her tiny hand and say, "Shhh." She placed a small, glittery stone in Prince's hand. A diamond.

"What's this?" he asked, watching it sparkle in the light.

"That's for my ring, silly."

"What ring?"

"The one you're going to give me when I grow up."

Prince furrowed his brow and I stooped down to her level. "Maizy, where are the rest of these?"

"I hid the treasure," she declared.

"Tell me where they are, honey."

"I don't want the bad guys to get them."

This was going nowhere. Maizy once hid a bag of licorice I brought home from the store. She refused to tell where, even when mom took away all her dolls and movies as punishment. We found the candy seven months later inside a pair of old loafers in the hallway closet. A trail of ants led us to the scene of the crime.

Prince rose to his feet and stared at the diamond in the palm of his cupped hand. "Here," he finally said, extending his arm toward me.

"No!" Maizy cried.

Tears sprang from her eyes and he immediately palmed it and bent over. "It was only in jest," he said with a warm smile. She pouted, as if he had made fun of her. "I promise to keep your treasure safe and return it to you someday, little one. You have my word."

That was all she needed, and Maizy shyly turned away. Denver had walked off several paces, staring at the cars that belonged to my father and the Mage. They would have to dispose of them. Maizy tugged on the hem of his shirt and he peered over his shoulder at her. She watched him patiently until he mashed his lips together to suppress a grin.

"C'mon, Peanut," he said. "Let's go home." She held up her arms and without a word, Denver bent over and lifted her up as he walked barefoot down the road.

"Lock up tight," Austin yelled out to him. "We'll stay behind and clean up."

<hr />

Maizy must have told a doozy of a story after Denver took her to the new house, because when my mom called to check on me, she was in a state of panic. It took a while to calm her nerves and assure her it was all over. I changed into a fresh pair of clothes and sat in the maroon recliner, staring at the black television screen. Two Breed lawmen had arrived to collect the body and interrogate us. Because the crime took place on Austin's territory, he was within his rights to protect his pack and his home. Austin covered for Prince for reasons I didn't understand.

"Why don't you shift again," he suggested, walking into the living room and looking down his nose at me. A slightly crooked nose, because it looked like someone had broken it a long time ago and he chose not to heal. Or couldn't.

"I'm fine. We went over this already," I said, feeling despondent about the turn of events.

"You were shot, Lexi. You're not fine."

He had a point.

"I'm just shaken up a little, I guess. I'm not sure how to feel about what's going to happen to my father."

"Don't hold on to a shred of guilt for a man who never loved you. He wouldn't have blinked if your sister got hurt, and he sure as hell didn't blink when he put a bullet in your arm," Austin growled.

I tried not to notice Austin was still shirtless. Not to mention he had picked up a golden tan that afternoon. I looked away and closed my eyes. Austin knelt in front of me and pulled off my shoes so he could rub my bare feet. God, his warm hands felt exquisite against my sensitive skin.

"Stay with me, Lexi. I'm asking you to choose my pack and make it official. You can have all the freedom you want, no strings attached. We'll look after you, and my brothers will help you get started with the business. I'll even let you have first dibs on any room in the new house."

"That's a mighty fine offer," I said in a soft, melodic voice.

"Is that a yes?" he asked gruffly.

How's a girl supposed to say no to a man giving her a foot massage? I decided to draw out the suspense until he finished circling his thumb around the middle of my arch. Austin caught on, and I shrieked when he tickled me.

"Is that a yes?" he said, holding my ankle firmly and continuing his relentless tickling.

Someone was going to get hurt with all my kicking. Finally, I gave in. "Yes!"

Austin slid between my legs and placed his head in my lap. His soft brown hair weaved between my fingers as I stroked it eagerly. The energy between us changed and the tingling returned, but it had nothing to do with being in heat. It had to do with my attraction to Austin as a man I admired.

"You make things so difficult," he murmured.

"I'm not the one with my head in your lap."

He looked at me and propped himself up on his elbows. "What's that supposed to mean?"

"It means I have no idea what's going on here. Are these repressed feelings you've had for me or am I misreading you?" My fingers drummed on the armrest of the chair.

Austin sighed through his nose. "I've never thought of you in a sexual way."

Which went down in my books as one of the most insensitive things a man had ever said to me. I wanted to bolt before I burst into tears from the embarrassment, especially after the intimate night we had spent together. But Austin held my hips firmly and wouldn't allow me to move.

"Let me finish," he insisted.

"Let me go!" I pushed his shoulders and the recliner began rocking; Austin was too strong for me to fight off. "I'm serious, Austin. Let go of me."

"You were a *child* for Christ's sake!"

"Not when I was *twenty*," I argued.

We were almost face-to-face, except he was a little lower because his arms were pinning me down. "To me you were, and the last thing I wanted was to have sex with you."

"Oh God, just let me up!"

I threw myself over his shoulder to toss him off balance, which worked. But not to my advantage as he flipped me over on the rug and covered me like a blanket. "Lexi, listen to me." I writhed beneath him, trying to break free. "Stop it!" he shouted, pinning me by my wrists.

Stupid wolf in me listened.

"Didn't you ever notice how I looked at you, Austin? I had a crush on you forever, and you hardly gave me a second glance."

"Whatever you felt for me was just instinct. We're alike, and you were drawn to me for that reason."

I shook my head. "No. You're wrong." I was about to remove the filter and say what I'd kept bottled up inside me for a lifetime—

something I'd always wanted to admit but never had the courage. "I've loved you since I was five years old. Longer than I can even remember. You were always in my life, and I looked up to you. It had nothing to do with this whole alpha wolf thing. It was *you*, Austin. It was the way you laughed at my jokes and stood up for me. You winked at me whenever I was feeling down, and I loved that you pulled over on a busy road and took that injured dog to the vet when anyone else would have driven by. I've always seen the goodness in you. I've always loved you, and it made me crazy you didn't feel the same."

He inched his face in closer and settled his body over mine to keep me still.

"You're right, Lexi. I haven't loved you since I was five. I'm not going to sit here and lie to you about it."

My stomach knotted and I felt a stabbing pain in my chest.

"You were a stubborn and odd little girl who liked to catch butterflies and release them in your house. You seem to have forgotten you used to call me Elastic Man when I hit a growth spurt at age nine." His breath was on my face and I froze as he continued. "You also had a knack for dating every guy who didn't pass my test, and if it were my decision, you wouldn't have gone out with any of them. No, Lexi, I'm not going to tell you I've loved you since I was five, because it's not true. I can't lie to you."

My heart sank, and he let go of my wrists and stroked his fingers through my hair.

"In fact, I remember the exact moment I fell in love with you. It was June seventeenth, the summer before your senior year in high school. We went camping with a bunch of friends and I sat next to you by the lake while you hummed a Fleetwood Mac song, watching the moonlight shine on the water and wearing a silly pair of pajamas. We didn't talk, but that's the first time I really saw you as the woman you would someday become. You probably don't even remember it, but I do. I always will."

Somehow, all the air in the room managed to disappear and I could scarcely breathe.

Austin bit his lip and turned his head away, his pale blue eyes glittering beneath inky lashes. It was the look of regret—one that inevitably came with something you wished you hadn't revealed.

An avalanche of emotion took over, and tears welled in my eyes, rolling quietly across my ears and into my hair.

He slanted his eyes toward me and saw me crying. "Shit," he breathed. "I'm sorry, Lexi." His fingers wiped my tears and I shook my head. He just didn't understand.

"I've waited my entire life for you to say that to me, Austin."

His lips twitched and his voice softened to the growly, bedroom one I liked. "Then why are you crying?"

"Because I don't know if you still do. Did I blow it?"

All humor in his face evaporated. Austin tilted his head down and brushed his lips against mine. I'd never been kissed in the slow and reverent way that Austin delivered. Each kiss barely pressed against my lips. Sometimes they stuck together a little, and small wet sounds filled the quiet room. But beneath such a simple gesture, sparks ignited between us, and all my doubts melted away. I could taste him, smell him, and feel his warmth on my mouth and body.

I used to watch shows about unsolved mysteries and spontaneous human combustion. I had an idea what the cause could have been because I felt like a box of explosives.

His rough hands cupped my cheeks, and his lips moved their way around my face, kissing the curve of my jaw, my eyelids, and the tip of my nose, before returning to my mouth.

The tension multiplied between us when I caught his bottom lip between my teeth and gave it a tug. He slid his body up just a fraction and I felt the weight of him everywhere. I bent my knee and he fit against me like a piece of a puzzle locking into place.

Being in heat had nothing on a kiss delivered by Austin Cole. It was intricate and reckless all at once.

"Don't be so gentle," I encouraged.

A spark flickered in his eyes and his mouth came down on mine, tongue pushing in as his hips did a swivel. I moaned and ran my hand along his jaw, scraping my fingers just a little bit so I could hear the scratchy hiss of his stubble. He lifted his head and awareness burned in those crystalline depths. I loved his eyes—the way the black rims made it seem like they framed an ocean in his gaze.

Austin stared into the depth of me as he pulled the ends of my shirt over my head. When he dragged his gaze down to my chest, he froze.

"What's wrong?"

When he didn't answer, I got irritated. "B-cup not enough for you?"

His left hand firmly covered my mouth. "Will you be quiet for a moment while I drink you in? I've fantasized about this moment for the last seven years, so give me a minute. I'm not going to rush the first time I get to see your body beneath mine. That okay?"

I stitched my lips together and let him make love to me with his salacious eyes while my fingers memorized his broad, inked shoulders and firm biceps. His skin was sticky and taut beneath my hands and I wanted to taste him as he slid down the length of my body.

Austin's lips skimmed across the flat of my stomach and I sucked in, stretching my arms up. Then it occurred to me I'd waited too long to just lie around while he took his time exploring territory he had recently vacationed to. I grabbed a fistful of hair and yanked him up, kissing him hard on the mouth.

He ran his hand over the lace of my white bra and dragged his mouth to the soft curve of my neck. My heart thundered like the hooves of a hundred stallions.

"Seven years," I whispered. "We're almost strangers."

Austin quit fumbling with my bra, grabbed both cups, and pulled it apart. With a snap, it gave way. His mouth sucked ravenously on my nipple while his left hand curved around and squeezed, sending a bolt of pleasure all through my body. "Then let's get to know each other. Favorite band?" he murmured.

"Mumford and Sons. You?"

His mouth journeyed lower until his tongue leisurely circled around my belly button. I whimpered a soft moan and loosened my grip on his hair.

"Kings of Leon," he said, pinching my nipples with his warm fingers.

"They have like two songs I've ever heard."

"Yeah, but they're good songs." Then he swung his eyes up to mine and slowly sang the opening verse of "Sex on Fire."

Oh God, I melted listening to his lush, raspy voice. Austin had a singing voice he rarely used, but when he did, it was a force of nature on my body.

"How many girls have you dated?"

He took his sweet time sliding my shorts down, kissing the soft skin surrounding my panties. "Five," he murmured.

"Five?" I almost shouted. "Jeez, you make me feel like a slut."

"How many?" he asked, pulling my shorts away from my ankles. He knelt at my feet, staring up the length of my body.

I bit my lip. "Nine. But only two were serious."

Austin cracked a smile. "Not serious enough. None of them matter."

Then he fell over me and the clash of our heated bodies intensified the tension building between us. I was swimming in a pool of desire and close to drowning in the deep end.

"You still own those brown cowboy boots?" he asked, kissing my neck roughly. Then his hips took on a life of their own as he rocked them against me.

I moaned some kind of desperate sound, struggling to pay attention as his tongue moved in slow circles between the sucking. "No, the heel broke."

"Good. I hated those damn boots."

Well, that was just insulting. "Hey, what about your 'I'm so badass' fringed leather gloves?"

He pinched my nipple and put me in my place as his hips thrust against mine.

"Still got 'em, and I'm still badass."

I nipped his jaw and licked at his ear, making him shudder. "If I see you in them, I'm cutting off those fringes."

A grin stretched across his face. "Don't even try it."

Then his mouth was on mine.

"Pudding," I said in a quick breath.

"What?" He didn't stop kissing me.

I turned my head to the side, allowing him to taste my neck and shoulder. My fingers weaved through his hair slowly. "You wanted to know what I craved when I shifted from wolf form. It's pudding."

He lifted my leg, grinding against me, and I moaned. "Chocolate or vanilla?"

I was tired of talking and my breath sounded as if I had run a marathon. Austin cupped between my legs and massaged as he spoke against my lips. "Answer the question."

I wasn't sure I wanted to if this was the punishment. He stroked his finger deep.

"Chocolate!"

I made a complaining sound as he shifted on top of me again.

"What's wrong?" he asked, lifting his head to look at me.

"The floor hurts my back."

The next thing I knew, Austin stood up and pulled me into his arms. My legs were wrapped around his waist like pythons and he pushed me up against the wall. A painting crashed to the floor and the frame split. We were too busy trying to determine how far we could get our tongues into each other's mouths.

I was trembling all over; never had I felt so aroused by a man.

Then I started working my hips and he turned around, trying to figure out what to do with me as we backed up against the window. I ripped the drapes down and the rod knocked over a picture frame on the TV stand.

"Oh God!" I cried out, so completely taken by his mouth all over me, the feel of his chest against mine, the smell of him.

"Shit, where?" he grumbled out.

"The chair," I said, staring at the hideous recliner.

When Austin sat down with me in his lap, we almost went flying forward again. He pulled the lever and reclined back as I unbuckled his belt and pulled down the zipper on his pants.

This wasn't the romantic scene I'd envisioned because let's face it, I'd never envisioned anything romantic with Austin. It was always unadulterated, feral sex.

His fingers worked diligently removing my panties, and I wiggled my body so I could at least get them off one leg.

Then his mouth was all over me—sucking and rolling his tongue in rhythmic circles. While he tasted my breast, his hands were trying to shuck off his jeans. In the process, he knocked over the glass lamp and it broke into pieces. A strangled moan escaped from my lips as his hand slid between my legs.

Austin's words came out in a heavy breath. "God, you're so fucking wet."

Somehow, stating the obvious was never sexier.

There was a moment between us when everything ceased. Our eyes met, our bodies calmed, our breathing fell in sync. As he kept his pale eyes locked on mine, Austin slid himself deep inside me, grabbing my hips and pushing me down to the hilt. Our eyes simultaneously hooded, struggling to maintain eye contact without closing and completely losing ourselves.

That moment would live in my mind for the rest of my life, because it was the first time I'd felt Austin look into my soul. That secret part of me I revealed to no one and saved only for him.

He shook his head. "You were my single biggest regret, Alexia Knight. I'll never get that time back. I'm not letting you go."

I cupped his face in my hands and kissed him warmly with soft lips and a gentle touch. "It wasn't the right time. Maybe it took all those years apart for us to be right for each other. But you have me now, Austin. Love me *now*," I said, my voice falling to a whisper.

And then he couldn't get enough of me. His arms hooked over my back, gripping my shoulders from behind as I rode up and down. He felt thick and delicious and oh God, I couldn't stop. His fingers gripped my ass so hard I actually cried out his name.

"Harder!" he demanded in his alpha voice.

I reached for the back of the chair and in a split second, the room tilted as the recliner fell back and bucked me off. Austin's legs went over and he roared in laughter as he fell on top of me.

Afraid the chair was going to topple over, I turned over and crawled toward the carpet on my hands and knees.

"Christ, Lexi, you're killing me with that view!"

The next thing I knew, Austin came up from behind and stroked my hips sensually with his rough hands, and my fingers gripped the long fibers of the carpet. He slid his shaft in slowly… all the way to the hilt. Never had I felt so connected with another man. It felt so right that I curved my back and pressed against him, taking him even deeper.

Austin released a strangled moan.

I fell to my elbows as he drove into me, stroking my back and thighs with his wandering hands. He was getting close judging by his chaotic rhythm, and right before he reached climax, I shouted, "Stop!"

Austin immediately pulled out, rolled me over, and stared me dead in the eye. "What's wrong?"

My heart was a banging drum. His cheeks were flushed and damn if his bottom lip didn't look swollen from my sucking on it.

"Nothing. I just wanted to see if you would," I panted.

"Why, did someone not stop when you asked?"

"No."

"I'm not an animal. If you say no, I back off. That's the deal."

My hands slid around the back of his neck and I smiled. Beckett had lied to me when he said a man couldn't stop; he just didn't *want* to with the other woman. I didn't mean enough to him when I caught them having sex in the back of my car. But I meant enough to Austin.

"Don't stop," I pleaded.

When he sank on top of me, I couldn't move. Austin shifted his hips teasingly as I wanted him back inside me. The heavy weight of his body held me right where he wanted, and he kissed me with a deep stroke of his tongue. It was a slow and steady burn.

The front door suddenly clicked open and Denver called out, "Hey, Aus. I know you missed me, so I'm chillin' out with you guys tonight." His keys jingled as he hung them on his nail by the door.

In the blink of an eye, I shifted into my wolf. Panic set in and the last thing I wanted was for one of his brothers to see me like that—naked on his tacky rug.

"The guys wanted me to stay here and watch over—"

Denver filled the doorway and my wolf snorted, wiggling around Austin's naked body. One thing I'd learned was that I could remember the shifting, but only the first minute or two before my wolf took complete control.

Austin stood up erect (in every way) and faced his brother.

Denver's jaw hung lax and his eyes were saucer-wide. He pointed a finger at me and I wagged my tail. "That is just *wrong* on so many levels. You need help, Austin. I'm outta here. You two do... *whatever.*"

The door slammed and I shifted back, staring up at Austin from all fours. "Great, now he thinks you're into my wolf."

Austin's laugh filled the room—loud and full of life.

I glowered at him as he folded his arms and looked down at me. "Aren't you going to go after him and explain?"

His brows lifted thoughtfully. "No. Actually, it's funnier if I don't."

CHAPTER 30

MAKEUP (AFTER GETTING SHOT) SEX was the best sex I'd ever had. Austin and I just fit in a way I couldn't explain. An undeniable chemistry existed between us—not just physically, but mentally. And in some ways, emotionally. Everyone has a person in life that just "gets them." They get all your idiosyncrasies, inside jokes, tells, and the subtext that lies beneath a comment or a wink of an eye. They know you inside out and upside down.

Austin got me.

We spent the next three weeks moving everything from their old place, Mom's house, and my apartment, over to the fixer-upper that Austin had purchased. Maybe it needed a little work, but it was cozy with charm and personality. It was a place I could call home.

Mom quit her job so she could help get the house in order in addition to feeding the crew of hungry men. In return, Austin not only compensated her with a room, but insisted that he pay her. Mom felt weird about it at first, but I convinced her what she was doing was legitimate work. Shopping, laundry, cooking, decorating—all in addition to becoming the matriarch of the house. I didn't think the arrangement would last; eventually Mom would insist she was doing it because she loved to. It was a good way to get her mind off my dad and everything that had transpired. I never found out what Lorenzo had done with him, and I didn't want to know.

"Denny! Time for ice cream," Maizy called out from the bottom of the stairs.

"Mr. Denny," I corrected her.

"No. That's Mr. Reno," she said, pointing to Reno as he carried a bright red toolbox down the hallway. "And then there's Mr. Cole,

Mr. Jericho, Mr. Wheeler, Mr. Ben, and Denny! He's not a Mister. He's just Denny."

"Why?"

Maizy shrugged. "'Cause he just is," she argued with six-year-old logic.

"Why don't you and Denny go treasure hunting for diamonds?" I suggested.

Denver did a little hop step coming down the stairs, wearing tattered jeans, flip-flops, and a Pink Floyd shirt.

"Jericho's going to kill you if he catches you wearing that," I said.

He brushed his fingers through his short locks of sandy-blond hair. "Yeah, yeah. Been hearing that for decades. They sell this stuff vintage on the Internet."

"I'm ready!" Maizy called out from the doorway. Actually, she was swinging on the door, holding onto the brass knobs and wrapping her legs around either side.

"Are you stopping by the old house today to see if she'll show you where she buried those diamonds?" I asked him in a quiet voice.

"For what?"

"Because she may forget someday, and that's fifty million in your backyard."

"So? It's just money," he said, fishing out his wallet. Denver thumbed through a few bills, doing a count. "Think it'll make your life better? No, it'll make it complicated. People covet money and do stupid shit over it. We're happy, we got a house, and I need to get this girl a strawberry cone before she tears up the door," he said, flip-flopping across the main room. "Skedaddle!" he barked at her.

Maizy squealed and ran out the front door toward his yellow pickup.

Denver had taken over as her watchdog, and apparently it wasn't uncommon in a pack for a wolf to step in as the protector for a fatherless child or woman. It wasn't a parental role, as Denver was more of a brother to her, but it gave me peace of mind knowing my family would be looked after. A pack bonded in ways humans didn't, and it was a way of life that felt natural the more I became immersed in it.

I heard coins jingling and spun around. Austin stood in the hallway, twirling the key ring around his finger and giving me a peculiar look.

"What?"

"Busy?" he asked.

"Well, I was going to go to the movies later with Naya. I think she misses me being right next door. She mentioned something about how the new tenant that just moved in is seventy and single. Plus, I need to talk to her about the whole Shifter thing she kept from me." I gave him a look. "Why?"

"Let's take a drive," he said, holding my hand and lacing his fingers with mine.

My brown summer skirt swished below my knees and matched the bohemian sleeveless top that tied behind my neck. I didn't wear skirts outside of work, and I could tell Austin enjoyed seeing me in something feminine. He didn't mention where we were going, so I rolled the windows down in his black muscle car and switched on the radio.

"Wheeler helping you sort things out?" he asked.

"He seems reluctant to get involved, but he's helped me out with a few things. Maybe I won't be so bad running a business after all; I'm learning a lot."

Once the initial shock had worn off, April totally stepped up to the challenge. I bought a cell phone so she could call me at any time, and we had live meetings on the Internet. The first order of business was that she lost her cherry earring, and that segued into a discussion about our work gear, which I didn't want to change.

April seemed to be going through some personal problems. I wasn't sure if it was family or money, but I could hear it in her voice. I wished she'd open up to me, but some people had a harder shell to crack. She revealed she had been riding the city bus to work because her car had crapped out. I didn't much care for that because April closed the shop late at night. She also had a fear of the dark, which is why she always went in the back room and turned on the main lights. I offered her my car, but she wouldn't accept. April was like that—never accepted help from others. You can't force your help on someone; you just have to trust they know what they're doing. We went over the current state of affairs with the shop and I couldn't help but start mentally planning the future of Sweet Treats.

"Okay, that's it. Where are you taking me, Austin?"

He grinned fiercely with pressed lips, giving me the impression he had a secret. Austin had a very subtle cleft in his chin that was always more prominent when he did the lip-press thing.

The car rolled up to a rest stop just off the highway. The kind with dilapidated picnic tables and foul-smelling restrooms.

"Need to go to the little boy's room?" I teased.

The engine purred to a stop and butterflies fluttered in my belly when I saw a group of men standing beneath a Texas live oak tree, watching us. Austin walked around the car to open my door and I realized he was taking me to them. I pulled the visor down to fix my lipstick.

"You look fine," he said with a soft laugh, tugging my arm.

Tiny pebbles on the concrete scattered as I dragged my sandals across the sidewalk. Then Lorenzo turned around and a golden shower of sunlight melted across his shoulders, illuminating his dramatic features. Skin taut around his chiseled cheekbones—high and proud—and straight brown hair that touched the top of his skull and crossbones tattoo on his upper arm. He wasn't smiling.

Austin squeezed my hand reassuringly. "Don't worry, they don't bite."

Only Austin could make me laugh in the face of danger.

"Cole, we didn't know if you changed your mind," the older man said, staring at his watch. "She's a fine-looking bitch."

Austin's arm stiffened, but he made no attempt to correct the man. That's when I knew this guy held a higher rank. Perhaps there was a pecking order among the Packmasters.

Including Lorenzo, there was a total of four men. One was a tall, handsome black man with swoon-worthy eyes and freckles across his cheeks. The other guy looked like someone had picked him up at a truck stop—scruffy beard, shaggy hair, and sloppy clothes. The older man who'd spoke to Austin was a Sean Connery body double;

I was certain of it.

"I've brought the Packmasters from neighboring territories here to be witness," Sean Connery said.

"Uh, wait a second," I interrupted, getting cold feet all of a sudden as to what exactly was about to go down. "Witness to what?"

"She doesn't even know why she's here?" Lorenzo said through clenched teeth.

And with one subtle gesture, Austin put Lorenzo in his place. He lifted our clasped hands and slowly kissed the back of my fingers, keeping his eyes locked on Lorenzo. A gesture that sent an unequivocal message to everyone present—I was *his*.

"What's your name?" The older man looked me over and arched a brow.

"Alexia Knight."

"Full name."

I flicked a glance at Lorenzo. "Alexia Talulah Knight."

He scribbled something in a small booklet and handed it to me with the pen. "I'll need your signature to show that you're entering this pack of your own free will until such time as you see fit to leave. If any Shifter commits a crime against you, then your pack has full rights to seek justice on your behalf."

I signed my name and handed it back to him. He gave it to Austin. "By signing your name, you agree to watch over this young Shifter as a member of your pack, look after her well-being, and protect her with your life."

On that note, Austin signed the paper, tapped the pen against it, and flipped it back around to the man. Didn't even blink.

"Is that it?" I asked.

The Packmaster laughed so hard it sounded like a wheeze. "She's funny," he said to Austin, tucking the pen behind his ear. "Alexia Talulah Knight, I hereby declare you an official member of the Weston pack. How's that? Official enough for you? I'll be sure to circulate the news. Come on boys, let's leave these two alone," he said, laughing into a fit of coughs.

As Lorenzo crossed in front of me, he stopped and brushed his hand tenderly across my cheek. He looked at me differently now, as if he had accepted the decision and decided to pursue me no further.

"Take care, Alexia. You should come visit with your family sometime."

His eyes slid over to Austin and they exchanged a look before Lorenzo walked off and got in his black truck.

"That felt weird," I finally admitted. "Like we just got hitched or something."

"Would that be so bad?"

My face turned red and I looked down at my shoes. "Depends if you leave the seat up or down."

Austin wrapped his arm around me and we started walking. "Come on, smartass. Let's go for a ride."

————•••————

The summer wind was a fragrant perfume on my skin, filled with the aromatic scent of sunshine and freshly cut grass. The sun dipped low in the western sky, casting a radiant gold across my arms and hair. We drove into a rural area and Austin pulled over on a dirt road by an overlook. He reached in the back seat and grabbed a few things I hadn't noticed before, bundling them under his left arm.

"What are you up to?" I asked, clicking open the door.

"No," he warned, pointing his finger.

I let go of the handle and watched Austin walk around the front of the car, never removing his eyes from mine. He opened my door like a gentleman and draped his arm over the top of the frame, letting his eyes drag down the length of my body.

"I like that skirt on you," he said with a suggestive wink. I thought the delivery of his compliment was all off because my skirt didn't show much leg.

Austin reached in the back and messed around with some things before slamming the door. He casually walked toward a grassy area near the slope of a hill and spread out a quilt in the sun. The car was just a few feet behind us, the engine popping and clicking from the heat.

It felt good to kick off my shoes and sit down. "This is nice."

"It gets nicer," he promised, placing an oversized paper bag in the middle.

He reached in and pulled out a bucket of fried chicken.

"Oh my God, Austin Cole. I love you."

He smirked while taking a seat on the blanket. "Is that all it took? Had I known it was that easy, I would have given you a breast and a thigh a long time ago."

A large container of coleslaw appeared, along with a cooler full of ice-cold bottles of root beer. Then he slowly pulled out a few cups of chocolate pudding and winked. "This is for later."

We shared the coleslaw and I picked out the best-looking piece of chicken. Austin laughed at how particular I was.

It was a perfect moment, and a light breeze cooled my back as I finished up the last bit of my meal and sucked down some of the root beer.

"Baby, you treat me so good," I said, smiling at him warmly.

"You were always too easy to please. I should have brought sushi or something better."

I didn't like the apology in his voice, as if it wasn't good enough.

"This is perfection," I said, leaning over and kissing his cheek. "I love that you know me, Austin. No one else knows me like you do."

He picked up his phone and sent a text message while I put our trash in the paper bag.

"Why don't you go grab the bottle of wine I left in the car before the sun goes all the way down? It's in the driver's seat," he said.

I carried the trash back to the car and set it by the tire. When I opened the driver's side door and looked inside, I saw a bottle of wine in the passenger seat. I got in and leaned over for a closer look. Attached to the neck of the bottle with a string was a note.

I carefully unrolled the paper and read the following:

Lexi,

Wes was all I ever knew in a best friend, and I feel honored to have known him. His life was cut too short and I regret that I won't see him grow old and have a family of his own. Wes loved you, and I don't know if he ever told you that, but he did.

Nothing in life is certain. I guess that's why I'm writing you this note, because I don't want the same thing to happen again.

All these years I've been lost, wondering if Wes's death was that void in my life. He was a brother, and I have so many stories to tell you about him that you've never heard. I've only cried twice in my adult life. The first time was the night the trooper showed up at your house, breaking the news when they found his body. Your mother's scream still haunts me to this day. The second time was when you ran after my car outside Dairy Queen, leaving who I thought was your daughter sitting at the table. Now that I'm home, I know what I've been missing for the last seven years. All this time, I was missing <u>you</u>.

Wes brought you into my life, and I strongly believe that was his purpose.

I've watched you grow into a devoted woman who puts her family first. Be my best friend, Lexi.

(Here's the part where I get mushy)

You turn me on, and I don't mean just physically. You turn on my mind and my heart. I love the animated way you tell a good story, how the sunlight looks in your hair, watching you sleep next to me, and I'm even crazy about that silly laugh of yours. I know when you're upset because you drum your fingers, and yet I still feel like I don't know everything about you. Your eyes soften when you look at me, and I sometimes wonder if it means what I think it does. You've carried a heavy burden taking care of your family, making you the strongest woman I know, and I'd like to take away some of that burden. You are the memories of my past, and I want you to become the memories of my future.
I love you.

I've loved you for so damn long that it kills me to think about the time we've lost since I left you all those years ago, and for that, I'm sorry. You needed me, and I wasn't there for you. But I promise to be here for as long as you'll let me, and I hope that's forever. Maybe I can bribe you with this candy to love me back, even just a little bit. I wish I was more of a poet, but hope that after tonight, we can start over again.

Together.
Yours always,
Austin

I wiped the tears from my cheeks and covered my mouth, allowing sorrow and joy to consume me like a storm. Austin had written this letter with the intention of confessing his love on the night Beckett had attacked me. He didn't just show up at my door with candy, but he showed up with his heart on his sleeve.

Beside the bottle was a CD with a yellow sticky note attached. *Put this in the CD player*, it said. I peeled the note away and handwritten on the label was:

Austin and Lexi

I turned the car key halfway and glanced up. His hands were deep in his pockets and he was staring at the ground, kicking up a few plumes of dirt. I slid the disc into the player and suddenly a haunting acoustic melody filled the car, playing the strings of my heart. The same song that was playing at the lake the night Austin fell in love with me.

"Landslide," by Fleetwood Mac.

Our song.

I jumped out of the car and ran straight into his arms. Austin swung me around once and delivered a kiss to go down as one of the great ones in my life. His right hand curved around the nape of my neck, and the other tenderly stroked my cheek. He wiped away a stray tear on my chin and smiled with his eyes. The song filled the air like a warm breath of life.

"Never let me go again," I whispered.

"Turn around, Ladybug, or you'll miss it." Austin wrapped his strong arms around me from behind and we faced the setting sun. Ripples of melon, rose, and daffodil filled the sky like glowing embers dying out.

"See that down there?" he asked, pointing his finger at a silver object.

In a clearing between the trees, I spied a familiar sight. "What is that? Wait a minute… is that my car?"

And then it exploded.

I shook from the thunderous detonation and gripped his arms. A fireball rose in the air with a billowing cloud of black smoke not far behind. My heart sped up and I stood still, watching the broken pieces of my past burn as Austin held me tight.

Forget flowers and candy. Austin blowing up my car was the most romantic thing any man had ever done for me.

I spun around on my heel. "You just blew up my car."

Austin smiled and kissed my nose. "Feel like going for a *ride?*" He reached in his back pockets and pulled out his fringed, fingerless gloves, stretching his hands in them slowly as he swaggered back to the Challenger.

As if on cue, the music blaring on the speakers switched to the Kings of Leon song Austin had sung during our first time.

Yeah, I got the tingles.

Austin stopped in front of his classic Dodge Challenger, stripped out of his T-shirt, and seductively leaned against the hood on his elbow. A sly grin crossed his expression and he winked, gently patting the hood of the car with his left hand.

Damn, that lean.

Made in United States
Orlando, FL
04 June 2022

18499060R00198